Wednesday Wives Club

By
Cynthia A Clement

Cover design by Robin Ludwig Design Inc.
www.gobookcoverdesign.com
Photography from Depositphotos.com

Dedication

To my sisters.

Lynn who loves to quilt.
Theresa, who loves to sew.
Michelle, who loves to cross-stitch.
All my love and thanks for the years of companionship.

Acknowledgements

Many thanks to John, Kim, Den, and Shawna for all of their support, advice, and editing. The encouragement of readers such as Nancy and Andrea, persuaded me to remain committed to finishing this novel.

Ella

Chapter 1

Ella needed advice about her marriage.

She didn't want a divorce, but she couldn't live with Gerry's mistress.

She glanced at the three women sitting in the living room and wondered if they could help her make the toughest decision of her life. For three years, they had been meeting every other Wednesday to quilt and discuss their lives. They talked about trivial things like their children, decorating, and recipes; never anything as devastating or as personal as this.

This group of quilters were the only friends she had. She'd spent most of her adult life working at her husband's business and raising their three children. After her twin daughters had left for university last year, she'd gone back to school to study landscape design. She associated with her fellow students, but they were too young to understand this problem.

She couldn't talk to her family. They would never understand. They'd insist that she keep the marriage together no matter what because divorce was unheard of in her family. A woman had limits. She needed advice and her fellow quilters were the only ones she could turn to.

She took a deep breath.

It was now or never.

Before she could speak, Brenna, their hostess, plopped the spool quilt she had been hand piecing down on her lap. "I have an announcement."

Brenna was in her mid-forties, slender and tall, with wavy shoulder length brown hair and hazel eyes. She was always calm and in control. Her home, which was on a forty-acre hobby farm outside of Dearston, was immaculate and furnished with a tasteful mix of antiques and leather. Her passion was breeding dogs, King Charles Spaniels to be exact, and she had people booking puppies a couple of years in advance.

Ella put down the floral block she'd been stitching and reached for her cup. Her hand shook as she brought it to her mouth. She'd been granted a reprieve; a few more minutes to gather her courage.

"Peter is seeing a dominatrix."

Ella had taken a sip of tea and choked at Brenna's announcement. Lara rushed to her side and pounded on her back. It took several seconds for the liquid to go down properly. When she had swallowed it, she inhaled a shaky breath. Brenna's husband, Peter, was a talented and ambitious lawyer. Submissive was not how Ella would have described him.

"Thanks." She put her cup down. It clattered on the glass coaster. "Give me a warning next time you drop a bombshell like that."

"There's no easy way to say it." Brenna clenched her hands on her lap. "I've been struggling with this for days and I don't know what to do."

"Are you certain?" Alisa picked up two diamond shaped pieces of fabric and pinned them together.

Alisa was exotically beautiful with long, black hair and light-green eyes. Her father had owned Fairman's Hotels, an international chain of luxury hotels. She'd settled in Dearston, ten years earlier, so that her son, Bert, would have a stable upbringing. Her husband, Henry, had taken over as CEO of the company after her father's death and traveled extensively for the business.

Alisa looked up from her work. "Peter doesn't strike me as the adventurous sort."

Lara settled back into her vacated seat. She was a petite woman and looked like a child sitting in the large chair; her golden hair a contrast to the deep burgundy color of the leather furniture. She recovered her needle and secured it in the crazy patchwork quilt she had been working on. "Did he tell you?"

Brenna shook her head. "I found her card in his suit pocket."

"It's obvious." Alisa flipped her long black hair over her shoulder and shrugged. "She's a client."

"That's what I thought at first." Brenna's voice cracked. "I even called his office, but Lisa, his secretary, had no record of her."

"It wouldn't be the first time a man has indulged his sexual fantasies." Lara's voice held a hint of sadness.

"But doesn't a dominatrix inflict pain?" Ella didn't hide her shock. "No person in their right mind would want that."

"It's not about the pain. Although pain can be pleasurable." Alisa threaded her needle and stuck it into the diamond pieces. "Being dominated is the main allure."

"He wants someone to control him?" Brenna frowned. "I've known Peter for over thirty years and he's never suggested that."

Alisa shrugged. "I think it's seen as an expression of love."

"Not if a stranger is doing it." Lara's voice was quiet. "Has Peter ever asked you to spank him?"

"No." Brenna's voice rose in disbelief. "We've always had a normal sex life."

"What's normal nowadays?" Lara leaned over and squeezed Brenna's hand. "A lot of people are into fetishes."

"I can't believe there's a dominatrix in Dearston." Ella shuddered.

"It's happening in the rest of the country, why not here." Alisa's voice was nonchalant.

"Because this is our hometown." Ella picked up square of floral material and jabbed a pin into it. "What if our children find out?"

"I think they're old enough to understand." Lara's voice was matter of fact. "Besides, the younger generation is much more open about sex."

Brenna's eyes widened. "Are you suggesting that my sons know about this? What will they think about their father?"

"Your boys probably don't know a thing about Peter's sexual explorations." Lara's voice was soothing. "I meant that they are more aware of these fetishes than we were at their age."

Brenna heaved a sigh of relief. "I couldn't bear them finding out. I know they're young adults and at university, but I'd hate to have their image of their father destroyed."

"Going to a dominatrix doesn't make Peter less of a man," Lara hesitated a second before continuing, "Lots of men like the freedom that a dominant woman gives them."

"What do you mean?"

"Men that have very stressful lives can forget their problems while they are being submissive to a woman." Lara bit her lip. "I know it sounds crazy, but not being in control gives them a huge sexual charge."

"So I'm not enough woman for him?" Brenna's voice quivered. "I should have been more demanding?"

"That's not what I said." Lara shifted in her seat. "How old is Peter now?"

"He's forty-eight."

"How long have you been married?"

"Twenty-four years." Brenna frowned. "Are you suggesting that Peter is bored with our marriage?"

"Not bored." Lara shook her head. "He might want to experiment a bit."

Ella almost snorted. She knew all about experimenting. Gerry had been doing that for the last year and a half. A dominatrix was a different story. It was public and it might even be illegal.

"That kind of exploring is going to make him vulnerable." Ella's voice was serious.

"She won't hurt him." Lara's tone was matter of fact. "It's consensual and safe words are used so that it doesn't go too far."

"Ella isn't talking about physical harm. She means blackmail." Alisa bit off the end of her thread. "You need to protect him, Brenna."

"Peter is a high-profile, defense lawyer. Any hint of scandal would ruin his reputation and career." Ella picked up a piece of white fabric and started pinning the floral print onto it. "There is nothing more damaging than a sex scandal."

"What if he won't stop?" Brenna worried her bottom lip with her teeth.

"I suppose you could wait and hope he comes to his senses." Ella's voice was hesitant.

"Is that what you'd do?" Alisa snapped. "Just let him call all the shots, destroy you and your family, no matter what?"

A sharp pain shot through Ella's stomach.

How had Alisa known?

She'd been struggling with how to handle Gerry's ultimatum for days now. Was she that transparent? Tears pricked her eyes. She tried to hold them back, but the dam of self-control she'd built to hold her emotions in check, burst.

Brenna jumped from her chair, and grabbed a tissue box. Ella took a few and buried her face in them, her sobs growing more uncontrollable with each passing second.

"Why do you have to be so blunt?" Lara hissed at Alisa. "She was trying to help."

Brenna wrung her hands and sat down again. "It's all my fault. I should never have asked for your advice." Her voice shook. "I just had nowhere else to turn."

"Alisa needs to show more compassion." Lara crossed her arms. "Just because she has the perfect marriage."

"I never said that." Alisa's eyes narrowed. "How was I to know that Ella was so sensitive?"

"Stop." Ella's voice rang out. "I'm the stupid one."

"No." Alisa denied in a sharp voice. "You're just too trusting of men."

"I'm a fool." Ella sniffed. "Every word that Alisa said is true. I've let Gerry do as he pleases even when it's destroying me. I thought he would eventually come to his senses."

Brenna leaned back in her chair. Lara tilted her head and Alisa raised an eyebrow. None of them looked surprised by her outburst. Maybe Gerry hadn't been as careful as he'd claimed.

"What has he done?" Alisa was the first to speak.

"He has a mistress."

"A mistress?" Brenna repeated under her breath.

"How long?" Lara's voice was emotionless.

"Over a year and a half."

"The bastard," Alisa swore. "Why didn't you leave him?"

"I thought it was a mid-life crisis. Something he'd get over." Ella hiccupped. "He's been very good about the whole thing."

Brenna glanced at Lara and Alisa. "You've discussed this with him?"

Ella nodded. "He calls it polyamory."

"That's just a fancy name for adultery." Alisa crossed her arms.

"Gerry says this is a way of life for many couples."

"Name two." Alisa's tone was wry.

"It's not a club." Ella stuck out her chin. "It sounds worse than it is."

"So you approve of Gerry sleeping with this woman?" Brenna's voice didn't hide her distaste.

"No. I mean yes." Ella dropped her head into her hands. "I just want things back to normal."

Ella's world had been ripped in two by Gerry's affair. She'd been living with this for over a year and only the fear that others would find out and judge her, had kept her silent. It wasn't until Gerry's recent demands that she'd known she couldn't live with the situation any longer.

"How old is this woman?"

Ella shrugged. "She can't be more than twenty-seven. She graduated from university with a Master's degree in business. That's why she came to work for Gerry two years ago."

"She's a trophy." Alisa pursed her lips. "What did he say when you asked him to stop seeing her?"

"He refused."

"That's when you should have left him." Brenna's voice was firm.

"He wants me to let his mistress live with us." The words exploded from Ella's lips. She'd been holding the secret for so long that it was a relief to finally have it out in the open.

There was silence for a few seconds.

"You mean you'd have to share the same bed with them?" Lara's voice was doubtful.

"I don't think anything that drastic." Calm descended over Ella. She'd actually admitted her deepest secret and no one had judged her for it. "He says that he's being honest with me and I should accept it. I'm the mother of his children and he respects that, but he doesn't find me sexually attractive."

"He actually told you that?" Alisa's lips were a thin grimace.

Ella nodded. "He says I need to think of myself and the children. Staying married means that there will be no disruption in our lives or the business."

"I'll bet he doesn't want you suing for divorce." Brenna's tone was matter of fact. "I've heard a lot of excuses for protecting the marital assets and that is exactly what it sounds like Gerry is doing."

"He'll probably have you sign an agreement." Alisa shook her head. "Don't believe a word that snake tells you."

"We started the business together." Ella's fingers crushed her quilt block. "He has to know that I'm legally entitled to half. I don't want a divorce or for my marriage to fail."

"It sounds as if it already has." Brenna's voice held sympathy.

Ella swallowed past the lump in her throat. It was impossible to just let twenty-one years of marriage go without a fight. Divorce wasn't done in her family. She'd suggested couple counselling, but Gerry had refused. She smoothed her quilt block out on her lap. There had to be some way to make Gerry realize a mistress wasn't the answer.

Lara's voice broke the silence. "I have a confession too."

"Don't tell me you're having an affair." Alisa leaned forward. "I knew David was too old to satisfy you for long."

David was Lara's husband. He'd made his first fortune in the early years of the Internet with a search engine company that he'd sold before the bubble burst. When he'd sold the company, he'd also left his first wife and children. Since then, he'd built up a successful video game design company and married Lara. He had more than enough money, but computers were his passion and making money, his hobby.

Lara ran shaking fingers through her long blonde hair. "I have always been faithful to my husband."

"Is David stepping out on you?" Alisa's voice rose in disbelief. "The man should slow down at his age or he'll have a heart attack."

"For goodness sake Alisa," Brenna interjected. "He's only fifty-two. Peter's almost the same age."

Alisa rolled her eyes. "You know what I mean. Lara is twenty years younger than he is."

"Age has nothing to do with sex drive." Ella had stopped crying and was focused on Lara. "What happened?"

"He hasn't done anything yet." Lara's voice was hesitant as if she were struggling to find the right words. "He says he wants us to swing."

"What?" Alisa and Brenna yelped at the same time.

"I don't understand." Ella frowned. "Why does a grown man need a swing?"

"Not a swing," Alisa explained. "He wants to swing."

When Ella just stared at her blankly, Alisa added. "As in swapping partners."

"You mean you would have to sleep with someone else?" Ella squinted her face. "What if you didn't like the person?"

"You get to choose." Lara's fingers pulled at her embroidery. "You all meet at parties and then you pick a partner."

"Sounds as if you've done a little research into this." Brenna threw the miniature spool quilt she had been working on into her basket.

"David has given me the information." Lara's lips tilted into a tight smile. "He has been relentless, showing me invitations, websites, and books. The man is on a mission and frankly, I don't think I can resist him anymore."

Alisa turned to Lara. "Do you want to sleep with other men?"

"No, but what choice do I have." Lara sighed. "I'm not a prude, and David knows I was sexually active before we married."

"Tell him no."

"That's easy for you Alisa. Your marriage is fine."

"Henry wants us to experiment with a ménage a trois. He says it might be exciting to have another woman join us in bed." Alisa threw the words down like a gauntlet. "So much for my perfect marriage."

Ella inhaled a sharp breath. Nothing was sacred if Henry, Alisa's staid and conservative husband, wanted a threesome. He had always seemed to be devoted to Alisa and her father's business. If a man like Henry, could want more, then there was no pleasing any husband.

Lara's hand went to her mouth. "I had no idea. I thought Henry adored you."

Pain flickered in Alisa's light green eyes. "He swears it's only a mid-life crisis thing. Once he gets it out of his system, everything will be back to normal."

"But will it?" Ella whispered.

Ella looked at her three friends and wondered why things had gone wrong in their marriages. On the surface, it seemed as if everything was great. But one announcement had caused all the bricks of their seemingly perfect lives, to come tumbling down.

"So none of our husbands are happy." Brenna's voice was matter of fact.

"And we're all miserable," Alisa added.

The truth hit like a sledgehammer. Ella had spent weeks agonizing about Gerry's ultimatum. She'd debated over whether to burden her friends and ask for their advice, all the time imagining their pity. Never once did she consider that they might be hiding similar problems.

"It doesn't have to stay this way." Ella straightened her shoulders. "There must be a way to keep our husbands at home."

"You mean submit to their demands." Alisa shook her head. "You've already tried that."

Brenna leaned forward, a glitter of excitement in her eyes. "We beat them at their own game."

Ella stared back at her as if she were mad. "How?"

"If Peter wants a dominatrix, then I will give him one."

Alisa tilted her head. "You're going to hire one?"

Brenna shook her head. "I'm going to be one."

A slow smile twisted Alisa's lips. "So we give them what they want, but we control it?"

"Exactly."

Lara's eyes widened with understanding. "So I should go with David to these swapping parties and then flaunt my conquests."

"Make him jealous." Brenna nodded. "He'll get bored soon enough."

Lara smiled. "I'll make sure the green-eyed monster is his constant companion."

"And you, Ella, need to find a man to have an affair with." Brenna's voice was firm. "I think you should find someone younger, just like Gerry did."

"I wouldn't know where to start." Shock ripped through her body.

"If Gerry wants polyamory, then you give it to him." Brenna squeezed Ella's hand. "Tell Gerry that he'll have to accept having your lover move into your house."

"I know lots of guys who would jump at the chance." Alisa giggled.

Brenna turned to Alisa. "And speaking of men. No one said that a ménage had to be two women and one man."

"I'll choose the third person." Alisa's voice shook with excitement. "And I'll pick a hunk of a man."

"It's agreed." Brenna sat back in her chair. "We're all going to give our husbands what they asked for."

"With our own particular twists." Alisa flipped her black hair over her shoulder.

"This won't be easy, especially if we want to save our marriages." Lara's voice was quiet.

Ella's stomach clenched with fear. There had only been one man in her life and that was Gerry. The thought of going out into the world and trying to pick up a man was terrifying. She swallowed her trepidation and straightened up in her chair.

"I'll do it. I won't promise he'll be young, but I'll find a man and have an affair."

Chapter 2

Ella opened her door and was greeted by silence. An empty house had become familiar over the past several months. Gerry no longer tried to hide his absence or his affair. She went into the kitchen and plopped her sewing bag on the table, before opening the refrigerator for the pitcher of lemonade.

She had just finished pouring a glass when the front door slammed shut. Footsteps sounded down the hall and into their bedroom. That could only mean one thing.

Gerry was home.

It was the first time in over a week. She sipped at her lemonade and glanced at the clock. At three in the afternoon, it was too soon for supper. She finished her drink and put the glass in the dishwasher before sauntering to their bedroom. Before she made any decisions about her plans to have an affair, she needed to talk to Gerry.

She found him coming out of the master ensuite. He had a bar of soap, shampoo, and a box of new razor blades in his hand. He threw them into a black duffel bag that was on the bed. There was a pile of dirty clothes on the floor. It looked as if he'd dumped the bag upside down and was now starting to refill it.

"This is a surprise." Ella's voice was mild with reproof. "Are you staying for supper?"

"Marta is waiting outside in the car." Gerry gave her a quick glance before he pulled a dresser drawer open. He rummaged through the clean shirts, tossing a few into the bag and then slamming the drawer shut. "Where's my company polo?"

"I haven't seen it." Ella leaned against the doorjamb. "Maybe you left it at Marta's place."

"I threw it into the laundry last week." Gerry put his hands on his hips and glared at her. "You've nothing to do all day. Is it too much to expect my clothes to be cleaned?"

"If you were home more often, I'd know what you needed." Ella pushed back her anger. This was an old argument and she didn't have the energy for it today.

"What do you do all day?" Gerry's voice rose in disgust. "I only ask for a few things and when I come home, nothing is done."

"Why don't you ask Marta to do your laundry?"

"She works."

"So does your wife." The knot in Ella's stomach tightened. "I go to classes and keep this house up. That's a full-time job."

"You can't even hire someone to fix the guest house." Gerry gestured to the outside. "I've been asking you to do that for months now."

"All the contractors are busy." Ella pushed away from the door. "You're never home, so why do we need that fixed anyway?"

"We need someplace for the kids when they come home."

"They have the house."

"We need more privacy than that. All we do is argue." Gerry zipped his bag shut.

"It doesn't have to be that way." Ella tried to keep her voice neutral. They'd had this conversation so many times in the past and Gerry never budged from his demands.

"I've told you what I want." Gerry picked his bag up. "You have to accept that Marta is in my life for good."

"You can't have both of us." Ella's voice shook.

"She's important to me. If you truly loved me, you'd understand and accept her." Gerry's eyes hardened. "I need her close. Having Marta move in here is the perfect solution."

"Do you actually expect me to let Marta live with us?" Ella's voice rose an octave.

"I'd be home more often." Gerry's voice was matter of fact. "At least you wouldn't have that to complain about."

"What role do you see me playing?" Ella held back her outrage.

"The same as now."

"I would do the laundry, clean the house, and cook meals?" Ella crossed her arms over her chest.

Gerry heaved a sigh. "You say that as if there's something wrong with my plan."

"If you want a housekeeper, then hire one." Ella's voice came through gritted teeth.

"I provide for you. You just finished telling me that you have a full-time job taking care of the house." Gerry's voice was a snarl. "I don't need to pay for two women."

"So you see me as the hired help?" Ella's voice exploded with anger. "I'm your wife. If anyone is getting paid, it's Marta, your mistress."

Gerry shook his head. "I want Marta. There's no negotiation about this. I will continue to take care of you because you're my wife."

"How would you feel if I had an affair?" Ella threw the taunt at Gerry.

He started to laugh. "Go ahead."

"Two can play your game." Ella's hands clenched into fists.

"You're being ridiculous. You're my wife and I will always provide for you." Gerry pushed past her and went to the front door.

The knot of frustration in Ella's stomach tightened. "Don't you care about our marriage at all?"

"Of course I care. Our children would be devastated if we divorced. Try and understand that I want more than one woman in my life." Gerry opened the door. "There's no reason for things to change between us, but you have to accept that Marta is part of our life."

Ella jumped as the door slammed behind him. A part of her died every time her husband left the house to be with Marta. There was no stopping the way she felt. For twenty-one years, she'd loved him, and she didn't want to let that go. It was too frightening to think of what the world would be without Gerry by her side.

She turned back to the bedroom and picked up the dirty laundry. As she went to the hamper, she glanced at the mirror. She pushed back her shoulder-length, auburn curls and ran a hand down the side of her face. She'd been blessed with good skin. Her face was still wrinkle free. Working outside, gardening, had given her a healthy glow. Her eyes showed the true story though. Green, fringed with black lashes, they were dull with exhaustion and weariness.

It didn't sound like having an affair was going to make a difference. Her marriage was already in trouble, so anything was worth a try. She had nothing left to lose. She might be frightened for the future, but one thing was certain. If she didn't do something fast, she wouldn't have a marriage left.

Chapter 3

Her mission was clear.

She needed to have sex with a man, preferably a younger one, so that she could throw her affair in Gerry's face. Then he'd understand the pain she felt at his betrayal; the constant ache and emptiness that he'd forced her to live with. He'd experience the anger that tied her stomach into knots every time he lied about where he was going. There was only one problem with the plan.

She didn't have a clue about where to find a willing man.

Ella drummed her fingers on the steering wheel. Class had run late today. All she wanted was to get home. Instead, she found herself behind a large crane truck that was delivering concrete blocks to a new luxury townhouse development in the neighborhood. It was the first of a series of six buildings, all slated to be built, by the end of October. At least someone was getting work done. She'd been trying for weeks to hire a contractor to renovate their guest house. They wouldn't even return her calls. Everyone was too busy.

Ella's gaze roamed over the construction area, stopping when she spotted the tall, muscular figure of a workman. He moved with an ease that sent her pulse racing. Her mouth went dry as she watched him directing the truck's crane operator.

He was gorgeous.

He was also younger than she.

Ella shook her head and looked away. She wasn't going to listen to Alisa's advice to find a younger man. She had always preferred older men. Gerry was older than her by eight years. Her eyes wandered over to the hunk again. Now, he was standing beside a rusty, red, pickup truck, drinking from a water bottle.

His head was thrown back, and the muscles in his neck were emphasized with each gulp of water that he swallowed. His biceps were tense and every sinew of his hard, muscular body was evident beneath his tight T-shirt. She clenched her hand around the steering wheel and looked away. Thinking about what it would feel like to stroke a finger down his body was not helping.

She twisted the steering wheel to the right and parked behind the delivery truck. Gerry always said she was too timid. Now was the time to prove him wrong. She needed someone to fix the guesthouse. She wasn't going to give Gerry another reason to criticize her. If she had to beg, she would.

She climbed out of her car and straightened her shoulders. The guy at the pickup had thrown his water bottle into his truck. She walked over to him. Her legs shook, and her stomach twisted with anxiety, but there was determination in every step. He raised an eyebrow when she cleared her throat.

"Do you know if your boss would be willing to renovate a guest house for me?"

He stared at her for a few seconds before giving her a lazy grin. "We're booked up for the next six months."

Ella bit her lip. "Is there any way he could fit in a small job?"

The man wiped his arm over his forehead. "We don't do small jobs."

"Never?"

He shook his head. "C & J is a large contracting and engineering firm."

Ella looked over at the half-finished project and the concrete blocks that were being piled beside the foundation. There were workmen everywhere, busy hammering forms and moving the blocks into place. It was a hive of activity.

"How long before you're finished here?"

"We have a six-week deadline."

"If you finish early could you do my guesthouse after that?" Ella held his gaze. "I'll pay extra."

He frowned. "Did you try someone local?"

"I have." Ella sighed. "Everyone is too busy to even come and look at the job. I know it's not big, but I'm willing to pay."

"Why the rush?"

"My husband wants it done before the children come home from school."

"Boarding school?"

"Hardly." Ella stopped herself from snorting. "University. I have three grown children."

The man crossed his arms over his chest. "I find that hard to believe."

"I'm not lying." Ella's breath caught in her throat at the once over he gave her.

"You're much too young for grown children."

"If you don't want to ask your boss, I understand. There's no need to try and flatter me." Ella turned to leave, but a hand on her arm, stopped her.

"I wasn't trying to." His voice was low with regret. "Why don't you tell me about this job you want done."

Ella hesitated before she turned back to the worker. He was smiling and she noticed the crinkles at the edges of his gray eyes. His skin was tanned, probably from hours spent outside doing construction work. He had black hair that was cut over his ears and above his collar. Not military short, but neat. The other thing she noticed was that he wasn't as young as she had first thought. He was probably in his early thirties. It didn't really matter. He was still too young for her to be thinking about him in any other way than as a business contact.

He tilted his head at her scrutiny.

She felt a flush of embarrassment heat her face.

"Are you serious, or just trying to placate me?"

"I'm trying to help." His voice was sincere.

She'd been willing to beg a few minutes ago. What did she have to lose?

"I live a couple of blocks away." Ella opened her purse and started to rifle in it for pen and paper. "If I leave you with my address, could you give it to your boss?"

"I'll give it to him, but I already know the answer." He cleared his throat. "After we finish here, we're scheduled to do an office building in Chicago."

Ella stopped rummaging in her purse. Her shoulders sagged and she turned to walk back to her car. There was no point in continuing. She'd given it a try. It was time to move on and find another way to get the job done.

"Look, I'm sorry." His regret was sincere.

Ella smiled back at him. "It's not your fault. I thought I'd take a chance."

"Good luck." His words hit her just as she reached the edge of the curb.

She stopped.

"What about you?"

He was putting on a hardhat, but hesitated at her question. "I don't understand."

"Could you do the job yourself?"

He waited a couple of seconds before answering. "I really don't have the time."

"Please." She had nothing to lose. "I'll make it worth your while."

"I don't need to moonlight."

Ella took a deep breath. "I will beg if I have to."

He shook his head. "You can't be that desperate."

"I've tried everything."

He twisted his hardhat in his hands and looked at the construction site. "Let me talk to the supervisor. Wait here."

Ella watched him walk over to a man talking to someone holding a set of papers. There was some gesturing of hands and then they both looked over at her. Embarrassment flooded her, but she stood firm. She needed this job done. After a few more minutes, the workman sauntered over to her.

"I can leave for dinner now. I need to look at the job before I agree to do it."

"Thank you." Ella could have hugged him she was so relieved. "Do you want me to drive?"

He shook his head. "I'll follow in my truck."

Ella got into her car and leaned back against the driver's seat. She waited until her heartbeat slowed and then she took a deep breath. That had been one of the hardest things she'd ever done. She hated to admit it, but Gerry was right. She was too timid.

When the workman got into the battered red pickup truck, she pulled out from the curb and drove to her house. She glanced in the rear view mirror to make certain he was following and then continued the three blocks to her home.

It was an upscale neighborhood that had been built about fifteen years ago. They'd bought one of the first homes on the street. Gerry had insisted that they needed the biggest and newest house. To him, it was a status symbol. For Ella, it was a lot of rooms to clean. She'd loved their old turn of the century house near the university. It had been a home, not the showplace they now lived in.

She pulled into the driveway and waited for the workman to get out of his vehicle. She walked toward him and held out her hand. "I'm Ella Powell."

He shook her hand. "Jesse Caldwell."

She walked to the house. "The guesthouse is out back. It was built with the rest of the house, but we've never used it."

Jesse glanced over the front lawn and across at the neighbor's place. "This is a fairly recent subdivision. You can't need much renovating."

"You'd be surprised." Ella unlocked the door and waited for Jesse to follow her inside. "Kids can be rough on a house. My husband wants everything upgraded, but I'll settle for the guesthouse."

She went through to the kitchen and threw her quilting bag on the table before opening the sliding glass door. It led onto a stone patio that extended about twenty feet from the house and stopped at the in-ground pool. The stones surrounded the pool and a path led to a small building at the rear of the yard. It had windows across the front and brick siding that matched the house.

"Nice." Jesse nodded as he looked around. "It must be relaxing out here."

Ella shrugged. "The kids loved it. I don't swim, and my husband is never home, so it's pretty empty now."

"Is that the guesthouse?" Jesse pointed to the rear building.

"It's pretty primitive inside."

"Let's take a look."

Ella led the way. She opened the door and let Jesse go in first. A wall of humid, stale air hit her when she entered. The building hadn't been opened since last summer. She inhaled a quick breath and started opening the windows that lined the north wall that faced the pool. A cool breeze filtered into the main area.

Jesse was looking up at the vaulted ceiling and then around the rough-hewn board and batten that lined the walls. "Very rustic." His voice was edged with sarcasm.

"I warned you."

He frowned. "This is a big job. It'll cost a fortune. Are you certain you want it done?"

"My husband is insistent." Ella shuddered when she remembered his last scathing remarks about her inability to get the work done. "You'd be doing me a huge favor if you took it on."

Jesse continued to look around with his hands on his hips. "Do you have a design in mind?"

"No." Ella waved her hand around the main area. "This should be a living and kitchen area, and there is room enough for a bathroom and bedroom in the back."

"What about the plumbing?"

"We had it roughed in when we built the place."

"One less expense." Jesse sighed and turned back to her. "I'll do it, but only because you asked so nicely."

"Thank you." Ella resisted the urge to hug him. "I'll pay you double the going rate."

"I'll do it for the regular price, but it'll have to be evenings and weekends. I can't let the crew down on this job."

"I wouldn't want you to." Ella shut the windows and moved outside. "If you have any extra time, I do have a room that needs to be done inside the house."

"We'll see how fast I get this finished." Jesse shut the door behind him. "I'll order the materials tomorrow. You can set up an account at the lumber yard if you don't already have one."

"I'll do it first thing." Ella didn't care what Jesse wanted, she'd do it. Just knowing that the guesthouse would be done was enough.

"Show me the room in the house."

"It's the den. According to my husband, everything needs to be redone, but the guest house is the most pressing."

Ella led him into the house and down the hallway to a large room that had once been a playroom for the kids. They had emptied it last year. Bare walls and a dirty carpet was all that remained of the room.

"It needs flooring and at least one wall of floor-to-ceiling bookcases."

"You're looking for a library." Jesse looked around and nodded. "Do you want those windows left, or would you prefer French doors that opened to the patio?"

"Doors would be nice, but if you don't think you'd have time, then just leave the windows."

"No point in doing a job half ass. You'll only want it redone later."

"I was just thinking about your time."

"Don't worry about me." Jesse walked out of the room and back to the kitchen. "You weren't kidding about this being a big house."

"It's what my husband wanted."

"But not you?" Jesse looked at her.

Ella shook her head. "I like older homes with character. A smaller house means a closer family. In this place you can go days without seeing each other."

"And you don't like that."

Jesse's gray eyes held her gaze. A shiver of awareness raced up her spine. Ella's mouth went dry and her heart raced. This was crazy. Jesse was only here because he needed some extra money. He wasn't interested in her.

Ella looked away.

The spell was broken.

She cleared her throat and went to the fridge. "Would you like me to make you something for your dinner? You did sacrifice it to come here."

Jesse grinned. "I have my lunch in my truck. I'd best be getting back."

Ella walked him to the door. "Will you be here tomorrow?"

"Definitely." Jesse went to his truck. When he reached it, he turned back to Ella. "As long as you're here, I'll be back."

A warm tingle settled in Ella's belly. Jesse might be too young for her, but he was going to make the next few weeks enjoyable. And she intended to be home as much as possible, in the evenings and weekends.

Chapter 4

"Have you had any success in finding another man?" Alisa reached for a pink micro-dot fabric and held it up to her unfinished star block.

Ella tightened her hold on her needle. It had been two weeks since their last quilt meeting, and she was no further ahead in her search for a man. "I don't know where to look."

"You need help." Lara's soft voice was filled with understanding. "Gerry's been your whole world since you were a teenager."

"He was my first and only." Ella's hands shook. The thought of change and the unknown paralyzed her. "I was so young when I met him that I never considered the possibility of pregnancy."

"Stop blaming yourself. Gerry was old enough to know better." Alisa looked at her. "He was twenty-four, a grown man. You were sixteen."

"Isn't there anyone you know?" Brenna finger pressed the last seam she'd sewn to the side. "There has to be someone in one of your classes."

"They're younger than my son." Ella frowned as she considered her landscaping classes. "Perhaps one of my professors, but I wouldn't know the first thing about how to approach them about an affair."

"Ask them out first." Lara looked up from the embroidery thread she was separating. "Dinner is a nice beginning."

"Then, you can suggest a coffee back at your place." Alisa threw the pink fabric back into her bag and pulled out a blue floral. "Let nature take its course after that."

"Are you speaking from personal experience?" Brenna's voice was dry.

"I love Henry too much to cheat on him." Alisa grinned. "You'd be surprised what information you can find on the Internet and in romance books."

"It sounds like it might work." Ella shrugged. "I don't want to do anything until I've spoken to Gerry."

Brenna threw her quilt block onto the table. "You were supposed to do that two weeks ago."

"He hasn't been home for more than two minutes at once." Ella tried to curb the defensive tone of her voice. "He promised me he'd be home tonight."

"Talk to him." Brenna shook her head. "The longer this goes on, the more problems you'll have if you divorce him."

"I'll speak with him tonight and if that doesn't work, then I'll approach one of my professors."

"I'm sure Gerry will come to his senses." Lara's voice was full of sympathy.

Ella reached over and gave Lara's hand a grateful squeeze. "I know it seems foolish to cling to a man who has betrayed me, but we did have a good life together. I just want my husband back."

Alisa leaned back in her chair. "That's what we all want. Call me if you have a problem getting a date. I might know someone."

Ella pushed back her panic. She didn't want a divorce. Her only goal was to convince Gerry to leave Marta and focus on repairing their relationship. A part of her doubted that anything would change Gerry's mind. If the threat of an affair would convince him that she was serious, then she'd try it.

"David has been researching swinger groups in the area. It seems you have a choice about what you do when you swap partners." Lara spoke in a soft voice.

Ella frowned. "Does that mean you don't have to have sex with them?"

Lara nodded. "You can do what they call a soft swap, which only involves kissing and touching."

"Then, you go back home with David, and have some good loving?" Alisa nodded. "That sounds like it might be helpful for a relationship."

Lara bit her lower lip. "David wants a full swap."

"He wants to sleep with other women." Brenna whistled. "How are you going to repair your marriage that way?"

"People in the lifestyle insist that it brings them closer together." Lara picked up her needle and threaded it with yellow embroidery floss. "It might be true, but you have to be able to talk with each other."

Alisa looked up from the material she was tracing her template on. "That's the most important thing to a successful marriage. Henry and I have always had good communication."

"Yet, he still wants a threesome?" Ella wrinkled her nose as she pinned a piece of floral fabric to a solid blue square. "I don't understand why. It sounds like you have a great marriage."

"He's comfortable enough to tell me what he wants." Alisa shrugged. "I'm not sure if it's really a fantasy of his, or just a way to provoke me."

"Have you figured out what you're going to do?" Brenna frowned down at the block she was finishing.

"I'm going to see if I can find someone that interests me at the Country Club."

"One of the pros?"

"If they fit. There's a couple of cute waiters that might work."

"I'd love to hear that conversation." Lara giggled. "A side order of sex with that steak please."

"It sounds so horrible when you put it that way." Alisa shuddered. "I'm hoping someone will come along and I'll know right away that they're perfect."

"And if they don't happen by?" Brenna pushed her needle into her seam allowance and backstitched a knot.

"I might hire someone."

Ella gasped. "Pay for sex?"

"Men do it all the time." Alisa picked up her scissors and cut into her material. "I'll only use it as a last resort."

"Is it safe?" Brenna took a stitch and pulled the thread through, before looking up at Alisa. "You could get arrested for soliciting prostitution."

"I saw an ad for male escorts on the bulletin board at the gym." Alisa's voice was hushed. "That's not all. I was doing research on-line and found this."

She put her scissors down and rummaged in her quilting bag. She pulled out a piece of paper and handed it to Brenna. Brenna glanced at it and gasped.

"You can't be serious?"

"Why not?" Alisa grinned. "School is the best place to learn a trade."

Ella took the paper out of Brenna's hand.

Learn to be a Dominatrix was plastered over the front of the sheet.

"You can take classes in dominating?" Ella handed the paper to Lara. "Is that legal?"

"Why not?" Alisa shrugged. "There's no sexual contact."

"It's more legal than hiring an escort." Lara's tone was dry. She handed the paper back to Brenna. "It might be a good way to learn some of the nuances of being a dominatrix."

"I hadn't thought about going to a school." Brenna's voice rose an octave. "I didn't know you could."

"The world's changing." Alisa went back to cutting her fabric. "BDSM is almost mainstream."

"That's a scary thought." Brenna folded the paper and slipped it into her bag. "I'll have to think about it."

"Don't take too long." Alisa's voice was brisk. "At the rate we're going, our husbands will have forgotten what they asked for by the time we deliver."

Ella's head was spinning with everything she'd learned today. By comparison, learning to piece a Mariner's Compass was easy. In two short weeks, they had gone from making quilts to hiring male prostitutes, and going to a dominatrix school.

"Maybe that's a good thing." Ella's voice was hesitant. "Some of these things could get us arrested."

"You can't afford to wait." Lara's voice was quiet. "Gerry's already flaunting his mistress. You need to take action now."

Chapter 5

Ella took out a bunch of carrots from the fridge and plopped them on the counter. The house was empty and she was preparing supper. Usually she ate alone. Over the past year, she'd learned to deal with it. Tonight would be different because Gerry had promised to be home.

A sharp rap at the kitchen door sent the peeler in Ella's hands careening off the carrot, just missing her finger. She turned to see Jesse, standing outside. She motioned him in.

"I didn't mean to startle you." Jesse grabbed a glass from the cupboard near the sink and turned the tap on. "I ran out of water."

Ella smiled. "I meant to bring you some lemonade. You're working too hard in this heat."

Jesse leaned against the island, so that he faced her. "It goes with the territory. Besides, I promised to get this job done quickly."

Ella brushed back a stray curl from her eyes. "You're a rarity."

Jesse's eyebrow slanted upwards. "How so?"

"You're a man of your word." Ella sighed and threw the carrot down. "I know you only agreed to renovate the guest house and den because I begged, but I'm truly grateful."

Jesse shrugged, his firm muscles rippling beneath his tight shirt. "It's what I do."

"Did you have a nice visit with your friends?" Jesse asked as he put his empty glass on the counter.

Ella felt her cheeks burn. Jesse had arrived at the house just as she was leaving for the quilting group. "It was interesting." Her voice rose on the last word.

"Now, that does have me wondering."

Ella frowned. "About?"

"What you were really doing? Somehow, quilting doesn't strike me as interesting."

"You'd be surprised."

They'd spent most of the meeting discussing whether Brenna needed to go to dominatrix school. Between hand-piecing material blocks, and fixing marriages, their Wednesday meetings were evolving.

"You'll be able to meet my husband, Gerry, tonight. He's going to be home for supper." Ella kept her eyes on the carrots she was peeling. The nearness of Jesse was causing her heart to beat quicker. She took a cleansing breath as she picked up the next carrot.

"I've been here two weeks now and never met him. He must be a busy man."

"He travels a lot." Ella forced her voice to remain steady. Lying wasn't her strongpoint. Then again, she wasn't really lying.

"What does he do?"

"Powell's Transmission." Ella grabbed a chef knife and a cutting board.

"They have franchises throughout the country." Jesse's voice held a note of admiration. "Do you work there too?"

She started chopping the carrots into coin shapes. "Not now, but I was there at the beginning. I kept the books. Now, he can afford to pay people to do that."

"Impressive."

Ella paused in her chopping and gripped the knife tighter. If she'd stayed doing the books, Gerry wouldn't have hired Marta to be his accountant.

No Marta.

No affair.

Who was she kidding? If it hadn't been Marta, it would have been someone else. Gerry had stopped paying attention to her years ago.

Jesse moved over to stand beside her at the counter. "How long have you been married?"

"Twenty-one years."

He shook his head. "You must have been a child bride."

"I'd just turned seventeen." Ella gathered the cut carrots and threw them into a pot. "It was the usual story."

"You were pregnant." Jesse's words were a statement.

Ella sighed. "Gerry Junior was born three months later. Two years down the road and we had the twins."

"That must have been hard. Three young children to look after and a business." Jesse's voice was sympathetic. "My mom only had me and I was tough enough."

Ella pulled the bag of potatoes close. "I find it hard to believe you were a difficult child."

"You'd be surprised what one boy alone can do."

"I doubt it." Ella's voice was dry. "Why don't you stay for supper? I'm making Chicken Cordon Bleu and I have more than enough."

Jesses pushed away from the counter. "Beautiful, artistic and a gourmet chef. How can I refuse?"

Ella watched him walk back to the guesthouse. His steps were unhurried and sure. Broad shouldered, tall, dark, and muscular. Jesse could make a woman's knees weak. He was gorgeous. She feasted on him until he was out of sight. With a sigh, she returned to her potatoes.

The last thing she needed was to start mooning over a younger man. She had to be at least eight years older than him. He could have his pick of women. Why would he look twice at a dowdy, plump woman with grown children?

Ella gave herself a mental shake. She was acting like she was in her dotage. She was only thirty-eight and looking never hurt anyone. Ella pursed her lips and attacked the potatoes with renewed vigor. She had better hurry if she wanted dinner to be ready before Gerry returned.

She was putting the prepared chicken in the fridge when the front door slammed shut.

Gerry was home.

She brushed back her auburn hair and adjusted her top, before leaving the kitchen. She took a deep breath and straightened her shoulders. He was still her husband and she intended to fight for their marriage. She found him in the bedroom, loosening his tie.

"You're home early," she said with a smile. "I'm making your favorite for dinner."

Gerry frowned. "Don't bother. I'm spending the night with Marta."

Ella's heart constricted as she sat on the bed. "You've been out every night this week."

"It can't be helped." Gerry threw his tie on the floor. "The accounts are a mess."

"You promised you'd be home tonight." Ella blinked back tears. "I was hoping we could talk this evening."

"About what?" Gerry turned to her, his brown eyes unwavering. "I told you there is nothing between us. What more is there to discuss."

"Our marriage." Ella clasped her hands together to stop their shaking. She was determined to give Gerry one last chance.

"I'm still your wife."

Gerry took a deep breath and shook his head. "And Marta is my mistress. She's also the company's accountant. I need to meet with her for business."

"Every night of the week." Ella wrinkled her nose. "I'm not a fool."

"Don't act like one."

Gerry pulled out a pale-pink polo shirt. He unbuttoned half of his dress shirt, pulled it over his head and threw it on the floor, before he slipped the polo on.

"Perhaps you're right." Ella bent over and picked up the discarded shirt and tie. For twenty-one years, she had been picking up Gerry's clothes. It was time things changed.

"You've explained polyamory, but it's just an excuse." Ella clenched the shirt tight, trying to control her anger. "You want to have your fling and make sure your laundry is done on time."

Gerry stopped tucking his shirt in and looked at her with a scowl. "I've been honest with you. You're the mother of my children and I respect you."

"I'm your unpaid maid." Ella stood up. "No more."

"You're my wife." The muscles in Gerry's throat tightened. "I have provided you with the best."

"You treat me like a slave." Ella threw the clothes into the hamper near the door.

"I work hard so that you can live in this mansion." Gerry waved his hand at the room.

"I never wanted this house." Ella lifted her chin. "In case you haven't noticed, I work too."

"You stay at home." Gerry's eyes bulged and his voice sputtered. "How is that work?"

Ella clenched her hands at her side. "I manage the house and go to school."

Gerry rolled his eyes. "Landscaping is a hobby, not a career."

"I intend to work as a designer when I'm finished."

"Good luck." Gerry's voice dripped with derision. He glanced at his watch and then grabbed his jacket from the chair. "I'm late."

Ella grabbed Gerry's arm before he could leave the room. "Don't go. Give our marriage another chance."

Gerry sighed. "No." He pulled Ella's hand away from his arm. "You're the one who refused to share a bed with me. Unless you've changed your mind, there's nothing to talk about."

"You can't expect me to make love with you after you've just come from Marta." Ella's voice cracked. "How would you feel if I had been with another man and then expected you to make love to me?"

Gerry grinned and then shook his head. "What man?"

Ella shrugged. "I can find someone."

Gerry threw back his head and laughed. "Go ahead," he said with a grin. "Nothing would surprise me more."

"Women have affairs every day." Ella tilted her head.

"You could never do it."

A surge of anger raced through her. "I might surprise you."

Gerry patted Ella's arm. "I appreciate your effort to make me jealous, but you have to be realistic. There is no way you could bring yourself to have a fling."

"You did."

"And you can't accept that." Gerry started to walk to the door. "You're too caught up in your middle-class beliefs to even think about sleeping with another man."

"So you wouldn't object to me having an affair then?"

"I dare you." Gerry smirked. "Who knows, it might make you more interesting."

He walked out of the room. She stood staring at the empty doorway long after he'd gone. She was numb. Her husband had dared her to have an affair, and then without a backward glance, he'd left to spend the night with his mistress.

She wanted to scream, but she was too stunned to do more than walk into the kitchen. She sat at the table and put her head in her hands. When had her marriage gone so wrong?

That's how Jesse found her.

"I thought I heard a car." Jesse was in the patio door opening.

Ella lifted her head. "It was Gerry. He's been and gone."

Jesse grimaced. "Does that mean dinner is off?"

"I was just going to put the chicken in the oven."

Ella straightened her shoulders and pushed away from the table. She was tired of letting Gerry ruin her plans. She'd promised Jesse dinner and she meant it. She turned the oven on and pulled the prepared Cordon Bleu from the fridge. While the oven was preheating, she turned the carrots and potatoes on.

"It'll be ready in forty minutes. Why don't you come in and wash up?"

"You don't have to do this if you aren't up to it."

"I'm looking forward to eating a meal with company for a change."

Jesse nodded and shut the outside door behind him.

He walked by her and down the hall to the washroom. She heard the tap running and sagged against the countertop. Gerry's words had been harsh, but worse, was his taunting. She'd prove him wrong. She would and could have an affair.

Jesse coughed behind her.

She inhaled a sharp breath.

All six feet of him was standing in the doorway with a huge grin on his face. Her mouth went dry when he stretched an arm up along the doorjamb. His chest and arm muscles bulged beneath the thin cotton of his gray T-shirt. What would it be like to be held within those arms?

He grinned. "How can I help you?"

Chapter 6

She blinked. He wasn't reading her mind. He was referring to dinner, not her. He could have any woman he wanted. Besides, he was too young. Ella swallowed the lump in her throat.

"The plates are in the cupboard, if you wouldn't mind setting the table."

"My pleasure." Jesse reached over her head and grabbed a couple of dinner plates. "It's been ages since someone cooked for me."

Ella inhaled his musky scent. He was temptation wrapped up in a gorgeous body. She gave herself a mental shake and put the chicken in the oven. The potatoes and carrots were simmering. She tossed a green salad with oil and vinegar dressing and put it on the table, along with the white wine.

She handed Jesse the corkscrew. "Would you do the honors?"

Jesse picked up the bottle and read the label. "Nice. Your husband doesn't know what he's missing." Jesse opened it and poured out two glasses.

Ella sat and handed him the salad.

"Gerry would rather spend the evening with his mistress." The words were out before she could stop them.

Ella slapped her hand over her mouth.

Jesse's eyes widened and his chair jumped back as he sat upright. "Then, he's a fool."

"I never meant for that to come out." Ella shook her head. "You don't need me dumping my problems on you."

Jesse reached for his wine. "Have you spoken with your husband?"

"I've tried." Ella shook her head. "The truth is, we argue rather than talk."

Jesse took a sip from his glass. "How did you find out?"

Ella put some salad on her plate. "He was never home, constant business trips, and then he got careless, and put the receipt for the apartment he was paying for Marta, in with the household accounts."

"Sounds like he wanted to be caught." Jesse scooped out some salad for himself.

"He calls it polyamory." Ella snorted. "What the hell is polyamory anyway? Have you ever heard of it?"

Jesse shook his head. "Never."

"It's the new religion of middle-aged men, an excuse for adultery." Ella leaned back in her chair. "He gets to screw around, and I get to do his laundry."

"How long have you known?"

"Over a year now." Ella inhaled a sharp breath. "I've been a fool to let it go on for so long, but I really wanted to make the marriage work."

"You can't do it on your own."

"I've tried." Ella took a sip of wine. "Diets, exercise, courses, and counsellors. Nothing I do seems to have any effect on my husband."

"You shouldn't have to change for someone else."

"Gerry thinks I'm all used up. I should be happy to remain his wife because I have no skills and I'm unattractive."

Jesse laughed. "As a man, I can tell you that is totally false."

"He needs a wife who can mingle with clients, and I'm not comfortable doing that." Ella shrugged. "When the business took off, I stayed at home while he went on the road."

"That's an excuse." Jesse leaned forward. "When a man truly loves, nothing will keep him away. Trust me, a man in love would never cheat."

Jesse's eyes never left her face. A tingle of awareness skittered across her skin and she had to force herself to breathe. His voice was sincere and for a few seconds she thought he was talking about them.

The timer for the oven went off.

The spell was broken.

She pushed away from the table and stood. A few minutes later, she returned with carrots, potatoes, and a platter of chicken. Jesse rubbed his hands together and started loading his plate with food. A glow of satisfaction settled within Ella. It had been a long time since someone had enjoyed her efforts.

"So tell me about yourself." Ella put some carrots on her plate. "Have you been married?"

Jesse grinned. "I've never found the right woman. My timing was always off."

"How so?"

"The good ones were taken."

Again, Ella had the sensation that he was talking about her, but she brushed it aside. She was older than him, at least twenty pounds too heavy, and as Gerry insisted, all used up. She needed to get out more. She'd met so few men that she couldn't tell when they were flirting, or just making conversation.

"At least you know what you want."

"My luck is changing."

Her stomach lurched at the thought of him with another woman.

"Good." She kept her smile plastered on her face. "What about your parents? Are they still married?"

"Thirty-five years." Jesse raised his wine glass in a salute. "They're still happy and planning a cruise for their anniversary."

"I always wanted to go on one." Ella clicked her glass with Jesse's "A toast to many more years of happiness for them."

After taking a few sips of wine, Ella couldn't resist asking. "How did they meet?"

"They were in the same class at university. My father took one look at her and knew she was the one."

"How romantic."

"He claims he was struck by lightning." Jesse took a bite of chicken. "He spent the next year convincing her that he was serious."

"He was persistent. Most men would have given up."

"I'm the same." He winked at her. "When I know what I want, nothing stops me."

"You should go into business for yourself." Ella's voice was dry. "Gerry and my son are exactly the same. Persistent and driven. Gerry Jr. is doing his MBA."

"What about your daughters?"

"Clarissa is very self-conscious about how others think. She has to have the right clothes, right school, and the right career."

"What's she taking?"

"She's planning on law school, but that's a long way away. She's just started her second year at university."

"Are they identical twins?"

"Fraternal." Ella's tension eased as she talked about her children. "Christina's a sweetheart. I think she might go into something like social work, but she hasn't decided yet."

Jesse pushed away from his empty dinner plate and picked up his wine. "You must be proud of them."

"I am, but it gets lonely around here." Ella started to gather the empty plates. "When the girls left for school, I spent the first year redecorating the house."

"I like it." Jesse stood and helped her carry dishes to the counter. "It's comfortable."

"Gerry wants a showpiece." Ella started stacking the dishes in the dishwasher. "That's why the renovations."

"That reminds me. I won't be here for the next couple of days."

"Abandoning ship?"

Jesse shook his head. "A meeting in Chicago for the new building. I can't miss it."

"I appreciate that you're fitting my work in around your regular duties."

"I'm enjoying it." Jesse rubbed his stomach. "Fine cooking, like that, is a bonus."

"It's one of my hobbies." Ella glanced at the clock. "It's too late for you to continue tonight, especially if you have to travel tomorrow."

"I'll pick up my tools and lock the guesthouse before I go." He hesitated a second. "Don't believe your husband. You're a beautiful and talented woman. He's nuts to let you go."

Ella watched Jesse leave and then turned the dishwasher on. The problem was that Gerry wasn't letting her go. He wanted her to stay and keep his house while he traveled and made love to another woman. She'd been crazy to let it go on for so long.

It had to change.

She was living a lie.

Ella straightened up. Gerry had made it clear that he didn't care about her sleeping with another man. He had challenged her and she meant to prove him wrong. She would follow through on her threat and rub it in his face. If an affair would make her more interesting, then she'd have two. Hell, maybe she'd even have three.

Ella pulled open the freezer and pulled out a carton of heavenly hash ice cream. She grabbed a spoon and dug in. Each spoonful strengthened her resolve. She went through a mental list of all the men she knew. It was only a question of which one would make the perfect lover.

Chapter 7

Ella patted the soil in place and then swiped a gloved hand over her forehead. That was the last of the tomato seedlings. Like a cat, she stretched her back, letting her arms reach high above her and then moved away from the potting table.

It was hot inside the greenhouse.

She had volunteered to help with potting the seedlings, but now she'd have to move fast if she were to make her design class and meet with her professor. She pulled off her gloves and reached for her backpack. She glanced at her watch. She had five minutes before Professor Darnell's office hours ended.

Ella rushed out of the greenhouse and took the stairs two at a time to the third floor. Darnell's office was at the end of the hall. She arrived just as the professor was shutting his door.

"Not a moment to spare, Mrs. Powell." Darnell winked. "What's so important you couldn't wait until tomorrow?"

Ella took a shuddering breath. "Sorry, I stayed too late in the greenhouse."

Darnell nodded. "Walk with me. I have a meeting with the Dean. We can talk as we go."

Ella snuck a glance at Darnell. He was a few years older than her and quite handsome despite his thinning hair. He had gentle hazel eyes that lit up when he became enthusiastic about ecology.

"Is this about an extension for your term paper?"

Ella shook her head. "Actually it's personal."

Darnell stopped and looked down at her with a questioning look.

Ella cleared her throat. "I wondered if you'd care to have dinner with me some night."

Ella thought she'd faint before she got the words out. Darnell was the first man she had ever asked out. Her fingers twisted around the strap of her backpack. Dinner sounded harmless, but Ella wanted more than that. Professor Darnell would make the perfect lover.

Darnell's eyes widened and for a moment Ella thought he was going to walk away without answering her.

"Forget I asked," Ella blurted out in a high voice. "There's probably a rule about seeing students outside the classroom."

Darnell smiled. "It is frowned upon."

Ella nodded. "It was stupid of me not to think of it."

She turned to go, but Darnell touched her arm. "I think there's been a misunderstanding. You're a mature student and there'd be no problem with us having dinner, but I have a partner."

Ella wished the floor would open and swallow her. "I didn't realize you were married. God I feel like such a fool."

Darnell gave her a slight smile. "I'm not married."

She bit her lip. Embarrassment must have slowed her brain because she sensed that he was trying to tell her something, but she couldn't figure it out.

"I'm gay."

"Oh." Ella's voice cracked. "I had no idea."

"There's no reason you should." Darnell glanced at his watch. "Is there anything else you need to talk to me about?"

Ella shook her head. "I've said more than enough."

"I'll see you at class tomorrow." Without another word, he walked away.

There had to be a special place in heaven for people as clueless as she.

She'd be at the front of the line.

It had never occurred to her that Darnell was gay. She'd been so caught up in her fear of trying to find someone that she'd forgotten the rules of the game had changed. It had been more than twenty-one years since she'd dated and Gerry had been the first and last man she'd gone out with.

Having an affair was imperative, so that she could bring Gerry to his senses. The sooner, the better. For a brief second she considered Jesse, but rejected him. He was too young for her. Besides, she wanted sex with no strings attached.

She wanted a quick fling with a man she could sleep with and forget. Jesse conjured up images of now and forever. She needed someone who wouldn't be hurt by being a pawn in her effort to save her marriage. Unfortunately, she was all out of ideas.

Ella sat on a bench outside and took a sip of lemonade before pulling out her phone. Her sister, Patty, had been widowed for two years. She must know a couple of available men. If that didn't work, then she'd take Alisa up on her offer to set her up on a blind date.

She wasn't going to let her marriage die without a fight.

It was now or never.

Chapter 8

The delicious aroma of roast beef filled the kitchen. Ella resisted the urge to check the oven for the tenth time and took a gulp of the red wine she had poured for herself. It was her second glass.

Tonight was the night.

Gerry was away and Alisa had been true to her word and arranged a date for her. An intimate dinner date at home with the end result being sex. What could be simpler?

Why was she so nervous?

Ella couldn't shake the feeling that she was going to regret this evening. A knot had settled in her stomach the moment she'd made the plans with Alisa yesterday. She was beginning to wonder if an affair would bring Gerry home. His indifference to her and their home couldn't be ignored any longer. Flaunting an affair wasn't going to change his attitude.

She walked into the dining room and refolded the forest green napkins and lit the candles. Antique china, crystal flutes, and golden yellow roses, were the perfect setting for a romantic evening. Her date would be here in a couple of minutes.

Ella twisted the champagne bottle in the ice bucket and stood back to admire her handiwork. She took another sip of her wine. She leaned forward to straighten a rose, just as the doorbell rang.

He was here.

Now what?

Answer the door, you idiot. Ella gulped down the last of her wine and rushed to the foyer. She reached for the doorknob and then hesitated. What if he didn't like her? She couldn't handle another rejection.

She ran a hand over the skimpy, black dress she had bought for tonight. It had a plunging neckline that displayed her best asset and hid her extra pounds. She adjusted her bra and took a deep breath. No man in his right mind would look beyond her bosom.

She opened the door to a Nordic god.

A six-foot tall, muscular, blue-eyed man stood there. Ella's stomach fluttered, her mind went blank, and all she could do was stare.

"I'm Lance Fowler. You were expecting me?"

Heat flooded Ella's cheeks. "Come in."

She opened the door wider and ushered him into the house. He moved into the living room with its deep blue furnishings and casual decor. It was a room of comfort more than style.

"This is nice." Lance's deep voice held a note of approval. "Not what I would have expected from the neighborhood."

"I'm glad you approve."

Ella's nervousness evaporated. Lance might be breathtakingly handsome, but he was also approachable. A flutter of excitement settled in her stomach. She was beginning to look forward to this evening.

"Can I get you a drink?"

"Scotch on the rocks if you have it."

Ella went over to the portable bar she had set up at the far end of the room. She put a couple of ice cubes in a glass and half-filled it with a single malt scotch. Then she poured another glass of wine for herself.

She handed Lance his drink and then sat down in a chair beside the fireplace. "I hope you like beef."

"I love it. Your friend mentioned you were looking for a boyfriend experience. I'm glad I accepted." Lance sat in the sofa a few feet away from Ella. "It's a treat for me to get a home-cooked meal."

"Don't you cook?"

"I usually eat out." Lance smiled. "It comes with the territory."

Ella was just about to ask what he did when the oven timer went off. She stood. "Stay and finish your drink."

"Nonsense." Lance followed her into the kitchen. "I can help."

Ella pulled the beef from the oven and put it on a platter. She arranged the roasted potatoes around the meat and pushed the platter toward Lance who stood at the island sipping his drink.

"Would you carve the meat?"

"My pleasure." Lance picked up the carving set, and started slicing the prime rib. "My mother was the last woman to ask me to do this."

Ella poured water into the roasting pan, scraping the bottom as she began to make gravy. When that was finished, she put the carrots and green beans into serving bowls and carried everything into the dining room. Lance followed with the platter of beef.

Ella motioned Lance to sit and then handed him the bottle of champagne. "Would you mind?" she asked. "I can never do it without making a mess."

Lance took the bottle and twisted the wire off. He placed his napkin over the cork and eased it out of the bottle. A gentle pop and it was open.

"You've done that a few times." Ella passed her glass to him.

"In another life, I was a waiter." Lance winked. "I come by it honestly."

"What do you do now?"

"This and that." Lance handed her a glass of bubbles. "Whatever pays the best."

Ella took a sip of champagne. Its effervescence tickled her nose and the liquid burned its way down her throat. She loved it.

"To us." Lance raised his glass in a toast.

His deep voice sent a shiver through Ella. She clinked glasses with him before gulping down her champagne. She might regret what she did tomorrow morning, but she would enjoy tonight.

After dinner, they made their way into the living room. Lance sat down on the sofa and pulled Ella down beside him. The raw sexual desire she saw in his deep blue orbs mesmerized her.

He reached out and ran a finger across the seam of her lips. Ella's breath caught in her throat and her heart beat frantically in her chest. Her mouth went dry and she licked her lips. Heat flared in Lance's eyes.

"You're tempting me." His low voice sent a shiver down her spine.

Ella's brain was numb from the wine and champagne. She was past caring about the consequences. It had been too long since she had felt the touch of a man and that was all she wanted tonight. To feel.

Lance didn't disappoint. He leaned closer and feathered his mouth across hers. Ella gasped at the intense shudder of delight that exploded within her. He deepened the kiss, thrusting his tongue into her parted lips.

A blur of sensations bombarded her. Excitement, anticipation, and heat coursed through her. She cast aside her inhibitions and luxuriated in the waves of pleasure that radiated throughout her body.

She shifted her weight and leaned closer to Lance, but with a lingering touch of his lips, he ended the kiss. Disappointment flooded her. She tried to pull him back, but he shook his head.

"We have all night." His voice was thick.

Ella wanted to scream. Instead, she nodded. Lance was right. It had been over two years since a man had made love to her and she wanted to enjoy every second. His slow touch was already building a fire that would last the night.

"More champagne?" Lance reached for the bottle he had brought in from the dining room. He filled their glasses.

She took a gulp of the effervescent wine, before putting her glass down. Her throat was dry and she couldn't take her eyes off of him. He was stirring his champagne with a finger, his gaze didn't waver from her. He took a sip before setting his glass on the table.

He ran his finger across her lips before capturing her mouth with his.

Lance's lips were hard and demanding. Ella couldn't resist. Her tongue darted into his mouth. He tasted of champagne and sex. She wrapped her arms around him and pulled him close.

The fire he had started burst into flames.

She moved restlessly against him, silently urging him to join her. Lance's free hand feathered across her back sending shivers of excitement to the tips of her toes. The kiss deepened, until she was lost to the world.

When he released her, he was breathing heavily and his eyes had taken on the color of deep midnight blue. She melted. All thought vanished as she surrendered to the promise of passion in his gaze.

Lance took an ice cube from the wine bucket and held it between them. Ella jumped when a drop of cold water fell onto her chest. He ran the cube over her exposed skin. Before she could protest, he licked the water off. Heat suffused her body. Pain and pleasure mixed as one. Ella's breath came in gasps as he continued to bathe her in ice and fire.

The melting water dripped between her breasts and Lance's tongue followed its trail. When her dress blocked access, he unzipped her from behind and pulled it off her shoulders.

Ella fought the urge to cover herself, forcing herself to relax back against the sofa. Lance's tongue was building an inferno that even the freezing water could not quench. She was on the edge of bursting into flames.

Lance's teeth snapped open the front clasp of her bra and her breasts spilled out. Ella was beyond the point of embarrassment.

"Your breasts are beautiful," Lance whispered. "Perfect and full."

His tongue flickered across one of her nipples sending a quiver of excitement to her lower body. He then rubbed the ice cube around the areola making larger and larger circles until he reached her ribs. He did the same with her other breast.

When she was slick with water, Lance used his mouth and tongue to sip it from her. She was throbbing with need. Her pounding heart roared in her ears. She was gasping for breath, yet still Lance continued his slow perusal of her breasts.

Only when she thought she would explode, did he finally relent. His mouth covered her nipple and suckled, sending waves of shimmering bliss across her body. Her inner core throbbed with need, but he didn't hurry. His expert and slow seduction enthralled her. He was a master, and she could only groan her approval.

She reached to touch him and he pulled away. "Later," he growled. "I was hired for the whole evening."

Lance's words penetrated the fog that clouded Ella's brain. "Hired?"

Lance leaned back. "Alisa took care of everything. All you need to do is lay back and enjoy."

"What did she pay you for?" Ella's fingers fumbled with her bra fastener.

"For my services." Lance moved her hand away from her chest and raised it to his mouth. "They are too beautiful to cover."

Ella pulled her hand away. "Are you a gigolo?"

"That's too harsh a word." Lance tried to tap her lips, but Ella moved away. Instead, he sighed and took a sip of champagne. "I provide a service to women."

"What's the difference?" Ella pulled her dress up.

Lance shrugged. "I am hired to do many things. Tonight, my job is your pleasure."

"You're a male escort." Ella's head swirled with the implications. "That's illegal."

"I won't tell if you don't."

Lance handed Ella her champagne, but her hands were shaking too much to hold it. Nausea threatened to overwhelm her. Why hadn't she questioned Alisa more about her date? She had just assumed it was one of Alisa's friends out for a good time.

"Why don't we continue?" Lance's voice was low and seductive.

Ella shook her head and stood. Her mind refused to believe that she had sunk so low. It was one thing to cheat on her husband, with a willing man, and quite another to pay for sex. Technically, she wasn't paying for it. Alisa was.

Dare she ignore her rules and do what felt good?

She'd enjoyed Lance's caresses, and her body screamed for release, but where would that leave her in the morning?

She'd have had the sexual fling she threatened Gerry with, but she'd be the one who would carry the shame. At thirty-eight, she knew who she was, and that wasn't going to change. No matter what Gerry had done, Ella had to live with herself. A night of hot sex wasn't the answer.

She wanted love, not sex she had to pay for.

She straightened her shoulders. She had to end it now before it went further. "It would be best if you left."

Lance put his glass down. "You are such a responsive woman. It would be a shame to leave with both of us unfulfilled."

"It wouldn't work for me." Ella's gaze shied away from the temptation of his body. "I'm sorry. I didn't mean to mislead you."

"As you wish." Lance stood and walked to the door. "I'm here to do your bidding. Thanks for the dinner. You really are a terrific cook."

Ella clasped her arms together and waited until Lance had closed the door behind him before she collapsed. She dropped onto the sofa and buried her head in her hands. She had almost allowed herself to be seduced by a professional.

He was good.

Too good.

Ella sighed. Her body still ached with need. She couldn't fault Alisa. She had given her what she asked for, an affair without strings.

Ella groaned. All she had to show for tonight was a messy kitchen. She had struck out twice now and she didn't want to try a third time. An affair wasn't the answer to her marriage woes. It was time she confronted Gerry once and for all.

Chapter 9

Ella threw her books on the counter and walked to the kitchen door. The sky was clear and the sun's reflected light made the pool sparkle like jewels. The larkspur and columbine that edged the patio were in bloom and the wick wick song of a Flicker filled the air.

She couldn't resist. Gerry still wasn't home from his weekend with Marta, and her thoughts had been too jumbled to focus on school today. Jesse's truck was in the drive when she'd pulled up, but there was no sign of him. She stepped onto the patio and took a deep breath. She wandered to one of the flower gardens and started pulling weeds. In seconds, she was lost in nature.

She'd been working for about ten minutes when footsteps broke the silence. She glanced up, shading her green eyes from the sun with her hand.

"Enjoying yourself?" Jesse's deep voice sent a shiver through her.

"Completely." Ella stood and brushed the dirt from her pants. "Plants are relaxing."

"Building is like that for me." Jesse looked down at the flowers. "I confess to getting frustrated when it comes to gardens, though."

"Me and hammers don't mix." Ella's voice was wry. "I tried renovating when I was younger and it took several professionals to fix my mistakes."

"Then, we're agreed. If you stay away from hammers, I'll leave you to the gardens."

Ella chuckled. "That should be easy."

She felt at ease around Jesse. A few words with him and all of her problems disappeared. After the humiliation of the past weekend, it was a relief to be talking to someone who made no demands on her.

Jesse gestured to the guesthouse. "It's finished."

Ella's eyes widened. "I expected you to take another week."

He shrugged. "I put in a few extra hours in the mornings when you were at school."

"Can I see it?"

Jesse motioned for her to follow him. "Your approval is all that remains."

Ella fell in step with Jesse. "Everything looked perfect the last time I looked."

"Peeking wasn't allowed." Jesse's voice sounded stern, but there was a twinkle in his eye. "There was a penalty clause in my contract."

"You mean the verbal one you signed?" Ella grinned up at him.

Jesse opened the door of the guesthouse. "It's those picky details that catch me all the time."

Ella stepped into the house and the beauty overwhelmed her. The golden yellow of the room bathed the main area in sunlight. Flawless walls rose up to the exposed wooden beams of the cathedral ceiling. The north wall was a bank of French doors that looked out to the pool. Comfort and space radiated from the room.

"It's perfect." Ella roamed around, letting her hands touch the walls and woodwork. "It seems so spacious."

Jesse stood at the doorway, his arms folded across his chest. "The color and height of the walls add to the illusion."

Ella walked into the kitchenette. An island with a granite countertop divided it from the living area, and there was a small dining alcove to the side. It was the same color as the main room. The absence of upper cupboards, and a mini-sized refrigerator, let it visually blend with the rest of the room.

There was a pocket door a few feet from the dining area. Ella slid it open to reveal a small hallway leading to the bedroom and bathroom. The north wall of the bedroom was a bank of windows, mirroring the main area. The walls were a deeper yellow than the main area, giving the room a warmer, cocooning feeling.

"What guest wouldn't want to stay here?" Jesse walked over to the French doors and stood looking out. "You might not be able to get rid of them."

"Gerry wanted the house done up for the children." Ella joined him at the window. "In case any of them needed a place to stay."

"Not enough room in the house?"

Ella shrugged. "The house is too big for us. I have no idea what he's planning."

Suddenly, a thought hit her like a brick. What if Gerry didn't want this for the children? Had he planned to install Marta, his mistress here? Ella almost gasped aloud at the thought. A shudder shook her. Even Gerry couldn't be that cruel.

"Are you okay?" Jesse touched her arm, his gray eyes full of concern. "You're pale."

Ella clutched at the window frame. "I'm fine."

"You should sit down." Jesse took her arm and guided her out of the room. "You look too weak to stand."

Ella forced a smile. "I was in a rush this morning and forgot breakfast. It'll pass."

Jesse glanced at his watch. "It's past one. You need to eat."

"I'll get something in a bit." Ella patted her stomach. "Besides, a few missed meals won't hurt me."

"You almost passed out."

He took Ella by the arm and led her out of the guesthouse, stopping under a crab apple tree near the edge of the pool where there were two chairs and a small table. Jesse grabbed a lunchbox from the table and pulled out a sandwich.

"Lunch is on me." When Ella hesitated, Jesse took her by the shoulders and sat her in the chair. "It's ham and Swiss cheese."

Ella eyed the thick sandwich Jesse held out to her and sighed. She might as well relent. Besides, she was hungry. The whole-wheat bread was fresh, and the sharp tang of the cheese complimented the ham. It was delicious.

"That wasn't so hard," Jesse said when she had finished. "I hope you weren't starving yourself on purpose."

Ella brushed some crumbs from her lap. "Not today, but a diet isn't a bad idea."

Jesse snorted. "You look perfect."

"I could lose at least twenty pounds."

"I've never understood why women don't believe men when we say that they don't need to lose weight."

"Because experience has taught us differently." Ella winced as she remembered the constant criticism she had heard from Gerry on the subject of her weight. "We have to compete with all the thin girls out there."

"Is that what your husband wants?" Jesse crossed his arms. "When I make love to a woman, I want to feel curves."

"You say that now, but after you've been married for a few years you'll think differently." Ella stood and walked to the house.

"I doubt it." Jesse walked beside her.

"You're unique."

Ella entered the kitchen. It took a couple of seconds for her eyes to adjust to the darker light. She went to the fridge and pulled out a jug of lemonade and then took down two glasses from the cupboard.

"What about Marilyn Monroe?"

Confusion filled Ella. "I don't see the connection." She poured the lemonade and held one glass out to Jesse.

Jesse took it and put it on the counter. "Men lusted over her and she was a voluptuous woman."

Ella took a sip of lemonade, savoring the tangy liquid as it slid down her throat. "She lived over fifty years ago. Men's preferences are different today."

Jesse eased Ella's glass from her hand. His gray eyes smoldered with an inner heat that sent a scorching shock through her. He took a sip from her glass and then handed it back to her.

"My tastes never change."

Without another word, he picked up the lemonade she had poured for him and walked out of the kitchen. She watched him until he was out of sight and then sank against the island. Her whole body tingled with awareness.

Ella shook herself out of her reverie. Men never flirted with her, but there was no mistaking Jesse's meaning. It was flattering, but she had other things to worry about.

Her revelation in the guesthouse still haunted her. Her shock had passed, but she needed time to digest this new twist to Gerry's possible motives. She had been naïve to believe in Gerry's honesty. There was no saying what devious plans he might be plotting.

She picked up the phone and dialed.

It was answered on the second ring. "Brenna, I need the name and number of a good divorce lawyer."

Chapter 10

Ella was in the kitchen doing homework, when she heard the door slam. Jesse was hammering in the den, so that meant Gerry was home. She looked at the clock. It was almost noon on Tuesday. Gerry hadn't been home after the weekend; not even for clean clothes.

She closed her books and went looking for her husband. She found him in their bedroom throwing clothes into his duffel bag.

"Are you going somewhere?" Ella picked up a rumpled polo shirt and folded it before putting it back in the bag.

"I'm out of here for a few days." Gerry flung a pair of shorts onto the bed, missing Ella by a couple of inches.

Ella ignored the shorts and sat down. "Business?" she asked, even though she knew the answer. Gerry's clothes were for the golf course, not a boardroom.

"I promised Marta a couple of days in Denver."

Ella's jaw clenched. Her hands tightened into a fist and she fought the urge to throw the duffel bag at Gerry. She couldn't remember the last time Gerry had taken her anywhere.

"What about me?"

Gerry shrugged and pulled out some socks from his top dresser drawer. "You'll have the house to yourself. Plenty of time to study."

"That's not what I mean." Ella took a deep breath. "When was the last time you took me away?"

"Stop acting so foolish." Gerry leaned against the dresser. "You're my wife. You can do anything you want."

"As long as I don't interfere with you?"

Gerry turned back to his dresser and pulled out a pair of boxer shorts. "I'm tired of discussing this. Marta needs my attention."

"So do I." Ella's raised voice, echoed in the room. She took a deep breath and continued in a softer tone. "I can't go on like this."

"I've been honest with you." Gerry threw the boxer shorts into his bag. "I could never hurt you. You mean too much to me."

"Not as much as Marta."

"Nonsense." Gerry zipped his bag shut. "You're my wife."

"This arrangement is not working." Ella straightened her shoulders. "You might believe in polyamory, but I don't."

Gerry hoisted the duffel bag off the bed. "What more can I do?"

"You can stay home this weekend." Ella locked eyes with him. "That would show me that you are serious about our marriage."

Gerry scowled. "I've already told you where I stand. I provide a good life for you. What more do you want?"

"Love."

Gerry rolled his eyes. "You're the mother of my children."

"I want passion, not obligation."

Gerry hesitated for a second and then turned away. Ella's stomach sank as she watched him walk to the door. He opened it and then looked back at her. For a brief second, she saw uncertainty in his eyes and then it was gone.

"I'll be back Friday," he said in a cold voice.

Without another word, he walked away. The front door slammed closed. Ella blinked back tears. For the past year and a half, she had clung to the hope that Gerry would come back to her. That wasn't going to happen. Marta's hold on her husband was too strong.

Ella tried to move, but her body refused. Intuitively, she had always known that Marta would win. She had expected Gerry to have some difficulty with the decision. Instead, it had taken him all of five seconds to decide to go with Marta.

A sharp rap at the door interrupted her thoughts. Ella swung her head around. Jesse stood there, concern evident on his face.

"Are you okay?" His voice was soft and comforting.

Ella sniffed. "Gerry had an unexpected trip this weekend."

Jesse tilted his head. "Sound travels in a house, especially raised voices."

"You heard."

"It was difficult not to." Jesse walked into the room. His steps quiet on the hardwood flooring, an odd contrast to the heavy work boots he wore.

Jesse picked up the tissue box from the bedside table and handed it to her. The bed sank lower as he sat beside her. She pulled out a couple of tissues and wiped her eyes before blowing her nose. There was no point in hiding her discomfort.

"He says I have no reason to complain about his cheating. He's been above board with everything."

"Isn't that a contradiction?"

Ella's mind was full of cotton wool. "I don't understand."

"How can a cheater be honest?"

Ella winced at the sarcasm she heard in Jesse's voice. "He thinks I should be happy because he's not hiding it."

"So you don't mind."

The past year of pent up emotion exploded all at once. Her voice shook with fury. "He's my husband. He should be home with me, not screwing a younger woman from the office."

Jesse pulled her close. "You've been acting like it didn't bother you."

"It eats me up when I think about it. What am I supposed to tell the children? Sorry kids, your father is never home because he's having an affair with his accountant?"

"They're old enough to understand."

Ella leaned her head against Jesse's chest. "If I let Gerry get over his fling, I look like a fool. If I put my foot down, I lose him."

"I'm glad to see you've accepted this."

Ella glanced up at Jesse. "Are you laughing at me?"

Jesse grinned. "Nope. Just happy to see you're not wallowing in self-pity."

Ella rolled her eyes. "I have behaved like the perfect wife for the last year and a half, but no more."

"Good." Jesse got up from the bed. "He's a jerk."

Ella's throat felt thick. Jesse was staring at her with admiration. He was proud of her. For a second, she went numb with shock and then a shiver of excitement went through her.

"You're better off without him."

"I have my children to think about."

"Grown children." Jesse leaned close. Ella could feel his breath against her cheek and her mouth went dry.

"You deserve better." Jesse's husky voice made the hair on the back of her neck stand on end. "I'll be here when you've decided what to do."

He reached out and ran his finger down her cheek. Ella's heart beat wildly. Time was suspended as she sat there staring into Jesse's molten eyes that seemed to promise a world of undiscovered delights.

Jesse straightened up and left the room. Ella released the breath she'd been holding and fell back onto the bed. She didn't understand what had just happened, but she couldn't remember the last time she'd been so affected.

She ran her hand down the cheek Jesse had touched. It still felt hot; as if she had been branded. Branded as his. A shiver of anticipation raced through her. She'd forced herself to think of Jesse as a friend. Her mind had shied away from anything else because of his age. Perhaps, she'd been wrong about that.

For the rest of the week, she was either thinking about Jesse or watching him. He never said or did anything different from before, but there was a definite change. His gaze was intense and heated. A charge of electricity filled the air when he walked into the room. Her mouth went dry at the sight of him, and every cell in her body longed to be near him. The attraction was an ache that longed to be soothed.

All she had to do was reach out for Jesse and he'd be there. Before that could happen, she had to make a decision about her marriage. She couldn't continue as things were. Either she was married or she wasn't. She needed Gerry to come home to finalize everything.

Gerry was true to his word. He came slamming into the house Friday afternoon. He went into the bedroom. She kept reading her book on landscaping until he called her into the living room.

"Where are you going now?" Ella couldn't keep the exasperation from her voice.

"San Francisco." Gerry was in the foyer. "I'll be gone at least seven days, maybe more."

"Is Marta going with you?"

"It's business." Gerry's voice rose in anger. "She's the company accountant. Of course, she's coming."

Ella leaned against the living room doorway. Gerry had already packed and had his bags in the car. Emotionally she was drained. Nothing Gerry did affected her anymore, but she needed to know where things stood between them. It was past time for a change.

"I refuse to be a third party in this marriage." She kept her voice calm. "You can't have us both."

Gerry crossed his arms. "Are you threatening me?"

Ella shrugged. "Take it however you want, but you have to make a choice."

Gerry's eyebrows rose. "Between you and Marta? You have to be joking."

"Are you willing to try to save our marriage?"

"I've already explained that I will honor my vows to you."

"You broke those vows when you took a mistress." Anger burned in Ella's stomach. "I need to know if you intend to leave her."

"Or what?" Gerry snorted. "Do you honestly think you can do better than me?"

"Yes."

Gerry laughed. "You're used up. No man would find you attractive. Hell, I can't even bring myself to touch you anymore."

Ella winced at the venom of Gerry's words. His cruelty cut to her core, but she refused to let him see that. She had loved this man for over twenty years, but until this moment, she had never realized how much she disliked him.

"Did you ever love me?"

"No." Gerry's answer seemed to echo through the house.

"Then why marry me?" Ella clenched her hands into fists.

"You got yourself pregnant."

"I suppose I did that all by myself?" Ella couldn't believe his audacity. "I was only seventeen. A couple of months earlier and it would have been statutory rape."

"I never coerced you."

"That's not what I said. You were twenty-four and experienced. Why didn't you take precautions?"

"I paid for my mistake, but I refuse to keep paying." Gerry's jaw clenched. "I took care of you and the kids. I've earned the right to love whomever I want."

"I was foolish enough to believe you loved me." Ella's voice was sad.

Gerry ran his hand through his hair. "You're the mother of my children."

"That's not good enough." Ella took a deep breath. "If you won't try and save our marriage, then I want a divorce."

"No."

Ella's mouth dropped open. Gerry glared at her, his brown eyes flashed anger and his mouth had thinned into a line. It was his mule look. She usually acquiesced when he was in this mood, but not today.

"You've just admitted you don't love me. Why stay married?"

"The business is mine. There is no way in hell I'm going to give you half of it."

At last, she had the truth.

Money trumped high ideals and polyamory every time.

Ella could have kicked herself for being so blind. What a joke. And she had played the fool.

"If it wasn't for me, you never would have gone into business for yourself. You'd still be working downtown in Joe's garage."

"I built that business from the ground up. It's mine."

"Have you forgotten I was there too?" Ella looked at him in disbelief. "I kept Gerry Jr. in the office with me during the day, and in the evenings when he slept, I did all the bookwork."

Gerry's eyes shied away from her. "You haven't been involved with the business for years."

Ella pushed away from the doorway. "We agreed the children needed me home with them, especially when you started franchising the business."

"And you've done a wonderful job raising them." Gerry's voice softened. "It's the children I'm thinking of now. Gerry Jr. is planning on taking over the business when I retire. You can't deny him that."

"But you would deny me what is rightfully mine?" Ella's voice shook with disbelief. "What is that going to teach our son?"

"I give you everything you want now." Gerry's tone was conciliatory. "It's selfish of you to demand a divorce. Wait a few more years, until I can get the business straightened out."

"Until you can hide all the assets?"

"I have always treated you fair." Gerry raised his hands and walked toward her. "I need time to finance our new expansion."

Gerry pulled her toward him in a hug. "Besides, in a couple of years, you may feel totally different about this."

Disgust welled up within her. For over twenty years, she had lived with this man and never once seen him for whom he was. How could she have been so blind? Worse yet, she had been willing to try to save their marriage.

"I think you had better go." Ella's voice was devoid of emotion. "I wouldn't want you to be late."

Gerry chuckled and gave her a quick kiss on the cheek. "I knew you would understand. I could always count on my Ella to do the right thing. We'll talk about this when I get back."

"I'm sure we can work something out."

Gerry smiled. "I'll always be honest with you Ella. I think that is why we deal so well together."

Numbness kept Ella at the door as she watched Gerry leave the house. He pulled out of the driveway without a backwards glance. She supposed that was the way it had always been. She just hadn't taken the time to notice before.

In Gerry's compartmentalized world, she only had one role. She was the mother of his children and nothing more. He would never see her as a partner or even a lover. She had been a responsibility and as long as he took care of her, his obligation was over.

The revelation ripped her heart apart. There was no one to blame but herself. She had allowed Gerry to manipulate her and never once had she protested. Well, no more.

She was still a young woman and she deserved love. She was tired of being just a mother. She wanted more from life and was determined to get it. Gerry might have controlled her in the past. She was the one in charge now.

She picked up the piece of paper with the lawyer's information from Brenna.

She dialed the number.

Chapter 11

Ella threw her gloves on the ground. She'd been trying to ease the knot in her chest by exhausting herself with work. It hadn't helped. She was working in the gardens in the sweltering heat of the midday sun. Sweat poured down her back and she needed a break. She stood and walked to the house. Killing herself with work wasn't the answer. The blast of cool air in the kitchen sent a welcomed shiver across her skin.

She'd seen the lawyer this morning and he'd started the paperwork for the divorce. There would be no contest because of Gerry's blatant affair. The lawyer said she could consider herself separated and he'd ensure she got her fair share of the assets. She'd come away from the meeting feeling scared and relieved at the same time.

It had been four days since Gerry had left for his extended business vacation in San Francisco, and she had done nothing but think since then. She oscillated between feeling selfish and feeling guilty because the divorce would tear the business and family apart. She needed to take care of herself and her future. She'd worked just as hard as Gerry. It wasn't fair that she was expected to walk away with nothing.

Gerry Jr. could still work in the business even if she owned half. The children were old enough to understand that she couldn't continue in a marriage where her husband openly flaunted his mistress. The more she considered her options for the future, the more depressed she became. Work was the only solution.

With a groan, she leaned back and stretched. Every muscle in her body ached, but the pain in her heart was worse.

Her marriage was over.

The words were a mantra that kept playing themselves, over and over, in her head. If she were being honest with herself, her marriage had been over the day Gerry had announced that he had a mistress.

She'd been too frightened and weak to recognize it. Her world was shattered. She wished she knew how to pick up the pieces of her life. She would have to tell all her friends and family, and then, the children. Her stomach clenched at the thought of telling her children. It would destroy them.

"Enough," she said aloud. "What I need is a drink."

"Alcohol?" a male voice asked.

Ella jumped. Adrenaline shot through her, causing her heart to beat at a furious pace. She turned and let out a gasp when she saw Jesse standing there, hands on his hips, a wide grin spread across his face.

"Did I startle you?" Jesse's low voice sent a shiver up Ella's spine.

"I forgot you were in the house." Ella turned back to the fridge and pulled out a pitcher of lemonade.

"So it's non-alcoholic." Jesse reached past her for two glasses. "Probably safer."

A shock of awareness skittered up Ella's back at Jesse's nearness.

"You're quiet." Jesse poured the lemonade into the glasses. "Or did I interrupt something."

"I was thinking aloud."

Jesse took a swallow of his drink. The long line of his throat mesmerized Ella. His muscles tightened in his neck as the liquid made its way down. She bit her lower lip and resisted the urge to touch him. Never had she been more aware of a man.

Jesse emptied his glass and put it down on the counter with a bang. "Aren't you going to drink yours?"

Butterflies fluttered in Ella's stomach and for a second she didn't think she had the strength to lift the glass, but she pushed past that. She was behaving like a lovesick teenager with a crush. She took a small sip and almost sighed as the icy bitterness freshened her mouth.

"Better?" Jesse was looking at her with concern.

"Much."

Ella finished her glass and then poured another for both of them. She hopped onto the counter and rested her head on the upper cabinets. She hadn't done this since she was a kid and she relished the feeling.

Freedom.

Jesse leaned against the island. "You're in a strange mood. When I came in this morning, you were so busy outside that I didn't want to disturb you."

"I had a rough night." Ella ran her finger around the top edge of her glass. "Gardening always centers me."

"Care to talk about it?"

"It's messy." Ella sighed. "And complicated."

Jesse folded his arms across his chest. "I doubt it."

Ella shrugged. "Gerry's away for a week, but before he left, I told him I wanted a divorce. He asked me to wait until he could straighten out the business."

"And are you?"

Ella shook her head. "I've been a fool. The only reason he's been stringing me along is because he doesn't want to give me a share of the company."

Jesse took a sip of lemonade. "I thought that might be the case. You didn't have a prenuptial?"

"We were kids and Powell's Transmission didn't exist until I convinced Gerry to take a risk."

"You deserve your half."

"He's making it difficult." Ella gave Jesse a wry smile. "He knows my weaknesses and he's using them against me. A divorce will mean that our son, Gerry Jr., won't get the business intact when Gerry retires."

Ella's stomach tightened as the familiar guilt washed over her. She'd been wrestling with it since Gerry had left. How could she be so selfish as to deny her children their future?

Jesse looked pensive. "You're not buying that are you?"

"It seems selfish if I don't let Gerry Jr. have it." Ella banged her head back against the cabinet. "I worked just as hard to establish the business, but what kind of mother would I be if I destroyed it?"

"You're asking for your half. If the business is stable, then that shouldn't be a problem." Jesse cleared his throat. "I would be more concerned with what your husband is doing while you hold off on seeing a lawyer."

"You mean what assets will he be hiding?" Ella rolled her eyes. "I must have sucker written across my forehead. Even a child could have seen through Gerry's stalling."

"Not necessarily." Jesse reached over and squeezed her hand. "You wanted to try to save the marriage. There's nothing foolish about that."

"Most people would disagree with you." She was filled with the familiar weariness that descended when she thought about her marriage. "There are some things beyond repair."

"Too many people are willing to throw away a relationship at the first signs of trouble."

"A mistress is more than a little problem."

"So you trusted your husband." Jesse shrugged. "That isn't a sin, or a judgment on your intelligence."

Ella smiled. "Are you trying to make me feel better or worse?"

"Neither." Jesse leaned closer. "I just want to know if your marriage is over."

"I spoke to a lawyer this morning and the paperwork for the divorce has been started. Tomorrow, the locksmith will be coming. Gerry no longer lives here."

A flutter of excitement danced in Ella's stomach at the intensity of Jesse's gaze. His gray eyes had softened to molten silver. The smell of lemons and musk mingled and tickled her nostrils. She inhaled deeply.

"Then, there's nothing to stop me from doing this," he said in a husky voice before his lips captured hers.

Shock coursed through her, until the delicious sensations that Jesse was creating took over. She shuddered with delight as quivers of pleasure raced throughout her body. He thrust his tongue into her mouth and she brushed hers against his. The taste of lemonade and lust set her body on fire. An explosion of fireworks shimmered through her.

She felt alive.

She craved more.

Jesse brought his arms around her and pulled her close. His heart beat furiously against her chest. He was as aroused as she. Never had she experienced such overwhelming passion. It was intoxicating.

Jesse ended the kiss, gently nibbling and sucking her lips until he had eased away. She shook with yearning as an explosion of heat pulsed through her. His thumb brushed her jaw. She gasped at the intense jab of desire that twisted in her womb.

"I've wanted to do that, since the moment I first saw you." Jesse's voice shook.

Ella's eyes widened. "I looked a mess that day."

"You looked adorable." Jesse rubbed his nose against hers. "I had to see you again. That's why I agreed to do the renovation work for you."

"You're too young for me." Ella tried to move away, but Jesse held her firm.

"I'm thirty-three. A grown man who knows what he wants. And I want you."

Ella bit her lip. Jesse's gaze didn't waver. There was no denying that she was attracted to him and he was only five years younger than her. Technically, it wasn't cradle robbing.

The simple truth was, she loved being with him. He'd been a friend when she had no one else. Time ceased at that moment. It was an effort to breathe as her chest tightened with indecision. She was at a turning point and the road to Jesse led to the edge of a cliff.

Did she dare jump?

What did she have to lose? Her marriage was over. Her children were grown. She'd be known as a cougar, and society would condemn her, but her friends would cheer her decision.

Then, there was Jesse's kiss.

Unforgettable and life changing.

She took a deep breath. "I'm thirty-eight years old. I'm a grown woman who has never been kissed like that before. I want you."

Jesse gave her a slow smile. "I'll prove that age doesn't matter."

This time, when their lips met there was heat, but time slowed, as did Jesse's kisses. Sighs and groans filled the air as his hands moved down her back. He held her close, drinking from her mouth, until she thirst for more. He didn't disappoint. His lips moved from her mouth to her neck.

A shiver of delight raced across her skin.

Jesse pulled at her blouse, until the buttons popped. Cool air brushed her skin, followed by the smooth caress of his fingers. Flickers of heat followed until she was burning with need. Jesse's lips moved to her breasts. With one swift motion, he disposed of her bra and shirt. His hand enclosed one of her breasts and his thumb brushed against the sensitive tip.

A shudder of desire ripped through her.

"God, you're beautiful." Jesse's voice was hoarse. "How long has it been since a man has made love to you?"

"Gerry hasn't touched me in two years." Ella groaned as Jesse's lips encircled her nipple and suckled. "I don't think any man has ever loved me."

"Then, I'm the first."

Jesse moved to the other breast and kissed and nibbled, until the embers of the fire that burnt within her burst into flames. Frantic fingers pulled at her clothes, unzipping and peeling her jeans and panties. His hands roamed up her calves and stopped at her thighs.

He pushed her legs apart and bent down to the juncture between then. A part of her brain was aware of what he intended, and she put a hand out to stop him. Jesse looked up with a raised eyebrow.

"No one's ever touched me there with their mouth."

Jesse smiled. "You're in for a treat."

He spread her legs. Ella's heart almost pounded out of her chest and she clung to the edge of the counter with her fingers. The wet lave of Jesse's tongue across her sensitive inner core sent a jolt of intense pleasure to deep within her entire being.

His tongue caressed and teased.

She shattered with climax within seconds.

Wave upon wave of bliss permeated through her body. She gasped with wonder and disbelief. She'd lived almost forty years without experiencing such intense ecstasy. She leaned her head back against the cupboard and shivered.

Jesse's lips were brushing her inner thighs, when she came back to earth. She moved to get off the counter, but he held her in place. This time, his lips moved up to her abdomen while his fingers brushed her clitoris. She'd barely recovered from her first orgasm, when her body shuddered with another release.

Jesse's fingers eased their pressure. His tongue circled her areola and a surge of liquid heat flooded her. His mouth moved to her lips and captured them in heated hunger.

"You're so responsive." His voice was a husky whisper that sent shivers of excitement through her. "Do you have protection?"

It took her a second to realize what Jesse was asking. Her stomach sank. Gerry's vasectomy had taken care of any birth control concerns she'd had, and she'd never strayed from her marriage. It was a whole new world. One in which she was ill equipped.

"No." Her voice was low.

Jesse stroked a finger down her cheek and cradled her chin in his hand. "No worries. I have one condom for emergencies, so we'll have to make do for now. I'll come prepared next time."

Ella almost groaned with relief. She needed to feel Jesse inside of her, to be connected intimately with this man who made her pulse race. Never before had she been so frantic to make love. She pulled open his work shirt and ran her hands over his hard muscled chest.

A spiral of tension built within her. The scent of his skin was a drug she couldn't get enough of. She licked and tasted every inch of his chest before kissing her way up his neck. She wanted to lose herself in him. Her body vibrated with need. Her hands reached for his belt and undid it within seconds. His jean snap proved trickier.

Jesse moved her hands away. "Let me."

Within seconds, his pants were around his ankles.

Hungry kisses and urgent fingers roamed his body. Heat raced through her as the frantic beat of his heart increased. His feet wrestled with his boots and then she heard the fling of his pants onto the floor, followed by the sound of a plastic wrapper being ripped open. She clung to his shoulders, feeling the firm muscles tense as Jesse lifted her from the counter. Her lips never left his. She savored the strength and urgency of their passion.

Jesse lowered her body until she felt him pushing to enter her. She leaned back and moved her hips to give him easier access. He entered her with a slow, steady motion. She moaned as waves of pleasure washed over her. He filled her completely.

"Perfect." His voice was hoarse.

"My feelings exactly." Ella captured his lips and let him feel her joy.

She eased up and then down. Her body shuddered with the thrill. Her hips moved in a measured, unhurried, and tantalizing motion. She wanted the sensations they were creating together to last forever. Never had she thought such bliss existed.

Jesse moved with her to the kitchen table. She hung on and let him take the lead. Every motion this man made was divine. He laid her on the table and then he thrust deep, touching her inner core. Shudders of ecstasy exploded, as her orgasm hit with the force of an earthquake. He held himself tight against her, so that her pleasure was increased.

When the last tendrils of bliss had faded, she opened her lids and looked up at him. His gaze was heated and tender. Sweat had beaded on his forehead. God she loved him. The realization was sudden and true. Her eyes widened and Jesse grinned. Surely, he hadn't heard her thoughts?

"Again?"

She didn't trust her voice, so she nodded.

This time, he rotated his hips as he thrust, hitting an area that sent a flood of moisture to meet him. He continued to move within her, building a taut coil of exquisite tension. He pulled her legs high onto his hips, his fingers caressing and teasing every inch of her, as he drove them both to a shuddering release.

Ella bit back her cry of exultation as she drifted back from pulsating rapture. Never had she experienced such perfect happiness. Jesse was gazing at her with tenderness. He leaned over the table and pulled her up close to him. His hands brushed over her back and his lips lingered on hers. It was a slow, lethargic descent from the heights of heaven.

"That was truly spectacular." Jesse's husky voice vibrated through to her.

Ella gave him a lingering kiss and then shifted on the table. He sighed and moved away, turning his back as he disposed of the condom. Ella jumped off the table, steadying herself with her hand, before picking up her jeans and top. She didn't bother with her bra. Her hands were still shaking too much to fiddle with its hooks.

When she turned around, Jesse was already dressed in his workpants and T-shirt. He was sitting and pulling on his boots. She held her breath and waited for him to look up. She'd never done anything like this before. Would awkwardness destroy the beauty of what they'd shared?

What happens now?

Jesse stood and looked at her. His eyes were soft gray with apology. He gathered her close and kissed the top of her head. This was the moment she dreaded. He regretted making love.

"I have to get back to my crew." He lifted her chin and kissed her nose. "I'm on a schedule and they need me."

Ella swallowed the lump in her throat. "Will I see you again?"

His thumb caressed her cheek. "Try and stop me."

The lead weight in her stomach shifted. He wanted to see her again. She hadn't made a complete fool of herself. She stood up on tiptoes and kissed him. Her lips clung as a jolt of desire burned through her veins. Even after all they'd shared, she wanted more.

"You're insatiable." Jesse's breathing was ragged. "I'll be back, and this time I'll have plenty of protection."

She walked him to the door and leaned against it, watching as he wheeled his truck out of her driveway. She didn't know how it had happened, but she'd made a huge mistake. She was supposed to have a fling, a quick affair to safeguard her marriage. Instead, she'd made wild, passionate love on her kitchen table.

She'd broken the rules.

She'd fallen in love.

Chapter 12

Twilight had descended and with it a cool breeze to relieve the heat of the day. Ella took a sip of white wine as she gazed out her patio door. A couple of the brighter stars were noticeable in the night sky, even though the streetlights hadn't turned on yet. Everything was calm and peaceful, which was the exact opposite of how she felt.

Having sex on the kitchen table did that to you.

She took another sip of wine. Jesse had run off with a promise to return. That had been hours ago. The longer it took to hear from him; the greater her insecurities became. Who was she fooling? No man who looked as good as Jesse would want to be with a woman her age. His looks alone guaranteed he never lacked dates, never mind how fantastic a lover he was.

That was an understatement.

A shiver of remembered ecstasy raced down her spine. She'd never imagined that lovemaking could be so wonderful. All of her years of marriage hadn't prepared her for the mind blowing, heart wrenching, pleasure she'd experienced this afternoon. There was no way she'd ever return to the cold and clinical sex she'd shared with Gerry, which had been more duty, than desire. For the first time since she'd found out about Marta, she was happy.

Relieved.

Free.

The fairy lights, strategically placed in the gardens surrounding her pool, were just beginning to flicker to life, when she heard the doorbell ring. Her heart stopped for a second and then raced. Her hand shook as she put her wine glass down and straightened her blouse. She forced herself to take steady, even steps to the door. As much as she wanted to run, she didn't want to show up out of breath. She still had some pride left.

She took a deep breath and then opened the door.

Jesse stood outside.

With a boyish smirk, he presented a bouquet of flowers and a box of extra-large condoms. "I came prepared this time."

Before Ella could say anything, he pulled her into his arms. His lips clung to hers as he walked her back into the house and slammed the door shut. His hand held her head close to him as he spun her around the foyer. Hunger and renewed passion sparked between them. Ella surrendered to the sensations and let Jesse sweep her off her feet.

The kiss ended when both of them came up for air. Jesse's hand brushed her hair away from her face and then, his finger traced a line down her cheek. His chest was heaving, but his gaze was tender as he looked down at her. A flutter of excitement settled in her stomach and Ella couldn't stop the smile of contentment that spread across her lips.

The truth was in his eyes.

He did care about her.

"It was so late, I didn't think I'd see you tonight."

"Nothing could have kept me away." Jesse's voice was a husky whisper that sent shivers of delight up her spine. "The taste and feel of you has haunted me since I left this afternoon."

Ella moved out of his arms. "Would you like some wine?" She took his hand and led him into the kitchen. "I just opened a bottle of Chardonnay."

"Wine sounds great." Jesse accepted the glass from Ella and raised it. "Here's to us."

Ella took a sip and then leaned against the counter. "How did your meeting go?"

Jesse grimaced. "The project is behind schedule."

"I hope that's not because you've been working here."

Jesse shook his head. "We had some unexpected complications. As it is, I need to head up to the city soon. I have a couple of projects that need my attention."

Ella's stomach sank. Jesse had a perfect excuse to leave because of job demands. There was nothing she could do about it. Would he remember her when he was gone? She gave herself a mental shake. He was here tonight and she intended to enjoy every moment.

"When do you leave?"

"Not for a couple of days." Jesse grabbed the bottle of wine. "Let's go outside. It's a beautiful night."

Ella couldn't agree more. The moon was rising, and the tiny sparkles of illumination from the garden lights gave the pool and courtyard a shimmering glow. It mirrored her feelings. Tingles all over and flickers of excitement. There was magic and romance in the air, and she didn't want to miss a second of it.

Jesse put the wine on the table and went to stand by the pool. Ella followed him. As much as she wanted to reach out and caress his arm, she kept a small distance between them, in case she'd misread his intentions. He was frowning as he gazed down at the smooth mirrored surface of the pool.

"What are you thinking?" Ella's voice was hesitant.

"For all the time I've spent at your house, I've never used this pool."

"You're welcome to swim if you want." Ella motioned to the newly finished guest house. "I have plenty of towels and extra bathing suits, if you need them."

"I've never seen you use the pool." Jesse turned to her. "Why don't you swim?"

"I never learned." Ella shrugged. "I sometimes go in and cool off, but that's all."

"It's time for a change."

Ella's eyes followed Jesse, as he put his wine glass down on the table. He pulled his T-shirt over his head and set it down on one of the chairs. God, he was gorgeous. All firm muscle with a lean physique. A rush of heat suffused her body, as she remembered how it had felt being held in his arms.

She swallowed back her desire. "I'll get a couple of towels."

She came back from the guesthouse carrying a stack of plush beach towels. Jesse was still in his jeans and had moved back to the edge of the pool. He motioned for her to join him. She couldn't deny him. Not tonight. She put the towels on one of the chairs and walked to him.

When she reached him, he unzipped his jeans and stripped. "Let's go skinny dipping."

"I couldn't." Ella's voice shook. "The neighbors might see."

"No chance. The fence is too high and the shrubbery and distance between the houses guarantees privacy."

"You've thought this out."

"Haven't you?" Jesse grinned and grabbed her hand. "Either you take your clothes off, or I'll pull you in with them on."

"You wouldn't dare."

Jesse tugged her close and kissed her. Their lips clung together, and she could feel the hard pressure of his arousal against her. She moaned and rubbed against him. He broke off the kiss and looked down at her. The heat of his gaze seared through to her soul.

"Two can play this game." He undid the top button of her blouse.

"I can't swim." Ella nibbled at his lower lip.

"I'm not interested in doing laps." Jesse's fingers finished with the rest of her buttons and pulled the blouse off her shoulders. "There's something very sensual about the feel of water against bare skin. Let me teach you."

A bolt of excitement shuddered through her and settled in her womb.

"If you promise not to let me go."

Jesse unclipped her bra. "Never. I will always be with you."

Jesse's fingers brushed against her heated skin. They fluttered against the side of her now bare breasts and smoothed across the front. The sweet thrill of anticipation fired her blood. He feathered his thumbs across her sensitive nipples and then circled them with a slow, deliberate teasing motion.

Moist heat centered in her lower abdomen.

"You have too many clothes on." The soft whisper of his voice tickled her cheek. "Let's get naked together."

How could she refuse?

With shaking fingers, she unzipped her pants. Her heart raced as Jesse's gaze followed her hands. His breathing became ragged, as the cool cotton of her pants slid to the ground. His fingers caressed her skin. When she stepped out of her slacks, he stopped.

"Beautiful." His voice vibrated with passion.

A warm glow of delight ran through her. There was no doubting the sincerity of Jesse's feelings. For the first time in her life, she was basking in the approval of a man she cared about. It was a powerful aphrodisiac.

She reached her arms up to his neck and pulled him close. "How about those lessons you promised?"

Jesse grinned. "Ready?"

She nodded.

The next second she was in the pool gasping for air. The water was cold and a chill raced up her spine. Panic threatened to overcome her, but Jesse held her close. His hand rubbed up her back in reassuring comfort. Her body relaxed as the initial shock of the water eased.

"I told you I wouldn't let you go."

"I wasn't expecting to jump in."

"It's always best to take the plunge in one swift motion." Jesse brushed her hair out of her eyes. "You get the unpleasantness over with, all at once. After that, it's pure enjoyment."

"I'll have to trust you on that one."

Ella leaned back in his arms and looked up into his face. He was in the shadows. The sun had set completely. The only light they had was from the moon and the garden lamps. It added mystery and a surreal atmosphere to the night. It was the perfect setting for love and romance, and Ella had waited her whole life for this. The tension eased from her body.

The water had warmed against her skin.

It was now a silken caress that tantalized.

Jesse pushed off from the bottom of the pool and took her with him. They floated over the glassy surface, arms and bodies entwined, until they reached the opposite side. Their bodies remained below the surface as they embraced. The back and forth motion of the water added to their lovemaking.

Fingers touched and stroked.

Lips clung with hunger.

Shivers of pleasure raced across her body. The world was spinning all around her, and she didn't want it to stop. She surrendered to the passion and the beauty of the night and let her body sing with the joy of being in Jesse's arms. This was a man who made her forget everything as she luxuriated in the sensations he created within her.

He lifted her at the waist and positioned himself to enter her. She twisted her hips and with one fluid downward motion they were joined. Bliss permeated throughout her. Jesse thrust deep and she tilted her pelvis to accept all of him. Together they moved. Pleasure and tension spiraled until she was at the screaming edge of climax.

Jesse's hold on her hips tightened and he turned them around in the water, letting its buoyance hug their bodies. Their heated pace increased until they both exploded with ecstasy. The water continued to embrace them as they descended from the heights of heaven. Their heartbeats slowed to normal and the languid ease of afterglow spread through them.

"You were right about the water." Ella gave Jesse a light kiss on his neck.

"You're superb." Jesse nuzzled her ear. "I've never held a woman so responsive before."

"You're no slouch."

Ella's heart soared. Being with Jesse was more than she had ever expected. She wasn't crazy though. It couldn't last. She might have been foolish enough to fall in love with him, but she wasn't expecting anything in return. She'd accept whatever time they had together and hold it close to her heart. After her divorce from Gerry came through, she'd probably be spending a lot of nights alone. That's when she would pull out these precious moments with Jesse and relive them.

Jesse floated them to the side of the pool where they'd first jumped in. He put his hands on her waist and lifted her onto the patio before joining her. Water dripped off their bodies and the cool night breeze brushed her skin, sending a shiver through her. She reached for the towels she'd brought outside and handed one to Jesse before she wrapped herself in its warm plush comfort.

Jesse reached over and pulled her close. His hand rubbed her arm in a brisk warming movement. "It's beautiful out here."

"It's my sanctuary." Ella snuggled closer, letting his body heat warm her.

Jesse smiled down at her. "Did you design it?"

"Everything except the pool and guesthouse. Gerry had those installed and left the rest for me."

"I take it you also did the work."

Ella shrugged. "I didn't lay out the patio stones, but I did the landscaping and gardens."

"You're very talented." Jesse stood and pulled her up beside him. "You should start your own landscaping design business."

"I will, once I finish my College course."

She lifted her face to Jesse and welcomed his kiss. His lips soothed and teased. His tongue slid over the seal of her mouth, until she opened for him and then he darted in. It was a slow lingering exploration that rekindled the embers of their passion. Her body burned with renewed interest. She didn't want the kiss to end.

Jesse was the first to move away. He wrapped his towel around his waist. "Let's take this inside."

Ella secured her towel under her arm. "Not the house. There's too many bad memories there for me."

"The guesthouse then." Jesse pulled her close. He grabbed his box of condoms and they walked to the small building he had renovated. "Is there any furniture, or should we grab a couple of blankets."

"I think you'll find it quite cozy."

Ella let Jesse go in first and waited as he flicked on the light. His eyes widened. The main room was furnished with a brown leather sofa and chair. Throw pillows in red and yellow floral fabric added warmth to the leather furniture. One of her quilts was thrown over the back of the sofa.

In the kitchenette, a small wooden table with two chairs stood against the wall. The stain of the wood matched the large exposed beams in the cathedral ceiling. Matching stools stood in front of the island that divided the space. Throughout the room, pictures of flowers and the outdoors adorned the walls.

"It's beautiful. When did you do this?"

"The furniture was delivered a couple of days ago. I had to finish the decorating after that." Ella ran a hand over the brown granite of the kitchenette island. "Do you like it?"

"I love it." Jesse walked over to the large windows that looked out over the pool. "It's a fairyland. I can't wait to see what you did to the bedroom."

Ella opened the pocket door.

Jesse grabbed her hand and pulled her through the doorway.

A four-poster, king-sized bed stood against the far wall. It was covered with another of Ella's quilts; a Dresden plate done in numerous scraps of floral fabric. It looked like rounds of miniature gardens. Pillows in reds and yellows were scattered over the top of the bed. A narrow table stood against the opposite wall and had two crystal table lamps at each end. Ella flicked them on and marveled at the warm ambiance that filled the room.

Jesse shook his head and turned to her. "You're one very talented lady."

"You did the hard work. Decorating was the fun part."

"I'll gladly do the renovations if you're going to finish it." Jesse dropped his towel on the floor. "Come here."

Ella fingered the edge of her towel and looked out the window. "Won't the neighbors see?"

"Not if you turn the lights out."

The desire that had been banked began to burn again. Ella turned the lights off and shut the door before dropping her towel. The illumination from the garden lights gave the room the flickering fantasy of candles burning. Jesse was right. It was a special night and beautiful. She went to the patio door and opened it wide. The cool breeze of a summer night and the scent of roses filled the air.

Jesse threw the covers back on the bed and patted it. "Now where were we?"

Ella reminded him by brushing her lips against his.

"How could I forget?" Jesse pulled her down beside him. His lips and fingers caressed her and rekindled the embers of passion.

Chapter 13

Ella put two cups of steaming coffee on the table and then screeched when Jesse grabbed her waist and swung her down onto his lap. Two nights and one glorious day had passed since Jesse had shown up on her doorstep. Nothing in her life had ever been so perfect. They'd talked for hours, made love, ate, and swam. Jesse had insisted on giving her swimming lessons.

Their time was almost over.

"I wish you didn't have to leave." Ella sighed as she straightened the buttons on his shirt.

"It's only one week." Jesse lifted her chin. "I promise to return as soon as it's over."

Ella blinked back her tears. They'd had a wonderful time together and she was crazy to wish it wouldn't end. Fear threatened to overwhelm her. Doubt clouded her emotions. As much as Jesse insisted he would be back, a part of her expected never to see him again.

"I'll be waiting."

"Trust me." Jesse's voice was a low whisper.

He leaned closer and brushed his lips over hers. The passion between them that was never far from the surface, flared to life. Ella wrapped her arm around his neck and clung to his lips. Their tongues teased and stroked until the world had spun away.

"What the hell is going on here?" A loud voice roared from the patio door.

Ella jumped at the sound of Gerry's voice. Jesse didn't release her immediately. Instead, he let his lips linger on hers for a few seconds before pulling away with a sigh. He glanced over at Gerry.

"I would think it's pretty obvious." Jesse's voice was dry as he straightened up in the chair. "If I'm not mistaken, you're trespassing."

Gerry's eyes bulged and Ella had to hide a smile. Gerry hated not being in control. She patted Jesse's chest and edged away from him. He didn't' release her. Her eyebrows rose, but Jesse held her firm.

"I can handle this." She kept her voice low.

Jesse glanced over at Gerry and then back at her. "You don't need to do this alone."

"I know, but this is between Gerry and me."

Gerry had entered the kitchen with hands clenched at his side and eyes narrowed. His anger was palatable. She understood Jesse's concern, but she'd lived with Gerry long enough to know when not to push him. This was definitely one of those times.

"He won't hurt me."

"Don't be so sure of that. What happened to the lock on the front door?"

Gerry threw his keys on the kitchen table. They clattered and skidded across the surface before coming to rest in front of her and Jesse. Ella's hand reached for the keys and she snapped the old house set off the ring and put them into her jean pocket. The locksmith had changed the locks yesterday and the sooner Gerry understood he didn't live here, the better.

Jesse's grip loosened.

He set Ella on her feet and then stood with his arms crossed over his chest. "You're not welcome here."

"This is my house." Gerry's voice rose to a shout as he took a step toward Jesse. "You're the intruder."

"Ella invited me." Jesse's voice remained calm.

Ella put her hand on Jesse's arm and stopped him from saying anything else. She had hoped to avoid this conversation, but it was necessary. She wasn't under Gerry's control any longer. She was a woman who could make her own decisions and stand by them. Gerry's reaction and anger didn't frighten her.

"I'll walk you out." Ella grabbed Jesse's hand and tugged. "You don't want to be late for your meeting."

Jesse tilted his head. "Are you sure."

She nodded. "I'll be fine."

At the front door, she stopped him. "Thank you for understanding."

"I don't want him steamrolling you into changing your mind."

"Nothing will do that." She stood up on tiptoes and brushed her lips across his. "After this weekend, I could never go back to that sterile excuse of a marriage again."

Jesse put his arms around her waist and pulled her close. He captured her lips in a kiss that took her breath away. He poured all of his hunger and passion into the kiss and Ella responded. She gave him all of her love. She might have doubts about their relationship, but her love was real and lasting.

When the kiss ended, Jesse put his forehead on hers. "I don't want to leave."

"It's only for a week." Ella swallowed back her tears. "That should give me time to sort things out with the lawyer."

"I'll call every night."

"And I'll be here." Ella straightened up and opened the door. "Drive carefully."

Jesse caressed her cheek with his hand before leaving. She watched him walk to his truck and drive away. Only when he was out of sight did she shut the door. She leaned against it and pushed away her fears. She had to trust that what they'd shared was more than a fling. Jesse would return when he could.

She straightened her shoulders.

Her old life was over, but she still had to tie up the loose ends.

Gerry was pacing in the kitchen when she walked in. She sat at the table and took a sip of her coffee. It had already started to cool. She didn't care. It was something to hold and that gave her strength. She became concerned when Gerry started to slam the cupboard doors.

"Dammit Ella. How could you have that man in this house?"

"He's been here for several weeks." She took another sip of coffee.

"That's not what I meant. You slept with him."

"Actually, very little sleeping was involved."

Gerry's eyes bugged out. For a second she thought he was going to have a stroke, but then he seemed to recover. His lips turned up in a sneer. "You whore."

"You told me to take a lover." Ella was surprised at how calm her voice was. "I thought you believed in polyamory?"

"Don't try and play smart with me. You're my wife for God's sake. You should behave with a little more decorum."

"Like you do?" Ella tilted her head. "Do you think people don't know you're sleeping with Marta? I'm sure I'm the byword for a fool down at the office."

"Nonsense." Gerry pulled his shirt down at the waist. "I've been very discrete."

"You've thrown your affair in my face at every turn." Ella twirled a finger around the rim of her cup. "No more. I've called a lawyer. You no longer live here."

"You can't do that." Gerry shouted. "I'm your husband and I make the decisions."

"You mean decisions about how you hide your assets?" Ella's voice rose. "My lawyer has already found them. Half of everything, including your pension is mine."

"Over my dead body." Gerry spit the words at her.

"In that case, everything will go to me." Ella took a deep breath. "In a few months, you will be my ex-husband. Adultery is grounds for a divorce, and you have certainly been guilty of that."

"What about you and the handyman?" Gerry's hand shook as he pointed at her.

Ella shrugged. "I was already legally separated when Jesse, and I became lovers."

"You stupid bitch!" Gerry picked up a cup from the counter and threw it. It crashed on the floor sending shards of broken glass skittering across the marble tiles. "My lawyer will tear you apart."

"I thought you wanted us to remain married?" Sugar would have melted on her voice. "When did you hire a lawyer?"

"The moment I knew I couldn't live with you any longer."

"Now the truth comes out." Ella nodded. "You thought you could string me along until there would be nothing left for me."

"You were stupid enough to go along with it."

"I was trusting and faithful." Ella's voice held a note of exasperation. "Just because I wasn't prepared to throw away twenty-one years of marriage without a fight doesn't make me stupid."

"It doesn't matter." Gerry leaned back against the counter and laughed. "I was almost finished with you, anyway."

Ella's eyes warmed when she noticed where Gerry was leaning. It was the exact spot that she and Jesse had first made love. In the past, she would have blushed at the thought, but not now. Jesse had taught her to enjoy her sexuality. She had nothing to be ashamed of.

"You forgot to clean your desk out when you left for San Francisco."

Gerry stopped laughing. "What are you talking about?"

"All those off shore accounts."

"That has nothing to do with you." Gerry straightened up.

"That's not what my lawyer said." Ella's voice was sympathetic. "He says that it proves you've been systematically robbing the business and putting the money in your personal account."

"That's a lie."

"The papers in your desk say otherwise," Ella declared. "It also happens to be a crime."

"You can't say that." Gerry's voice sputtered. "I had a right to the money."

Ella shook her head. "Theft is theft. Your attorney has probably been trying to find you for the past two days, but you turned your phone off."

"How would you know that?" Gerry's shoulders sagged.

"The police came here looking for you."

Ella took another sip of her now cold coffee. She didn't care. Seeing the expression on Gerry's face was worth it. Never had she been so in control of a situation with her husband. He'd always had the upper hand until now. She'd found proof of his activities in his locked desk drawer. After her meeting with her lawyer, she'd gone looking for the evidence that he had been hiding assets. What she'd found had been a treasure trove of information. Information that her lawyer had used.

Gerry sat down and reached a hand out to her. "You can't do this Ella. You're my wife. What about the children."

"They're adults." Ella pulled her hand away. "They'll survive."

"Gerry Jr. expects to take over the business."

"You should have thought of that before you stole all of its liquid assets. The forensic accountant that my lawyer hired says it's a miracle the company hasn't gone bankrupt already."

"I'll put the money back."

Ella shook her head. "I'm not certain that's what is best for me."

"What are you talking about?" Gerry spat the words at her. A red flare of anger flashed across his cheeks. "You're always droning on about the business and how concerned you are for it."

"I'm starting a new life."

"With that bum that was just here? He must be years younger than you." Gerry snorted. "He's having a fling and taking you for a ride."

Ella shrugged. "Maybe, but it's been one hell of a ride."

Gerry took a deep breath. "I know I've neglected you lately, but there's still a chance we can work out our marriage."

"No."

"That's not like you Ella." Gerry's voice took on a whining tone. "I'm begging you to drop the divorce. I'll put the money back."

"My lawyer thinks you'll lose the money and the business." Ella stood and took her mug to the sink. "A stint in jail might give you a better perspective on the life you threw away."

"You think going to jail will save our marriage?"

"There's nothing left to save." Ella turned back to the room. "Jail will give you time to reflect on your mistakes, though."

"Now, you're just being vindictive." Gerry stood, throwing his chair to the floor. "To think I've trusted you all these years."

"That does seem to be the root of all our problems. Trust." Ella crossed her arms over her chest. "I trusted you and you betrayed that trust."

"I was honest about Marta."

"You lied and stole." Ella's voice hardened. "You played me for a fool and controlled me throughout our marriage. No longer. I'm a free woman and I intend to enjoy my life."

"What about me?" Gerry patted his chest. "I worked hard for that business."

"That might have been true in the beginning, but you let lust and greed rule you. You had a good wife and family, but you threw it away."

"I made a few mistakes. You still love me."

Ella picked up the phone. "You used it up. I have no feelings left for you."

"Give me another chance." Gerry's voice became desperate. "I'll get on my knees and beg if that's what you want."

"Don't bother." Ella dialed a number on the phone.

"Who are you calling?"

"My lawyer." Ella listened to the phone ringing. "I don't want to see you here ever again. This is my house, not yours. I'm sure you'll get your fair share once your legal problems are sorted out."

Gerry's eye's widened. "I paid for this house and everything in it."

"As did I." The phone was answered on the other end. "This is Ella Powell. My husband has forced his way into the house and is refusing to leave."

Gerry grabbed the phone from her and disconnected the call. "I'll leave. I need my stuff."

Ella pulled a ticket and key off the bulletin board and handed them to him. "This is the location of the storage locker where I had your things shipped."

"You really thought this out." Gerry took the paper and walked to the patio door. "You will regret this. You're old and used up. No man is going to want to stay with you for long."

"At least I'll have the freedom to choose."

"I offered you security." Gerry pushed the screen door open.

"For how long?" Ella followed him to the door. "You were planning on leaving me destitute. Don't pretend you cared."

There was the sound of police sirens in the distance. Ella doubted that they were coming for Gerry, but he seemed to consider it a possibility. He scurried to the side gate and left. She locked the patio behind him before going to the front window to watch him back out of the driveway.

It seemed she was wrong.

A police cruiser blocked Gerry's exit.

Chapter 14

"I can't believe you let Dad go to jail."

Ella winced at the tone of disgust in her son's voice. "I had no choice."

"He's your husband." Gerry Jr. threw himself down in the kitchen chair. "You had him arrested in broad daylight."

"What will the neighbors think?" A shudder went through Clarissa.

"Your father broke the law."

Ella tried to keep her voice sympathetic. She knew the children had been shocked by the news of Gerry's arrest. It didn't matter to them that she had convinced the prosecutor to refrain from going forward with the charges. Gerry had agreed to cooperate with her lawyer. The money he had stolen from the company was returned and a settlement was being worked out. It was better than Gerry deserved. She had done it for the children's sake. Now she wondered if it had been worth it.

It had been one week since Gerry's arrest and this morning the children had shown up on her doorstep. They'd already seen their father, and were returning to school after visiting with her. Their mission was clear. Keep their parent's marriage and business together, no matter what the cost.

"Dad says he found you in the house with a younger man." Her son's lip curled in a sneer. "The handyman."

"He works for a construction company." Ella crossed her arms over her chest. "He has a job and is respectable. He doesn't deserve your disdain."

"How could you?" Clarissa's voice was a high whine. "My friends will think you're a cougar."

"He is younger than me, so I suppose they would be right." Ella bit her lower lip so she wouldn't smile. "What difference does it make? I'm still your mother."

"I think it's wonderful." Christina's voice was hesitant. "Mom deserves some happiness."

"How long do you think it will last?" Gerry Jr. pointed a finger at her. "She couldn't keep Dad. How do you expect her to find someone else?"

"That's not fair." Ella's voice rose. "You're father lied to me. You're old enough to understand that not all marriages last."

"Why now?" Gerry Jr.'s voice was filled with disgust. "You've put up with Dad's affairs for years. We didn't think it mattered to you."

Years? Ella pushed back the pain in her chest. She'd only known about Marta because Gerry had told her. How many others had there been? She must have been blind not to have known her husband was unfaithful. She shut her eyes for a brief second and then straightened her shoulders. It didn't matter how her children felt. The marriage was over.

"I didn't know he was cheating on me." Ella's voice was quiet. "When he told me about Marta, I tried everything to make things work, but I couldn't do it alone."

"You don't give a damn about the business, or you wouldn't have pushed Dad for a divorce." Gerry shifted in his chair. "That's the only reason he took the money."

"I started Powell's Transmission with your father." As painful as it was to hear her children's criticism, she refused to lie any longer. "I was the one who pushed your father to go out on his own. I supported him and the business. In the early years, before the money started coming in, I worked at the office."

"I remember you used to take us with you." Christina put her hand on her mother's arm. "It was fun."

Ella smiled at Christina, the youngest of her twin daughters. She had the same strawberry blonde hair and blue eyes as Clarissa. The resemblance ended there. Clarissa kept her hair styled short and wore designer clothes. She always looked as if she had stepped off the pages of a fashion magazine. Christina's hair was shoulder length and usually pulled back in a ponytail. She wore jeans and a faded denim shirt. She dressed for comfort, not style.

Gerry Jr. looked like his father. He was tall and muscular with light brown hair and brown eyes. He was usually attired in a dress shirt and sports coat. Today, he was glaring at her and his tie was loosened from his collar. He might understand business, but he had a lot to learn about life, especially if he thought his father was blameless in his actions.

"If you cared about it so much, why did you almost destroy it?" Her son shook his head. "It will take years to recover from this."

"Your father did that." Ella's eyes narrowed. "He lied to me and stole from the company."

"Why didn't you just walk away then?" Her son's gaze was intense. "Dad must have explained that the business was going through an expansion and that money was tight."

"I deserve a fair share and your father wasn't willing to do that." Ella pushed back her exasperation. "I thought I brought you up better than this. Since when did money become more important than honor?"

"It's business." Gerry Jr. looked down at the table and shook his head. "You have no right to criticize. You're only after the money."

"I lived with your father for the past year and a half, knowing he was sleeping with another woman, because he said it was best for the business and the children."

"That sounds reasonable." Clarissa cleared her throat. "Women did that in the past before divorces became popular."

"So, I should have stayed with your father for the sake of appearances?"

Clarissa nodded. "You had already done it for over a year and it was working out."

"It was hell."

"Dad says he was honest with you, but you wouldn't understand." Clarissa sat down beside her brother. "Your sudden decision for a divorce doesn't make sense."

Ella shook her head. "I refused to have his mistress live in this house. What would your precious neighbors have thought then?"

"Dad would never do something like that." Clarissa's voice was filled with horror.

"Why do you think he wanted the guesthouse renovated?" Ella relaxed her shoulders. "Your father made it unbearable, but he had no intention of being honest with me. He was systematically hiding money, so that when he decided he wanted a divorce, there would be nothing left."

"You don't know that?" Gerry Jr.'s voice held a hint of doubt.

"You're a businessman. How would you describe his actions?" Ella paused to see if her son would answer, but he looked away. "You're father has treated me horribly and all you can do is blame me."

"I think you did the right thing, Mom." Christina's voice was strong with approval. "Dad has tried to make us take sides, but I love you both."

Ella hugged Christina. "I never wanted any of you to know this. I love all of you, but I can't continue to live in the past, not even for you."

"I don't expect you to." Christina blinked. "You deserve to be happy."

Just then the doorbell rang. Ella moved to answer it, but Christina put out her hand. "I'll get it."

Gerry Jr.'s eyes followed his sister out of the kitchen and then, he turned back to Ella. "Do you have to take half of the business?"

"I worked just as hard as your father. If he hadn't stolen from the company, he could have given me a settlement."

"Is there no way you can work it out?" Gerry Jr.'s voice softened. "I always hoped to take over the business."

"You can still do that, but the expansion will have to wait a few years." Ella felt a twinge of guilt denying her son what he wanted, but her husband had gutted the business in his effort to hide assets.

"I don't want to wait." Gerry Jr.'s tone was mulish.

Footsteps were approaching, signaling Christina's return from the front door. Gerry Jr. didn't seem to notice.

"You just want the money for your boy toy." Gerry Jr.'s voice rose in anger. "It's disgusting to think you'll be wasting all of Dad's money."

"I'm perfectly capable of supporting your mother if that's what she wants."

A familiar voice spoke from the doorway. Ella's heart soared as her eyes fell on Jesse standing beside Christina. She hadn't expected him for another day. He gave her a lopsided grin and then walked over to stand beside her. She reached out for his hand.

"You're early."

"I rushed the meeting as much as possible to get back." Jesse squeezed her hand. "You shouldn't have to go through this alone."

They'd spoken on the phone every night since he'd left, so Jesse was familiar with what had happened after the police had arrested Gerry. He knew about her agreement not to press charges in exchange for an honest division of their assets. What he wouldn't have expected was for her children to be home. They'd shown up this morning, unannounced.

"You might fool my mother, but not me." Gerry Jr. pushed back from his chair and stood. "You're a handyman. There's no way you can support her."

Ella interrupted her son. "I don't need someone to look after me. I'm a grown woman and capable of working."

"You haven't worked in years." Gerry Jr.'s arm waved around the kitchen. "You're used to living in luxury and ease."

"I wasn't born into this lifestyle." Ella lifted her chin. "Money doesn't bring happiness. I don't care what I have to do to support myself. Anything will be better than living the lies I was forced to do with your father."

"Fine words considering you're expecting a settlement from Dad." Gerry Jr. shook his head. "You'll have more than enough money to support the two of you."

Jesse straightened his shoulders. "I have a confession to make."

"Here it comes," Gerry Jr. scoffed. "You need money because you have debts you need paid, or a wife you forgot about, but were planning on divorcing, or children that need support. You'll admit to anything so long as you can con my mother out of her money."

"I was going to say I don't need your mother's money." Jesse's tone was harsh. "I understand you're angry at your parents for divorcing, but you're an adult. There is no excuse for your behavior. Your mother deserves respect."

Gerry Jr.'s nostril's flared. "How dare you tell me how to treat my mother?"

"I dare because I love her." Jesse straightened away from the counter. "Your mother has made a tough decision and you should be supporting her. She waited until you were old enough to understand, but she needs to live for herself now."

"I agree." Christina spoke up from the doorway. "Mom deserves to be happy."

"Why does her happiness come at the expense of the business?" Gerry Jr. continued to glare at Jesse.

"If a business is viable, it will survive." Jesse kept his voice even. "You're in business school, so I don't have to tell you that."

"We're planning an expansion, and giving her a settlement will make that impossible."

Ella rubbed the back of her neck. Nothing she said was going to convince her son that she wasn't deliberately trying to destroy Powell's Transmission. She had thought that her children would understand the reasons she needed to end the marriage.

"So the expansion is delayed." Jesse shrugged his shoulders. "You're lucky that you can do that. If your mother hadn't stopped your father when she did, you'd be starting from scratch, with a new company."

"What do you know about business?" Gerry Jr. shook his head. "You're a carpenter."

"Carpentry isn't all I do. I'm an engineer."

"You're still just an employee." Gerry Jr.'s eyes narrowed. "Things look different on the other side of the equation."

"True." Jesse crossed his arms over his chest. "I own C & J Construction. It's a family company that my grandfather started and passed onto my Dad. My father is C and I'm J. My Dad's semi-retired, so I run the company now."

Silence followed Jesse's announcement.

Ella's hand fluttered against her chest as a flood of color filled her cheeks. She'd never guessed that Jesse was anything but a laborer at the company. He'd never told her differently, either. He'd let her go on thinking that he was a workman with no responsibilities, when all along he ran the company. Worse, he'd led her to believe that he was working at her house for extra money. That was clearly not the case.

"Why didn't you tell me?" Ella's voice was a whisper.

"It wasn't important." Jesse's voice soothed. "You needed someone to do the work, and I had the time."

Ella shook her head. "I feel so stupid. I should have guessed when you said you had meetings to go to. I just assumed it was something like employee safety."

Jesse touched her arm. "I didn't want you to know."

"So why tell her now?" Gerry Jr. pushed his chair back under the kitchen table. "Are you planning on leaving her?"

Jesse rolled his eyes. "You were complaining that I didn't make enough to support your mother and now I make too much?"

Gerry Jr. started to speak, but Ella raised her hands. "Enough. I don't need a man to take care of me."

"Are you sure Mom?" Clarissa, who had been silent through most of the conversation, spoke up. "I don't want you living in squalor just because of your pride. Staying with Dad would be better than that."

"I think being destitute would be better than staying here." Ella could have laughed at the expression of dismay on her daughter's face.

"You're not serious." Clarissa's eyes widened.

"I have no intention of embarrassing you, Clarissa." Ella motioned to the doorway. "It's time you all left. I'm not changing my mind about divorcing your father."

"At least consider what you're going to do with the business." Gerry Jr. paused at the door. "It would be best if you waited for your money."

"Maybe you could continue to live here," Clarissa added.

"The house is too big and the memories too sad." Ella walked with her children to the front door.

Christina hugged her. "Be happy. I think Jesse is a fine man."

"Thank you."

Ella turned to Clarissa. "Try and understand. I'm not doing any of this to hurt you."

Clarissa pouted. "It affects me."

"Only if you let it." Ella gave her a hug and watched the twins leave before turning to her son.

"Are you going to placate me with some lame excuse?"

Ella shook her head. "Only time will help you understand why I need to do this. I can't change your mind."

Gerry Jr. sighed. "I don't want things to change."

"I know, but we have no control over that. Fighting it will only make you bitter. I don't want that for you."

"I can't change how I feel."

"I'm not asking you to."

Ella hugged Gerry Jr. He was his father's son and the only way he'd ever accept her decision was for him to see the damage Gerry had done to the business for himself. Her lawyer said that it was quite a mess, and she would be lucky to walk away with it still intact. She hoped that was true for her son's sake.

When they'd left, she shut the door and leaned back against it. Dealing with her children's anger was more difficult than she had expected. Hopefully, the worst was over. Now she needed to consider what Jesse had revealed. Her head was still spinning from his admission to being the owner of an international engineering and construction firm. There was no way he'd want to stay with an older, less sophisticated woman.

There was no point in delaying the inevitable.

She walked back into the kitchen.

Jesse had poured two large glasses of lemonade and placed them on the countertop. When she entered the room, he pushed one of the glasses toward her. She picked it up and wrapped her hands around it, trying to gain strength from its cold surface. She wasn't a coward. She'd learned a lot about herself in the past couple of weeks, and even though she loved Jesse to distraction, she was finished with relationships that were one-sided.

"I never meant to hide my business from you." Jesse's voice was low. "At the time, I only wanted an excuse to be near you."

"You thought I was vulnerable."

Jesse shook his head. "Never. You practically begged me to do your renovations and I didn't have the heart to refuse. It wasn't until I started working here that I started to hope that something could build between us."

"Did you think you were humoring me? Telling me what I needed to hear." Ella fought to keep her voice steady.

"I have never lied to you." Jesse put his glass down and walked to her. "What we share is more than I ever hoped to find."

"Now I know you're stringing me a line." Ella turned her face away from him.

"I love you."

Ella's heart stopped for a second and then reason took over. They barely knew each other, and he had another more important life to go back to. He couldn't mean what he'd just said. She was tired of believing men who lied to her. Even though Jesse had been there when she needed someone, his words felt like a betrayal.

"You don't have to say what you think I want to hear." Ella inhaled a sharp breath before turning to look at him. "I knew I'd fallen in love with you the day we first kissed. I also accepted that you couldn't possibly return that love."

"Why? Is there something wrong with me?"

"You're younger than me." Ella forced herself to hold his gaze. "You could have any woman you wanted."

"So you think I would lie?" Jesse's voice hardened. "What kind of man do you think I am?"

"You've already lied to me once." Ella clenched her glass tighter.

"I didn't tell you the whole truth." Jesse's pushed his hand through his hair. "It didn't seem important."

"I think you're a good man Jesse and I love you with all my heart." Ella patted his chest with her hand. Her voice cracked on a sob, but she continued. "We can't build a relationship on lies. I'm not the type of woman who could attract someone like you."

"You're wrong about me." Jesse lifted her chin with a finger and gazed at her with a tender expression. "You had me twisting from the first moment I saw you."

"That's not true." The breath caught in Ella's chest.

Jesse took the glass of lemonade from her fingers and put it on the counter. "Nothing about our relationship has been easy."

Ella frowned. "I don't understand."

Jesse pulled her into his arms. "Until you made a decision about your husband, I couldn't say anything. If I'd told you how I felt, you would have sent me packing. Instead, every day I'd come to work and you would drive me crazy."

"I didn't mean to." Ella leaned back so that she could look him in the eye. "I'm older than you. I never thought that you could possibly be attracted to me."

"Watching you work in the garden drove me nuts. You'd wear the skimpiest tops. The moisture from your sweat outlined every delicious detail of your breasts." Jesse's voice was a low rasp. "There's not that much difference in our ages either."

Ella's gaze roamed over his face before settling on his gray eyes. They had softened and glimmered with emotion.

He was sincere.

"You really love me?" Ella's voice was a hushed whisper.

"Since the moment I first saw you." Jesse's eyes darkened. "My heart almost pounded out of my chest and it felt as if a huge weight lifted from me. Light seemed to surround you."

"It was a sunny day." Ella forced her voice to remain light.

"I couldn't let you walk away." Jesse gave her a light kiss. "It felt as if I was going to miss out on the most important thing in my life."

"That's why you agreed to do the renovations?"

"It was all I could think of to keep you close." Jesse grinned. "I know you're going through a huge change in your life. I wouldn't ask you to make a major decision about us right now."

"I have a lot to learn about doing what makes me happy." Ella's voice shook.

"I want you to do that too." Jesse brushed his lips across hers. "I just ask that you not push me away. Who knows, you might find out that I'm part of what makes you happy."

Ella giggled. "I think you already know you make me happy."

"I'm more than a boy toy." Jesse nibbled at her ear. "I have staying power."

"That you do." Ella felt a shiver of renewed desire.

"I'm serious." Jesse looked down at her. "I want to be the one you reach for, when the dust settles."

"Always." Ella couldn't fight her feelings for Jesse any longer. Right or wrong, she loved him. "I need you."

"Good, because when you're ready, I intend to marry you."

Jesse didn't wait for her to answer. He captured her lips and the world spun away. Ella was certain that they would have to push past more obstacles in the future, but she didn't care. She had done everything that was expected, and all it had done was make her miserable. She was determined to live the rest of her life differently.

Her love for Jesse was new and untested, but it felt right.

Chapter 15

Ella pulled out the floral pinwheel block she was working on and relaxed in the leather wing chair. The quilt meeting was at her house today, and she was excited to give the group her good news. She'd found love and within a couple of weeks, she'd be divorced. Life was full of surprises.

"You've repainted the house." Lara pulled her work from a bag. "Did you have a designer in?"

Ella shook her head. "I needed a change."

Ella had made a clean sweep of everything. Gone were the deep blue walls and furniture. Instead, there was a neutral color on the walls, and brown leather furniture. It was more showroom than a place to live, which suited her future plans perfectly. She was speaking with a realtor this week and then the house was going to be sold. She couldn't bear to stay living where she'd been so unhappy.

"It's not what I would have picked for you, but it's beautiful and rich looking." Lara turned back to her stitching.

"Peter has gone out of town for a few days." Brenna looked up from her stitching. "He did mention something about refusing to defend Gerry."

Ella's chest tightened.

For a second, she considered telling them it was a mistake, but she dismissed it. These were her friends and they had started out on this journey together. There was no embarrassment in them knowing how bad things had become between her and Gerry.

"Gerry was stealing from the company."

Silence as all three women stopped what they were doing and looked at her.

Alisa was the first to speak. "How long?"

"Since he started seeing Marta, a year and a half ago." Ella took a deep breath. She was past most of the pain Gerry's betrayal had caused.

"Was he arrested?" Alisa asked.

"The children were furious with me, but I had no choice about involving the police. The company was close to being bankrupted."

"There was nothing in the papers." Brenna picked up her quilt bag and pulled out some solid red cotton. "What happened?"

"The prosecutor was ready to press charges, but I convinced him to wait." Ella fingered her quilt block. "Gerry is putting the money back into the business."

"It sounds like he escaped with a slap on the wrist." Alisa's voice was dry. "Most men do."

"There'll be consequences." Ella smiled. "Gerry will no longer have control of the company."

"Good." Alisa said. "He just needed a reminder that he wasn't above the law."

"He certainly got that." Ella pulled out her needle and thread.

"I wish something like that would happen to David." Lara measured and snipped a length of embroidery floss for her Crazy Quilt block.

"Is he stealing?" Brenna's voice rose in shock.

"No. He needs to realize that things don't always go his way." Lara clenched her fabric in her hands. "I want to try counselling for our marriage, but he's insisting that variety is the only answer. He is adamant that we take up the swinging lifestyle."

"My marriage was beyond repair, I just didn't realize it." Ella's voice was solemn. "I was frightened to follow through with our plan, yet doing so, gave me the courage to end my marriage. I have no regrets."

"So you think I should accept David's demands that I sleep with other men?"

"Only you can answer that." Alisa reached over and touched Lara's arm. "Ella is just asking you to take a closer look at your marriage, and see what is right for you."

"Even if the outcome is different from what we originally envisioned?"

Brenna nodded. "Ella has given us hope."

There was silence for several minutes before Lara spoke. "So swapping partners will save my marriage?"

Lara

Chapter 1

Lara's marriage was held together by a thread.

She was ready to start a family, but her husband craved sexual excitement. He wanted to try swinging, but she didn't think swapping partners was the best way to generate intimacy between a couple already having problems. She wasn't a prude, but sleeping with other men seemed contrary to her marriage vows.

Marriage wasn't easy.

Compromises were required.

A marriage couldn't survive if it remained stagnant. It needed to grow, just as the individuals within the marital unit did. Lara had watched her parents go through a bitter divorce. Years later, her mother had confessed that she'd wished she'd tried harder to keep the marriage together. That's when Lara had promised herself that she would do whatever it took, to keep her husband happy. If he wanted to experiment with sexual fetishes, then she would be there with him.

She'd never thought that would mean swapping partners.

Lara finished the last French knot in the string of flowers she'd embroidered on the black velvet material of her crazy quilt block. Everything was in a perfect, symmetrical line along the seam that joined the velvet to a piece of red silk. If only her marriage could be as ordered as the stitches of her quilts. Her relationship was a mess and no amount of wishing was going to make it better. Action was needed to mend it.

David, her husband, had made his first fortune in computer software. When he'd sold that company, he'd divorced his first wife, and left her to raise their two children. Lara had met him when she was twenty-five, and he had seduced and wooed her until she agreed to marry him. Seven years later, she was still in love, but she wasn't so sure about David. Her husband's second company was now successful, and he was looking for new challenges.

"David has been leaving pamphlets about the local swapping group all over the house." Lara knotted her thread and pushed the needle into her material. "He isn't going to let this go."

"I thought you decided to give it a whirl." Alisa pinned two diamonds pieces together. "What's the hold up?"

Alisa was strikingly beautiful with long, black hair and light-green eyes. Lara still had difficulty believing Alisa's husband, Henry, wanted a ménage a trois.

Lara rested her hands on her lap. "I'm not convinced."

Brenna looked up from the scraps of fabric she'd been sorting. "I know you think you have to do it, but it could destroy your marriage."

"Is that what you think Ella?" Lara leaned back in her chair.

Ella flattened her floral fabric out across her knee. "My threatening to cheat on Gerry didn't work."

"That's because the minute Gerry asked you to accept his mistress, the marriage was dead." Brenna punctuated each word with a thrust of her finger.

Alisa giggled. "That dominatrix training you've been taking is paying off."

Brenna's cheeks reddened. "I haven't gone yet."

Alisa's voice rose in mock disgust. "So you're not learning to be a dominatrix, and Lara isn't swapping partners yet. What about you, Ella?"

Ella's eyes widened with surprise. "You already know I'm divorcing Gerry. It was my lawyer who discovered that Gerry was stealing from the company. If I hadn't started divorce proceedings, we'd never have known."

"That's not what I was talking about. You were supposed to sleep with a younger man." Alisa's voice was gentle. "I even arranged for one to go to your house. He said that you didn't want to consummate the arrangement."

"I couldn't sleep with someone who was being paid. That's not what I want." Ella's voice was defensive. "I appreciate that you were trying to help, Alisa, but that would have only made things worse."

"How? Gerry was already flaunting his mistress in your face."

"I would have hated myself." Ella's voice was a low whisper. "Gerry destroyed my self-esteem. Paying for sex would have made it worse."

"I agree." Brenna picked up a blue micro-dot fabric. "Ella has taken the first step in getting her life back on track. She's divorcing the swine."

"What about men?" Alisa didn't hide her exasperation. "She's not yet forty. She needs to have a man."

"Not everyone wants a man." Lara crossed her arms. "I was doing just fine before David swept me off my feet."

"That's all right for you," Alisa said. "You have your design business and other interests. Ella has always stayed at home with the children. How is she going to find someone?"

"I do have a man." Ella's voice was firm. "His name is Jesse, and we're happy."

Brenna dropped her fabric. "Why haven't you mentioned him before?"

"I didn't want you to criticize him."

"What's wrong with him?" Alisa's voice was suspicious.

"Nothing. He was doing the renovations at the house." Ella inhaled a deep breath. "We love each other."

"Great." Brenna went back to her fabrics. "Gerry treated you poorly. You deserve love."

Lara reached over and squeezed Ella's hand. "I'm happy for you. How long have you known him?"

"A couple of months. I met him after we all decided to do something about our marriages." Ella gave a lopsided grin. "I was a bit embarrassed because he is younger than me."

Alisa laughed and reached over and hugged Ella. "Here I was worried about you finding a man, and you already had one lined up. Good for you."

"Thanks." Ella looked at Lara. "I think you need to do what's in your heart. I tried to make things work with Gerry for over a year, but once a marriage is gone, there's no retrieving it."

"I suppose that's the question. Is the marriage salvageable?" Lara sighed and leaned back in her chair. "When I met David, I thought there was nothing I wouldn't do for him. Now, I'm not so sure."

"It's what he wants." Alisa squinted her eyes as she threaded her needle. "He seems very serious about it."

"He's obsessed with it." Lara shook her head. "When he gets onto a subject, there is no turning him around."

"His perseverance made him a rich man." Alisa's voice was matter of fact. "I'm assuming that's one of the things that attracted you to him."

"He pursued me relentlessly." Lara smiled. "He's been so distracted lately that I've forgotten what it felt like to be the center of his attention."

"He wants to swing with other couples." Alisa shrugged. "I can't see it interesting him for long. Once he has it out of his system, he'll be his usual self. The only way to cure him, is to go along with it."

"Only if that's what you want." Brenna's tone was sharp. "Don't let us, or David, bully you into something you don't desire."

"That's the problem." Lara folded up her crazy quilt patch. "I'm so confused that I don't know what will make me happy."

"Then take time to figure it out. Jumping into bed with someone else isn't going to solve the problem. On the other hand, you might enjoy it." Brenna pinned two pieces of fabric together.

"She's not cheating if her husband wants her to do it," Alisa reasoned.

"Lara has to work this out for herself." Brenna turned to Alisa. "What have you done about your husband's request for a ménage?"

"I'm working on it. It's not easy finding a young man who wants to be with both of us."

"Why don't you hire one?" Ella raised an eyebrow.

Alisa gave a sheepish grin. "Probably for the same reason you didn't want to. In the end, I might have to go that route."

"Let's hope not." Brenna frowned as she picked up a block of yellow fabric. "Giving our husbands what they need, is more complicated than we bargained for."

"I'm not giving up." Alisa's tone was adamant. "There's an answer out there for all of us. Look at Ella. She found a younger man and is happier for it."

"But her marriage is destroyed." Lara couldn't hide her dismay. "When I married David, I took my vows seriously."

"Ella and Gerry were finished long before we set up our plans." Alisa threw her diamond patches into her bag. "There was nothing she could do to save it."

"Alisa's right." Ella's voice was filled with sadness. "Gerry planned to divorce me after he finished hiding the assets of the business. That's the only reason he was staying with me. I was too blind to see it."

"There's nothing wrong with trusting your husband." Brenna sighed. "I still can't believe Peter is seeing a dominatrix."

"That's why you have to take those classes. If he wants to see one, then let it be you." Alisa leaned back. "It's what we all agreed to."

Brenna straightened her shoulders. "I'll learn to be the dominatrix that Peter wants."

"I will continue to sleep with my younger man." Ella giggled.

"And I will find the perfect man to make up the ménage a trois that Henry wants."

Lara nodded. "I'll let David have his swinging parties. I'll sleep with the most attractive men there and enjoy every minute of it."

Alisa stood and picked up her bag. "Now, let's give our husbands what they think they want."

Chapter 2

Lara pulled out a light-blue suit from her closet and carried it to her dressing area. She was already wearing an ivory silk blouse, and she slipped the suit's pencil skirt on, zipping it up behind before shrugging into the jacket. She pulled out two pairs of pumps from her shoe rack and took them into the bedroom.

"Did you read that information I left for you?" David was still lounging in bed.

"Which one?" Lara looked up from the shoes.

"The invitation to the party tomorrow night." David rubbed a hand over his cropped hair. "We've been invited to the Burkett's."

Lara frowned. "I don't remember meeting them. Are they clients?"

"They're swingers." David's voice was harsh. "I told you about them last week. Are you just completely ignoring me now?"

Lara blew a wisp of blonde hair out of her eyes. "It must have slipped my mind. I've been busy working on a new design job."

"This is something that is important to me, and you just brush it off." David sat forward in the bed, a vein bulging at the side of his temple. "I've been setting this up for weeks. They just don't accept people off the street. I had to fill out an application, give photos of us, our medical history, and our income level."

Lara's stomach lurched with nausea. "They know what we look like? How could you do that without asking me first?"

"They're going to see every inch of you tomorrow what difference does it make?"

"It's a violation." Lara sat at the window seat and put on the shoes that were closest to her suit color. "I haven't agreed to do this."

"You'd better." David's eyes were narrowed. "I've given you enough time to get over your hang-ups. I don't see what the big deal is. Before we were married, you dated a lot of guys. You were far from a virgin."

"It's different now."

Lara picked up a purse and held it against her skirt. The blue leather was a slight tone darker, but it would do for today. Her stomach was churning and the sooner she ended this conversation with David, the better. She needed to have a clear head for work today.

"I've given you permission. It's not cheating."

Lara dumped the contents of yesterday's purse into the new one. "It will change everything about our relationship."

"Not if you don't let it."

Lara fought back a scream. "Can't you see what a mess our marriage will become?"

"It will make it stronger." David crossed his arms over his bare chest. "I want this and if you love me you'll do it."

"That's emotional blackmail." Lara turned on her heel and started out of the room.

"Don't you dare leave in the middle of a discussion." David's roar was so loud that Lara felt it reverberate through her body.

"I thought you'd said everything you wanted to." Lara refused to look at him.

"If you truly love me, then you will explore this with me."

"What if I don't?" Lara held her breath.

"It's not an option." David's voice was cold. "It's either this or the marriage is over."

"Just like that?" Lara turned back to her husband. "We took vows before God."

"And you signed a pre-nup." David exhaled in exasperation. "I'm asking you to be adventurous and open yourself to new experiences. Most wives would jump at the idea."

"You expect me to be happy that you want to screw around with other women?"

"Jealous?" David's voice was smug. "It's working then. Our marriage has been flat for years. It's time we spiced it up a bit."

"We've only been married for seven years." Lara didn't bother to hide her outrage. "You weren't bored before you started obsessing about swinging."

"I just never told you."

"What's that supposed to mean?" Lara frowned. "Have you been unfaithful?"

"No." David's eyes skittered away from her. "It's not because of lack of opportunities."

"We made a commitment. I would never think about cheating on you."

There was a tremor of pain that ran through her words. She loved him. To hear that he'd been bored with her for years, cut like a knife. Lara inhaled a deep breath.

"I have to go to work. We'll talk about this tonight."

"There's nothing to discuss." David's voice was a low growl. "We're going to that party and having a good time. I've earned this."

Lara escaped the room before she said something that she'd regret. She grabbed her briefcase from the kitchen table and rushed out of the house. There was no point in arguing with David. He'd been fixated on this alternative lifestyle for months. His personality wouldn't let him change his mind. It's what made him such a good businessman, but a horrible person to live with.

She got into her BMW and drove out through the iron gates at the end of the driveway. Soon she was maneuvering through traffic and her mind was focused on the day ahead of her. When she had met David, her business was new. It had been slow-to-grow, with mainly David's friends and clients using her design services in the early days. She'd built a name for herself and her business was successful because of her talent.

Focusing on designing was positive.

Thoughts of her marriage were depressing.

She used the Bluetooth on her steering wheel and dialed Alisa. Her friend answered almost immediately.

"David is demanding that I go to a swapping party tomorrow night or the marriage is over."

"He's determined." Alisa's yawn could be heard at the other end.

"He thinks I'm too old fashioned in my views about sex."

"You were pretty wild before your marriage." The sound of running water came over the phone.

"He thinks that's why I should go along with his plans." Lara put her blinker on and switched lanes. "I settled down after marrying David."

"True."

"I'd like to start a family and all David can think about is having sex."

"Do you think he has a problem?" Alisa sounded doubtful. "I know they have groups for people with sex addictions."

"He's addicted to the chase." Lara's tone was scornful. "The more difficult the pursuit, the better. I think that's why he married me. I didn't fall into his lap."

"That means he likes to work for your affection." Alisa paused for a second. "The swapping could work in your favor. If David sees other men vying for your attention, then that could renew his own interests."

"This morning he told me he was bored with our marriage." Lara's voice didn't hide the ache his words had caused.

"Jealousy should get rid of his ennui." Alisa's tone was heavily laden with sarcasm. "I don't know what he has to complain about. You're young, beautiful, and you love him."

"He's so different from the man I married." Lara braked for a red light. "He swept me off my feet with his extravagance. It was nothing for him to fly us to Paris for dinner or to New York for coffee. Everything he did was romantic. How could I not fall in love with him?"

"That was his intention." Alisa tone was dry. "His money and persistence convinced you that he loved you."

"So you think I was a trophy to be won?" Lara gripped the steering wheel tighter. "I wanted to better myself, but David's money never seduced me to marry him."

"That's not what I said." Alisa's voice took on a soothing quality. "David wanted you, and he used every trick in his arsenal to get you, including his money."

Lara bit her lip. David had dazzled her with his elegance and money.

"So you think he never loved me?"

"Only you can answer that." Alisa sighed. "If you want your marriage to work you know what you have to do."

"I'm thirty-two years old. I'm ready to start a family, and David always promised me that we could have children someday."

"So maybe the swapping is a phase he's going through." Alisa cleared her throat. "Lots of people live that lifestyle and have children."

"But will David?" Lara turned onto the street where her office was. "Having a baby is no guarantee that he'll stay. He left his first wife and children."

"Maybe going along with this lifestyle will bring you together."

"You might be right." Lara slowed her vehicle down. "I'm at work now, so I'll tell you how everything goes at the next quilter's meeting."

She pulled into the parking lot of Knight's Interior Design and shut her engine off. Alisa had given her a lot to think about. She still had qualms about swapping. It didn't feel right to openly cheat on her husband even if he was doing the same thing with another woman. She shook off her doubts and focused on business.

Pulling up to her office always gave her a sense of confidence. She had built the business from the ground up. She'd started off in a small cramped one room office and now she owned the building. She'd come a long way. She had talent and years of training. Those things were necessary to prosper in a design business, and succeed she had.

When Lara opened the door to her workplace, her assistant Margery was waiting for her. Lara bit back a groan. Margery was mouthing something at her and jerking her head toward her office. Lara looked over and her door was closed. That meant only one thing.

She had a client waiting.

Chapter 3

"Did I forget an early appointment?" She glanced down at her watch. She still had ten minutes before her usual start time.

"There's a Vince Warner in your office." Margery's voice was a low whisper. "He doesn't have an appointment, but he insisted on waiting."

Lara put her briefcase down on a chair and shrugged off her coat. "Do I have anybody scheduled for nine?"

Margery walked over to her desk and flipped through the appointment book. "Mrs. Henderson isn't coming in until eleven."

"No problem."

Lara straightened her shoulders and opened her office door. Walk-in clients were unusual, but she wasn't in the habit of turning business away. That's what had made her successful. She worked when others didn't.

A tall man in his mid-forties stood when she entered the room. He was well-dressed, in a tailored, black suit, white-collared shirt, and black tie. His dark hair was cut short and there was a trace of gray at his temples. Dark-blue eyes with a hint of sadness in their depths, assessed her as she held out her hand.

"Mr. Warner, I'm Lara Knight. How can I help you?" Lara walked over to the chair beside him and sat. She motioned for him to join her.

"Your receptionist mentioned making an appointment, and normally I would, but I was in the neighborhood and saw your office. I thought I'd stop in and try to speak with you."

Lara waved a hand in dismissal. "I have no appointments scheduled right now. What did you want to see me about?"

"My house." Mr. Warner cleared his throat. "I'm relocating to Dearston and bought an old Victorian that needs a lot of renovation. Your name was given to me by one of my clients, Nicholas Weatherton. He claims you're the best designer in the city."

"That's very generous of Mr. Weatherton." Lara folded her hands on her lap. "What were you planning for the house?"

"It needs to be totally updated, but most importantly, it has to be kid friendly."

Lara nodded. "How many children do you and your wife have?"

"Two. I'm a widower." A muscle tightened in his jaw. "I lost my wife to cancer nearly three years ago. That's part of the reason for the change. It's time the children and I moved forward with our lives. A new town and a different house is what we need right now."

"I'm sorry, Mr. Warner. I had no idea." Lara's voice was soft with apology. Now she understood the sadness in his eyes.

"Please call me Vince."

"Vince it is. I'm Lara, by the way." She stood. "We should schedule a time when I can see your house and then I'd be better able to tell you if I can help."

"How about now?" Vince's voice was eager. "Unless you have something else to do."

Lara walked to her desk and flipped through her calendar. She had some drawings she wanted to complete for a client that she was seeing later in the day, but other than that, she was free. She looked up at Vince, and the expectant look on his face convinced her. The drawings were almost done, and Mrs. Henderson was her only morning appointment.

"Where's the house?"

"It's over on Willow."

Lara stopped herself from giving a low whistle. That was one of the most elite neighborhoods in Dearston and there were only a couple of Victorians on the street. Both of them, were mansions by anybody's standards.

She grabbed her briefcase. "Let's go. As long as I'm back at the office by eleven, it'll be fine."

"Let me drive." Vince held the door open for her.

She walked into the outer reception area and gathered her coat. "Margery, Mr. Warner is taking me to see his house. I should be back in time for my next appointment."

Fifteen minutes later, they were at the house. Lara's eyes widened when they drove up the winding driveway. The house was huge, and Vince had been right. It needed attention badly. Foliage was covering most of the driveway and overgrown shrubs hid the porch.

It was a beautiful Victorian, complete with a turret and gingerbread dentil details. Intricately carved and scalloped wooden corbels supported the porch roof. Curved bargeboard covered the gable ends and spindles decorated the rest of the roof line. The siding, which had been painted in the distant past, was now peeling and cracked. There were signs of decay in the upper windows and the porch wasn't safe. Still, it had charm, and with a lot of money and time, it could be restored to the grand old lady it had once been. The question was, did Vince Warner have the time and the money?

"It's not much better on the interior." Vince's voice was rueful.

Lara stepped out of the car. "There's nothing I like more than a challenge."

Vince grinned. "Well this should tickle your fancy."

"Whatever possessed you to buy this place?" Lara started up the overgrown walkway to the house.

"It reminded me of myself and the kids. We need the same loving care that this place does."

"You miss your wife a lot."

Vince cleared his throat. "She was the heart of our family. Nothing is the same without her."

"So this is your way of helping your family and the house."

"Exactly." Vince helped her navigate the broken floorboards of the porch and then unlocked the door. "The real estate agent thought I was going to bulldoze the place and build something new, but that seemed sacrilegious."

"With time and money, it'll be beautiful when it's finished."

"Luckily, I have both."

Vince went to the rear of the house and into the kitchen. It was a disaster by today's standards. There were no permanent cupboards, the linoleum on the floor was peeling, and there were no outlets for a modern stove or refrigerator. The only recognizable thing was an old porcelain sink that looked big enough to bathe in.

Vince swung his hand around the room. "I'd like a large modern chef's kitchen here."

"A place where the family can gather?"

Vince nodded. "The kitchen is the heart of the house and family."

"You'll have to gut everything. It needs new wiring and plumbing. There'll probably be a few structural problems too."

"It won't be easy."

"Are you planning on living here during the renovations?"

"I'm not a lunatic." Vince chuckled as he walked into the south facing solarium attached to the kitchen. "We haven't moved yet. When the house is finished, I'll pack up the kids."

Lara bit her lower lip. The house was a huge project, and she was already fully booked for the next few months. Still, she loved the feel of the place. Restoring this old beauty would be a labor of love. Knowing that she was making two motherless children happy in the process was a huge incentive.

"Is it too much?" Vince's voice was quiet.

"It would be fun to do."

Lara walked over to a window and looked out over the unkempt yard. The remnants of large flower beds were still evident along the stone fence. It must have been a grand place in its time.

"I'm sensing a problem."

Lara shook her head. "I was debating on how to fit it in with the commitments I've already agreed to."

"I can be flexible with the time."

Lara tilted her head. "Are you sure? I could give you the name of a couple of other designers."

"No." Vince's tone was firm. "I want you. I already sense that you have a love for the place, and that's what I need for the house to become a home."

"I can't promise to give it my full attention for at least a month."

"That's fine with me." Vince held her gaze. "Do you think it might be livable by the fall though? It would be nice to move the kids in before the new school year."

That left her three months to have the house renovated. "Do you mind which contractors I choose?"

"I'll give you full control of the project."

"I'll have to get an architect and structural engineer to look the place over and draw up whatever plans need to be done. Will you be available to okay those?"

"I'm a phone call and a fax away." Vince led her outside and locked the door. "I'll drop off a set of keys to your office today."

Lara ran her hand over the paint chipped oak door and made her decision. "I'll do it."

"Great." Vince grinned. "You can draw up the contract and I'll stop by the office later to sign it."

"You're the easiest client I've ever dealt with."

"I'm a desperate man." Vince opened the car door for her. "I had visions of living in the middle of repairs that I'd have to do myself."

"Not very appealing." Lara climbed into the passenger seat.

"And very dangerous. I'm not much of a handyman. Computers are more my forte."

"What do you do?"

"Security software." Vince looked over his shoulder as he reversed the car. "A larger driveway with a turnaround would be perfect also."

"I'll put it on the list."

The return trip to her office was spent discussing the particulars of the house design. Vince wanted as open and informal a layout as possible. By the time he dropped her at her door, she had a good idea of the look he desired. She'd firm up the colors and finishes once she'd had the architect and engineer in to look at it.

Her morning went by fast, but at the back of her mind was the meeting she'd had with Vince Warner. The man had obviously loved his wife, and he'd been willing to do anything for his children. That was the kind of love she wanted, but it worked both ways.

Was she willing to do anything for David?

David was right. She had become old fashioned and conventional. She didn't like the idea of having to sleep with another man in order to keep her husband happy. Still, she believed in making a marriage work. David was more adventurous than she was, so that meant she was the one who needed to change.

By the end of the day, she was exhausted. She still had to work out what she was going to do about the swinging party before going home. There was no way she could face another battle with David. His personality was stronger than hers, and he would win. She bit her lip. Maybe that was her answer. She wanted to keep her husband happy, and he was determined to make this swapping happen. It would be better if she just went along with it.

Her course was clear.

Tomorrow, she would have sex with another man because that was what her husband wanted.

Chapter 4

Lara clutched her purse tight and forced her legs to move forward.

David held her elbow. Even if she wanted to turn around, he'd made certain it wasn't an option. The bright lights from inside the house made everything look cheerful and happy. All Lara felt was dread.

"Do we have to do this?" Her words were a whispered plea.

"Everything is in place." David pulled her up the front stairs. "These are nice people and they're looking forward to meeting you."

"I'll bet." Lara hissed the words under her breath.

Before David had a chance to reply, the door was opened and a woman in her mid-to-late thirties stood there. She was wearing a floral dress with short sleeves that sat below her shoulders. It accentuated her large breasts. David seemed to pulse with interest beside her. Lara's heart fell.

"I'm glad you made it." The woman held out her hand. "I'm Anna Burkett."

"Our beautiful and charming hostess." David's voice was filled with admiration. "It's wonderful to finally meet you."

Anna gestured for them to step inside. The foyer was large with a massive staircase on the right side. A huge crystal chandelier hung from the two-story ceiling and reflected rainbows of light. Lara glanced at the original watercolors on display, the neutral wall tone, and the dark hardwood floor. It was impressive. A very talented interior designer had decorated the Burkett's home.

"The rest of the party is in the living room." Anna reached for Lara's suede coat. "They're very eager to meet the two of you."

The coats were hung in the nearby closet. David and Lara followed Anna into a spacious room. A baby-grand piano was situated in a bay window at the far end, and was flanked by two white upholstered wing-back chairs. There was a white leather sectional and another two wing-back chairs in front of a floor-to-ceiling stone hearth. The floor was the same dark oak from the foyer and showcased the furniture perfectly. The decorating was the work of a genius.

"Do you have children?" Lara turned to their hostess.

Anna grinned. "They're older and when they're home they use the recreation area in the basement."

"This room is stunning." The tension eased from Lara's shoulders.

"Let's meet the rest of the party."

Anna led them to the seating area. There were five other people there. Three men and two women. All of them stood when Lara and David walked up. They ranged in age from mid-thirties to early fifties.

"This is Lara and David." Anna introduced them. "This is their first time swinging, so be gentle with them."

There was a soft rumble of laughter and Lara's tension returned. She wanted to run out the front door and never come back. A good-looking man with gray hair that brushed the edge of his shirt collar held out his hand.

"I'm Frank, Anna's husband." Lara took his hand and liked the firm grip. "It's been a long time since we've had virgins, so to speak, in the group. Welcome."

Another man with curly brown hair and a receding hairline cleared his throat. "I'm Bobby. It's a pleasure to welcome you here."

The man winked. Lara looked at David to see what his reaction was, but he was oblivious to the attention she was getting. David was busy talking to a woman with long, black hair standing beside Anna. She turned back to the last gentleman when he touched her arm.

"I'm Steven." He was a tall man with thinning dark hair and vibrant blue eyes. He put his arm around her waist and led her to the sectional. "Why don't you join us? Your husband is busy meeting the girls."

Lara sat, and was immediately surrounded by the men. They stared at her as if they were starved and she was a choice steak. She shifted on the couch and they all moved back a bit. It had been a long time since she'd had this much male interest. A tiny spark of excitement flickered within her.

She looked over at David.

He was encircled by women.

He had his arm around two of them. Their hostess, Anna, was showing him where he could sit. A glitter deep within the depths of David's eyes told her that he was fully engaged. She squashed the flicker of jealousy that was forming a vice grip around her chest.

She could play the game too.

She put her hand on Steven's lap. "How long have you been swinging?"

Steven grinned. "Almost ten years. My wife, Tracy, and I decided that the only thing that would keep our marriage together was a bit of variety."

"So this helps your relationship?" Lara tried to keep the disbelief out of her voice.

"You bet." Bobby answered. He leaned close to her. "Janice and I would have divorced long ago if we hadn't started swapping. It adds a bit of danger to the relationship."

"Danger?" Lara's voice was hesitant. "I thought this was a safe environment."

"It is." Frank Burkett sat on the coffee table in front of her. "What Bobby is referring to, is the excitement of the chase."

"So you're chasing me right now?" Lara was intrigued.

"You got it." Bobby brushed a hand down her arm. "How are we doing so far?"

"You're certainly making me feel special." Lara's voice took on a sultry tone. "Do you do this for all the women or just those here for the first time?"

"Depends." Steven shrugged. "First timers are fun and like you, they can be a bit skittish."

"It's that obvious?" Lara swallowed the lump in her throat. "I'm not certain about all of this. It's my husband who wants to try this lifestyle."

Bobby rubbed his hands together. "That means we'll just have to work harder to make you stay."

"What happens at these parties?"

Frank swept his arm around the room. "It's like any other party. We have some drinks, play a few games, and let nature take its course. Speaking of drinks." Frank stood. "How about a glass of wine? Red or white?"

"White."

Frank handed her a glass and Lara sniffed the floral bouquet of the wine before taking a large gulp of courage. Her tension eased before the wine hit her stomach. She smiled up at Frank and then leaned back into the leather couch. Being surrounded by three attentive men might not be such a bad way to spend the evening.

"Now what?" Lara took another sip of wine.

"We get to know you." Bobby inched closer. "What do you do for a living?"

"I'm an interior designer." Lara tilted her head at him. "And you?"

"I'm a writer." Bobby's voice held pride. "Mysteries and thrillers. One of my books has been optioned for a movie."

"That's exciting."

"Not as much as you." Bobby leaned in and sniffed her neck. "What's that perfume you're wearing?"

"I'm not." Lara giggled. "I respect that some people have allergies to scents."

"You're considerate." Steven stepped into the conversation. "That's a wonderful trait in a potential lover."

There was a second of silence. Lara took another gulp of wine. This was becoming very real and she had to gather her thoughts. She would be sleeping with one of these men tonight and the thought was terrifying.

What if she didn't measure up?

What if they didn't?

"Way to stop the conversation Steven." Frank gave him a light swat on the arm. "Lara, you are free to do whatever you wish. If you want to take it slow that's fine by us."

"If you want to try all of us tonight, that's also fine." Bobby's tone was playful.

Lara's eyes widened. "Is that normal? What about the other women?"

"No that isn't normal, but no one is going to stop you from having more than one partner if that's what you want. You make the rules." Frank's calm voice eased her tension. "We're here to have fun and enjoy ourselves."

Lara threw back the rest of her wine. She handed her glass to Frank for a refill. She was going to need lots of alcohol tonight. Already, she had more than she bargained for with three men vying for her attention. She planned on sleeping with only one, though. Even David couldn't convince her that she should participate in an orgy.

"You're frightening her." Frank handed her a second glass of wine. "We like to start these things off informally. It helps everyone get comfortable."

"Maybe if we kept to safer topics for a while." Lara exhaled a shaky breath. "Steven, what do you do for a living?"

"I'm in real estate." Steven pointed at Frank. "Frank's in manufacturing. How about hobbies? Do you have any?"

"I quilt." Lara gripped the stem of her wine glass tighter. "Every other Wednesday, a group of friends get together. I find it relaxing."

"My grandmother quilted." Bobby leaned back. "I can remember watching her as a boy. One day she'd be working on small scraps and the next she'd have a whole new quilt put on the bed."

Lara relaxed. "She sounds like an amazing woman."

"She was." Bobby smiled and something twisted inside of Lara. He might be the one tonight.

Frank cleared his throat. "Anna is waving us over to the table. She wants to play a couple of games."

"Strip poker." Steven hooted as he stood. "I always win."

"You cheat." Anna pulled out a chair. "I thought we'd start with something old fashioned."

One of the other women held her hand out to Lara. "I'm Tracy. I'm glad you're joining us tonight."

The other woman waved at her from beside David. "I'm Janice."

Tracy led Lara over to one side of a big round table. She sat beside her and they were joined by Anna and Janice. The men sat on the opposite side. Anna place a plastic bottle in the center of the table. A chorus of groans came from the men.

"Not spin the bottle?" Steven shook his head. "We're not kids."

"It's the perfect ice breaker." Anna's fingers stroked the bottle. "David and Lara are new to our group. I don't want to scare them away before the fun begins."

Steven rolled his eyes as he pulled out a seat at the table. The first person to spin was Anna. The plastic bottle twirled around the table top for a couple of times and then landed on Tracy. A jolt of surprise went through Lara. She hadn't considered that they were going to be doing anything bisexual.

"Don't look so concerned." Anna touched her arm. "If the bottle lands on the same sex, you just kiss their spouse."

Anna stood and pulled Steven from his seat. She wrapped her arms around his neck and pulled his head down so that they were mouth to mouth. Her tongue flicked out and brushed across the seam of his lips and then she captured his mouth with hers. The kiss was hot. Their bodies rocked against each other and Steven's hands roamed across her back and lower. When they were finished they were gasping for air.

"Kids don't kiss like that." Steven grinned. He was visibly aroused and proud of it. "That's what I call foreplay."

Anna handed the bottle to Lara. "Your turn."

Chapter 5

"So soon?" Lara gave a half laugh and then looked up at the eager eyes watching her. The only person not showing any interest was her husband. Lara straightened her shoulders and looked away from David. If he wanted to play the disinterested spouse then she could do the same. She tightened her grip on the bottle and sent it for a spin.

It went around a couple of times and then started to slow. Lara's heart beat sped up with each rotation of the bottle. Her hands were clasped together tight in front of her, and she fought the urge to shut her eyes. What was she so uptight about? It was only a kiss.

The bottle stopped.

It pointed at Steven.

Lara forced a smile to her lips and stood at the same time as Steven did. They met at the head of the table.

"Ready?" Steven grinned and then pulled her close.

Lara inhaled and forced her shoulders to relax. She was behaving like a schoolgirl anticipating her first kiss. It was ridiculous, but a part of her couldn't ignore the fact that her husband was sitting at the table watching her every move.

Steven's lips were hungry and they devoured her mouth before she had a chance to take a breath. There was no romantic touching or exploring, just hot, sexual need. A flicker deep inside of her responded to the raw energy that Steven exuded, and she relaxed into the kiss. If he wanted heat, then she could provide it. She ground her pelvis into his and bit at his tongue. Steven's body hardened in response and he gripped her buttocks, holding them tight to him as he thrust his hips into her.

Fire exploded.

Then the kiss ended.

Lara eased away from Steven. His eyes had turned a deep blue and his grin was gone. In its place was a look of interest that sent her body temperature soaring. Steven had given her a taste of what having sex with him would be like. She wasn't disappointed. Given the chance she would have continued with their kiss to see where it might lead.

"Okay you two. Give the rest of us a chance." Bobby's voice interrupted their silent appraisal of each other.

Lara's cheeks heated as she remembered that they had an audience. Steven's kiss had made her forget everything, including the fact that David had watched it. Her hand went up to straighten the collar of her shirt. She glanced at David, but he was talking with Tracy. So much for caring about what she did.

She sat down and watched the others spin the bottle and waited. When David's turn came he was all smiles. He winked at Tracy and then gave the bottle a twist of his wrist. It went round a couple of times and then landed on Tracy. If she hadn't seen it with her own eyes, she would have thought that he'd fixed the game.

David bowed to Tracy and then pulled her up beside him. His arms went around her and he leaned in for the kiss. Lara's stomach tightened and she had to force herself to continue watching them. David held Tracy's head in place with one hand and his other roamed over her back. The kiss seemed to go on forever. David might justify the swapping, but this felt like cheating.

Her husband was kissing another woman.

She was powerless to prevent it.

When their kiss ended they stood back and smiled at each other. Lara knew that David had every intention of sleeping with her later. It was in his eyes. She'd seen that same determined, seductive look the first time they'd met. David was on the hunt.

Anna stood and clapped her hands to get everyone's attention. "Before we decide who we want to spend a bit more time with, I thought we'd have some dancing."

"Slow music and close embraces." Frank added.

"This time we'll chose our partners by letting the men pull names from the hat." Anna dropped four pieces of paper into a hat and held it out to Bobby. "You first."

Bobby reached in. He read the name he'd picked and then looked at Lara. "It looks like it's our chance to turn up the heat."

David picked Janice as his partner, which left Anna and Steven, and Tracy and Frank together.

A sultry jazz song filled the room. Bobby grabbed her close and they started to move to the music. Bobby's arms were like an octopus and Lara forced herself to relax. She usually refused to dance with men who couldn't keep their distance, but this wasn't the normal situation.

The song ended and Anna clapped for their attention again. "Switch partners."

Frank gathered her close as Bobby released her. He was a wonderfully smooth dancer and they glided around the room with ease. Lara enjoyed his expertise and was sorry when the song changed again. This time Steven caught her close to his chest.

He wasted no time in picking up from where they'd left off with the kiss. His hands pushed her close to him and he massaged her buttocks. They moved standing in place. It was more sexual foreplay than dancing. Lara's insides started to melt as a flame of desire sparked to life within her.

The music ended and Lara stepped back to straighten her clothing. Anna was clapping for attention when the front door of the house opened. There was laughter and a bit of chatter before four young men came into the room.

"Sorry Mom and Dad, I didn't realize you were entertaining." One of the young men gave a sheepish grin.

"Dennis." Anna's voice was a high squeak. "I wasn't expecting you home tonight."

"Just me and the guys looking for a place to watch the game. Our television went on the fritz tonight. Is it okay if we spread out in the rec room downstairs?"

"Of course." Anna's voice was motherly. "Do you need anything?"

"We brought all the munchies with us." Dennis nodded to his father and then he and his friends went downstairs.

For a second, there was silence and then Steven pulled her close and laughed. "All that fooling around for nothing," he whispered in her ear.

Lara giggled. She didn't know if it was because of the situation, or the relief she felt at not having to follow through with the evening. Whatever the reason, she was floating on top of the world. She'd been saved and was grateful. No matter how exciting she had found being the center of attention, she still didn't feel right about cheating on David.

"I'm so sorry." Anna's voice was a hoarse whisper. "I had no idea that Dennis was coming home tonight."

"This is the first time one of our parties has been interrupted." Frank's voice was apologetic. "We're very careful to only schedule parties when the kids are away."

"It happens." Steven released Lara and walked over to his wife, Tracy. "It just means we'll have fun with ourselves tonight."

"That's for sure." Bobby grabbed Janice's hand and walked to the door. "I'm not wasting this buildup. We'll see you later."

Steven and Tracy left at the same time. That left her and David. She went to her husband and clasped his hand. He looked down at her and scowled. She refused to let her mood be dampened. Her body was screaming for release, and like the others, she intended to go home and make love to her husband.

"Thank you for inviting us." Lara tugged David closer to the door. "It was a very interesting experience."

"We'll be having another party next weekend." Frank held the door open for them. "You two are invited."

"Thank you." David shook Frank's hand and then turned to Anna. "We'd love to see this through."

"No interruptions next time. I promise." Anna glanced behind her and rolled her eyes. "You think you have everything under control and then the unexpected happens."

Lara and David walked to the car in silence.

David drove fast. Lara kept glancing over to see if she could gage his mood, but his face was impassive. He didn't speak the whole ride home. He let her off at the front door and then he moved the car into the garage. She watched him go with a sinking feeling in her stomach. She'd seen him upset before, but this was the first time he had refused to speak.

She let herself in and headed straight for the bedroom. She kicked off her shoes and slipped out of her shirt and pants. What she needed was a shower. She needed to clean away the horrid way she felt at having been kissed and groped by other men. She turned the water on hot and when the room had filled with steam, she stepped into the glass-enclosed shower.

She lathered the soap, but before she could wash, the door clicked open. David was standing there nude and very aroused. He pulled the door closed and stepped close. His eyes roamed over her body and settled on her breasts. He reached out and flicked his thumb over one of her nipples.

Heat suffused her body.

He pushed her against the shower wall and held her hands over her head. "I saw you with those other men. You were hot for them. I haven't seen you that interested since we were first married."

"I did what you asked me to."

"And I was right. You're panting for it."

David ground his lips onto hers and thrust his tongue inside. There was nothing gentle about the kiss. He devoured her mouth and sucked on her tongue until she moaned. Then he lifted her high against the shower wall and thrust deep within her.

She clasped her legs around his hips and moved with him. It was a fast-paced race to the heights of ecstasy and ended with an explosive climax. They were both gasping for air when it was over. David moved away from her and lathered up the soap and washed himself before handing her the bar.

"Next time, you won't be so reluctant to come to the party." David opened the shower door. "You can't deny it's improved our sex life."

Chapter 6

"David and I went to our first swinger's party on Saturday." Lara looked up from the row of triple feather stitches she'd just completed.

Ella's eyes widened. "I thought you were unsure about whether you were going."

"I was." Lara pulled out two strands of yellow embroidery floss from her skein and threaded them through her needle. "I still am. It seems that swinging parties and children don't mix."

"I would have thought that was obvious." Alisa tilted her head at Lara. "Are you telling us that the party ended abruptly?"

Lara grinned. "We were all primed to pick partners, and then the couple's son showed up with some of his friends from college. It put quite the damper on the whole thing."

"So what was it like?" Brenna leaned forward. "Did you know who you wanted to sleep with?"

Lara shrugged. "There were a couple of men I found attractive. It was difficult to think about going through with it. David was in his element. He had his hands full with the other women, while their partners never left my side."

"I bet that made you feel wonderful." Alisa's voice was dry. "What woman doesn't like to be the center of attention?"

"It was exciting and for a while I forgot about David being in the same room."

"So what did you do?" Ella held her hexagon floral block close to her body. "Did you get to pick, or did they pull names out of a hat?"

"It was much like any other party except there was a lot of touching and sexual innuendoes."

"In what way?" Ella's voice was a shocked whisper.

"We played spin the bottle."

Alisa snorted. "We did that as kids."

"Our kisses were X-rated." Lara buried the knot of her thread in the seam and took her first stitch with the yellow thread. "The guy I kissed started grinding into me. I could feel every inch of his arousal."

"Was he the one?" Alisa's voice held mild interest.

"He certainly had the equipment."

"Lara!" Ella's tone was of embarrassed shock. "Is he the one you would have gone to bed with?"

She shrugged. "One of the guys I danced with wasn't so bad."

"How many men were at this party?" Brenna looked up from the spool quilt she'd been quilting.

"Three."

"That's not much choice." Alisa frowned. "What if you didn't like any of them?"

"David thought it would be easier for me to participate if there wasn't a crowd." Lara took a deep breath. "He was right. Before the kids showed up, I was pretty relaxed and ready to choose a partner for the night."

"What about David?" Brenna's eyes narrowed. "Was he jealous?"

"To be honest, I don't think he knew I was there." Lara took a deep breath to release the knot of pain in her chest. "He was so enthralled by the women, that he didn't even notice what I was doing."

"He doesn't sound like a very committed husband." Ella's voice was doubtful. "How will this help your marriage?"

"Lara and David are exploring ways to make their marriage more exciting." Alisa's voice was matter of fact.

"So did it spice up your relationship?" Brenna's voice was full of curiosity.

Lara leaned back in her chair and considered what had happened when they returned home. David had been eager to make love, but was it because she was convenient and he needed a release, or because he desired her?

"We made out in the shower." Lara's voice was hesitant. "He wanted me and the sex was hot."

"You don't sound certain." Alisa stopped stitching and looked at her.

"He hasn't touched me since."

"That's not good." Alisa frowned. "Have you tried to seduce him?"

"I've tried everything but standing on my head. He isn't interested." Lara didn't hide her frustration. "All he talks about is the swinger's party this Saturday."

"You're going?" Ella asked.

"What choice do I have?" Lara threw her block down on her lap. "David is insistent that this is how he wants our relationship to proceed."

"You could say no." Brenna's voice was quiet. "You don't have to put yourself through this if you aren't comfortable."

"I want to keep my marriage intact."

"Just don't lose yourself in the process." Brenna shook her head. "If David truly loved you, he wouldn't ask you do something you're uncomfortable with."

"That's what I keep telling myself, but you should have seen him at the party. It was as if he were another man. He was energized and alive."

"How did you feel?" Ella folded her block in half. "I know that when Gerry asked me to accept his mistress, I felt as if he'd robbed me of all my self-esteem and self-worth. When I tried to have an affair, it made things worse."

"Being with the other men made me feel sexy again."

"Then it sounds as if you want to go to this party." Alisa's voice was matter of fact. "Don't fight it."

"Go and enjoy myself?" Lara sighed. "You're right. I won't know if this is the lifestyle for me, until I sleep with these men."

"Make certain to rub it in David's face." Brenna's words were said without malice. "A dose of reality may make him realize what he is giving up."

"Make him jealous," Ella agreed. "If he loves you, then he won't want other men pawing you."

"What if he doesn't care?"

Lara's voice was a low whisper. The thought of David's rejection after the party still stung. If the only thing that could make him touch her was being frustrated by other women, then there wasn't much hope for the marriage surviving.

"He'd be a fool to let you go." Alisa's common sense tone eased Lara's mind.

"The reason you're doing this is because you want to show David that he needs only you in his life. The thrill of being with these other women will wear off." Brenna's words were convincing.

"You're such a lovely woman, both inside and out." Ella reached over and clasped her hand. "David will realize that. He isn't a fool."

Lara tried to smile. "That's what I'm hoping for."

"It's why you're doing this." Alisa's tone was brisk. "A few encounters, and he'll get it out of his system."

"We'll see." Lara put her quilt block in her bag and stood. "This weekend there will be no children to interrupt the activities."

Chapter 7

Lara's stomach muscles clenched tight.

It was the same house, the same people.

A whole week had passed, and she still wasn't certain that this was what she wanted. David had been like a caged tiger all day long. Lara had been five minutes late getting home, and he'd ripped into her about her lack of enthusiasm.

"Smile." David growled. "You've met these people already. Your hesitancy is no longer cute."

"I don't want to do this." Lara kept her voice low. She could hear footsteps from the house. "How can you insist on sleeping with other people if you love me?"

"Grow up. This isn't about love." David clenched her elbow. "You're the one who said you'd do anything to keep the marriage together."

Lara took a deep breath.

Anna pulled the door open and ushered them into the house. There was no more time for arguing. David had already decided the direction he wanted their marriage to go in. She either went along for the ride, or walked away. Maybe Alissa was right. She needed to relax and enjoy.

Steven stood when she paused at the living room doorway.

Lara took a step toward him and was stopped by Bobby before she had a chance to enter the room. He caught her by the waist and pulled her in close. "Where are you going pretty lady?"

"Aren't we gathering at the couch?" Lara's voice was hesitant.

Bobby shook his head. "It's been decided."

"What?" Lara looked for David, but he had disappeared. So had Tracy.

"It's you and me tonight."

Lara's stomach rolled with nausea. "I thought I could decide."

Bobby guided her down the hall. "Not tonight. The rules have changed."

"That's not what I want."

"I'll just have to convince you." Bobby nuzzled her ear. "Your husband already agreed to this."

David had taken away her choice?

Her stomach tightened and she fought to control her anger. How dare he? It had been one thing when she thought that she could pick someone that she fancied, but to know that her husband got his choice and she didn't, was unacceptable. Bobby would not have been her pick for a partner. Being forced to have sex with him was a violation.

Lara planted her feet on the floor.

Bobby tried to pull her. She refused to move. Either the rules were the same for both of them, or she wouldn't play.

"What's the matter?" Bobby's voice held confusion. "I thought we got along fine last week."

"Did David get to select who he would sleep with?"

"He arranged it ahead of time with Tracy. She called me and gave me the news."

"So we have been manipulated into this situation by my husband." Lara pulled away from Bobby. "Is that how swapping is supposed to happen?"

Bobby shrugged. "There are no hard and fast rules."

"I don't have anything against you. At this moment, I wouldn't be very good company."

"Are you refusing?" Bobby's tone of disbelief was almost laughable.

"I will make my own choice tonight. If that happens to be you, great." Lara swung around and headed to the living room. Steven and Frank were sitting on the couch with their wives. When she walked into the room the men's eyebrows rose. Their wives stood and came over to her.

"Is something wrong?" Anna touched her arm.

"It seems my husband thinks he calls the shots in this arrangement. Is this the normal way for you to introduce people into your lifestyle?"

Janice shook her head. "What happened?"

"David decided that Bobby and I would be together tonight. He didn't consult me."

Anna's eyes widened. "He told us that you'd made your decision ahead of time."

Janice turned to her husband. "Were you part of this?"

Bobby gave a lopsided grin. "Tracy called me. I didn't know that Lara wasn't informed."

Lara let Bobby's lie slide. She had no intention of being passed around like a piece of property. She went and sat between Steven and Frank. It took a second for her heart beat to slow, but the gradual warmth of the room and the glass of wine that Anna handed her did the trick. All the men were looking at her with concern, and she forced a smile to her lips.

"I'll be fine. I wasn't expecting to be pulled into a bedroom the minute I stepped into the house."

"I wasn't forcing you." Bobby's voice was indignant.

"You didn't let her take her coat off." Frank eased her jacket off her shoulders, and handed it to Anna. "We're not usually so brutish."

Lara leaned back against the couch. "How do you decide these things?"

"You can pick a name out of a hat, or wear a blindfold to choose, if you don't have a preference." Frank cleared his throat. "You did get a chance to sample a bit last week, so you might already have a preference."

Lara looked at the three men and decided to take a chance. "Let's go for the blindfold. You three line up and I'll make a choice."

Anna clapped her hands together. "You're being adventuresome tonight. I'll get a scarf."

Lara stood and straightened her skirt. She didn't really care which man she chose, however it must be her decision not David's. She positioned herself in the center of the room and waited while Anna tied a dark scarf over her eyes. Her heart started to race and a twinge of excitement curled in her stomach.

This might be fun.

She heard the three men move and stand in front of her. When they were in place, she walked to the first one. She held her arm out in front and when she touch him, she began to pat her hand over his chest. It was firm and muscular. Next, she leaned in and inhaled his scent; spicy with a touch of bergamot. The last thing she did was brush her lips across his.

Instant sparks.

Their lips clung for a few seconds, their tongues glided and tasted. She savored the sensations he was arousing. Someone cleared their throat and she broke off the kiss.

Her hands felt the next candidate. He was shorter, with a soft abdomen. He smelled of whisky and cigarettes. She fought the urge to wrinkle her nose. She kissed him, almost gagging at the taste of stale smoke. She pulled away and went to the last man.

He too was tall not muscular, not fat, just broad shouldered and steady. He smelled of expensive cologne and when she kissed him, his expertise had her head reeling. His tongue twirled around hers so that he heightened the connection. Delicious shivers ran down her spine. This was a man who knew how to make love. She wouldn't go wrong picking him.

Two of the men were keepers.

"Number two is out."

"Damn." Lara recognized Bobby's voice. A surge of relief went through her.

"Do you need another inspection?" Janice's voice was full of laughter.

"Maybe another kiss?" Anna's suggestion was met by a groan from Bobby.

Lara nodded and reached out for the first man.

He didn't make her wait. He pulled her into his arms and kissed her with a passion that had her head spinning. She hadn't expected this. Her body tingled and her knees were weak. She let herself get lost in the spell he was weaving with his lips and hands. Shivers of delight raced through her. His tongue glided over the seam of her mouth and then plunged into her moist interior, sliding and sucking, until she shook with need. Only then, did he release her.

She turned to the last man.

He gathered her into his arms and kissed down her neck and around to her mouth before smoothing his lips over hers. He eased his tongue into her mouth with a finesse that had tremors of excitement racing through her body. Every lick and brush of his tongue sparked the fire of arousal deep within her. He ended the kiss just as she was responding to him. He left her wanting more.

It wasn't going to be an easy decision.

Passion.

Or expertise?

She stepped back and cleared her throat. "You both make it very difficult to decide. Are you sure I can only chose one?"

"For now." Anna's voice was low. "If you want, you can come back for more later in the evening."

"They won't have that kind of stamina." Bobby's sarcasm helped her make her decision. Passion burned bright and hot. It would be best to take it now. She didn't want to risk it sizzling out.

"Number one." Lara pulled off her blindfold and looked straight at Frank Burkett.

Her eyes widened.

"Surprised?" Frank's voice was quiet with concern.

She had thought it would have been Steven. It was an interesting twist on how her perceptions could be completely wrong. She hadn't associated passion with Frank. Looks were definitely deceiving.

"I knew it wasn't Bobby."

Steven laughed. "Bobby is a poor loser."

"I'm not a prize to be won." Lara's voice was firm.

"You're a woman of incomparable beauty who deserves to be wooed." Frank held out his hand. "How about a dip in the hot tub?"

Lara nodded and let him lead her out of the room. When they had reached the quiet of the patio, he pointed to a tiny, cedar-clad building. "You can borrow a bathing suit if you want and there should be a couple of robes for us."

Lara waited until the butterflies had settled in her stomach. She walked over to the change rooms and went through the door labeled girls. A long wooden bench was on one side and several shelves on the other. White cotton robes hung on hooks next to the shelves. She reached for a robe and started to undress.

She picked out a skimpy, neon-pink bikini and grabbed a second robe before she stepped out into the warm night air. The house was located on several acres at the outskirts of the city and provided complete privacy. When she reached the hot tub, Frank was already lounging nude in the water. Two glasses of white wine had been poured. She dropped the robes, stepped into the water, and took the glass he handed her.

She eased into the warm water and took a refreshing sip of the wine. It was delicious. It would take several sips, if not glasses, before she would be relaxed enough to have sex with Frank, though. She took a large gulp and eased against the side of the hot tub.

"Sex isn't mandatory."

Lara almost choked on her drink. "Is it that obvious?"

"I've been at this for many years. I don't think I've ever seen anyone as nervous as you."

Lara twisted so that the pulsing water jets were aimed at the small of her back. "I'm not a prude. I'm old fashioned and think that marriage means fidelity."

"I'm the same." Frank picked up the wine bottle and filled her now empty glass. "After our first party, Anna insisted we continue the lifestyle."

"I suppose you wanted to stop?" Lara took a long swallow of wine.

Frank laughed. "I want what's best for my marriage. It's been many years since I've been truly interested in the playing."

"Why?" Lara's head was spinning as the wine began to take effect.

"We see the same type of people at these parties." Frank shrugged. "You're the first person in years that I've truly desired."

Lara's heart skipped a beat.

Frank was looking at her with an intensity that sent shivers across her back. Her temperature rose and even in the hot tub, she felt the searing heat of his desire. His kiss hadn't lied. Passion simmered just below the surface.

"Do you need more wine?" Frank's voice was a low whisper.

Lara looked down at her empty glass and nodded. She moved closer to Frank and held the glass out with a shaking hand. She was way over her limit and didn't care. Nothing about this evening seemed real, so she might as well enjoy it through an alcohol haze.

"I bought this bottle especially for you. I remembered that you prefer white wine, so I thought you'd like this. It's a rare vintage and worth every penny." Frank leaned close to her. "I knew you probably wouldn't choose me, but I wanted to be ready, just in case."

"You did that for me?" Lara couldn't remember the last time David had done something special for her.

"For us." Frank clicked his glass against hers. "I promise to make this evening special."

A couple more sips and the rest of the world had faded away.

All that existed was Frank.

He pulled her close and started to knead her shoulders. "You're starting to relax."

Lara let his fingers work their magic and soon her body was limp. Tension and inhibitions had drifted away. The jets of the tub had her pushed against Frank and there was no hiding his arousal. He was ready for sex.

She turned to face him. "Shouldn't we take this slower?"

"No need." Frank unclipped the bra of her bikini and flung the pink top onto the patio. "I took a pill, so I'll be good to go all night long."

Lara giggled. "You've gone to a lot of trouble."

Frank rubbed his fingers over her breasts. "It's my pleasure. This evening will be memorable for both of us."

Lara groaned. Frank's touch was tantalizing and erotic. She leaned closer and shivered when one of his hands moved lower. He pushed beneath her bikini bottom and pulled on it until he'd dragged it down over her legs. It was thrown over his shoulder. His fingers caressed her clitoris, sending heat vibrating throughout her body.

"Do you like that?"

"You know I do." Lara moaned with pleasure.

"Come for me," Frank whispered.

Her body was screaming for release. Frank nipped at her ear and an intense bolt of pleasure shot to her womb just as she climaxed. She shook as waves of bliss pulsed through her, each more intense than the last, until she was exhausted by the sheer power of her body's response. Frank's fingers eased their pressure and she leaned against his chest.

"I sense your tension is gone."

She was too drained to do more than smile. "You planned that didn't you?"

"It was the fastest way to get your attention." Frank lifted her until he had positioned her above his erect penis. "Now take me for a ride."

The hard thrust of Frank entering her, jolted her back to reality. "What about protection?"

"I've got a clean bill of health. All of us do. Proof of that is part of the admission into the group." Frank clasped her waist and held her close as he tilted his hips in an upward thrust. "I've had a vasectomy so there's no chance of pregnancy. All you have to do is enjoy."

Frank was gazing at her with hooded eyes and his hands were propelling her hips to move. She reached up and grabbed his shoulders, moving her fingers to massage his neck. She let him guide her. They moved together in a fast-paced rhythm that sent rapture spiraling through her. Tighter and tighter the tension was coiled, until they both exploded in a shattering release.

Lara gasped at the power of the climax that ripped through her body.

Frank leaned back against the hot tub wall. "That was fantastic."

Lara eased away and sat on the opposite seat. She sank down into the warm heat of the water and let it cleanse and relax her body. Her head was still fuzzy from the wine, but she was aware of what she'd just done. She'd had sex with a man who was almost a stranger. There was no love involved, just mutual gratification. Guilt wouldn't let her admit that she'd liked it. Not yet.

Frank emptied the wine bottle into her glass and handed it to her. "It wasn't so bad."

She shook her head. "It still feels like cheating."

"Give yourself permission to enjoy." Frank picked up his wine glass that was still half full. "Once I have a few minutes rest, I'll be ready to go again."

Chapter 8

"Here?" The word ended on a raised squeak. If she stayed in the hot tub much longer she'd look like a prune.

"You'd prefer a bed?" Frank grinned and finished his wine. "Let's go."

He jumped out of the tub and held out her robe. Lara forced back her embarrassment, pushed herself to the edge and stood. She wrapped the robe around her naked body, tied it tight, and then followed Frank into the house. No one was in sight. They skirted past the kitchen where Frank picked up another bottle of wine, glasses, and a corkscrew.

"This'll make it even better." Frank grinned and turned to the rear of the house. His hair was damp and clung to the back of his neck. Lara had to give herself a shake at the unreality of the situation. She felt as if they were teenagers sneaking into the house past curfew.

Why had she agreed to this?

Why was she enjoying it so much?

She didn't want to question her motives too closely. Not now. There would be plenty of time to examine everything tomorrow. Tonight, she was going to go with the moment and enjoy. She followed Frank down a long hallway and entered the room he directed her to.

She was blinded by the brilliance of reflected light.

The room was floor to ceiling mirrors.

She turned at the sound of the door closing behind her. "You have to be kidding?"

Frank put the wine glasses on a small table near a king-size bed. "This was my daughter's dance studio. When she left home, we appropriated it."

"Do you need this many mirrors?"

"You'd be surprised how erotic their effect is." Frank pulled the cork out of the second bottle of wine and filled their glasses. "We call this the Fun Room. When we feel like group sex, this is where we come"

"How often is that?" Lara's voice was hesitant as she took the wine glass that he held out to her.

Frank shrugged. "Not often. We're getting pretty tame in our old age. The room was reserved for you tonight."

"Me?" Lara took a sip of wine. "Why on earth would you do that?"

"It's your first time." Frank's voice was serious. "It's special, and this room will make it memorable."

"It's David's first time also."

Frank shook his head. "I doubt it."

Lara was about to object when he motioned for her to finish her wine. She gulped the delicious liquid and put the empty glass on the table. Frank took her hand and led her over to the mirrored wall. There was a ballet barre attached to it and she ran her hand over the smooth wood.

"Do you dance?"

She shook her head. "I always wanted lessons as a child, but it was too expensive."

"You're graceful enough without them." Frank's hand moved down her sleeve and feathered across one of her hands. "Hold onto the bar."

A twinge of excitement shot through her. "Why?"

"You'll see." Frank nuzzled her ear. "Do as I say."

Lara clasped the bar.

"Both hands."

She hesitated and looked up at Frank's reflection.

"Trust me." Frank's voice soothed. He shrugged out of his robe and stood behind her naked. "All you need to do is enjoy."

Lara took a deep breath and forced the tension from her muscles. She clasped the rail with both hands and eased back into Frank's arms. She gazed into the mirror and watched as his fingers brushed against the back of her wrists. A jolt of sensation raced up her arm. Frank's fingers moved up to her shoulders and then fluttered across the back of her neck. Tingles spread throughout her scalp, sending a twist of awareness to her inner core. He pulled the robe from her shoulders, and lifted each hand from the railing as he eased it off her arms. The robe fell open to her waist.

Her breath caught in her throat.

He undid the tie.

Her wrap dropped to the ground leaving her completely exposed. Her fingers twitched and just when she was going to release the barre and cover herself Frank put his hands over hers.

She wanted to hide.

There was nowhere to turn.

"You're beautiful." Frank's voice held a note of awe. "Your face is so expressive. I want you to watch as I pleasure you."

A pulsing need began to build within her.

"Promise you won't let go." His hands lifted away.

Lara bit her lip and nodded. Every cell in her body wanted to follow where Frank was leading. Excitement and thrills of desire clamored for fulfillment. Never had she experienced such an erotically sensual situation. She had slept with men before her marriage, and even though she loved David, he had never aroused her to such a fevered pitch. Frank knew exactly what to say and do.

Frank's fingers traced up her arm.

A delicious shiver raced through her.

He nipped at her earlobe, and she leaned her head back against his shoulder. Both of his hands moved to her breasts and fondled and kneaded until she moaned with delight. His thumbs circled her nipples before flicking across their sensitive tips. A jolt of raw desire shook her.

"Are you watching?"

She nodded. Her eyelids were half open. She could see her reflection in the mirrors and was awed by the beauty of the scene that Frank was creating. Every movement of Frank's fingers was magnified both in the mirrors' reflection and her body's reaction. Moist heat pooled between her legs, and she ached to have it assuaged. Frank was in no hurry. His was a slow and tantalizing seduction of her body that aroused and left her on the edge of release.

"You're so responsive."

Frank leaned into her. His erection pressed into the small of her back. He was as excited as she was and that added to her pleasure. She wasn't the only enjoying this. Somewhere at the back of her mind she wondered if he wooed all of his partners with such care.

His fingers caressed the side of her body.

"Spread your legs."

A boneless, weakness overcame her. If she hadn't been holding onto the barre, she would have fallen. Still, she obeyed. Frank smoothed his palm over the juncture at the top of her legs and rubbed.

"A natural blonde." There was a hitch in his breathing. "I sense everything about you is genuine."

"You seem pretty real yourself."

A husky laugh tickled the skin of her neck. "Lean forward."

She put her weight on the barre. The tip of Frank's penis nudged for entry at her vagina. He moved closer and stroked her clitoris with his fingers. An exquisite thrill of pleasure pulsed through her when Frank penetrated her.

He thrust with a slow and steady rhythm that had her panting for release. She trembled with the fire and need that flowed through her, struggling to catch her breath. Every inch of her body tingled with sensations of bliss.

"Are you watching?" His voice was a husky whisper.

She opened her eyes and was transfixed by the intense vulnerability she saw in Frank's expression. He was straining to delay his release. She moaned and sank back, letting her hips gyrate against him. She gained control and power with each tilt of her pelvis. Shudders rippled across Frank and he clasped her close to him, his arms around her lower abdomen, his fingers stroking her clitoris while time seemed to stand still.

Her release came in a cataclysmic climax that she felt to the tips of her toes. Frank thrust deep and then shuddered. Together they sagged against the mirrored wall, their chests heaving from their exertion. A low chuckle rumbled from deep within Lara.

"What?" Frank's voice was shaky.

"I thought you said we were going to use the bed."

"The evening isn't over yet."

Lara shook her head. "You couldn't."

"Tonight, everything is possible." Frank gave her a quick kiss on her neck and disengaged himself. "What we need now is sustenance."

"Food?"

Lara resisted the urge to cover her nakedness. What was the point? Frank had seen all of her anyway; numerous times, if you considered the mirrors. To be honest, she was too relaxed to care. She was totally satiated.

Frank led her over to the bed. He poured her another glass of wine and handed it to her. "You stay here and I'll raid the refrigerator."

"Dressed like that?"

Frank looked down at his naked body and gave her a rueful look. "See the effect you have on me. I forget the simplest things."

He picked up his robe and tied it tight before heading out the door. Lara fluffed up several pillows against the brass headboard and then leaned back. She drank her wine and marveled at how great she felt. Better than she had in years. She'd forgotten how good sex could be. She pulled the bed sheets up around her and snuggled into their freshness.

The evening had gone from fear and trepidation to delight and pleasure. For a second, she wondered how David had fared, then she shook off the thought. He'd left her alone at the door and she didn't care. David could take care of himself.

Frank came back with another bottle of wine, cheese, grapes, and strawberries. He put the food on the bed and the unopened bottle on the table. He refilled her wine and poured himself a glass before sitting beside her. Lara took a sip of the deliciously cool wine and smiled.

"We won't be able to walk out of here."

"Is that a problem?"

Lara popped a green grape into her mouth. "At least you don't have to drive."

"Have the party at your house next time."

"I just might."

Lara leaned back and watched Frank through half-closed eyes. She could get used to this, but it was a fantasy and she wasn't going to be silly enough to confuse it with reality. She picked up a strawberry. She might as well enjoy what little of the evening they had left.

After her second glass of wine, her head was spinning again. Frank moved the food off the bed and pulled the sheets away from her. He threw his robe off and climbed in beside her. Lara could see the renewed passion in his gaze. He hadn't been kidding when he said anything was possible.

"Are you sufficiently rested?" His voice was husky.

Lara nodded.

"Then let's not waste what little time we have left."

Frank's finger touched her cheek and then started a slow, sensual path down her body. Shivers of anticipation skittered across her skin. Tantalizing and teasing, he roamed over her body with a velvet touch that had her twisting with need. Lara reached out to stroke him and he pushed her hand away.

"Tonight is for you." Frank's gaze was intense with sincerity. "Lay back and enjoy."

"That's not fair."

"Giving you pleasure is more erotically stimulating than anything I've ever experienced." His voice was gruff.

Frank's mouth replaced his fingers.

He kissed her until the world was spinning and a spiral of tension had built to a screaming pitch within her. She arched her hips, silently begging him for relief, but he ignored it. Instead, he trailed his kisses down her legs, lingering at the sensitive inner skin of her knees. Only when he reached her feet did he move up beside her.

His tongue darted and moved across her neck and breasts. Heat rushed through her and settled in her inner core. She clenched the sheets within her fists as her hunger grew. When he finished with her breasts, he moved down her abdomen, licking and nipping as he laved every inch of her body.

She shook with the need for release.

He thrust inside her.

Bliss exploded.

He moved back and then lunged again. Stroke after stroke, he penetrated deep within her, sending spirals of pleasure to every nerve in her body. Frank held her tight to him, as the dam exploded in a fiery blaze of ecstasy. From a far distance it registered that he had shuddered with his climax at the same time. He collapsed on her and they drifted back from the heights of passion. Their breathing eased and their bodies started to cool. Frank pulled the covers over them.

Exhaustion claimed both of them. When Lara awoke, the house was quiet. She pushed back the sheet and sat up. Frank yawned and looked over at her with surprise.

"How long did we sleep?"

Lara shrugged. "I haven't a clue. Why didn't someone come and wake us?"

"It's against the rules." Frank threw the sheet off and stretched his arms over his head. "I put the Do Not Disturb sign on the door."

"I'm surprised David didn't demand I leave sooner."

"No big deal." Frank stood and picked up his robe. "I'll go and get our clothes from outside. No need for both of us to freeze."

"Thanks." Lara gave him a lazy smile.

Frank was a generous and considerate lover. She'd been lucky to have spent her first time swapping with him. It had been a truly unique evening, and she doubted that any future encounters would equal it.

Five minutes later, Frank returned with an armful of clothes. He placed them on the bed and sat down beside her.

"The hot tub is still going if you want another dip."

"I'd better not." Lara picked up her underwear. "David will be angry enough."

"He understood the rules when he joined the group." Frank's voice had a note of steel that Lara hadn't heard before. "The party wasn't just for him."

Lara pulled on her panties and skirt. "Thank you for tonight. You made it special for me."

"I enjoyed it too." Frank handed her bra to her. "It was a privilege to introduce you to the lifestyle. You will always remember me as your first."

"You went to so much effort to make me feel comfortable." Lara closed the clasp of her bra. "I realize you didn't have to."

"You made it easy." Frank hesitated a second. "Too easy actually."

Lara tilted her head. "What do you mean?"

"It would be dangerous for us to be together too often." Frank pulled on his pants. "With swapping, you have to be careful not to get emotionally involved. That spells the end of your marriage."

"Which defeats the purpose."

"We're trying to bring excitement into our marriages, not break them up." Frank held her blouse out so she could slip it on. "You could make me forget my vows."

Lara's heart skipped a beat.

She turned to Frank and saw the truth in his eyes. She hadn't been wrong when she'd felt that he'd taken more care with her than he usually did. She swallowed the lump in her throat. She fought the temptation to throw caution to the wind and tell him it didn't matter. She wanted to be with him again.

Instead, she nodded. "We shared something special."

"You deserve to be treated with respect." Frank grimaced. "I don't want to interfere. Are you certain that your husband loves you? He doesn't act like a man in love."

"David used to care." Tears pricked her eyes. "I'm not so sure, now. He's restless and angry, and he blames me for everything."

Frank put his hand over hers. "If you need someone to talk to, I'm here for you."

"Thank you." Lara swiped a hand over her eyes. "That might be dangerous."

"True." Frank stood and helped her up. "Some things are worth taking a risk for."

She was pulled into his arms and held close. He gave her back a soothing rub and then leaned back. "You take care."

Lara nodded. "You too."

Frank kept his arm around her shoulders as they walked out of the room. The house was quiet and only a couple of lights were on in the kitchen and hallway. It looked as if everyone had gone home. She slipped into her shoes and picked up her jacket and purse at the door.

"I called you a taxi." Frank flipped the outside light on. "When I came out to get our clothes, I noticed that David's car was gone."

Again, Frank had shown her more consideration than her husband. Lara swallowed back her pain. She wasn't going to let David's behavior spoil her evening. He'd insisted that she come to this party and sleep with another man. She'd done what he'd asked, and he would have to live with the consequences.

She straightened her shoulders. "It's probably for the best. I don't think I could face him right now."

"The others have left also."

"Will your wife be upset?" Lara's voice was a low whisper.

Frank shrugged. "Probably, but like you, I'm here because it's what she desires."

"You don't want to swap partners?"

"I never did." Frank leaned close and lowered his voice. "It's a lifestyle she enjoys, and I want to keep the marriage together."

"I don't think it's been much of a hardship for you." Lara's voice was wry.

Frank laughed. "Especially not tonight."

The lights of a car pulling into the driveway flashed through the window. Frank opened the door and walked with her to the cab. He leaned in through the window once she was settled inside.

"Take care. I'd like to see you again, but I don't think your husband has plans for another party with us."

Lara opened her mouth to object, but Frank had already moved away. She watched him walk back to the house with a sinking heart. What happened when Frank had left her alone in the room? Had he had a run in with David? Whatever it was, she would have to wait until she saw her husband to get to the bottom of it.

When she arrived home, all the lights were out, including the one at the front entrance. David had done it deliberately to show his displeasure. She paid the cabbie and walked up the front pathway to the door.

Inside, she reset the alarm and then made her way upstairs. David was probably asleep. She needed a shower and she didn't care what time it was. She flipped on the bathroom light and was shutting the door when the irate voice of her husband stopped her.

"Where the hell have you been?"

Chapter 9

"Where you abandoned me." Lara continued into the bathroom.

David stomped in behind her. "Everyone else left hours ago."

"Jealous?" Lara couldn't resist the taunt.

"You reek of sex." David grabbed her arm and pulled her around. "Don't be coy with me. What were you doing with Frank all night long?"

Lara's eyes widened. "Exactly what you were doing with Tracy."

"I didn't spend the whole night with her." David's mouth was twisted into a snarl. "I had plenty of time for Anna and Janice, and I still got home before you."

Lara's stomach dropped. Her husband had slept with all of the women at the party. No wonder Frank had said that he doubted she would be coming back. David had had his fun and now he wanted to move on. This wasn't the vision of swapping that she'd had in the beginning.

"You treated it like a buffet. Did you think you were supposed to sample a little of everything?" Lara couldn't keep the disdain from her voice. "I thought it was the lifestyle that you were interested in."

"I want to have sex with other women and I'm tired of lying about it." David spat the words at her.

Lara's breath caught in her throat. "How long?"

David didn't pretend not to understand. "A year after we married."

"And you blame me?" Everything was clear now. David had thought he'd found the perfect excuse to cheat on her. It would be guilt free as long as she was cheating too.

"You're young. I thought you'd be more adventurous and take more risks in bed."

Lara took a deep breath. He was angry and deliberately trying to hurt her, yet that didn't excuse his words. She loved him, and until he had brought up the need to try swapping, she'd thought they had a wonderful life together.

"Why is this the first time I'm hearing that you've been miserable?" Lara pulled a clean towel off the rack.

David had the grace to look shamefaced. "I've not been unhappy."

"What then?" Lara unzipped her skirt and let it slide to the floor.

"I'm restless." David shrugged. "You know I'm high energy. I have to be on the go all the time. You're working at your business and that leaves me with time on my hands."

"You told me you wanted a wife who had a career." Lara leaned against the sink countertop. "Debra stayed home with the kids and you said she was boring because she'd never been out in the real world."

"Keep my ex-wife out of this." David's hands clenched into fists.

"Why?" Lara crossed her arms over her chest. "She was always available and you weren't happy. If I quit my job, how would that make things better?"

David shrugged. "You never do what I want. I'm the one who is compromising in this relationship."

Lara gasped. "I never wanted to sleep with another man. You insisted."

"Why didn't you go with Bobby? He was perfect for you."

"You mean perfect for you." Lara forced herself to keep her voice low. "You were able to pick who you wanted. That means I should have the same freedom."

"I had time to sleep with all three women." David's voice rose. "You spent all night with one man. Don't tell me he was that good."

It was on the tip of her tongue to agree. Instead, she walked to the shower and turned the water on. There was no point in arguing with David when he was in this mood. He'd given enough away about his motives to leave her doubting her marriage.

"Don't turn away from me." David's voice reverberated around the tiled room. "I won't be dismissed. I'm every bit as good a lover as Frank."

He grabbed her from behind and pushed her against the countertop. One hand held her in place while the other ripped her silken panties off her body. Lara's heart beat frantically as she struggled to escape him. She didn't want him making love to her in this condition. With a final surge of power, she reared back against him, and broke his hold.

"Are you planning to rape me now?" Her tone was full of contempt. "Is that what swapping has done to our marriage?"

David stepped back as if she'd slapped him. "You made me angry."

"That's no excuse."

Lara was too furious to care about David's feelings. She bent down and picked up her discarded and ripped clothes before turning the water off in the shower. She left the washroom and slammed through her dresser drawers until she found some soft flannel pajamas and more underwear.

"I'm sleeping in the guest suite tonight." She pulled her robe off the inside hook of the closet. "There's a lock on the door."

"You're being ridiculous." David followed her out of the bedroom. "I'm not going to hurt you."

"I'm not giving you the chance." Lara held her clothes close to her body. "We'll talk in the morning."

She slammed the lock in place in the guest room and leaned back against the door. David had been angry in the past, yet never had she seen the kind of rage he'd just displayed. He had frightened her. She straightened away from the door and went into the washroom, turned on the shower and then finished undressing.

Hot water and soap did more than just cleanse her body, it helped clear her mind. She took a long, hot shower, letting the water ease her worries. There had to be an answer somewhere to her marriage problems. Swinging wasn't it. As much as she'd enjoyed being with Frank, she wasn't foolish enough to believe that all encounters were like that.

When she stepped out of the shower, the room was full of steam. She toweled off and wiped her hands over the mirror. She looked the same as when she'd gone out earlier in the evening, yet she felt years older. She combed the tangles out of her long blonde hair and slipped into her pajamas.

She needed sleep.

In the morning she would deal with the disaster her marriage had become.

The sun streamed into the bedroom windows earlier than she'd expected. The guest suite was on the east side of the house and she'd forgotten how early sunrise was at this time of year. She groaned. She wanted to throw the covers over her head and hide. It was morning and everything looked uglier in the bright glare of daylight.

David was already downstairs and he handed her a cup of coffee when she entered the kitchen. She sat at the granite countertop island and took a long sip. Caffeine was what she needed to clear the cobwebs from her head.

"Did you sleep well?" David's voice was neutral.

Lara nodded. "Morning came too soon. What about you?"

"I've been up all night." David gave her a sheepish look. "I'm sorry about last night. I acted like a jealous jerk."

Lara's tension began to ease. "At least you realize it."

"I insisted you go to the party." David sat beside her. "I still think it might be the answer to some of our marriage problems."

"I didn't think we had any problems until last night." Lara took another sip of coffee. "Wouldn't a marriage counselor be a better solution?"

"I don't want to talk to a stranger." David sighed. "I suppose I didn't expect you to be so late. I thought you'd have one go and then head for home."

"So you're upset because I enjoyed myself," Lara stated. "You had fun too."

"Not really. I slept with all of the women. I didn't find satisfaction with any of them. That's why I'm looking into another group."

"Changing partners isn't going to solve the problem." Lara felt as if a weight were pressing down on her chest. "All you're doing is running away. We need to sit down and discuss why you're unhappy. If you don't want to stay married to me, I can accept that. Just be honest with me and yourself."

"I love you." David's voice sounded strangled. "I want us to stay together."

"When did you decide this?" Lara looked at her husband and noticed the dark shadows under his eyes. "Before or after you slept with all three women last night."

"After I ran into Frank last night."

"When?" Lara forced her voice to remain calm. She'd suspected Frank had spoken with David.

"He was scrounging for food in the kitchen." David twirled his finger around the rim of his coffee cup. "I asked him how long he intended to keep my wife, and he said there was no time limit."

Lara nodded. "That upset you?"

"I saw red." David rubbed a hand over his eyes. "You know what my temper is like. I told him that I expected you to be ready to leave in five minutes. Frank told me to take a powder."

"Then what?"

"I took a swing at him." David shrugged. "He countered and held my arm behind my back. He said that men who considered their wives as property didn't suit a swinging lifestyle."

"That sounds reasonable."

"He's wrong." David looked at her. "I like showing you off and seeing other men admire you. It excites me. That's one of the reasons I was attracted to you in the first place. When I first met you, every man in the room wanted to take you home with him."

Lara's stomach clenched. "I was nothing more than a trophy."

David didn't answer. He picked up his coffee and took another sip. Silence filled the kitchen until Lara could stand it no longer. She pushed away from the island and went to the fridge for a yogurt and then turned back to her husband.

"I'm not a prize to parade around whenever it suits you." Her voice was low. "We are equals in this marriage. If you want our relationship to work, you'd better start acting like that."

"What are you planning to do?" David's voice was hesitant.

"I'm going to finish my breakfast and then get dressed for the office. I have some plans to work on. We'll talk when I get back." Lara took her last sip of coffee and put the empty cup on the counter. "That should give you enough time to decide if you want this marriage to work or not."

Chapter 10

Lara was bent over the designs for the Victorian house when Margery buzzed. "Mr. Warner's here."

"Send him in."

She straightened up and went to greet Vince at the door. It had been one week since the Burkett's party, and the fight with David. Life had settled down into a peaceful routine after David apologized. He'd said he wanted the marriage to work and he'd prove it. He was more attentive than he had ever been, and Lara thought the worst of their marital problems were behind them.

Vince came into the office with a smile. "From the sounds of your email you've been busy."

"The plans are finished and waiting your approval. The engineer has signed off and all of the permits are in place." Lara motioned Vince to sit. "We're ready to start."

"I timed this visit perfectly. Do you have the contractor hired?"

"I've got two for you to consider. Either one will do a good job." Lara picked up the plans from her desk. "Have a look through these and let me know what changes you'd like to make."

Vince put on a pair of dark rimmed reading glasses and started to leaf through the papers. Lara went back to her desk and gathered the information concerning the two different contractors. She sat beside Vince and waited.

"This looks spectacular." Vince looked up at her. His blue eyes peered over the edge of his glasses and were filled with approval. "I love the layout for the kitchen. I would never have thought about using the atrium."

"That will provide lots of natural light and a wonderful view of the ravine and gardens."

"Loads of privacy." Vince nodded.

Vince continued to peruse the drawings, asking questions about her color choices and the room placements. When he was finished, he took the information about the contractors from her and then handed her one back.

"This one looks good."

"I'll have the contracts drawn up for you to sign. They should start work on Monday."

Vince leaned back in his seat. "Do you have time today to go with me to the house?"

Lara gathered the plans together and then went to her desk. She scanned her day planner and then nodded. "I could meet you there in an hour. I have one more client this morning. After that, I'm free until the afternoon."

"Great. That'll give you a chance to meet my children." Vince stood. "I know they would love to see where their rooms are going to be."

"They can tell me if they have any color or design preferences as well." Lara led Vince out of her office.

She worked until it was time to meet Vince and his children. It was a sunny day with a cool breeze that moderated the temperature and humidity. A perfect day to get out of the office and enjoy the late spring weather. She parked the car in the newly-cleared driveway and took a deep breath, enjoying the fragrance of roses in the air.

The sound of children's laughter rang out. A rental car was parked in front of the house, and she assumed it was Vince's. She pulled out her briefcase with the plans, locked her car, and headed through the overgrown gardens to the side of the house.

Vince was chasing a small boy and girl among the large oak trees that lined the side of the house. He caught his daughter and started to tickle her. Shrieks of laughter were his reward. Then his son touched him on the back of his leg and ran. It seemed to be a game of tag because Vince twirled his daughter around once, and then took off after his son. Lara couldn't help smiling. Memories of her childhood flooded her.

Playing catch with her father.

Picnics with the whole family.

She walked over to the group. "Can anybody play?"

Vince turned at the sound of her voice. "Mrs. Knight." His chest was heaving from his exertion. "We've been waiting for you."

"It looks like you're having fun." Lara put her briefcase on the vine-covered stonework of a crumbling, patio wall. "I wish I'd worn different shoes."

"Kids, I want you to meet Mrs. Knight. She's the interior designer I was telling you about." Vince walked over to her with two children at his side. "This is Josh and Jessica."

Lara crouched so that she was on eye level, and greeted the two children.

Josh was younger than his sister. He had light brown hair and the same dark-blue eyes as his father. He glanced at her from behind his father's leg and then looked away. Jessica was about seven-years old with dark hair, features she must have inherited from her father as well. Solemn green eyes looked at her for a few seconds and then glanced up at her father. When he nodded, she walked over and held her hand out for a shake. Lara smiled, took the small hand in hers and gave it a gentle squeeze.

"Your father said you like the color purple." Lara reached for her briefcase. "Would you like to see the design for your bedroom?"

Jessica's eyes lit up. "Is it all purple?"

"It could be." Lara pulled out the room design and held it out for Jessica to look at. "I've given you the room at the back of the house. We can change that if you want."

"What about me?" Josh moved away from his father's leg. "Which room is mine?"

"There's a room that overlooks this yard." Lara stood and pointed up to a window on the northeast side of the house. "It's opposite from where your sister's room is. We can change it if you don't like it."

"What color is my room?"

"Blue."

Josh scrunched his nose. "I like green."

"Then I will change it." Lara pulled out the design page.

Josh pointed at the design. "What's this?"

"That's your bathroom." Lara picked up her briefcase. "Maybe it would be best if we went in and saw the rooms. If you want a different room, then you can pick it now before the work begins."

Vince nodded. "Great idea. Come on kids, let's take a look."

They went in through the front door, and the children started running from room to room, their scampering feet loud on the hardwood floor.

Jessica ran her fingers over the dusty windowsills. "Gross. Who will clean this?"

"Not me." Josh giggled and pointed at the cobwebs that clung to the wooden trellis in the arch between the living and dining rooms. "Are there spiders living here?"

"They'll be gone before you move in."

"I hate spiders." A shiver of revulsion went through Josh.

"So do I." Lara's voice was sympathetic. "My brothers used to catch them in jars and leave them in my bedroom."

Josh's eyes widened. "Really?"

Lara nodded. "They thought it was funny."

"What did you do?"

"I found a way to irritate them." Lara lowered her voice and leaned closer to Josh. "When they had girlfriends over, I would sneak into the room and sit between them and show their baby pictures."

Vince laughed. "That must have gone over well."

Lara nodded. "We came to a compromise. They stopped with the spiders, and I made myself scarce when they had dates."

"Cool." Josh looked at her with interest. "Why didn't you hit them?"

"They were older and bigger than me."

"You outsmarted them." Jessica's voice held approval. "My Dad says that's the best way to handle a situation."

"He's right." Lara walked toward the atrium at the rear of the house. "My brothers never tried to scare me again."

Vince chuckled beside her. "What did they do when you brought boyfriends home?"

"I didn't date much until I was in college. By then, I had moved away from home."

"Smart." Vince's voice was low enough that only she could hear. "I find it hard to believe that a girl as beautiful as you, didn't have dates."

"I had my nose in a book all the time." Lara walked over to the outer glass wall of the atrium. "I wanted to be a designer and that's all that interested me."

"You certainly succeeded." Vince glanced around the space. "Your ideas for this place are inspired."

A glow of pride filled Lara. She'd spent a lot of time coming up with the plans for this house. She had a soft spot for Victorian houses with their intricate woodwork details and large rooms. Vince Warner seemed to feel the same way. No expense was to be spared on the renovation of the house and property. Fitting modern conveniences into such a grand old house was a challenge that she would enjoy.

"I'm glad you like them." She pointed to glass that lined the south side of the atrium. "The windows will be replaced and lower kitchen cabinets will be built under them." She turned back to the main part of the house. "The engineer plans to take out that wall and once it's opened up, I think you'll be very happy with the space."

"So the east side of the house will be for the family and the formal dining and living rooms are on the west. I don't entertain at home often, but when I do, I like the fact that it will be separate from the living space."

Together they climbed the central staircase.

"I think it's easier, especially when children live in the house." Lara's voice softened. "They need a place that feels like a home, not a showpiece."

"It sounds as if you speak from experience." Vince paused at the upstairs landing. "How many children do you have?"

She shook her head. "Stepchildren and they're both grown. I have lots of nieces and nephews, though."

Vince walked into the master bedroom. "How big was your family?"

"Two brothers and one sister." Lara walked over to the large rear window. "My Dad was a teacher and my mother stayed home."

Vince joined her at the window. "My wife didn't work outside of the home either. She said the only thing she ever wanted was to be a homemaker and that was a full-time job. I've since learned how right she was. She spoiled us."

Lara glanced over at him. "I admire her. It takes courage to stay home when everything around you says that you need to have a career to be fulfilled."

"That's an unusual statement from a business woman such as yourself."

Lara shrugged. "I always envisioned myself someday juggling a family and work."

"What stopped you?"

Lara hesitated for a second. In the past she would have said that she didn't want children, but that wasn't the truth. When she'd married David he had wanted to wait and it hadn't been a problem. She was young and more concerned about getting her business off the ground. Now, she had a hole inside of her that only children would fill.

"Forget I asked." Vince raised his hand in apologetic gesture. "It's none of my business."

"I don't mind answering." Lara turned back to the room and leaned against the windowsill. "The short answer is that my husband is reluctant to have more children."

Vince rubbed his chin. "What about you?"

"It wasn't a problem before. Now, I'm not so sure." Lara stood up and straightened her shoulders. "Enough about me. I thought that we'd keep this as the master. Even though this is a fairly large room, I'd like to knock down the wall to the next room and make a sitting area, an ensuite, and walk-in closets."

Vince walked into the center of the space and nodded. "Are you going to keep the fireplace?"

Lara ran a hand over the antique marble mantle. "I wouldn't think of destroying it. A new chimney and liner and it will be good to go. If you want a gas insert, we could arrange that."

"Gas would be easier."

"Do you have any color preferences?

"What you've planned is great."

They were back on a professional level, and Lara gave an inward sigh of relief. She didn't want to examine the relationship she had with David too closely. Chaos and danger seemed to be around every twist and turn of her marriage. She was behaving like a coward, which seemed safer.

Lara walked toward the stairs. The children had been running from room to room and she and Vince tracked them down to the bedroom she'd planned for Josh. He was turning circles in the room, while Jessica was looking out the window. When Lara and Vince came through the doorway, both children looked up at them.

"Is this my room?" Josh's voice echoed in the empty space.

"Do you like it?" Lara asked.

"I love it." Josh ran to the window. "I can see when Daddy gets home."

Lara crouched down beside Josh. "There's going to be a new driveway and garden out front."

"What about a garage?"

"Right over there." Lara pointed to a flat area at the far side of the property and then stood. "What about your room Jessica?"

They spent the next couple of hours going over the small details of all of the rooms. When Lara left, the Warner family was heading out to explore the ravine at the rear of the property. It had been such a pleasant afternoon, ending with a pang of regret that it wasn't longer. The children had been delightful and Vince a perfect father.

It was past five when she finally arrived home. David's car was in the driveway. Maybe they would be able to spend a quiet romantic evening at home. Alone time with her husband would be perfect. Even though David had been very considerate the last couple of weeks, they still hadn't made love.

Lara opened the door and dropped her briefcase on the hall table. "I'm home."

She was taking her coat off when he came running down the stairs. "You're late."

She frowned. "This is my usual time."

David glanced at his watch. "It doesn't matter. You need to get dressed."

Her shoulders sagged. "I thought we had the evening free."

"I've been working all day on getting us an invite to the Coliseum Club." David's voice rose in excitement. "They're making an exception for us. Run upstairs and put on your sexy red dress."

Her stomach dropped as a nasty suspicion took hold. "Why?" She didn't bother to hide her wariness.

"It's the premier swingers club in the city and you're going to be the star attraction tonight."

Chapter 11

"The Coliseum is a swinging club?" A wave of dizziness raced through her and she put a hand on the table to steady herself. "Since when?"

The Coliseum was an exclusive nightclub that had opened in the city last summer. It was located several miles away from Dearston, but its reputation as an elite and exclusive club had been whispered around town. The Coliseum didn't advertise and entry was by invitation only. The club had been built in the lower level of a large building that had once been a hotel. Lara now understood why. The rooms were needed for the sexual activities of its members.

"That's not something they'd advertise." David's voice was filled with disgust. "What does it matter? I've pulled strings to get us admitted. Go and dress."

"I thought we were finished with swapping after the last party."

"Never." David's eyes narrowed. "That wasn't the right place for us. I've done my research and the Coliseum is where we want to be."

"Why."

"That's where the elite go." David pushed her toward the stairs. "Get dressed. We have a special invitation and being late wouldn't look good."

Lara stopped and straightened her shoulders. "I'm not going."

David's face twisted with anger. "That's not an option. The invitation was specifically for both of us. I won't become the laughing stock of this group."

Lara inhaled a quick breath. "No."

David grabbed her arm and twisted her around to face him. His face was inches away from hers and his eyes glared fire. "We're doing this. You agreed and I won't have you backing out at the last minute. You said you wanted to keep the marriage together."

"What's that supposed to mean?" Lara tried to keep her voice steady.

"Either you come with me tonight, or you pack your bags and leave."

Lara's breath caught in her throat as she stared into David's unblinking brown eyes. His lips were thinned into a straight line and his nostrils flared with each breath he took. Time seemed to stop as she saw the truth in her husband's eyes. He was serious. Either she went with him tonight or the marriage was over. It was blackmail.

What choice did she have?

Was she ready to end her marriage?

Lara gripped the stainless steel railing and forced her legs to move up the stairs. She'd thought that David had finished with swapping after their night at the Burkett's. He'd been so angry with her for being home late, and he'd confessed that he'd been disappointed. He'd promised to put more effort into their relationship. She should have seen it for the lie that it was. He was looking for a new sexual high.

He'd found it with another place to swing.

Her stomach clenched as trepidation filled her.

How could she have been so foolish? David never let a project go until he had exhausted all avenues. He was worse than a hound on a scent. She walked into the bedroom and saw her skimpy red dress spread out on the bed and a shiver of disgust shook her. She'd bought it on a whim last Valentine's day to tantalize David. It was indecently tight and she'd never meant it to be worn in public. How could he expect her to wear it in front of strangers?

"You have just enough time for a shower before we need to leave." David's voice boomed from downstairs.

Lara kicked off her shoes and clothes and headed for the shower. David had her cornered and there was no way to get out of tonight's party unless she was prepared to end the marriage, here and now. She showered and put body lotion on afterwards, smoothing the cool cream over her arms and legs.

The dress was so tight that every detail of her undergarments would show beneath it. Lara didn't need the support of a bra, but she wasn't leaving the house without panties. She put on red high-heeled sandals and pulled out a matching red purse on a silver chain. She put in a few essentials and some bills into the small clutch and took one last look in the mirror.

She tried to pull the dress lower because it stopped at mid-thigh. Bending over was out of the question. It clung to every curve, accentuating her tiny waist and full breasts. The shoes gave length to her legs and even though it was a designer dress she felt exposed and cheap. Her stomach churned and she fiddled with the chain of her purse.

Was this really what she wanted?

Just then, David came into the room. He stood at the doorway and gave her a long slow perusal. "The underwear has to go."

Lara shook her head. "I can't go out like that."

"You did when you modeled it for me."

"That was private and between the two of us. I never bought this dress so that others would see me in it."

David walked to her and pulled the skirt of the dress up to her waist and pulled her silk panties down her legs. She had no other option but to step out of them. David threw the undergarment onto the bed and then ran his hand up her legs. He pushed a finger between her thighs and swiped across her clitoris before pulling the dress down.

"I'm glad you shaved." He gave her a quick kiss on the lips. "You're primed for sex tonight and as excited as I am, so don't deny it."

Lara ran her hand over David's lapel. "Why don't we stay home and make love instead."

"Don't you get it? I want other women and tonight I mean to have my share." David laughed and pulled her out of the bedroom. "Let's go."

The entrance to the club was hidden in a side alley. It was a plain brown door and there was a bouncer in a tuxedo guarding it. David handed him a printed card and the large man nodded and opened the door. The nondescript exterior of the club didn't prepare Lara for the interior. Strobe and colored overhead lights lit the place up brighter than a Christmas tree. The music was loud enough that it reverberated through her body. People were gathered in small groups, holding drinks in their hands, or kissing and rubbing their bodies against each other.

The room smelled of sex and vodka.

Lara clasped David's arm. "Let's leave."

David shook her hand off and headed toward the center of the club. A waist-high platform was erected there. It was flooded with light, and people were starting to gather and lean on the edge of its outer wall. She rushed after David trying to keep within a few feet of him. She had to dodge some of the patrons who reached out to touch her as she moved past them. This place was eons away from the experience at the Burkett's and fear started to tighten in her stomach.

David was talking to a tall man in a dark suit with his shirt collar open at the neck. He was probably in his early forties, dark haired, and would have been handsome except for the upturned sneer of his lips. When she reached David's side, the stranger's eyes narrowed and he put his glass down.

"Turn around," he ordered.

Lara tensed. "Why."

David exhaled an exasperated breath. "Just do it."

Lara forced her shaking legs to do a slow turn and stopped when she was facing the man. "Is that what you wanted?" She raised an eyebrow.

"It'll do." He held his hand out to her. "I'm Jason. I run this place."

A shiver went up Lara's arm when she shook his hand. It wasn't pleasant and her inclination was to pull away and run. He winked and then turned to David. He leaned close and whispered something into her husband's ear.

David nodded. "Of course."

"The bidding starts in fifteen minutes." Jason picked his drink up and took a sip. "She looks nervous. Perhaps a glass of wine?"

David looked over at her and smiled. "My pleasure." He took her arm and led her over to the bar and ordered their drinks.

"What did he mean about bidding?" Lara tried to keep her voice from shaking, but she didn't succeed. Something was going on between the men and she sensed that it involved her.

"They like to initiate new couples."

A chill went through Lara. "How?"

"They bid on who gets to have sex with them." David shrugged. "It's meant to show that you're willing to embrace the club rules."

"What exactly are the rules?" Lara was sinking fast. She was in way over her head and she'd been a fool to let David coerce her into coming here.

"You're available to whoever asks."

"What?" Lara's heart skipped a beat. This had nothing to do with choices. "That's not what I agreed to when you insisted we try swapping."

"Not every club is the same." David handed her a glass of wine. "Drink. You look like you could use it."

"Are they bidding on you?" Lara took a sip of wine.

"Men do the choosing, not women."

"This isn't a swapping club." Lara clenched her jaw. Suddenly it was clear that David had lied to her. This was an anything goes, sex club.

"I'm going up there with you." David's voice was smooth. "Jason assured me that there would be several bidders to choose from."

"You can't just let men bid on me." Lara's voice rose. "I'm your wife for God's sake."

"Lower your voice." David's voice was stern. "You will do as expected if you want to remain my wife. I won't be embarrassed in front of these people."

Nothing was worth this. Lara shook her head and put the glass down. "I refuse."

"Too late." David grabbed her arm and pushed her to the center again. Jason was standing on top of the stage. He leaned over and grabbed her beneath the arms. Lara was lifted onto the platform and held tight by Jason. David climbed the stairs and was grinning from ear to ear.

David was in his element.

Lara was terrified.

This wasn't what she'd agreed to, or what she was comfortable with. She moved to leave. Jason tightened his grip.

"No need for nerves." He whispered in her ear. "You'll have the time of your life tonight. All these men are panting to be with you."

Revulsion snaked through her. The last thing she wanted was to be the center of attention in this group of partygoers. David stood beside her, relaxed and waving at the crowd. He didn't have a clue about how miserable she felt in the spotlight. He loved the attention. Lara pushed back her tears. She was here now and there was no escape.

Jason held his hand up and the music stopped. "We have a treat tonight."

All eyes turned to the stage. Lara wanted to shrink away as Jason held her shoulders in a tight clasp. The heat of the bright spotlight was causing beads of perspiration to form on her forehead, and she fought the urge to fidget with her dress. If she had to be on display, then she refused to slouch. She straightened her shoulders and forced a smile onto her lips.

"Tonight we have newcomers to the club, and you all know what that means." Jason spoke into a microphone. People started moving from there to the platform.

"Auction." The shout went up from the crowd.

Jason moved the mike closer to his mouth. "Are you ready?" The feedback from the mike was deafening. It took a couple of seconds to tone it down and then he placed her under the spotlight and moved away.

"This beautiful woman has asked to join our ranks." Silence filled the room. "Does anyone object?"

"Hell no." A bald man leaning against the platform gave her a toast with his drink. "She's a looker."

Lara looked over at David and he was nodding. She pleaded with her eyes for him to end this. He turned away. Lara inhaled a sharp breath and forced her tension to ease. She'd played the games at the Burkett's and this was just one more game. All she had to do was change how she viewed this whole thing. In the end, David would realize he was making a mistake. He was jealous when other men pawed her. She would use that to bring him to his senses.

Men pushed to the front of the dais. They were waving pieces of paper in the air and at first she thought it was money, but then she realized it was some kind of club currency. She didn't know what they had to trade for the bills, but they seemed pretty happy to offer them to Jason.

Several minutes later, five men surrounded her on the platform. They were looking at her as if she were a delicious dessert meant to be enjoyed. This was no different from what had happened at the Burkett's. There were more men here, but they didn't mean her any harm. The nausea in her stomach settled. The tension in her shoulders relaxed and she returned each man's look with an appraising one of her own.

They came forward one by one and ran a hand down the side of her body which caused tremors to race across her skin. They leaned close and sniffed at her neck and then stepped back before grabbing her butt. When the first one did it she nearly jumped a foot in the air. By the time the last one did his inspection she was prepared. She steadied her breathing and let her eyes wander over the men.

All in all they were a good looking lot, well-dressed, and self-confident. When the last man had finished, Jason moved to her side and patted her bum. "That wasn't so bad was it?"

"If you say so." Lara forced her voice to sound bored.

"Quite the beauty we have here gentlemen. Who'll start the bidding?"

The paper club chits were thrown down in front of her as each man vied for her attention. Jason nudged her. "You're supposed to choose one by picking up their credits."

The choice was still hers.

All the club had done was narrow down the number of men she'd have to choose from. They'd make it easy for her. She almost laughed with relief and looked down at the credits on the platform in front of each men. A couple had thrown a large bundle and she looked up at them with interest. They were obviously very attracted to her.

"Can I check them out like they did me?"

Jason shook his head. "No. You have to decide now."

She looked over each man before settling on a man with short blonde hair and light-green eyes. He was dressed in a loose jacket and jeans, with a stance of self-assurance. It might not be the best way to choose a partner for the night. Right now it was her only option. She raised her hand and pointed at him.

"Sam." Jason turned around and shouted it out to the crowd. "Sam is the lucky bidder."

Sam grinned and picked up his club chits. He handed them to David and then pulled her into his arms and kissed her. It wasn't a tentative kiss. He had complete domination of her mouth and tongue. His hand roamed down her backside and reached under her dress to squeeze her bottom.

A surge of excitement and fear rushed through her.

She struggled to push away.

He wouldn't release her.

He ground his hips into hers and she fought back her panic. Surely he wasn't going to have sex with her in front of the crowd? Just as quickly as he'd possessed her mouth, he released it, and grabbed her arm.

"We need a room. Now."

Chapter 12

"Follow me." Sam winked at her. "We need privacy for everything I want to do with you."

He grabbed her hand and led her down the side stairs. He pulled her close as they moved through the crowd. People were reaching out and touching her, their hands on her hair, breasts, buttocks, and legs. Sam moved at a slow pace, lingering and letting the men and women caress and stroke her. It was oddly erotic and she realized it was their way of welcoming her into their group. Her tension drained away and her fear subsided.

David wasn't the only man who could fulfill her, and the sooner he came to that realization, the sooner they could work on keeping their marriage together. Sam's hand had moved lower, and he was now stroking the side of her breast. Shivers of pleasure raced through her and he leaned closer to her.

"You like that." Sam's deep voice tickled her ear. "By the time we reach the room, you'll be primed for your first orgasm."

Sam stopped and positioned her so that she stood in front of him. He pressed his body close enough that she could feel his arousal. He clasped both of her hands together with one of his and held them close to her waist.

"This is where I let the others help. It's all part of your initiation." He nibbled her ear. "Relax and enjoy."

Lara frowned and turned to ask him what he meant when she felt his free hand move beneath her dress and edge up her inner thighs. She squirmed for him to stop, but he was relentless in his teasing. As if on cue men started to line up in front of her. The first in line was of medium height with balding hair and a short-trimmed beard. He reached out and stroked her breast before kissing her. The kiss was meant to seduce and it didn't disappoint. By the time he had finished, she'd melted into Sam's arms, letting her head rest against his shoulder. Then another man came forward. His tongue darted out and licked up the side of her neck before he captured her lips.

One after another came forward and kissed and stroked her until she was on the hot edge of explosive pleasure. Her seduction and arousal were on public display and she'd lost track of time and place. Her body was shaking with need and she didn't care who saw it. Throughout the initiation, Sam held her close and continued his soft feathering strokes, stoking the fires deep within her. When the last man had left, his finger dipped inside of her.

"If I wasn't so selfish, I'd strip this dress from you right here and let them all enjoy you." Sam exhaled a shaky breath. "Can you walk?"

Lara's knees were weak and when she moved she almost fell. Sam gathered her into his arms and picked her up. There was a roar of cheers when he carried her through the crowd. Lara put her arms around his shoulders and hid her head in his neck. Her body was jittery with need and all she could focus on was release. Everything else was a daze.

Sam carried her into an elevator and pressed the fifth floor button. "This is the room reserved for initiation. You'll love it."

"Do you initiate many women?"

"We haven't had new members in a while." Sam's lips brushed her neck. His arms still held her high against his chest. "You're one of the most beautiful I've ever seen. I'm going to thoroughly enjoy this evening."

"What about my enjoyment?"

He gave a husky laugh. "You won't have anything to complain about."

Sam stopped further conversation by kissing her. Tongues dueled and the fires that had cooled were blazing again. When the elevator stopped at their floor, he released her mouth and gazed down at her with eyes ablaze with passion. Lara shivered with a matching longing. He exhaled a shaky breath and tightened his hold on her as he walked to their room. There was a hook with keys beside the door, but it was open already, as if it'd been prepared in advance. He switched the light on, shut and locked the door, and eased her legs to the floor.

"Spread your legs." He dropped to his knees and pushed her dress up to her waist. "Hold onto my shoulders."

Lara had barely registered his intention before his mouth was on her. His tongue circled her clitoris, licking and teasing until she shook with a climax that had her reeling with its force. She would have fallen if Sam hadn't held her. He continued to taste and tease her until she shuddered with another climax and then another.

Only then did his mouth leave her sensitive inner core and started a journey up her abdomen. Each kiss exposed more of her body, sending fire deep within her with each caress. Inch by inch he moved higher, easing the dress off her as he stood. His tongue twirled over her nipples, nipping and sucking until she moaned with pleasure. When she was completely naked, he sat her on the bed and then stood in front of her. He shrugged out of his jacket and pulled his shirt over his head.

Her eyes devoured his firm and muscled chest and abdomen. He had a gorgeous body.

"Unzip me." His voice was a whispered command.

She ran her hand down the front of his jeans, a shiver of anticipation that she didn't fully understand raced through her when she felt the hardened length beneath the material. There was no doubt about Sam's arousal. She undid the waist button and then the zipper, before pulling the jeans down. Fully exposed, he was magnificent. She looked up at him with widened eyes. Her stomach flipped at his wicked grin.

"I was born to pleasure women." He kicked off his shoes and then his jeans. "Your turn to drive me crazy."

He was cocky and arrogant.

She was aroused enough to accommodate him.

Her tongue darted out and she licked from the base of his penis to its head. She twirled around the tip in a playful motion and then took him inside her mouth. She continued curling her tongue around the tip as her hand gripped his length and moved up and down. His groans signaled her to change her strokes to a quicker pace. His body shook in reaction. That's when she sucked him deep into her mouth.

"Enough." His voice was hoarse. "I'm going to explode before we start."

She released him and then leaned back on her arms to look up at him. "I thought you wanted that."

"Honey, your mouth is lethal." He lifted her high onto the pillows and then climbed onto the bed. "We'll play with that later."

He reached into a basket on a side table and pulled out a condom packet. It took a few seconds before he had himself sheathed and then he was pressing for entry. Lara leaned back against the pillows and shivered as he pushed into her. Delicious tendrils of sensation skittered across her body.

"You're so tight." Sam pulled back and pushed inside again.

A shudder of bliss raced through her.

Sam was on his knees and he grabbed a pillow and placed it under her bottom to angle her closer to him. He spread her legs wider and began to thrust deep. She rose to meet him. Every movement of his hips sent her swirling into a heavenly cloud of ecstasy. He drove in and out with a slow steady rhythm that had her skirting the edge of climax for what seemed like hours. Nothing existed but their labored breaths and the upward spiraling of tension.

They climaxed together in a shattering explosion.

Sam collapsed onto her, but Lara didn't notice his weight. Bliss and joy flickered through her as she floated on the after effects of their coupling. Sam shuddered for a few seconds and then he rolled onto his side. His fingers fluttered across her breasts in a lazy perusal, and Lara felt the stirring of renewed interest within her.

Sam pulled the used condom off and threw it into the trash bin. "You're fantastic."

"You're not so bad yourself."

Lara was feeling in a generous mood. There was no denying the sex was terrific even if it lacked an emotional element. She'd never been so orgasmic before, but the uncertainty of the auction, the initiation, and the foreplay had heightened her pleasure. It also helped that Sam was a very skilled lover. She'd been lucky.

She might as well enjoy herself.

She reached over and fondled him. His penis jumped to life, and that's when she knew he was ready to go again. Her fingers gripped him and stroked up his long length. He groaned and lay back with his hands behind his head.

"I'm all yours."

Lara got up on her knees and bent over him. She worked him with her mouth, tongue and hands until he was hard, throbbing, and ready. She reached into the basket, pulled out another packet, and rolled the condom down his long length before straddling him. She eased herself onto his erection and sighed as he filled her completely. There seemed no point in wasting such a delicious opportunity for pleasure, especially when her husband had given her permission.

She rode him long and hard.

Shivering pleasure and bliss filled her with every tilt of her hips until the world ceased to exist and all that matter was that they both reach climax. When it came, they both trembled with the electrifying release. She collapsed onto his chest. Sam had exhausted and fulfilled her completely. She was replete.

The spell was broken when Sam disengaged himself from her. "Time to go pretty lady."

She rolled over onto her side and watched him discard the used condom. There was an attached bathroom and he held his hand out to her. "Let's shower."

"Together?"

"Is there any other way?"

Lara shrugged and stood. Her body was boneless and limp with satiation. She followed Sam into the bathroom and waited while he adjusted the water temperature and flow. Together they stepped in and let the water rejuvenate them.

They took turns lathering each other with the soap. Teasing and tantalizing with each pass of the bar until they were both aroused and ready. He backed her against the shower wall and reached for a condom packet from a cup of them sitting inside the stall.

"They didn't miss a thing when they set this room up."

"Details are a must for a club like this. All members have a clean bill of health, but I refuse to risk an unwanted pregnancy."

Sam ripped the packet open with his teeth and when he was ready, he lifted her and thrust inside of her. She wrapped her legs around his waist and hung on as he took them on a deliciously erotic ride. Afterwards, they finished showering and got dressed. Lara slipped the slinky red dress over her head and pulled it down over her hips. Her blonde hair was still damp from the shower and all she could do was use her fingers to comb the long strands into place.

Sam looked as casually elegant as before, not a hair was out of place. When he was ready, he shook her hand. "It was great fun."

Lara nodded. "Thanks."

"I hope I get to see you again." Sam opened the door. "Do you want to go back to the club?"

"Just to find my husband and leave." She was finished for the evening. The sooner she got home, the better.

She hadn't a clue what David had been doing, but if there was an initiation for her, there was probably one for him. They were halfway down the hall when the elevator opened. Lara gasped when she saw who was in it.

Jason was there with David and another woman.

David glared at her. "What took you so long?"

"I didn't realize we were on a time limit." Sam's voice was casual. He turned to her and kissed her cheek. "I'll head back downstairs and leave you with your husband."

David muttered something under his breath, but Lara didn't catch it. She watched Sam walk through the door to the stairwell and then turned back to David. He was holding the red headed woman around the waist and glaring at her. She straightened her shoulders and scowled back. She'd had enough of his posturing.

Either he wanted this lifestyle or he didn't.

Jason rubbed his hands together. "It's my turn now."

Lara shook her head. "I've had enough for tonight."

"Sorry, but that's not what your husband agreed to." Jason grabbed her arm and pulled her down the hallway.

"I didn't agree to anything." Lara turned back to David.

"Your body was the price of admission." David opened the door to room 504 and ushered the redhead in. "You're Jason's for the rest of the night. He has my permission to do whatever he desires."

Chapter 13

Jason took a key from the hook beside another room and opened the door.

He pushed her inside.

"I want you naked and on your knees."

Lara shook her head. "This isn't what I agreed to."

"I saw you downstairs. You were panting for it." Jason unbuttoned his shirt.

"I'm serious." Lara's voice shook. "I'm going home."

Jason's eyes narrowed. "That's not what David promised me. I get to do what I want, for as long as I want."

"Don't you have enough willing partners without resorting to rape?" Lara's tone was full of disdain.

"All new members are vetted through me." Jason threw his jacket and shirt onto the floor. "That's the only way into the club."

"I don't want to be a member." Lara took a step backwards.

"Too late." Jason grabbed her by the waist and pulled her to him. "You're mine. Anything goes in this room."

Lara took a deep steadying breath. There was a glitter of determination in Jason's eyes that frightened her. She didn't want to escalate this. All she wanted, was to leave. She steadied her heartbeat and held her hands up in a conciliatory manner against his chest.

"Can't we discuss this?"

Jason shook his head. "I'm not in the mood. I waited for Sam to finish, but now it's my turn."

The skirt of her dress was pulled up to her waist. He backed her up against the wall and grabbed her hair with one hand, twisting it so she couldn't move her head. Panic flooded through her when she heard him unzip his pants. He had every intention of raping her. She tried to move her body, but he slammed her head against the wall.

She saw stars.

Her mind went blank for a second.

She felt his erect penis against her leg. "Stop. I don't want this."

"Too bad." Jason pushed her thighs apart with one of his legs.

"Don't do this." Lara's voice was a plea.

"You flaunted yourself downstairs, teasing and seducing all of us." He hiked her up the wall with his free hand and pressed closer to her so that her arms were pinned against him. "You want this as much as I do. You just won't admit it."

"I said no." Lara's words were lost in her sobs. "I want you to let me go."

"Not a chance." Jason looked down to position himself and Lara squirmed her hips to keep him away. His jaw tightened and he glared at her before slapping her across the face with his open palm. "Settle down."

Shock and horror filled her.

Her tongue tasted blood from her split lip.

That's when she knew there was no escape. This monster was going to rape her, and David had given him permission. He was too strong for her to overpower, and he'd already shown her that he wouldn't hesitate to hurt her. Her body shook with sobs. She felt him press for entry into her. He hadn't even bothered to use a condom.

She shut her eyes to block out his face, but that didn't stop her from having to smell the liquor on his breath. Her stomach churned with nausea. He pushed her higher on the wall just as a knock came to the door.

"Jason, you had better get downstairs now." She recognized Sam's voice.

"What the hell?" Jason muttered as he released his hold on her hair. Her knees were too weak to hold her weight so she slid down the wall. He crouched down beside her and put his hand over her mouth, before he answered. "I'm in the middle of something."

"I'm just warning you." Sam's voice was casual.

Lara tried to scream when she heard his footsteps moving down the hall, but Jason tightened his hold on her mouth. When the footsteps had faded, he released her. She gasped as she inhaled a gulp of air. Jason's eyes narrowed before he stood and zipped his pants. He picked up his shirt and jacket and dressed before he turned back to her.

"If you move from here, that slap will be the least of your worries." He grabbed her chin and forced her to look at him before waving a key in her face. "I'm locking you in. We'll finish this when I get back."

A tremor went through Lara.

Was there no escaping this man?

He left the room and she heard the key turn. She counted to five and then she stood and straightened her dress. She didn't care if she had to jump out the window, she was getting out of this room before he returned. If all else failed, she would hit him over the head with something when he came back in.

She ran to the window and pulled the curtain back. It was solid glass. There was no way to open it. She pushed back a sob and started searching for something to hit Jason with. That's when she heard the lock on the door turn. She rushed over to a table and picked up a vase. It would have to do. She raised it over her head just as the door opened. She started to throw it when she realized it wasn't Jason.

Sam was standing there.

He hung a key back on the hook outside the room.

She kept the vase in her hand. She didn't know why he'd come back. He might have been sent to guard her until Jason return.

"I thought you might like to leave." Sam looked back into the hall. "You don't have much time before Jason gets back."

Lara dropped the vase and then grabbed her purse from the floor. "I should find my husband."

Sam took her hand and headed down the hall in the opposite direction of the elevator. "From what I heard downstairs, your husband gave you to Jason in exchange for admittance to the club."

Lara stumbled. "He knew what was going to happen?"

Sam gave her a compassionate look. "Jason was very specific about what he wanted. There could be no doubt about his intentions."

She was numb with shock.

David must have misunderstood Jason.

Sam tugged on her arm and she forced her legs to move. She couldn't risk staying here in case Jason returned. Whatever the truth, she could work it out at home.

He pushed open the door to the stairs and they both ran down to the ground level. Lara waited while Sam opened the exit door which led to an alleyway. Sam looked outside before motioning for Lara to follow. The headlights of a vehicle glared back at her.

"I sent for a cab." Sam pushed her toward the vehicle. "My advice would be for you to go home and not come back."

"I will."

"This club is about consensual sex, not coercion. There are plenty of places to go if that's what you're into."

"Will you get in trouble?" Lara's voice was hesitant.

Sam shrugged. "Jason might wonder, but he can't prove anything. Besides, this place was getting boring."

Lara reached out and clasped his hand. "Thank you for everything."

Sam gave her a crooked grin. "My pleasure."

He stepped back into the building and Lara ran to the cab. Freedom and safety were within reach and she couldn't risk having that snatched from her. She clutched her purse to her body and climbed into the taxi. Once she'd given her address, she leaned back against the seat and counted the minutes until the car pulled into her driveway. She didn't relax until she was in the house and the security system was armed. Only then, did she allow herself to react.

She went upstairs to her bedroom and took the dress off. It had been foolish to allow David to convince her to leave the house with it on. She had trusted him. He had planned to have her hurt and humiliated tonight. Those were not the actions of a jealous man. She rolled the dress up and threw it into the trash.

When she'd showered and changed into a pair of flannel pajamas, she crawled under the bed covers and only then did she break down. Tears racked her body and it was a long time before she'd finally cried herself out. She didn't have any answers to what had happened tonight.

One thing was certain.

She couldn't live with David any longer.

It was dawn when David walked into the bedroom and switched the lights on. Lara was sitting up in bed. Her mind had been too busy with the horrifying details of the encounter with Jason to allow for sleep. Instead, she had waited for David so she could get answers to her questions.

"Did you have fun?" Her voice startled David who turned to her with narrowed eyes.

"I thought you'd still be out."

"You expected Jason to keep me captive is what you really mean."

David threw his jacket on a chair. "Don't be ridiculous."

"Did you know he meant to rape me?"

"You went to the club of your own accord." David unbuttoned his shirt. "There was no rape."

"The man slapped me and held me against a wall and didn't stop when I said no. That's what I call rape." Lara's voice was firm.

"It was a safe setting. You should have let yourself enjoy the experience."

"Are you telling me that you knew what he intended?"

David shrugged. "You're too narrow in your attitudes toward sex. You needed an awakening."

Lara fought back her nausea as she saw beneath the surface of her husband for the first time. How could she have been married to him for seven years and not seen this side of him. He had deliberately arranged for her to be assaulted. Only a person who despised another could do such a thing.

The last shred of her love for him shriveled.

"I agreed to do the swinging because you insisted it was what you needed." Lara's words were tinged with sadness. "I wasn't comfortable with it and for the sake of our marriage I did it."

"You seemed pretty comfortable last night, letting all those men touch and caress you." David didn't bother to hide his disgust. "You looked like a streetwalker."

"You chose that dress." Lara's voice was choked with outrage. "You also insisted that I not wear anything under it."

"You went along with it." David sat on a chair and took off his shoes. "I don't understand why you're complaining now. Is it guilt because you enjoyed it?"

"I did not want to be sexually assaulted and hit." Lara's heart constricted as she watched her husband undress as if nothing had happened. This wasn't the reaction of a man who cared. "Did you ask Jason to do that to me?"

David rolled his eyes. "There was no need. He knew right away what you were, and he insisted that he have a shot at you."

"That's the second time you tried to make me sleep with someone." Lara's voice trembled. "Do you think I'm your property that you can pimp out?"

David tilted his head. "You acted like a whore, so I can understand if you see yourself that way. I married you because you looked good on my arm and I thought you might be more adventurous than you were. I knew you enjoyed a wild streak at college."

Words stuck in her throat at the casual admission. She blinked back her tears. There would be plenty of time for that later. Now she needed the truth if she ever hoped to understand her marriage.

"Did you ever love me?"

David shrugged. "I lusted for you and you took advantage of that by playing hard to get. Marriage was the only way I could have you."

Finally the truth.

"You said you weren't certain about having more children when we married, but that there was a possibility of a family later. Was that a lie too?"

"I had a vasectomy after my daughter was born." David stood and unzipped his pants. "I don't know what you're complaining about. I've given you a great life. You have money, a beautiful house, and all the clothes you can buy."

"Do you think that's what I want?" Lara kept her voice neutral.

"I need more than you've given me in the past, but I'm willing to continue with the marriage. It has to be on my terms, though. You will indulge my sexual fantasies." David walked into the bathroom and slammed the door shut.

Lara was numb.

Her perception of her relationship was shattered.

She had given him love, devotion, and commitment. None of that mattered. David was like a boy who'd never grown up and she'd been a fool not to recognize it. Her attempt to please him with swapping had only made him despise her. He thought he could do whatever he pleased with her.

Deep, raw pain throbbed within her.

She pushed it behind her. A decision was needed and the answer seemed clear. Without love, she couldn't go on. No matter what David thought, she'd married him because she'd loved him. The money and lifestyle were nice, but they weren't necessary. She threw her covers off and dressed. She grabbed her purse and car keys before she left the house.

She needed somewhere safe to think.

She was facing the toughest decision in her life. She'd always thought that marriage should be for life. Every couple had disagreements and problems, and she'd been naïve to think that as long as you were committed and made concessions, that things work.

Sometimes compromise wasn't possible.

The sun was high in the sky when she pulled up in front of Ella's house. She parked the car and dialed her friend's number. She needed to clear her head and talk to someone who would understand.

She needed advice.

Ella answered on the second ring.

"Is it possible to talk?" Lara's voice cracked on a sob. "I want to divorce David."

Chapter 14

Ella opened the door and grabbed Lara in a hug.

"I didn't know where else to turn." Lara choked back a sob.

Ella stepped away. "Oh my god. What happened to your face?"

"David set me up with someone last night." Lara's voice shook. "This is what the guy did when I refused to have sex with him."

Ella's eyes widened. "David planned this?"

Lara nodded.

Ella shut the front door and pulled her close in another hug before leading her to the rear of the house. "I want to hear everything."

The smell of brewing coffee lured her into the kitchen, but the sight of the strange man leaning against the countertop, stopped her at the doorway. Ella pulled her into the room.

"This is Jesse."

The man was gorgeous.

Ella hadn't exaggerated about his good looks. He was tall, dark, and handsome. His hair was damp as if he'd just come out of the shower, and he was dressed in jeans, T-shirt, and work boots. When they walked into the room, he held a cup of coffee out to Ella before glancing in her direction.

"You must be Lara." He scanned her face, his gray eyes rested on her cheek for a second, before he reached for a mug. "What do you take in your coffee?"

"Just cream." Lara turned to Ella. "I didn't realize you had company. I'll come back another time."

"Nonsense." Ella sat at the table and motioned for Lara to join her. "Jesse lives here now. He's not company."

"That's wonderful."

At least their plans had worked out for one of them. Ella deserved happiness after all she'd endured from her husband. Maybe there was hope for her too.

Jesse put her coffee on the table and pulled a chair out. "Sit. It looks like you need to talk to someone, and I'm leaving for the jobsite. You'll have plenty of privacy."

Jesse turned to Ella and kissed her. "I'll be back in a couple of hours."

Ella's eyes followed him as he left the room and then she turned back to Lara. "Start at the beginning."

Lara clasped her mug tight. "You know that David and I were going back to the first swinger's group last weekend."

"The one where the son and his friends had shown up unannounced?"

Lara nodded. "When we arrived, David had already planned who I was to sleep with that night."

Ella frowned. "Weren't you supposed to choose?"

"That's why I refused. Instead, I picked one of the other men."

"What happened?" Ella's voice had dropped to a whisper.

"It was wonderful. He was kind, considerate, and generous. I couldn't have asked for a better introduction to the lifestyle."

"How did David react?"

"He was livid." Lara took a sip of coffee. "He exploded, but he apologized afterwards. He was a changed man and I thought that he was finished with swapping until I got home from work last night."

"What did he do?"

"He wanted us to go to a sex club." A shiver went through her. "He had everything planned, including what I was to wear. He threatened me with divorce if I didn't go through with it."

"It sounds as if he didn't give you a chance to think about what was happening. Did he already have a man picked out for you?"

Lara shook her head. "There was an initiation and men bid on me. I had my choice of five guys."

"And that's the one who hit you?"

"No." Lara dropped her voice to a conspiratorial whisper. "Sam gave me fantastic sex. He claimed that he'd been made to pleasure women, and he hadn't lied."

Ella's mouth dropped open.

"I was a bit wild when I was in college and did a lot of experimenting. I had more than my fair share of one night stands." Lara gave a rueful grin. "I'd forgotten how much fun sex could be."

Ella pointed to her cheek. "If it was so wonderful, why the bruise?"

"Sam didn't do this." Lara glanced out the window and shuddered as the images of her encounter with Jason replayed in her mind. "David had gained admission to the club by promising my body to the club owner."

Ella gasped. "He sold you?"

"He gave me to him for the night, to do whatever he wanted."

There were several moments of silence.

Finally, Ella spoke. "You cannot stay with David. He is abusive."

Tears pricked Lara's eyes. "Why didn't I see it sooner?"

"For the same reason I didn't see through Gerry's lies. You trusted him."

"I feel like such a fool." Lara took the tissue that Ella handed to her. "I've been married for seven years and I never once suspected that this side of him existed."

"Did you talk to him about it?"

"He said that he'd lusted after me and that marriage was the only way he could have me." Lara wiped the tears from her eyes. "That's not true. I loved him and gave myself to him willingly. He was the one who insisted on marriage."

"So he's twisted the past to justify his actions." Ella's voice was matter of fact.

"How could I have been so wrong? My husband gave me to a man that he knew had every intention of hurting and humiliating me." Lara's voice cracked. "If Sam hadn't come back to help me, I don't know how bad it would have been."

"You're lucky you escaped alive." Ella reached over and squeezed her hand. "You can't let this destroy you."

"Where do I go from here?"

"You already know the answer." Ella's voice was full of sympathy. "If you're not ready to make a decision, then at least move out of the house."

A tremor of fear shook her. There was only one choice and as much as she didn't want to face the reality of her ruined marriage, she had to protect herself. David's anger and contempt were impossible to ignore.

"I need the name and number of your divorce attorney."

Chapter 15

Lara rushed into the office early Monday morning with a stack of papers in her arms and her briefcase strap over her shoulder. Everything in her life was in confusion, yet she felt free for the first time in years. Ella had supported her decision to divorce David, and she had phoned the attorney that afternoon.

Even though it was the weekend, Ella's lawyer had set everything in motion. David would have been served his papers of separation late Sunday night or this morning. Lara had returned to her house when David was gone on Saturday night and with the help of Ella and Jesse, packed up her possessions and left. Right now she was staying in Ella's guesthouse and this afternoon she'd lined up a couple of apartments to view.

She was busy working on a new client's plans when Margery buzzed her. "Mr. Warner is here."

Vince had said he'd stop by to sign the papers for the contractor this morning. He had one more day in town before heading back home with his children. Lara closed the file she was working on and pulled out the Warner papers. She'd already highlighted where the signatures should go, so all he needed to do was read the contract and sign. She walked out to the reception area to greet Vince when the outer door opened.

David slammed in.

"We need to talk." David walked right past her and into her office.

Her hands clenched the file folder and her heart started beating at a frantic pace. What did he want with her and why at her office? She forced a smile to her lips and handed Vince the papers.

"You can start reading these." She tried to keep the tremor out of her voice. "I shouldn't be long."

She went back into her office and closed the door with a quiet click. "What do you want?"

David threw a paper down on her desk. "What the hell is this?"

"I thought it was self-explanatory." Lara clenched her hands together. "I won't continue to be married to a man who doesn't love me."

"What does love have to do with our marriage?" David's voice rose. "You're in it for the money."

Lara struggled to keep her temper. "I married you because I loved you."

David snorted. "You're a gold-digger like all the rest."

Lara shook her head. "I want to be a wife and mother, and you've made it perfectly clear that you want to sleep around and pimp me out. We don't want the same things."

"You agreed not to have children when we married."

"You said we would consider it in a few years. You lied." Lara kept her voice low. "I was twenty-five when we married. I was too young to know what I wanted out of life."

"Are you suggesting I robbed the cradle?" David's shout echoed around her office. "You're just upset because you got slapped. What if I promise that won't happen again?"

Lara crossed her arms over her chest. "Our problems are deeper than that. You admitted you don't love me and you certainly don't respect me. I don't want this kind of relationship."

David grabbed her arm and shook her. "No one walks away from me."

"Let go." Lara clenched her jaw. "I'm not your property."

David flung her arm away from him. "So much for your words of love."

"You killed that last week." Lara rubbed her arm. "I've moved my stuff out, so there's no need for us to see each other again."

"You signed a pre-nuptial." David's voice was a roar of rage. "You're not entitled to anything."

Lara swallowed the lump in her throat. "I took my clothes. If you'd cared about where I was this weekend, you would have noticed my closet was empty."

"I bought the car." David motioned to the door. "I saw it parked outside."

"It's in my name. My lawyer says that I can keep it."

"We'll see. The lawyer I used when Debra divorced me was quite a shark. He'll make sure that you return everything."

"Did you notice who my lawyer is?"

A surge of satisfaction went through Lara. Ella had recommended the same lawyer David had on his first divorce. She might not be entitled to very much, but at least she'd walk away with her dignity.

David's eyes narrowed. "Do you honestly think you'll survive without me?"

"Yes." Lara's voice held sadness. "I have my business and my friends."

"A business I gave you."

"That's not true." Lara's voice shook. "I started it before we met."

"I provided the customers." David's tone was scornful.

"You referred your friends, and I appreciate that." Lara took a step closer to her office door. "They wouldn't still be using me if I didn't have talent. I provide them with a service they want."

David snapped his fingers. "One word from me, and they'll be gone."

Lara straightened her shoulders. She hadn't expected David to take the divorce well, yet she hadn't expected that he'd be out for revenge. So be it. She couldn't control his actions. All she could do was focus on her work and getting her life back on track.

"You can try." Lara cleared her throat. "If you don't mind, I have a client waiting."

"You'll regret this." David pushed away from her desk.

"I doubt it."

Lara opened the door, and watched David storm out of the building. She inhaled a deep breath and then forced herself to go into the outer office. It was a small space and judging by Margery's wide eyes full of compassion and curiosity, David's voice had carried out to the reception area.

"I'm sorry for the interruption." Lara turned to Vince Warner. "Do you have any questions about the contract?"

"It seems pretty straight forward." Vince stood and followed her into her office. When she shut the door, he put the file folder on her desk. "I signed the papers while I was waiting."

"Great. They'll start work this afternoon."

Vince sat and ran his eyes over her in a critical appraisal. "Are you all right?"

A flush of heat filled her cheeks. "Of course."

"Even makeup can't cover the bruise on your face." Vince leaned back in his chair. "Did you charge him?"

"David didn't do this." Lara's hand fluttered against her cheek. "He could have prevented it, though."

Vince nodded. "I won't pry. It sounds as if things are complicated between you and your husband."

"Soon to be ex-husband."

Lara sighed and sat in her chair behind her desk. There was no point in pretending that her conversation with David had been private. Vince was a client that she had come to like. He deserved an explanation.

"David and I have been growing apart for some time. Things reached a breaking point and I couldn't bend anymore; not even to save our marriage."

"I'm sorry." Vince stretched his legs out in front of him. "My wife and I had our fair share of arguments, but we always managed to remain in love."

Lara nodded. "I don't think David ever loved me. He saw me as a trophy and when I outgrew the role, he became angry."

"You loved him." It was a statement.

Tears pricked at the corner of her eyes and she blinked to keep them from falling. "Very much."

"It sounds trite, but time does lessen the pain."

"Keeping busy will help too. I'm thankful that I have my work."

Lara pulled Vince's file toward her and opened it. She glanced over the papers to make certain everything was in order and then shut it. She'd call the contractor when he left, and the project would be underway. A feeling of satisfaction surged through her. Knowing that construction was starting on one of her designs reassured her that everything was going to be fine.

Vince cleared his throat. "My timing is bad, but I promised the children I would ask you."

Lara frowned. "Do they want to change their bedrooms? I can draw up new plans."

Vince held his hand up. "It's nothing like that. We're leaving tomorrow morning and they asked me to invite you to join us for dinner this evening. I understand if you can't make it."

Dinner with two lively children would take her mind off her confrontation with David. Her only other option was to stay in Ella's guest house, and rehash every word that David had said. Her mother had always said that accepting invitations from people was the best way to get on with life and move past the pain. The alternative was to become stagnant and depressed.

She refused to let David destroy her.

It was time she moved forward with her life.

Lara flipped through her appointment book. "I have a couple of meetings this afternoon, but I'll be free after six. Is that too late?"

Vince stood. "We're staying at the Helsom Arms. They have a giant pizza oven in their rear restaurant."

"I know it well." Lara stood and went to her door. "Nobody in Dearston can pass up pizza there."

"Are you sure about dinner?" Vince pushed a hand through his hair. "I'll understand if you don't feel up to it."

"Staying home isn't going to make things better." Lara opened the door. "Pizza is the perfect solution. I'm honored the children wanted to invite me."

"I'll see you there then." Vince left the office.

Lara turned to Margery. "Did you hear every word?"

Margery bit her lip. "David was yelling and even though you were quiet, the walls are awfully thin."

Lara groaned and sat with her head in her hands. "How humiliating."

"It is past time you came to your senses and left that man." Margery snorted. "It's none of my business, but he never treated you properly."

"Margery!" Lara looked up at her secretary. "I never knew you felt that way."

"It wasn't my place to say anything." Margery crossed her arms. "You're a beautiful woman and you deserve a good man who loves you. David Knight cares only about himself."

"How long have you thought this?"

"Since you married him." Margery shook her head. "Did Mr. Warner ask about the argument?"

Lara shook her head. "He was very discrete."

"Now that's a gentleman."

"I was grateful he didn't pry." Lara stood. "I'll be out of the office this afternoon. I'm apartment hunting."

Lara went back into her office. She had calls to make and designs to finish, yet she couldn't help the flutter of excitement that twirled in her stomach. She was exhilarated. She still had to face months of legal wrangling with David, but he couldn't touch her anymore. She was beginning a new life, and for the first time since walking out of David's house, she felt relief.

Chapter 16

Lara was humming to herself as she pulled out her almost completed crazy quilt square. She smoothed her hand over the plush velvet of the material patches before picking up her embroidery needle. She was working on the last chain of feather stitches before moving on to another block.

"Are you going to tell us?" Alisa's voice was impatient.

"I left David." Lara looked up from her work. "I thought that was obvious because we're meeting in Ella's guest house."

"We figured that." Alisa leaned forward. "We want the details."

"Give her some space." Brenna laid out some scraps of material on her lap. "Lara will tell us when she's ready."

Alisa waved two diamond squares at Lara. "You can't keep us in suspense."

Lara glanced up at her friends. "Ella helped me leave him."

Ella shuddered. "That man was horrible. He was just like Gerry, wanting everything his own way. He didn't care if Lara was hurt."

"What happened?" Alisa's voice was low. "Did you hate the swinging?"

Lara shrugged. "The sex was great for the most part. David was a beast about it."

"So he was jealous just as we predicted." Alisa pursed her lips. "What went wrong?"

"He treated me like I was his property to hand out." Lara's fingers stilled on her block as she remembered the horror of her encounter with Jason. "I barely escaped being raped."

Brenna gasped. "I knew our plan would backfire."

Alisa waved away Brenna's objections. "Tell us about the great sex."

Ella shook her head. "Lara deserves some privacy."

"And we want the details." Alisa's voice was full of curiosity.

"We went back to the first group, and I chose a man who was kind and gentle with me. He knew it was my first time swapping so he made it special." Lara smiled at the memory of her night with Frank Burkett. "David was furious that I was out the whole night."

"Good." Brenna pinned two patches together. "It was his idea to begin with."

"His jealousy didn't last long." Lara cleared her throat. "One week later, David gave me an ultimatum and insisted I go with him to a swinger's club."

"There's a club in town?" Alisa scrunched her nose. "Why haven't I heard of it?"

"It's not in town. It's The Coliseum Club in the city, and to be honest, it's a sex club where anything goes." Lara swallowed as she remembered what had happened there. "We were new, so there was an initiation."

Alisa took a stitch. "Was the sex hot?"

"You're obsessed with sex." Ella shook her head.

Lara laughed. "I picked a guy who was fantastic, but things got ugly when David told me I had to go with the club's owner. Apparently my body was the price of admission to the place."

"What did he do?" Brenna's voice was a hushed whisper.

"He tried to rape me. When I fought back he slapped me, and if Sam, my first partner, hadn't come back, I don't know what would have happened."

"Do you think David knew that?" Brenna leaned forward.

Lara's head throbbed as the implications of what Brenna had suggested took hold in her mind. She rejected the possibility. "David hasn't taken the divorce well, yet I don't think he wanted me harmed. He only cared about joining the club no matter what the price."

"I hope not." Brenna exhaled a shaky breath. "We would never have suggested you try to make him jealous if we'd known how he'd react."

"It's not your fault." Lara shrugged. "I don't regret doing it. I would never have learned the truth about my marriage or found the strength to leave David."

"Maybe we shouldn't continue." Brenna's tone was doubtful. "Two of you have given your husbands what they wanted, and both your marriages have failed."

"I have no choice but to follow through with our plans." Alisa exhaled an exasperated breath. "Henry has been pressuring me for a ménage, and I still haven't found a man to join us."

"Are you certain that's what you want to do?" Lara's voice was cautious. "My experimenting with swapping showed me how flawed my marriage was. You seem to have a good relationship with Henry."

"I do." Alisa hesitated for a second. "Henry's so good to me that I just want to give him the one thing he's asked for."

"What if it destroys your marriage?"

"I have to trust in Henry's love." Alisa's voice became serious. "I love him enough to see where this goes. If he wants a ménage a trois, then I'm willing to give him that, but it has to be on my terms."

Alisa

Chapter 1

Alisa loved her husband. They'd been married for over eleven years, and she'd never once thought about being unfaithful until now. There was a question of whether it was truly an affair if your husband knew about it. Alisa frowned as she pinned her diamond star to the white inset piece of her quilt block.

Was a ménage à trois cheating?

Both parties participated.

Both parties agreed.

"Could I find one at this Coliseum Club?"

Alisa looked up from her work.

Lara shrugged. "It's possible. They were definitely into sex, and I'm not certain it mattered who they had it with."

"It's either that, or I advertise for someone."

"You could hire a male escort." Brenna gave Alisa a side look. "You thought that would work with Ella."

"That's a possibility." Alisa pursed her lips. "An escort wouldn't have any expectations afterward."

"Would that be wise?" Ella gave her a doubtful look. "Henry might think you're not serious."

Alisa rolled her eyes. "Henry only said he wanted a ménage. He didn't specify the terms. I don't think he expected me to go through with it. It's going to be difficult to pull this off without him guessing my real motivation."

"Aren't you doing it to help your relationship?" Brenna's voice was curious. "We decided to give our husbands a taste of their own sexual demands, but with a twist. I thought it was to save our marriages."

"Then we've failed." Alisa voice was serious. "Look at Ella. She found a younger man and divorced her husband. Lara's husband became abusive, and she was forced to leave him."

"Following the plan was not a failure for me. My marriage was over before I started this journey." Ella's voice was firm. "Gerry was a liar and a cheat, and I clung to the hope that I could save a sinking ship. If we hadn't made this pact, I would never have found Jesse and real love."

"I was successful too." Lara's voice was quiet. "Sleeping with other men showed me how inconsiderate and selfish David was."

"So the sex was that good." Alisa's eyes widened. "You still haven't told us everything."

Lara shrugged. "It was awkward in the beginning. My partners made certain I was fulfilled and satisfied by the time we parted."

"Would you do it again?" Brenna's voice was curious.

Lara shook her head. "No. There's more to life than great sex. I want a relationship with a man who will always be by my side. Sex without the emotion is just a physical release."

"It sounds cold." Brenna looked at Lara with sympathy. "You went through all of that because you wanted to keep your marriage together."

"I think David had been sleeping with other women for a while." Lara turned her block over and knotted her thread. "I didn't want to see the signs that the marriage was over."

"He'd never been abusive before." Alisa started to stitch her diamond star in place. "So you succeeded in making him jealous."

"Not really." Lara clasped her hands in her lap. "After the first encounter, David called me a whore."

"He was looking for an excuse." Ella reached over and squeezed Lara's arm. "His reasons for wanting to swap were wrong. He didn't care about saving the marriage."

"You're right." Lara's voice cracked. "I never expected him to treat me like his property. I thought men and society were beyond that."

"Most are." Brenna's voice was firm. "David was used to getting his own way. He's had great success in life, and no one denies him."

"He must have thought you'd refuse to sleep with someone else and that would have left him free to do what he wanted."

Lara frowned. "He set me up the first time. There was already an agreement in place between the two men. I threw a wrench into his plans by choosing a different partner."

Alisa looked up from her stitching. "I want to make certain that Henry understands that if we invite a third person into our relationship he has to accept the consequences."

"Do you think it's going to destroy your marriage?" Brenna's voice was hesitant.

"Maybe." Alisa damped down her panic. "It might increase our intimacy."

"Hasn't that improved since Bert went away to boarding school?" Brenna tilted her head. "I know that there was a huge reconnection between Peter and myself once the boys left for university. It was like we were teenagers again."

"I get to go places with Henry. He is so involved with the business and all of his associations, he doesn't even notice I'm beside him." Alisa pushed back her frustration. "For years, I stayed home with our son and did the mother thing. Now that I want to become involved with the business, Henry is blocking me."

"You mean he won't allow you to work?" Ella's voice rose in dismay. "I thought the company was yours."

Alisa stabbed her needle into her fabric. "My father built Fairman's Hotels into the multinational it is today. When Henry and I married, he made Henry sign a prenuptial agreement. He liked Henry, but he didn't believe that marriages lasted."

"So Henry can't claim the business if you divorce." Brenna looked up from the fabric she'd been cutting. "That makes sense. What was the agreement?"

"Henry owns ten percent of the business no matter what happens." Alisa took a couple of straight stitches along her seam to calm her thoughts. "I own seventy-percent, ten percent is in trust for any children I may have, and the balance is held by board members."

"It's definitely your business." Lara held a piece of red embroidery floss against the black velvet on her block. "Henry can't keep you from it."

"I've never worked at Fairman's before. To be honest, I've never worked anywhere." Alisa shook her head. "Henry tries to humor me with parties and socializing. He has no intention of letting me near the real operations."

"Is that what you want?" Lara asked. "Working in a business setting can be exhilarating, yet at the same time exhausting. You wouldn't have time to do your committee work or volunteer."

"I'm bored." Alisa's eyes widened. For months now, she'd been restless and unhappy. Until this moment, she hadn't realized the intensity of her boredom.

"Then you need to do something." Lara nodded. "I couldn't imagine how isolated my life would have been if I'd let David convince me to close my business. It's been my anchor through a lot of difficult bumps in our marriage."

"Henry and I haven't had any bumps, even though lately I think we're growing apart." Alisa sighed. "Does that make sense?"

"Completely." Brenna paused with her scissors in her hands. "When the boys were gone, I just wanted to do something. I loved being a mom, but other things in life were waiting for me. That's when I expanded my kennels and started entering my dogs in competitions."

"It's normal to want to spread your wings." Ella looked up from her quilt block. "Gerry wouldn't let me go back to work in the business, so I went to school instead."

"I already have my degree in business." Alisa leaned back in her chair. "Working at Fairman's makes the most sense to me. I just have to convince Henry that I can do it."

"Do you think arranging a ménage is going to do that?" Lara's gaze was intent.

"Henry doesn't think I'm capable of looking outside the box." Alisa's voice was low. "I think that's why he threw the threesome challenge at me. He believes I can't change and grow. He still sees me as the young woman he met at Princeton, while he's expanded his knowledge and expertise."

"That's so unfair." Ella's voice was full of outrage. "You're just as talented as he. He doesn't have a clue how much it takes to manage a household and children."

"I'm at my wits end with this problem." Alisa's voice cracked. "Henry doesn't see me as a business person. Just because I stayed home to raise our son doesn't make me incompetent."

"You're the cleverest person I know. You know what you want and how to get it. You'd be deadly in a business," Lara said.

"You own Fairman's. Why not just walk into the office and take over." Brenna had put her fabrics to one side and was leaning toward Alisa. "You're the real boss."

"It's not that easy. Henry might be the CEO, yet he still answers to the board. Even though I'm the majority stockholder, the best I could do is vote against them."

"And take a chance that the company doesn't survive." Lara's tone was matter of fact.

"I couldn't bear to take away my son's legacy. My father worked hard to build up his empire of hotels."

"You have the same problem I had with Gerry and the business." Ella sighed. "There's nothing designed to make a mother feel guiltier than to have to choose between your needs and those of your children."

"The children always win." Brenna bit her lip. "You're in a tough place."

"So it's a threesome or find something else to do." Alisa said. "If I show that I can be flexible in my sexuality, maybe Henry will realize that I can survive in the business world."

"Finding a new sexual partner does sound like fun." Lara's eyes twinkled. "It's a mission that would certainly get rid of your boredom."

A spark of enthusiasm settled in Alisa's chest. "I hadn't looked at it like that."

"That's because you were thinking of it like work." Ella smirked. "Trust me, when you let yourself embrace the challenge, you'll have fun."

"Ella!" Brenna's voice was shocked. "You used to be so shy and reserved. What happened?"

"Love and great sex." Ella pursed her lips. "There's nothing better to improve your outlook on life, and I think that is what Alisa needs. A new perspective."

"I couldn't agree more." Lara buried her needle in her crazy patchwork block. "I'm single now, with lots of time on my hands. I could help you with the search for Mr. Number Two in your life."

Tendrils of excitement twisted in Alisa's stomach.

She'd never thought of it as fun before.

Finding a man who would be part of a sexual encounter with her and Henry had seemed such a chore. It was obvious that Brenna still had her doubts. Not Lara and Ella. They'd taken the challenge, and in their minds, they had come out ahead. She had a strong marriage with Henry. That didn't mean there wasn't a need for change. He had to see her as a mature woman with needs and ambitions.

She was ready for adventure.

"When do we start?" She sat up in her chair. "Where do we start?"

Chapter 2

Alisa walked into the bedroom that she shared with Henry and dropped her towel. She glanced into her mirror and smoothed her hand over her small waist. She had the figure of a much younger woman. At thirty-six, men still turned to watch her pass by. She'd inherited her mother's exotic, dark-haired beauty and was careful with her diet and exercise, spending a couple of hours a day at the gym. She had thought that would be enough for Henry.

She was wrong.

He wanted to make love with another woman.

It didn't matter that he desired Alisa to be a part of the encounter. She loved him, and he wanted to experiment with a ménage à trois. He called it expanding her sexual awareness and acceptance. She didn't want her husband making love to another woman.

Alisa turned away from the mirror and put on her undergarments. If Henry was serious about the threesome, then she would arrange it on her terms. A man was what she was looking for. Henry was going to be in for a surprise if he expected her to find a woman. She would just have to see how sexually flexible and accepting he was. She pulled on her robe and sat at her vanity to brush out her hair.

When she heard the water in the shower stop, she turned to watch Henry enter the room. At thirty-eight he still had a good figure. His dark-brown hair was beginning to thin and turn grey at the temple. He was still the handsome charmer she'd fallen in love with when she was twenty-two. Looking at him still made her tingle, sending a charge of excitement through her body.

It was time to shake things up.

Alisa cleared her throat. "Have you thought about what I suggested last night?"

Henry threw his towel on the floor. "Are you still talking about coming to work for the company? I thought we'd decided that you would stick to your charities and society work."

"I want more."

Henry laughed. "Everybody wants more. The problem is that I answer to the Board, and they aren't about to give you a position just because you ask."

"Why not." Alisa turned back to put mascara on. She kept an eye on Henry in the mirror. "I own the majority share."

Henry paused in putting on his boxer shorts. "That's not a good reason to give someone a job."

"It seems a reasonable request." Alisa loaded a brush with bronze eye shadow. "You work there after all."

"Your father gave me the position when we married."

"Don't you think Daddy would have wanted me there too?"

Henry shook his head. "He was old fashioned in his views of where a woman's place was meant to be."

"True. At the time, I'd just had Bert." Alisa stroked on the eye shadow. "I wanted to stay home."

"You got your wish. I don't know why you want to alter things now."

"I've changed." Alisa turned around in her chair to stare at Henry. "How can you not see that?"

Henry sat on the bed and pulled on his slacks. "You're still doing the same things as far as I can see. Hell, you were at a quilter's meeting all yesterday afternoon. There's nothing more domesticated than that."

"You'd be surprised," Alisa muttered under her breath.

She turned back to the mirror and finished putting on her makeup. When she was done, she stood and went to her closet to pull out a white sleeveless dress and matching blue jacket. She laid the clothes on the bed and then untied her robe. Henry had finished putting on his shirt and tie. He pulled out a small suitcase and put it on the bed.

"Where are you going now?"

"New York." Henry put a couple of clean shirts into the case. "I'll be back at the end of the week."

"I could come with you." Alisa watched for Henry's reaction. There was an imperceptible intake of breath before he relaxed.

"I'm going to be too busy. It's one meeting after another."

"I'd shop during the day." Alisa walked up to him and ran her hand over his chest. "The evenings could be filled with lovemaking."

Henry's muscles tightened. "What about your charities? Don't you have a big fundraiser coming up?"

"They'll survive without me." Alisa's voice was low and seductive. "I could follow you on a later flight this evening. That shouldn't interfere with your meetings."

Henry jerked away. "Not this week."

Alisa fought back her anger. This wasn't the first time Henry had refused her company. She didn't want to let her mind think the worst, yet there was no way to stop it. Their son was away at boarding school, and she had nothing but free time on her hands according to Henry. There was no reason she couldn't join him. She'd half a mind to surprise him with a visit and see what was keeping him so occupied.

"Are you still serious about us exploring your sexual fantasies?" Alisa let her robe fall to the floor.

Henry dropped the socks he'd been carrying. "What brought that up?"

"You did say you wanted to try a ménage à trois." Alisa deliberately kept her voice nonchalant.

Henry picked up his socks and threw them into his case. "You don't have the nerve."

Alisa stepped into her dress and turned to Henry to zip it up. "Now why would you think that?"

"Deep down, you're a prude." Henry chuckled. "You come across all sex and sophistication. I know the truth."

"Do you?" Alisa slipped her jacket on.

"Yes. You're too worried about what others might think. You have your reputation to consider." Henry shut his case. "It's hard to believe that you and your father share the same blood."

"Are you implying something about my father?" Alisa's voice hardened.

Henry laughed. "Only that your father was ruthless, and you're the exact opposite. That's why I know you'd never succeed in business. You don't have the determination or hard-heartedness."

Alisa's eyes narrowed. "You don't think so?"

"You're too soft." Henry kissed her on the cheek. "I love you, Alisa. You wouldn't hurt a fly. You need a thick skin to succeed in business."

"I could surprise you."

Henry hugged her before picking up his case. "You'd let people walk all over you."

"Just because I allow them to get away with things, doesn't mean I'm blind." Alisa's voice held a note of steel.

"I love you. I don't want you to be stressed all the time with business. I take pride in the fact that I can provide you with a luxurious lifestyle." He glanced at his watch. "The car is probably waiting outside. I have to run. I'll see you in a week."

"So I have your permission to go ahead with my plans for a threesome?"

"I don't have time to discuss this." Henry exhaled a deep breath. "Do whatever you want."

He didn't wait for her answer before rushing out the door.

Alisa picked up his towel and threw it into the hamper. Another week alone. This time it would be different. When Henry came back from New York she would have picked out the man who would be the third person in their ménage.

Chapter 3

The sun was high in the sky. The bright-blue umbrella on the table provided protection without destroying the view. Alisa sat back in the wicker chair and took a sip of her strawberry daiquiri. The Dearston Country Club was busy this morning. That was no surprise on a weekend. Most members tried to make an appearance even if it was only for a quick drink.

This should be the perfect hunting ground for a man.

The place was swarming with athletic, handsome specimens, whether it was the golf or tennis pros, or the waiters. If she couldn't find what she needed here, then she was going to have a difficult time fulfilling Henry's challenge.

A purse was set down on the table. "I'm sorry I was late. My new landlord called and needed me to sign papers and give him a security deposit. It seems there was a couple snooping around the place, and he was going to give it to them if I didn't get the money to him right away."

Alisa pushed her sunglasses down, and gave Lara a quick perusal. As usual not a hair was out of place, and Lara was glowing with beauty. If she wasn't a friend, she'd be jealous. "When do you move in?"

"At the end of the month." Lara sat. "Ella's boyfriend Jesse has a truck, and they're going to help me move."

"I thought you left most of the stuff for David."

"I did, but my clothes and the furniture from my grandmother are mine." Lara started rifling through her purse. "If I'd left them for David, he would have burned them."

"True." Alisa took an assessing look at Lara. "Are you really happy?"

Lara pulled a handkerchief from her purse. "Very."

"Even after sleeping with all of those men?"

Lara dabbed the back of her neck with the cloth. "At first, I thought I'd be embarrassed. Not now. The sex club was in another town, so there's only a slim chance I'll run into anyone from there. If I do, I'm certain they'll want to keep their activities a secret too."

"What about the party in town?"

"They were nice people." Lara leaned back in her chair. "If things had been different, I could have become friends with them. David made that impossible."

"So having sex with another man wasn't the reason your marriage broke up." Alisa tried to keep the anxiety out of her voice.

"It made the end come sooner, that's all." Lara cleared her throat. "What's the real reason for your questions? Are you getting nervous about finding a man for you and Henry?"

"Am I that obvious?" Alisa motioned for the waiter. "I've analyzed the scenario in my mind until I think I'm going crazy. Nothing stops the butterflies in my stomach."

"They'll be there until you've actually taken the leap."

The waiter came and took their drink order. Alisa eyed him up and down behind her sunglasses. He was cute, in a young kind of way. He had dark hair that was slicked back, gray eyes, and an impish smile. When he left, she leaned close to Lara.

"What about the waiter?"

Lara frowned. "He seems a bit young. That might be a good thing."

"How so?"

"You know what they say about a young man's stamina in the bedroom." Lara pulled her sunglasses out of her purse and put them on. "This is wonderful weather. It's a shame to waste it eyeing up the help."

"It's not like that." Alisa sipped the last of her daiquiri and pushed it away. "Henry's in New York again, and he refused to take me."

Lara turned to her. "Do you have a reason for concern?"

Alisa bit her lower lip. "I'm not sure. Lately he's been having meetings out of town and refusing to talk about them. I don't want to think that he might be having an affair. What else could it be?"

"Why don't you fly up and surprise him."

"I've considered it and decided I don't want to know." Alisa's voice was low. "I'm a coward. If I don't confront him, it's only my superstitions."

"You love him that much?" Lara's voice held sympathy.

"It was love at first sight." Alisa grimaced. "It sounds so cliché, yet when I saw him across the courtyard at Princeton, it was as if I'd been hit by lightning. Nothing has changed, even after all these years."

"Why do you think Henry is asking for a threesome then?"

"He's bored?" Alisa voiced her greatest fear.

Lara looked at her for a few seconds and then shook her head. "I doubt it. He's hit his midlife crisis and thinks he's missed out on something."

"You don't believe he has a problem with me?"

"It's never been about you or me." Lara's voice was firm. "Our husbands were the ones asking for sexual adventures. All we've been doing is trying to accommodate them."

Alisa took a deep breath and forced back the whisper of doubt that twirled around her thoughts. She loved Henry, and she would do this for him. She was also doing it for herself. Henry thought that she couldn't have a life outside of their home, so she would prove him wrong. She was capable of change.

"So how do we go about finding this unknown lover?" Alisa asked in a determined voice.

"I picked up a copy of the Underground Voice." Lara pulled a newspaper out of her purse. "They always have the most interesting classifieds."

"Is this how others look?"

"Unless you have a friend in mind that you want to approach." Lara raised an eyebrow. "That would be the easiest way."

"I couldn't look them in the face again." Alisa started to giggle. "Can you imagine seeing them at a charity ball. What would you say?"

"It might be awkward." Lara opened the paper. "With a stranger, you risk finding someone who is dangerous."

"That's why I want to interview them first." Alisa leaned closer to the paper. "You'll have to come with me."

"No problem." Lara moved a finger down the lines of classified advertisements until she hit the personal columns. "Here's one. M looking for M/F. They don't seem to care what they get, so maybe a threesome will work for them."

Alisa pulled out a pad and pencil and took down the phone number. "It's worth a try."

They continued searching the paper until their drinks arrived, and then they sat back to enjoy the atmosphere. It had been ages since Alisa had relaxed at the club even though she was a regular visitor. Usually, she was trying to perfect her tennis serve or golf swing. The pros were generous with their advice and flirting.

If all else failed, she could ask one of the pros to complete the threesome. She would prefer not to choose someone she knew. Somehow, she didn't think Henry would like that. He enjoyed coming to the club when he had the time and having slept with one of the employees would probably ruin that for him.

"I think it's best if I don't approach anyone at the club." Alisa's head was spinning with the effects of her second drink.

"I agree." Lara slurped up the last remnants of her daiquiri. "I run into a lot of artisans in my line of work. I might be able to get a lead on someone who swings both ways."

"Sounds good." Alisa pushed her empty glass away. "The last resort is to hire someone."

Lara pulled out her phone and started dialing. "It's now or never."

"Who are you calling?" Alisa fought back her panic.

"The first guy on the list." Lara held the phone to her ear. It took her a while to negotiate a meeting place and then she threw the phone back into her purse. "He'll be here in fifteen minutes. I've arranged for us to meet outside the club gates where the parking lot meets the street. We'll take it from there."

"He's going to think it's you and I who want the threesome." Alisa's words seemed to be stuck in her throat.

"There's only one way to find out."

Lara stood, and the waiter came immediately. Alisa paid for the drinks and followed her friend out of the restaurant. Her stomach was tied in knots, and she didn't know if she'd be able to speak, but she felt completely sober. She'd heard somewhere that fear had that effect.

They waited in the parking lot near Lara's BMW. Beads of sweat were forming on her brow. Alisa wasn't sure if it was the sun or her trepidation.

"I think I'm going to be sick."

Lara nodded. "I know the feeling. The night I had to go to the first swinger's party, I thought I'd pass out."

Alisa took a deep breath. "I shouldn't be so nervous. This guy advertised, so he'll be prepared for whatever we ask."

Alisa straightened as a vehicle pulled into the parking lot. A man in his late thirties stepped out of a rusty van. A shiver of revulsion raced through Alisa. The man was well dressed, yet there was something about him that made her uncomfortable. Usually she trusted her instincts. She couldn't be certain this time. Her anxiety about this meeting was clouding her judgement.

"You'll have to be the judge. I can't be objective about this." Alisa whispered to Lara. "I don't trust him, though."

"I won't steer you wrong." Lara's eyes had narrowed as the man approached them.

"Are you the one who called?" He stopped with his hands on his hips. "You didn't mention you had a partner."

"This is my friend." Lara's voice sounded calm. "Is a partner a problem?"

The man shrugged. "I'm not into anything kinky."

"That's not what it sounded like from your advertisement." Alisa's voice was sharp. "What exactly are you into?"

"One on one." The man looked back at his van. "Which one of you wants to have some fun?"

Alisa's eyes narrowed. A warning shiver raced up her spine. "What's your name?"

"Fredrick." The man spat on the ground. "Are we going to get this thing moving or what?"

"Where did you intend to meet?" Lara crossed her arms over her chest.

"How about my van?"

Lara shook her head. "This isn't going to work."

"You don't know that yet." Fredrick's voice was a low growl.

"No." Alisa had a sudden urge to run. She reached out to Lara just as the man grabbed her arm and pulled her toward the van. She dug her feet in and twisted her arm to break his hold. Lara was hitting him on the shoulder. His grip seemed to strengthen.

The side door of the van opened, and two men jumped out.

A surge of adrenaline rushed through Alisa.

She screamed and swung her purse at her abductor's head. He cursed and slackened his grip. It was enough for Alisa to twist free and run. She headed to the club gates. Lara was beside her, and she could hear the shouts and footsteps of the men close behind.

They were gaining on them.

Just then a group of men with their golf clubs came through the club's gate.

"Help!"

Alisa's voice came out as a whisper.

Fear and adrenaline had made her mouth dry and her words silent. It didn't matter. The sight of the newcomers halted the men behind them. There were a few choice curses and then the sound of running in the opposite direction. She heard the slam of the van doors and the sound of tires spinning out of the parking lot.

She sagged against one of the stone pillars that anchored the rod-iron gate.

Lara collapsed beside her.

"Are you ladies okay?" One of the golfers asked. The rest of his party continued on to their vehicles.

Alisa nodded and waited until he left before turning to Lara. "That was a close call."

A shudder went through Alisa. The man's advertisement had said he was interested in a single man or woman. Who knows what he and his friends had planned. For the first time, she realized how very vulnerable she was making herself.

"It was too dangerous." Lara's voice was shaking. "I didn't like the looks of him when he stepped out, but I probably would have given him the benefit of a doubt."

"We might never have been seen alive again."

"Don't even think it." Lara wiped a hand across her forehead. "Your instincts were dead on. You didn't trust him."

Alisa shivered. "How am I going to find someone if this is the risk I have to take?"

"No more personal ads." Lara moved away from the gate. "I need another drink."

"How did they think they could kidnap us in broad daylight?"

"There were certainly enough guys in the van." Lara clasped Alisa's arm and they walked back to the club. "Who knows where they would have taken you if you'd been alone."

Alisa started to shake.

"This isn't going to work." She fought back the sudden urge to cry.

"Don't give up," Lara said after they'd been seated inside the restaurant and given a menu. "This is just a setback, not the end of the game."

"What do you suggest I do?" Alisa opened her menu with trembling fingers. "Stand on a street corner and wear a sign advertising that I want a man to take home and meet my husband?"

"That's not a bad idea." Lara's voice held a hint of laughter. "I'd hate to see who you'd attract from this place."

Alisa giggled. "Could you see the look on the manager's face?"

"He might be the first one to take you up on the offer." Lara's tone was dry. "I've seen the way he looks at you."

"He's old enough to be my father." Alisa could feel her heartbeat returning to normal.

"They're never too old to think about it." Lara grinned. "What about the other members? Most of them have known both you and Henry for years."

"They'd be shocked." Alisa grinned. "It might be worth it just to liven this place up a bit."

"You'd probably end up giving one of them a heart attack." Lara closed the menu. "There really is only one solution."

"What's that?"

"I'll have to find someone from my circle of clients and craftspeople." Lara said. "A few words in the right place should give us some results."

"Are you sure?" Alisa leaned forward. "Aren't you afraid of what they'll think about you?"

"I was initiated at one of the most notorious sex clubs in the area. I have nothing left to hide."

Alisa squeezed Lara's hand. "I appreciate you doing this for me. I'd have been at a total loss of where to go from here."

Lara smiled. "What are friends for? Besides, you stood by me through the whole swapping thing."

"This is different. Henry isn't demanding I do this, he just doesn't think I can."

"You're going to prove him wrong." Lara's voice sounded fierce. "You're a capable woman, and this is your chance to prove it. Together, we'll find the perfect man."

Chapter 4

It was Tuesday afternoon, and Alisa still hadn't found a man who was interested in having a threesome with Henry and her. She'd scoured the personals in the papers and checked out sites online. There just wasn't an easy way to find someone trustworthy who was sexually open to a ménage. She'd looked into Lara's sex club. It was closed to strangers, and they refused to give out any information to outsiders.

Lara had made good on her promise, though.

She'd found someone who was interested.

Trent was his name.

That's why Alisa was sitting at a patio table at the Coffee Bean Café. She was going to meet the best lead she'd had in a week. Lara said that one of her custom-furniture designers had suggested that Trent was sexually adventuresome and looking for a place to live for a few months. The arrangement was longer than Alisa had planned, yet if that was what it took to secure someone's interest, then she could arrange it.

She took a sip of her dark-roast coffee. The café was a safe enough environment to meet a stranger, plus Trent came with recommendations. She picked a table in the corner of the patio that backed against the brick wall of the building. There was privacy with a direct view of the exit. If an escape was needed, she could run.

A tall, muscular man walked onto the patio. He had dirty-blonde hair, styled and gelled into a windswept look. He sported a two-day old beard and was wearing dark glasses. He stood with his hands on his hips as he surveyed the tables and patrons. His glance rested on Alisa for a few seconds before he pulled off his sunglasses and walked to her table.

"Alisa?"

She stood and held out her hand. "Mr. Jackson?"

He grinned. "My friends call me Trent."

He was gorgeous.

A tingle went through her as she shook his hands, and her mind went blank as she stared up at him. She needed to say something and all she could do was motion for him to sit. After the waitress had taken his order, she leaned back in her seat and took in the complete beauty of this man.

His blue eyes lit with amusement. "Do you like what you see?"

"Very much." Alisa clapped her hand over her mouth. The words were out before she'd realized what she'd said.

Trent grinned. "I like a woman who says what she thinks."

"I didn't mean to be so blunt." Alisa's voice was apologetic.

"Considering what I'm here to discuss, I think the more honest we are, the better."

Alisa fumbled with her napkin. "I've never done anything like this before."

"I have."

The waitress returned, and Trent stopped speaking while she placed a cappuccino in front of him. When she left, he put a packet of sugar in the coffee and took a sip before looking back at Alisa. She had a chance to digest his words. Her heart was still beating at a rapid rate, but her breathing had returned to normal.

Trent was perfect for her needs. He had looks, charm, and experience.

"I should clarify my last remark." Trent gave her a rueful grin. "I've participated with two women before. Never a woman and a man. The women were friends of mine who were gay. They wanted to mix things up a bit, so we had some fun."

"Did the women remain a couple?"

Trent threw his head back and laughed. "Come to think of it, I didn't see them together afterward."

Alisa bit her lower lip. "That's what I was worried about."

"It could have had something to do with me moving away." Trent lowered his voice. "You sound pretty nervous about this. Are you sure this is what you want?"

"Positive." Alisa straightened her shoulders. "Tell me a bit about yourself."

"I'm thirty years old, single, and I don't have any children." Trent leaned forward with his elbows on the table. "I modeled when I was younger before drifting into acting. That's why I'm here in Dearston. A friend of mine is producing a play that he wrote. I promised to help out."

Alisa watched his long fingers touch his coffee cup handle. They were expressive hands. He caressed the handle with unconscious grace. A shiver went through her as she thought of what it would feel like to have those same fingers touch her. Her mouth went dry. Trent was a very masculine man, and he oozed sex appeal.

"What about you?" Trent's voice was a lazy drawl that sent a tremor through her.

"I'm thirty-six, happily married for eleven years and have one son." Alisa hesitated for a second. This man was going to share her bed and house. She needed to be completely honest. "I grew up rich and sheltered, and my husband has continued to treat me that way. I'm bored and even though I've tried to get involved in the family business, my husband refuses to give me a job."

"So you're doing this to get back at your husband?" Trent's voice was doubtful. "There must be more conventional ways to do that."

"I'm doing this to prove to him that I've changed." Alisa's voice was firm. "I'm capable of running a business."

"And experimenting with sex is a way to show that?" Trent tilted his head. "It's a stretch. A part of me understands your motivation."

"Why are you willing to do this?" Alisa cleared her throat. "A man with your talent and looks shouldn't have a problem finding a place to live. Why would you tie yourself to an arrangement that includes sex?"

Trent shrugged. "The idea was intriguing. Now that I've seen you, I'm even more interested."

"Are you flirting with me?"

"You're a very attractive woman." Trent's voice was low, sending multiple shivers up her spine. "I find it hard to believe your husband would want to share you."

Alisa grimaced. "He dared me to arrange a threesome. He thinks I'm too strait-laced to experiment."

"You know differently."

"I'm not the girl he married." Alisa took a sip of coffee. "I should also tell you that I think my husband is expecting me to find a woman, not a man, to complete his fantasy."

Trent leaned closer. "Now that is exciting. A woman who takes control."

"Are you still willing?" Alisa could see the dark rim around Trent's electric-blue eyes. She didn't look away.

"I don't have a problem competing with another man for something I want." Trent's gaze was steady. "I very much want you."

Alisa could have drowned in the desire she saw in Trent's eyes. Instead, she forced herself to look away. This man was dangerous. He knew every erotic button to push, and he didn't pull any punches. She usually walked away from men like him. Not this time. Henry had given her permission to find a partner. She was determined to get exactly what she needed.

She wanted Trent Jackson.

Alisa cleared her throat. "You're very direct."

"I thought that was why we agreed to meet." Trent reached over and clasped her hand. "If there wasn't any chemistry between us, I would have walked away."

Alisa nodded. "I'm attracted to you also."

Trent's thumb traced a pattern over her hand. Her stomach tightened and excitement settled in her womb. Her breath caught in her throat as she realized that not even Henry had this effect on her. The two men were polar opposites in character and that added to the attraction.

Things were moving fast.

She had no intention of putting the brakes on.

For the first time in her life she was going to do something just because it felt good. Wasn't that what having a sexual adventure was all about? Exploring taboos and letting your desires lead you?

Alisa pulled her hand away. "I think we're going to get along very nicely."

Trent tapped the table. "Is that a yes?"

"You know it is." Alisa drained her coffee and pushed the mug away. "Would you like to see where I live?"

Trent stood. "I thought you'd never ask."

Chapter 5

When they pulled into her driveway, Alisa parked in front of the garage, and waited as Trent parked beside her. He was driving a red truck. Before she could shut her engine off, he was already out of his vehicle and leaning against the front of it.

"You live in a nice neighborhood." Trent looked around with satisfaction.

"We bought this when we were first married." Alisa scanned the large Tudor styled mansion and felt a sense of satisfaction. "It reminded my husband of his family cottage."

Trent whistled. "His family must have had money."

"They lost it all." Alisa shook her head. "Most men would be bitter. Not Henry. He put himself through university, and he runs my father's company now. He's a whiz at business, and he could have built his own empire. Instead, he gave my father the son he never had."

"It sounds like you love your husband." Trent's eyes were soft.

"From the first moment I saw him." Alisa shut her car door. "I don't doubt his love for me. I just need him to stop thinking I'm still a girl who needs protection."

"You're definitely a woman." Trent followed her toward the garage. "Your husband is a lucky man."

Alisa sorted through the keys on her chain until she found the one to the apartment above the garage. She unlocked the door and motioned for Trent to go ahead of her. She could be risking everything with this man. He came with recommendations from Lara's friend, and she had to trust that. She was going to let him into her life. It wouldn't be too difficult to let him into her heart too.

The upstairs opened into a two bedroom apartment. The place hadn't been used for a while and there was the distinct smell of disuse. Turning the air conditioner on and opening windows would dispel that. Alisa unfastened the side windows that were attached to a bay window in the living area.

"We had the place renovated a couple of years ago for my son's nanny." Alisa went into the kitchen and opened the window over the sink, and then she opened the French doors off of the dining room. "This area is private from the house, so you don't have to worry about anyone watching you."

Trent followed her out onto the deck. "This is nicer than what I'm used to. Are you certain you don't want any money for it?"

"Positive." Alisa leaned over the railing and gazed into the wooded ravine that edged the house's property. "I'm a woman who treasures my friends."

"We don't know each other yet."

"I like to think that if I'm having sex with someone, then it's within the confines of a relationship."

Trent shook his head. "Your husband's right. You're old fashioned."

"Because I develop friendships?" Alisa raised her eyebrows. "Or is it because I'm considering the traditional meaning of ménage à trois, which described a domestic arrangement between people who lived in the same house and were sexually involved."

"As opposed to a threesome and a one-night stand?"

"Exactly." Alisa walked back into the apartment. "Is that going to be a problem for you?"

Trent glanced around the open-space living quarters. "Can I see the bedroom?"

"There are two."

Alisa led the way to a short hallway. There were two doorways on each side and a large bathroom with a separate shower and tub at the end. The bedrooms were spacious with walk-in closets. They were furnished with king-size beds, dressers, and a desk. The rooms were painted a delicate shade of beige, and except for different colored bedding and drapes, were exactly the same.

Trent inspected both rooms and the bathroom while Alisa waited in the living room. When he came back he was shaking his head. "This place is more than enough for me."

"I appreciate what you're going to be doing."

"You make it sound as if it'll be a hardship for me." Trent stood in front of her. "I find you a very attractive woman."

"You haven't met my husband yet." Alisa's heart beat quickened. "You might not want to stay."

"I'm a pretty reasonable guy." Trent reached a hand out to stroke down her arm. "Is he likely to be a problem?"

Alisa shrugged. "He doesn't know what I've planned."

"I promise to watch myself." Trent took a step closer. "You've gone to a lot of effort for this. Are you certain you want to go through with it?"

It was the moment of truth.

Alisa loved Henry with all her heart.

When she looked at Trent, her stomach did cartwheels. Excitement churned within her. A part of her wanted to fling herself into his arms and forget that she was a married women. It was different from what she felt for Henry. Her gut was telling her it was right.

"Remember I told you I fell in love with Henry the first moment I saw him."

Trent traced a finger down her cheek. "You don't have to explain. I know you love him and you don't have to sleep with me to get what you want. I could help you figure out another way."

Alisa inhaled a sharp breath. "You don't understand."

Trent frowned. "Continue."

"I felt drawn to you the moment you walked through the café door." Alisa touch Trent's mouth with a finger to stop him from speaking. "There's a connection. It's not the same way that I felt with Henry and yet I know it is right."

"So that's why you're willing to let me live here?"

"Yes." Alisa pulled her hand away from him. "I want to see where this goes. I think there's more here than a one night stand."

"Then you won't mind if I do this." Trent pulled her into his arms and brushed his lips across hers. "I've wanted to do that from the first moment I saw you."

Alisa shivered as a delicious spark of desire swept over her. Trent's tongue pressed against the seam of her mouth, and she moaned. His tongue darted into her mouth and slid against hers. She savored the taste of him. The world spun away as she lost herself in the sinful delight of being held in Trent's arms.

Sparks ignited.

Shivers of desire raced through her.

A deep hunger that she never knew she possessed took control. Alisa moved closer, letting her body mold with his, savoring the long length of his arousal pressed against her. She clung to him as need and longing burned through her. She lost track of time, letting passion replace reasoning. They were both gasping for breath when the kiss ended.

Trent continued to hold her in his arms.

His gaze never left hers.

A quiver went through her at the heated yearning she saw reflected deep within his eyes. He'd been as affected as she was by the kiss. It sounded crazy, but she wasn't prepared to walk away from this man. They were connected, and she wanted to see where it led.

"Are your instincts always so accurate?" Trent's voice was hoarse.

Alisa nodded. "Where people are concerned."

"I can't promise how long I'll stay."

Alisa rubbed her cheek against his chest. "Stay as long as you can. Just know that this is your home. I won't invade your privacy."

"What are the rules in your house?"

"All three of us will work that out." Alisa looked up at Trent. "Henry will be shocked. He loves me, and I know that he'll come around."

"You're one hell of a lady." Trent cleared his throat. "I don't know if I'd want to share you with someone else."

"If I understand the arrangement correctly, we'll be sharing each other."

"That we will." Trent kissed her forehead and then released her. "I can move my things in today."

"Great." Alisa pulled the key off her chain. "This is yours."

Trent took it and turned it around in his hand. "Do we get to share each other before I meet your husband?"

A surge of power raced through Alisa. For a second, she considered staying with Trent and living out a part of the fantasy. Her husband would see it as a betrayal. If this was going to work, she needed Henry to be in at the beginning. All of them meeting each other together before they settled their sleeping arrangements.

"It wouldn't be fair." Alisa didn't hide the regret in her voice. "I'll arrange a dinner on Saturday night, and then we'll all get to know each other."

Trent exhaled. "Two days. How am I supposed to sleep knowing you're a few steps away?"

Alisa ran her hand up his firm, muscular chest. "Denial is a powerful aphrodisiac."

A tremor went through Trent. "You're getting a thrill out of this."

"I thought enjoyment was the point." Alisa's hand caressed his chin. "I wouldn't want to spoil anything for you."

"Like I said before. You're one hell of a woman." Trent took a step away. "I just hope I'm up to what you have planned over the next few weeks."

Alisa glanced down at Trent's crotch where his arousal was obvious. "I don't think you'll have a problem."

Chapter 6

Alisa sat in bed with a book in her hands. She'd been waiting for Henry to come home since dinner time. She'd finally given up and went to bed. Sleep refused to come. Her book remained unread because all she could think of was Henry's reaction when she told him they had a guest staying in the garage apartment.

A flicker of light danced on the bedroom wall, and she recognized it as headlights. There was the sound of car doors slamming, and then a vehicle driving away. Henry was home. Her heart started pounding a furious tattoo in her chest, and her fingers gripped the book tighter.

The moment of reckoning had come.

Footsteps sounded on the stairs and the bedroom door opened. Henry threw his suitcase and suit jacket on a chair before he walked over to her. He looked exhausted. He bent and gave her a quick kiss on the cheek.

"I need a shower." He undid his tie and pulled it off his neck. "The plane was late taking off. There was some kind of security blunder, and we were waiting on the tarmac for a couple of hours."

Alisa put her book on the bedside table and sat up. "I was beginning to worry."

"Air travel is still the safest." Henry kicked off his shoes. "How was your week?"

Alisa pulled her knees up to her chest and wrapped her arms around them. Henry hated to talk about anything serious after a business trip. It was an unwritten rule that it was best for her to wait until the morning before starting a discussion. Tonight he looked more exhausted than usual. She was hesitant to broach the subject of Trent.

"Go get your shower." Alisa kept her voice causal. "We'll have plenty of time to catch up after that."

Henry raised an eyebrow. "That sounds ominous."

Alisa shook her head. "I had a wonderful week."

"It had to be better than mine."

Henry finished undressing and walked into the bathroom. A few seconds later she heard the shower start. Her husband was a creature of habit and after eleven years of marriage, Alisa knew how to handle him. After he'd showered and just before he fell asleep, she'd whisper to him that they'd talk in the morning.

She worried her lower lip with her teeth. Waiting until morning was best. It would be Saturday and even though he'd probably planned a golf game, he'd have enough time to listen to her. She'd make him listen.

Tomorrow night she was introducing the two men at dinner.

When Henry came to bed, Alisa snuggled close. Her husband fell asleep almost immediately. Alisa forced her breathing to steady. One more night wasn't going to change her news. Patience had never been her strong point because she'd never had to wait for anything. This was different. As much as Henry doubted her ability to follow through with his request, she wanted to see the expression on his face when she told him what she'd done.

The sun had barely reached the horizon when Alisa opened her eyes. Her body was tense with trepidation. Today was the day everything would change in her marriage. It was time to tell Henry. She snuggled close and kissed his ear. Henry groaned and tried to move away. She moved lower and kissed his neck.

"It's too early to wake up."

"It's morning." Alisa whispered. "I have news."

Henry stiffened. "How bad is it? Nothing has happened to Bert?"

"I would have phoned you if something had happened to our son." Alisa rubbed her hand down his arm. "This is about us."

Henry relaxed and turned onto his back. "Couldn't you wait until I woke up?"

"This is important." Alisa laid her head on his chest. "I'm too excited to wait."

"I spent last week running from meeting to meeting." Henry pulled a pillow over his head. "At least let me sleep in on Saturday."

Alisa moved away from him. "Don't you have a golf game planned?"

"Not until ten." Henry flipped back onto his side. "Wake me at nine."

Alisa got out of bed and grabbed her robe. She slipped it on before heading to the bathroom. "Don't be surprised if you find someone else waiting with me when you get back."

"What are you talking about?"

"I arranged for us to have a threesome this evening." Alisa walked into the bathroom and waited. When Henry didn't follow her, she showered. If he wasn't interested now, he would be tonight.

She walked into the bedroom, and Henry was sitting up in bed with his hands behind his head. The sheets were tented from his arousal.

"Look at what you've done."

"I thought you weren't interested in anything I had to say."

Henry pulled the sheets back and patted the mattress beside him. "I'm always keen to hear your stories. This one is a doozy. You have my attention."

Alisa tilted her head. "You don't believe me?"

"Not for a second." Henry winked at her. "You know how to bring me to attention."

Alisa glanced down at his erection. "Is that for me?"

"You know it is."

Alisa pursed her lips to stop from smiling. Henry thought she was joking about the threesome. What did it matter? Right now, he was aroused and ready to go. There was no point in arguing over the truth. He'd find out soon enough. She dropped her towel.

Henry inhaled. "You're beautiful, woman. Come here."

Alisa took a slow step forward. "Why?"

"So I can love you." Henry's voice was a husky whisper. "Don't make me beg."

"Would you?" Alisa released her hair from its loose tie and shook her head.

"You know it." Henry's eyes didn't leave her.

She stroked a hand down her side and took another step closer to the bed. "It has been a week."

"Did you touch yourself?"

Alisa shook her head. "Did you?"

"Every time we talked on the phone. That's all I did." Henry ran his hand up his penis. "You're the only one who can satisfy me."

Alisa pouted and took another step forward. "You weren't interested earlier. I thought you were too tired."

"I'm a fool." Henry's gaze sent a wave of heat through her.

Alisa put a knee on the bed and leaned closer to her husband. "Apologize."

"Get in this bed and let me show you how sorry I am." Henry's voice was a growl.

Alisa leaned back and let her fingers brush across her breasts. "Promise to make it worthwhile?"

A tremor went through Henry. "Always."

Moist heat filled Alisa, and she couldn't tease him any longer. She needed to feel her husband's body close and taste his kisses. She leaned forward and captured his mouth. He wrapped his arms around her and pulled her into the bed.

The kiss grew hotter.

Her need grew greater.

Henry's hunger was all encompassing. It had been a week, and he was making up for lost time. His tongue stroked against hers, sending shivers of delight throughout her body. The kiss teased and aroused until she was on fire. She squirmed in his arms until he pushed her onto her back and took control.

His lips roamed over her neck and moved to her breasts, while his fingers traced her inner thighs and eased between her legs. He found her clitoris and caressed her to the verge of climax. His tongue brushed the tip of one of her nipples before he took it between his lips and sucked. A shot of electric tension rippled through her. He didn't relent.

He teased and stroked her at the screaming brink of release.

It was a familiar and pleasurable love play.

Only when she was writhing with need, did he enter her. It was almost too much. Still, he didn't let her climax. He thrust deep within her with an easy, steady pace that kept her riding the wave of pleasurable sensations. His stamina had always been great, and this morning it was no different.

She looked up at Henry, noting the sweat that beaded on his forehead and she marveled at how well he knew her body. He edged her for what seemed like hours before he quickened his pace and deepened his penetration. They were both panting and hot for release by the time he pushed her over the precipice and followed her down the spiral of delicious orgasm.

He collapsed on to her.

It was several seconds before either of them was able to speak.

"Did I apologize enough?" Henry was panting for breath.

"That was fantastic." Alisa eased onto her side, stroking a finger across Henry's cheek. "You should go away more often."

"I would miss you too much." Henry turned onto his back.

Alisa kissed his cheek. "I love you Henry. Don't ever forget that."

"You make it sounds as if you're leaving." Henry turned to look at her. There was a question in his eyes. "Is there something wrong?"

Alisa shook her head. "I just want you to know that everything I do is because I love you."

He gave her a lazy smile. "You're a loyal wife and fantastic mother. You could never do anything that would hurt our family."

Tears pricked Alisa's eyes. "I might surprise you."

Henry leaned over and gave her a quick kiss. "I doubt it."

Alisa struggled with the words to tell her husband that she hadn't been teasing when she'd said that she'd arranged a threesome. Henry knew her well. She would never upset her family. Arranging for Trent to live with them wasn't harmful. It was going to shake up their lives. There was nothing wrong with familiarity, but a bit of variety was exciting.

Before she could say anything, Henry sat up. "Is that really the time? I've got to get ready for my golf game."

Henry climbed over her and headed to the bathroom. "Could you make me a quick breakfast?"

He shut the door. Alisa sat up and pulled on a pair of pants and top. There was no point in coming between Henry and his Saturday morning ritual. She went downstairs and put on a pot of coffee before making omelets.

Henry was dressed in cotton slacks and a green polo shirt when he came into the kitchen fifteen minutes later. His hair was still damp from the shower, and he smelled of spice cologne. She inhaled the scent and smiled. This was a scene that was familiar. A wave of happiness filled her. This would be the last time she'd enjoy this particular moment with her husband. After tonight, everything would change.

"I'm having a special dinner tonight."

Henry raised his eyebrows. "Company?"

Alisa shook her head. "Just us."

"What's the occasion?" Henry sat at the large island in the center of the kitchen. "I didn't forget an anniversary or birthday?"

"We're celebrating us and our marriage." Alisa leaned on the island and looked at him. "We were lucky to find each other, and I never want to take that for granted."

"Why do I sense you aren't saying what you mean?" Henry took a mouthful of omelet.

"Tonight is the start of a new beginning." Alisa's voice was low.

Henry finished his breakfast and pushed his plate away. His gaze never left hers as he brought his coffee cup up to his lips. He took a couple of sips before putting the cup down. "Have you been reading a new self-help book?"

"Nothing like that." Alisa picked up his empty plate. "Just don't be late for dinner."

Henry shrugged. "I've some things to do at the office. I'll be home for five."

"Great." She kissed him and walked with him to the door. "I'll be waiting."

Henry gave her another searching look before looking at his watch. "I'm going to be late."

Alisa stood on the porch and watched him drive away. Her eyes glanced over to the garage, and she shivered. Henry might think it was a normal dinner. He would be surprised. She had tried to warn him, and he hadn't been willing to listen. In his mind, she was the girl she'd been when he'd married her. He couldn't or wouldn't see that she'd changed.

Tonight he would learn otherwise.

Tonight she was introducing him to Trent.

Chapter 7

Alisa lit the last of the candles and blew out the match.

The sun was low in the sky, and even though Henry had promised to be home by five, she knew better. It was already past six and he wasn't home yet. She'd set the dinner up on the patio at the rear of the house. Everything was ready for a romantic evening. Trent was scheduled to arrive at seven-thirty.

She heard the front door open and took one last look at the table and patio before going to meet Henry. He looked exhausted and overworked. If only he'd let her carry some of the load, but he refused to let her help. All she could do was show him that she needed something more from life.

Henry gave her a whistle as he walked into the hallway. "You're dressed fancy tonight."

"Did you forget I planned a special dinner?" Alisa twirled around in her little red cocktail dress. She'd bought it especially for this evening. It had cost a fortune and was worth every penny. You only lose your threesome virginity once.

Henry hit his forehead. "It slipped my mind. I'll go and change."

Alisa gave him a kiss. "Dinner is ready. Hurry and get a shower."

"You're pulling out all the stops."

"Tonight is special" When Henry raised an eyebrow, she continued. "You'll understand at dinner."

Henry shrugged and then ran up the stairs.

Alisa was waiting for him in the kitchen when he came down a half hour later. He was showered, shaved, and dressed in dress pants and a short-sleeved shirt that was open at the neck. Her heart twisted with pride. He was a handsome man. Her fingers were crossed that he'd be open to what she had planned this evening.

She was serving an exquisite beef tenderloin stroganoff with Caesar salad. The stroganoff was already on the patio in a heated serving dish. All she had to do was bring in the salad and wine. She handed the bottle of Cabernet Sauvignon to Henry and mixed the salad before heading out the kitchen French doors. Henry picked up the cork screw and followed her. When they reached the table, he paused.

"The table is set for three." He pulled the cork out of the bottle. "I thought you said we weren't having company."

Alisa put the salad on the table just as Trent walked in from the side garden. He was dressed in casual pants and shirt, much like Henry. His hair was neatly combed and fell in a natural wave to his collar. He carried a vase of flowers. When he reached the table he handed the flowers to Alisa. She sniffed the arrangement of yellow roses and white lilies, inhaling the heavenly scent before placing them on the table.

"Trent isn't company." Alisa took Trent's arm and led him over to Henry. "He's part of the family."

Henry's eyes widened. "Is he a long forgotten cousin?"

Alisa shook her head. "Nothing so dramatic. Trent is the man who's agreed to be part of our ménage à trois."

Henry would have dropped the wine bottle if Alisa hadn't taken it from his numb fingers. She'd expected him to react. Going into shock wasn't one of the scenarios that had played through her mind. She handed Trent the bottle and led Henry to his seat at the table. Trent poured out the wine and took the seat Alisa pointed out to him.

"I did try and tell you this morning. You weren't in the mood to listen."

"I thought you were kidding." Henry's voice was a low whisper.

"I realized that." Alisa handed the salad bowl to Trent. "That's why I've arranged this dinner so we can all get to know each other."

Henry pushed away from the table. "I can't do this."

Alisa put a hand on his arm. "Stay. All I'm asking is for us to enjoy the meal I've prepared."

Henry hesitated before pushing his chair back to the table. "You deliberately misunderstood my meaning about experimentation."

Alisa took the salad from Trent and put some on her plate. "I understood what you wanted. It's not about you. You said I had free reign before you left for New York."

"I thought you knew I was joking." Henry's voice sounded strangled.

"I was serious." Alisa's voice was firm. She knew that Henry was in shock so she wasn't going to debate semantics with him right now. "We have a guest. Let me introduce you."

"Trent, this is my husband, Henry."

Trent reached a hand across and shook Henry's hand. "I can see I'm a bit of a shock. If it helps any, I've never been in a situation quite like this."

"You mean you don't regularly participate in threesomes?" Henry's voice was sarcastic.

Trent gave a sheepish grin. "I've been involved with two women before, but they approached me. I've never been with a woman and man, especially not a married couple."

"Are you a male prostitute?"

Alisa gasped. "I know you've been taken by surprise, but that's no reason to be insulting. Trent is employed and our tenant. He's staying in the apartment above the garage."

Henry put the salad bowl down with a bang. "Is there anything about my life that's the same?"

"I still love you." Alisa straightened her shoulders. "You've been ignoring my requests for change ever since Bert went to boarding school. You proposed the threesome and I've run with that."

Henry rolled his eyes. "I suggested gardening. You didn't do that."

Alisa grinned. "This sounded like more fun."

Trent threw his head back and laughed. "Henry, I admire your wife. She's quite the woman."

"You think this is funny?" Henry almost choked on the romaine lettuce. "I'm away on business and when I come home everything is topsy turvey."

"Your wife has taken your staid life and infused it with excitement." Trent kept his voice calm. "This could be a situation straight out of the movies."

"Nobody wants to live inside a movie script." Henry took a stab at a crouton on his plate. "I just want my home back to normal."

"You don't know that until you've tried something different." Alisa took a sip of the red wine she'd chosen for the meal. "I think this is the beginning of a beautiful relationship."

Henry threw his fork down. "You can't expect me to be pleased by the fact that you want to sleep with another man."

"Why not?" Alisa kept her voice calm. "You wanted me to watch you sleep with another woman."

"That's different." Exasperation filled Henry's voice. "Men have fantasies like that. It doesn't mean they act on them."

"Women have fantasies too." Alisa crossed her arms over her chest. "You said you wanted me to think about a threesome and then dared me to arrange it."

Henry pointed at Trent. "This isn't what I meant."

"You made the mistake of thinking I wasn't anything like my father." Alisa continued to speak to Henry as she reached over and clasped Trent's hand. "You're wrong. I might allow most things to slide, but not a taunt. Especially when it's my husband who thinks he knows me better than I know myself."

Trent raised her hand to his mouth and kissed it. "You have to love a woman with a mind of her own."

Henry leaned back in his chair and stared at the two of their clasped hands for several seconds before looking at Alisa. "Did I actually say something so priggish and arrogant?"

Alisa nodded. "You did, and more than once."

Henry groaned. "What a fool I was. I'm sorry."

"I accept your apology. That doesn't change my plans." Alisa reached over and took Henry's hand in her free one. "Trent is special. I want this to work out."

"What about diseases?" Henry's voice was deep with concern. "You can't expect me to let someone into our lives without making sure there won't be repercussions."

"Trent had tests done this week and there are no concerns." Alisa's voice was matter of fact. "I had to show Trent proof that we both have a clean bill of health, and that I'm on birth control."

Henry turned her hand in his and nodded. "I can see you're serious."

"Good. Now let's enjoy the meal and get to know each other." Alisa released the men's hands and picked up her fork. "I hope you like stroganoff, Trent. It's Henry's favorite."

"It smells delicious." Trent took a bite of salad. "It's been a while since I've been served a home-cooked meal."

Henry cleared his throat. "What do you do for a living?"

"I'm an actor right now." Trent shrugged. "I started out modeling in my late teens and when the jobs dried up, I changed careers. I've been acting for the last couple of years."

"Dearston is not the place to further your career."

"A friend of mine is producing a script he wrote, and I promised him I'd play the lead."

"So you're in town for a few weeks."

Henry's tone was neutral and Alisa recognized it as the voice he used to interrogate potential job applicants. She didn't put a stop to his questions. Trent seemed willing to answer, so she relaxed. Maybe this would help Henry accept Trent quicker. At least he wasn't screaming and throwing things.

"Carlos has me here for rehearsals. The play should begin in a couple of months." Trent shrugged. "Productions like this can be plagued with delays."

"So it's not set in stone." Henry nodded. "What theater are you going to be performing at?"

"The Charles Street Playhouse."

"That's a pretty high-profile place. Your friend must have some big connections."

Trent nodded. "What do you do Henry?"

"I'm CEO of Fairman's Hotels." Henry pointed at Alisa. "My wife's father left me in charge after his death."

Trent's eyebrow rose. "I had no idea."

"Alisa didn't tell you that she's Albert Fairman's daughter?"

"Not a word." Trent picked up his glass and gave her a silent toast. "That's why you said you were your father's daughter."

Alisa's face heated from the compliment. She hadn't wanted Trent to know her background in case he used it against her. Now that he and Henry had met, it seemed ridiculous to keep secrets. She pushed back from the table and stacked the empty salad plates. She filled plates with the main course and handed them out. When everyone had been served, she sat down.

Trent waited until she was seated before tasting the food. "This is delicious."

Henry nodded. "Alisa is a fantastic cook."

"Thank you." Alisa took a sip of wine before eating.

The rest of the meal progressed in small talk. Henry was on his second glass of wine before he started to relax. She left him on the patio and then she gathered the empty dishes and took them to the kitchen. She had started loading the dishwasher when Trent followed her in with the leftover food. He put everything on the island and then pulled her close.

"I think you deserve a reward for such a sumptuous meal."

Alisa eased back in his arms and looked up at him. "What might that be?"

Henry cleared his throat from behind.

"Am I interrupting?" Henry's voice was tinged with anger.

Chapter 8

"Are you two having an affair?" Henry's words were an accusation.

"No!" Both Alisa and Trent spoke at the same time.

"I just wanted to give your wife a hug." Trent dropped his arms from around Alisa's waist. "It was a wonderful meal."

Henry watched both of them with narrowed eyes. Alisa sensed his uncertainty, and she could understand it. If she'd walked in on him, with his arms around another woman, she would have been livid. This was no different. The problem was that the kind of relationship they were going to start wouldn't allow for jealousy or doubts.

Alisa went to Henry and rubbed her hand across his cheek. "I love you Henry. I met Trent this week, and he moved in two days ago. The only contact we've had is tonight, and the day he moved in."

Henry's gaze didn't leave her face. "What kind of contact."

"A kiss." Alisa's voice was low. "If there was no chemistry between us, there wasn't any point to pursue the relationship."

Trent cleared his throat. "I find your wife very attractive, but I would never overstep the boundaries."

"The very nature of a threesome is stepping over a line." Henry's voice was doubtful.

"It doesn't have to be."

Alisa gave her husband a deep, arousing kiss. She let her hands wander over his chest and down his abdomen before grinding her hips against him. She turned to Trent and kissed him in the same manner. By the end of the kisses she craved more. She couldn't risk moving too quickly. Henry had to be ready.

"I have enough love for two men." She turned to Henry. "Can you share me with another man?"

"I don't know." Henry shook his head. "This wasn't what I envisioned when I suggested a threesome."

"Thank you for being truthful." Alisa took both of the men's hands. "The only way this will work is if we're completely honest with each other."

"What about you, Trent?" Henry looked over at the other man. "Can you walk away from this when it's over?"

"I don't know." Trent lifted Alisa's hand to his mouth. "The more I get to know your wife, the deeper I fall."

"So are we talking about a permanent relationship?" Henry struggled to get the words out.

Alisa shrugged and dropped both of their hands. She picked up another bottle of wine and led the way out to the patio. "It's too early to put limits or conditions on this relationship. I love you Henry. Nothing is ever going to change that."

"I love you too."

"You were the one looking for change." Alisa pushed Henry into his chair and handed him his glass of wine. "That's the only reason you suggested we try a ménage."

"I was jesting."

"I'm asking you to be honest." Alisa and Trent both sat. "Why a threesome?"

Henry sipped his wine and looked out over the garden. It was several seconds before he finally turned back to her. "I'm away so often, that I didn't want you looking for another man. You have a healthy sexual appetite, and I was afraid you'd find someone else now that Bert is at boarding school."

Alisa pushed away her shock. She had never once considered cheating on her husband. He and Bert were her whole world. To think that Henry had worried about such a possibility sent her mind spinning.

"I was bored." Alisa admitted. "I was thinking of a job, not an affair."

"You don't need to work." Henry grimaced. "I put in long hours to make certain all of your investments remain intact. In fact, this past week I was finalizing a merger between Fairman's and Milton Hotels. I wanted it to be a surprise."

"Is that why you've been away so often?" Alisa could have kicked herself. "I thought you were having an affair."

"Never." Henry's voice shook with shock.

"It seems you two should talk more often." Trent's voice was dry. "Are you sure you want me here for this?"

"Definitely." Alisa reached over and squeezed Trent's hand. "You need to know what you're getting into."

"I have a pretty clear picture." Trent sipped his wine. "The question is do you still want me?"

"I do." Alisa turned to her husband. "If Henry was honest, so does he. He wouldn't have suggested this type of relationship otherwise."

"That's one of the problems with being married as long as we have. You can read each other's thoughts." Henry's lips turned up in a smile. "Stay Trent... at least for tonight. We'll explore where this goes."

They all raised their glasses in a toast. "To us."

Alisa sent Henry back into the house for another bottle and to turn some music on. The sun was setting and the candles she had lit on the table and around the patio planters were their only light. She leaned back in her chair and smiled at Trent.

"Having you here with us makes me happy."

"I'm glad." Trent stretched his legs out in front of him. "I like your husband."

Alisa giggled. "That makes two of us."

"You'd better." Henry put the open bottle of wine on the table and plugged in the portable speakers so that the music from the sound system in the house was audible outside. "Don't get too tipsy. I'd hate for you to forget the evening."

"I could never do that." Alisa stood and took her husband's hand. "Let's dance."

Henry took her in his arms and together they swayed to the soft rhythm of the song. The wine had relaxed her. The worry of her husband accepting the arrangement was lifted. All she wanted to do was enjoy the music and feel loving arms around her.

When the song ended, Trent tapped Henry on the shoulder and took his place. She let him lead her in a sensual dance that had their bodies touching and swaying together. Excitement stirred within her, and she let herself enjoy it. There was no guilt even though she was getting aroused by another man.

Henry stepped in for the next dance. He held her close enough that she could feel his erection, and then he nuzzled her neck. Sizzling sparks ignited, and she held on tighter. Henry's mouth captured her, his kisses demanding. His tongue dueled with her, and she was oblivious to everything else.

The tap on his shoulder was a surprise. A new song had started, and Trent gathered her close. He held the back of her head as his lips descended on hers. There was a brief caress and then it was hot hunger. He ground his hips into hers, letting her feel his arousal as they moved to the rhythmic beat of the music. By the time Henry cut in, she was out of breath.

Henry's hand caressed down her back and rested on her butt. He squeezed and kneaded while he nipped at her lower lip and tongue. He moved away from her mouth and brushed his lips across her eyes. She melted. His breath tickled her skin and every touch of his lips sent a jolt of sensation through her body. She was a pulsing nerve of need by the time the dance ended.

"Perhaps we should continue this upstairs?"

Alisa nodded. "I've set up the guest bedroom for us."

Henry leaned close and whispered in her ear. "Thank you for keeping the master bedroom just for us two."

"I know you better than you think."

Henry guided her back to the table. Trent had already blown the candles out and turned off the speakers. The only thing left was to enjoy the rest of the night in the arms of her husband and their new partner. The two men held her close, one on each side, as they moved to the downstairs guestroom.

Candles had been spread across all of the dressers and tables. She handed Henry the lighter and watched while he set each candle aglow. Soft flickering light was the perfect romantic backdrop for this evening. For the first time since she'd set out on this journey, the enormity of what she was going to do hit her.

She hadn't had sex with a new partner since she'd met Henry fifteen years ago.

She'd never had sex with two men at once or even dreamed of it.

Tonight she was going to do both.

Flutters of excitement and trepidation filled her stomach. Trent must have sensed her unease because he held her closer and kissed the top of her head. When Henry had finished lighting the candles, he switched on some soft music and then came back to stand in front of them. She could see the unease in his eyes.

"This is new for all of us." Trent's voice was a hoarse whisper. "The slower we take it the better."

Alisa nodded and went to the bed. She threw back the coverings before unzipping her red dress and letting it fall to the floor. She was wearing a sexy red bra, silk panties, a garter belt that held up silk nylons, and a pair of red stilettoes. The men's eyes widened, and they both took a deep breath. Alisa stepped out of her dress and put it on a chair.

She'd gotten their attention.

The next move was up to them.

Henry gave a low whistle. "You're trying to seduce us."

"It's working." Trent unbuttoned his shirt and dropped it to the ground. "It's every man for himself."

Henry ripped his shirt open and kicked his shoes off. His pants were next. Both men were undressed and standing in front of her naked before she had a chance to move. They were very aroused, and she inhaled a quick breath as she looked at them. Trent was muscular and lean. He was taller and larger than Henry as evident in the size and breadth of his erection. Henry was no slouch either. He worked out regularly, and even though he was smaller in stature than Trent, she'd never had any reason to complain.

She walked to them with deliberately slow steps, letting the tension in the room rise to a breaking point. When she reached them, she stopped and let her eyes roam over them before taking each man's penis in her hands. A swift up and down motion resulted in labored breathing from both of them as they shuddered in unison.

"I guess I am woman enough for two men." Alisa's voice was seductive. She held both men in her hands and shivered with excitement as she felt them pulse with need.

Henry was the first to touch her. His hand covered one breast, and he fondled it before pushing beneath the bra. "Is this necessary?"

Alisa shrugged. "You can take it off."

She gave them one last tease with her fingers before releasing them. Trent brushed a finger across the silk of her bra and then reached for the clasp in front. He flicked his wrist and it was undone. She shrugged her shoulders so that the flimsy material fell to the ground.

"You are so beautiful." Trent filled his hand with one of her breasts. "There's more than enough for two men to enjoy."

"I suppose I've been greedy." Henry's voice cracked.

Trent's thumb brought her nipple to a peak. "You've been lucky."

Henry feathered a finger across her other breast and then captured her mouth in a searing kiss. Hunger and passion were in each tantalizing twist of his tongue with hers. Alisa shuddered. It had been years since Henry had kissed her like that, and she moaned with heightened pleasure. As Henry kissed, Trent, stroked and caressed her other breast.

Heat settled in her.

She squirmed with arousal.

Trent moved his hand beneath her silk panties and pressed past her folds until his hand rested on her inner core. His palm rubbed as his finger dipped into her wet vagina. She trembled at the jolt of sensation that ripped through her body. Trent kept his arm around her waist as he stroked and caressed her until the tension burst into flames.

She shuddered with climax in the arms of two men.

Trent didn't release her. He continued to stroke and excite her to new heights. Henry ended the kiss, and she turned to Trent, running her tongue across his lips. He opened for her and sent his tongue plunging into her mouth. She sucked and nipped, letting her mounting passion take control.

Henry whispered in her ear. "I love you."

Henry's mouth trailed down her neck and continued to her breast. His lips and tongue replaced his hand and he licked and sucked until she was panting for another release. Trent broke off their kiss and knelt in front of her. Henry's arm moved to her back and held her in place as Trent ripped her silken panties off her body.

He nuzzled his face into her folds and then his tongue licked and teased, building the spiral of delight until she shattered with another explosive release. She would have fallen if Henry hadn't held her. She turned to Henry and kissed him in gratitude for letting her invite Trent into their lives.

"Thank you both." Alisa pulled Trent up to his feet and then led the men to the bed. "I think it would be safer if we continued lying down."

"I thought you'd never ask." Henry's voice was deep with hunger as he settled on the mattress. He sat up high on the pillows. Alisa laid her head on his chest, luxuriating in his support. His fingers combed through her hair and sent tiny shivers of sensation down her scalp.

Trent climbed up on her opposite side. He ran his hand up her nylon covered leg. "This is sexy as hell."

"So are you." Alisa pulled him close. "You're very generous too."

"It's my definition of an icebreaker." Trent's hand rubbed against her abdomen. "Ready for more?"

"Always." Alisa leaned forward and stroked down his penis. "It's my turn to play."

Trent groaned. "That's up to Henry."

"I'm a patient man." Henry stretched back and stroked his hand up and down his heavy erection. "Alisa knows I'm ready whenever she needs me."

"Good."

Alisa turned toward her husband and licked down his penis before taking him into her mouth. She sucked and twirled her tongue, massaging his testicles until he was shuddering. Only then did she release him, licking the tip of his penis. He was primed for climax, but she wasn't finished teasing him. They had all night.

Trent had leaned back on his arms to watch her.

"Ready?" Alisa's voice was low. "I'm hoping you have enough stamina for me."

Trent grinned. "Bring it on."

Alisa pushed him onto his back, and then she leaned over him. Her fingers stroked his firm pecs and abdomen, curling in the tight curls that covered his chest before moving lower. She inhaled a quick breath at the size of his erection. He was made for loving, and she was in the mood.

She clasped his penis in her hand and stroked down. He groaned. She stroked up and watched from half-closed eyes as his body tensed. She pressed her finger to the tip of his penis and edged him back from his release. When he relaxed, she positioned herself astride him and lowered herself onto him.

She eased herself down in a slow, steady motion until he filled her completely. She tilted her hips and pulled back before descending again. She felt hands on her hips, guiding her motion and thought it was Trent, but when she felt kisses feathered across her back, she knew Henry was joining them in their love making. A glow of happiness filled her.

Henry directed her rhythm in a steady pace until she found herself near the brink of climax again. She leaned back against her husband, letting him increase her pace. Henry's hands on her hips were replaced by Trent's as Henry reached around and caressed her clitoris, heightening the sensation of tension and need. She screamed her release a few seconds later.

Trent pushed her onto her back and took control.

Henry held her close in his arms as Trent thrust deep. She felt the spiral of tension begin again, this time shudders of sensation continued to splinter through her as Trent lunged deep and steady. Within seconds, Trent collapsed with his own release. He moved away and Henry eased her back against the pillows.

"My turn."

Alisa nodded.

Tiny shudders of ecstasy were still exploding within her when Henry drove into her. He set a familiar rhythm that continued to send shivers of delight throughout her body. Trent kissed her neck and shoulders, heightening her pleasure as Henry moved within her. She was boneless with satiation. Every thrust and withdrawal heightened her body's fulfillment. By the time Henry collapsed with his own release, she was exhausted from pleasure.

Henry eased away from her and moved to her side.

Trent pulled the covers up around them and snuggled close. Alisa was too tired to care. She turned on her side so that Henry could spoon her, and she rested her head on Trent's chest. She was asleep within seconds.

She awoke to someone stroking her clitoris.

Chapter 9

"I want more." Trent's whisper sent a shiver of arousal through her.

Alisa blinked her eyes and looked over at Henry. He was fast asleep. Trent's erection was hard against her leg. He was eager to please and be pleased. Wasn't this what she'd wanted? Excitement pulsed between her legs at the realization that two men meant having as much sex as she could handle.

"I'm all yours." Alisa moved onto her back and gave Trent access.

He leaned over her and brushed his mouth across hers. It was a slow, seductive caress and Alisa traced her hand across his neck and down his cheek. There was no hurrying their pleasure this time as tongues glided against each other and hands feathered sensations of delight across their skin.

Alisa savored the unhurried arousal, letting Trent set the pace as he stroked his fingers across her breasts and abdomen. The embers of the fire they had started earlier in the evening sparked to life until she was aching to feel him inside her. She stroked his long length and moved her legs apart for him to enter her.

He set a lazy rhythm, thrusting deep and sure.

The spiral of tension built until they were both straining for release.

Alisa felt a hand smooth her hair from her forehead and looked over at Henry. He was awake and watching. She reached for him and felt his erect penis. She gripped him and then was lost as Trent increased his stride, sending them both flying toward ecstasy. She surfaced from a bliss filled climax seconds later, to find that Henry had replaced Trent.

Her husband's lovemaking continued where Trent's had finished. She was riding the peak of pleasure within seconds and Henry's thrusts were fast and steady. She climaxed again as Henry pushed on to his own release. He collapsed on her with a moan and then rolled with her onto his side. She was still connected to him when he fell asleep.

Trent threw his arm around both of them and snuggled into her neck. "Is this what you envisioned?"

Alisa yawned. "Better. Thank you."

Trent kissed her ear. "I should warn you, I always wake up with a glorious erection."

"Promises, promises." Alisa was too exhausted to laugh.

"Pleasure and more pleasure." Trent moved his hips closer and sighed. "You're one special lady."

Sleep was swift and deep.

Alisa awoke to sunlight filtering through the slats in the window blinds and two men holding her close. She was replete with satiation and ached with renewed arousal. She didn't have a clue how that was possible after last night. She stretched her arms over her head and eased her body out from between the two men.

She needed coffee first.

She padded to the ensuite, slipped out of her garter and stockings, and put a robe on before going to the kitchen. She felt muscle twinges in places she didn't know existed. It was a pleasurable ache. She put the coffee pot on and finished filling the dishwasher from last night. By the time she was done, the coffee was ready. She poured a cup and sipped it until it had worked its way into her system. When she felt awake, she returned to the men with a tray of cups, cream, sugar, and an insulated carafe.

She was in generous mood.

After the pleasure they'd given her last night, they deserved to be spoiled.

The room was empty when she arrived. She put the tray down on a side table before opening the blinds. Their clothes were still on the floor in the piles they'd kicked them into. She bent and started sorting their things and folding them. It was only as she was shaking out her dress that she heard voices.

They were in the adjoining bathroom.

She put her dress over the back of a chair and peaked into the ensuite. There was a large tiled shower with glass walls and a door. It was large enough to fit six people. Now, two naked men were in it. Henry and Trent were showering together and they were laughing about something.

"Am I interrupting?"

Both men turned around at the sound of her voice. Trent winked and Henry gave her a sheepish grin. She recognized it as the same look her son Bert gave her when he'd been caught red handed. She couldn't prove it, but she'd bet they'd been talking about her. Two could play that game. She stepped into the room.

"What mischief are you up to?"

"We were rehashing last night." Trent didn't bother lying. She liked that.

"And washing away the evidence." Henry added.

"Is that good or bad?" Alisa raised an eyebrow.

"Definitely good." Henry's voice was firm.

"Why don't you join us?" Trent turned so she could see his front. He tugged at his half aroused penis. "I'm sure you'd like to come and play with the boys."

Alisa glanced at Henry for his reaction. He'd agreed to try a threesome for last night only. When he nodded, she dropped her robe to the floor and stepped into the shower. The water was hot and pulsing from the rainshower spout above their heads. Jets sprayed water on all sides, and for a few seconds she lingered as the water eased her soreness from the previous night.

The men moved aside and let her stand under the showerhead until she reached for the soap. That was their signal to start caressing her. They each took a bath scrubber full of suds and started to rub it across her body until she was lathered up, then their hands replaced the scrubber. They left no area untouched. Her skin tingled as their fingers moved between her legs and under her breasts.

Then they let her stand under the shower head again and continued to caress and brush her until the soap was gone. That's when their mouths replaced their hands. Henry kissed her neck and let his lips roam over her back. Trent caressed her breasts before kneeling and pressing his face against her mound. His tongue licked between her folds and sent a shiver of pleasure through her body.

He was a master at using his tongue.

He drove her wild.

She shook with need and if Henry hadn't held her tight in his arms she would have fallen. Only when she'd reached an exquisite climax did Trent stand and lean her against the tiles. He lifted her high and then position himself to enter her. He thrust deep and held himself tight within her as she exploded in another orgasm. That's when he began to move, sending shards of delight to every nerve ending in her body. She was panting with need by the time they both reached climax.

Trent eased away and let her slide down so that her feet were touching the floor of the shower. Henry brushed the wet strands of her hair away from her face and started to kiss her with a slow and seductive passion. Alisa was vaguely aware that Trent had finished showering and left them alone. Henry's kisses turned urgent. She was consumed by his need. She focused completely on her husband.

His hands caressed down the side of her body, and he pushed her thighs apart with his knees. His lips moved to her breasts. He kissed and sucked until she was frantic with renewed desire. Then he moved to her other breast and repeated his actions. Only when she could take no more did Henry lift her and position himself to enter.

He knew the exact moves and pace to set her body on fire. He continued to thrust and withdraw in a rhythm that had her on the screaming edge of ecstasy. His finger reached for her clitoris as he quickened his pace. The spiral of tension that had been built within them broke into delicious shudders of joy. Henry rocked his hips closer to wring the last shreds of pleasure from her body.

When they came back to earth, Henry was still holding her high against the shower tiles. His arms eased her down to the floor. He continued to hold her close. Together they stood under the shower head and soaped and rinsed themselves off. Henry held her with a tenderness she had never seen in him before.

She was protected and embraced by his love.

Never had she felt so close and intimate to her husband before.

"I love you." She turned in his arms so she was facing him. "Thank you for allowing last night to happen."

"How could I refuse you? You're the only woman I've ever loved." Henry kissed her forehead. "I want to give you pleasure always."

Their lips clung in one last lingering kiss before Henry stood away. "Time for us to dry off before we look like prunes."

Alisa stepped out of the shower and grabbed a towel. "What were the two of you laughing about?"

Henry wiped the steam off the vanity mirror and grinned back at her. "We were considering how likely it was that you'd be in the mood to satisfy both of us this morning."

Alisa gasped. "You were plotting together."

Henry laughed. "It worked."

Alisa rolled her eyes. "That was a given, considering how nicely you approached me."

Henry turned around to face her. "I can't remember ever enjoying a night so much. You were insatiable."

Alisa leaned up and kissed his chin. "So were you."

She picked up her robe and shrugged back into before she left the room. Trent was dressed and sitting in a chair with a cup of coffee. Alisa walked over to the carafe she'd brought into the room and filled a mug for herself before sitting on the bed.

"You make an excellent cup of coffee." Trent gave her a silent toast with his cup.

"You know how to make a shower interesting." Alisa took a sip of the hot brew and leaned back against the pillows. "You weren't kidding about pleasure in the morning."

"It's the only way to start the day." Trent stood and put his empty cup back on the tray. "I've got a meeting this morning."

Alisa glanced at the clock. "It's later than I thought."

Trent leaned over her and gave her a quick kiss. "I'd love to do this again. I'm not sure Henry is onboard."

"Give him time."

Alisa knew deep in her heart that she wanted to keep Trent in her life. She had to consider Henry's wishes. She loved him, and as much as she felt a connection to Trent, she couldn't ignore Henry's wishes. If he truly wanted to keep her happy, Henry would find a way to accept Trent in their lives. It would take some convincing.

"You know where to find me if you need me." Trent straightened up and left.

Henry came out of the bathroom a few minutes later. He had his towel wrapped around his waist. "I smell coffee."

"It's on the table."

Henry filled his cup and then sat on the bed beside her. "Trent has gone home?"

"He has a meeting today."

Alisa took another sip of coffee. She could sense the tension in Henry. Years of experience had taught her to be patient. He would tell her what was bothering him when he was ready. She leaned back on the pillows and waited.

"I've been thinking." Henry cleared his throat. "Last night was spectacular, but it can't happen again."

Chapter 10

"Alisa are you going to tell us what happened?" Lara pulled her crazy quilt block out of her bag.

"Tell us what?" Ella picked up a floral micro print and pinned a template to it.

"About her threesome." Brenna shook her head. "Don't you remember our last meeting? Alisa told us she was determined to find a man."

Alisa laughed. Their quilter's meeting was at Brenna's this week and Ella had been fifteen minutes late. They were in Brenna's studio sitting around her large cutting table. "Ella's too much in love to remember."

Ella blushed. "I didn't realize you were serious about following through with Henry's suggestion."

"Oh she was serious." Lara shook her head. "I met her at the Country Club, and we answered a personal ad together."

"Isn't that dangerous?" Ella's eyes widened. "There's no way to know who might answer."

"We did it just once." Alisa shivered as she remembered. "I was lucky Lara was with me."

"A man in a van showed up." Lara threaded her needle. "He grabbed Alisa."

"It was one of the scariest moments of my life." Alisa pinned two diamond pieces together. "He wouldn't let my arm go, and then two men jumped out of his van to help him."

"I hit him," Lara added.

"When I saw those men, I got a surge of energy and broke free." Alisa's voice shook. "We ran."

"They followed until some guys came out of the Country Club's gates." Lara shivered.

Brenna dropped her scissors. "We may never have heard from you again."

"It was scary." Alisa still remembered the horror of all the possible scenarios that had raced through her head. "I had visions of kidnapping and rape."

"The ad was specific for someone interested in groups." Lara started embroidering a daisy chain. "He said he was coming alone, so he lied. I don't think it would have ended well."

"I hope you stopped looking after that." Brenna bent down and picked up her scissors. "It was a crazy thing to do."

Alisa shrugged. "I didn't know where else to find someone."

"You could have hired someone." Ella looked up from her quilting. "That's what you tried to do for me."

"I felt the same way about it as you did. My self-esteem couldn't handle paying someone for sex." Alisa clenched her quilt pieces in her hand. "Even though it was only supposed to be for one night, I couldn't bring myself to do it. It seemed so impersonal."

"I agree." Brenna pinned her template to her fabric. "I hope you gave up the idea."

Alisa felt her cheeks heat up as she bit her lower lip. "Lara helped me find someone else."

"What!" Ella squealed.

"Who?" Brenna's voice was breathless.

"A friend of a furniture maker I work with." Lara leaned forward, and lowered her voice. "He needed a place to stay, and when I said he had to be sexually adventurous, Bryan, who makes the most beautiful custom tables, laughed. He said this guy would fit the bill perfectly."

"Now this is interesting." Brenna leaned back in her chair. "Did you meet him?"

Alisa nodded. "At the Coffee Bean Café. His name is Trent Jackson, and when he came outside to the patio, I knew right away he was the one."

"Did he have a sign on his forehead that said he was into threesomes?" Brenna's voice was dry.

"It was something in his stance." Alisa tried to pinpoint what it was exactly, but it was more of an instinct than anything else. "We talked for a bit, and then I showed him the apartment above our garage."

"So he was going to trade sex for rent?" Ella frowned.

"It sounds pretty horrible when you put it like that." Alisa smoothed out her diamond patch on the table. "He needed a place to stay, and there was an immediate connection between us. He said that if he hadn't been attracted to me, he wouldn't have agreed to the arrangement."

Brenna groaned. "Don't tell me your marriage is over too."

"Nothing like that." Alisa inhaled a steadying breath. "Henry and I are closer than ever."

"You didn't go through with it?" Lara questioned. "Good for you."

"Henry took a bit of convincing." Alisa hesitated. "In the end, he agreed to it."

"You slept with both of them?" Shock filled Ella's voice.

"I did." Alisa's heart was pounding after her confession. "It was the most spectacular evening of my life."

Brenna cleared her throat. "You and Henry are still married?"

Alisa nodded. "As crazy as it seems, it brought us closer together."

"We need details." Ella's didn't hide her curiosity. "Were both men with you all the time, or did Henry leave you alone with him?"

"We were together the whole night." Alisa shivered with the memory of the pleasure she'd experienced. "I slept in the arms of two men. I've never been so sexually satiated in my life."

"So what happens next?" Lara picked up her needle and continued with her embroidery. "Are you going to continue seeing Trent?"

"I want to."

"And Henry has agreed?" Brenna's tone was doubtful.

Alisa shook her head. "He said it couldn't happen again."

"There's your answer." Lara's voice was matter of fact. "You love your husband."

"I think he'll come around eventually."

"Why would you want to push Henry? You might lose him." Ella used a marker pen to trace around her template.

"The sex was over the top." Alisa's voice quivered. "Trent is a wonderfully generous lover."

"There's more to life than sex." Brenna put another cut triangle on the table.

"True, but it does make things fun." Lara winked at Alisa. "Why do you want to risk your marriage?"

"I really enjoyed the sense of power I had." Alisa struggled to find the right words to describe how she'd felt that night. "They treated me with care and consideration. I lost track of the number of orgasms I had. What I enjoyed most was being able to give both of them pleasure at the same time. That was a huge aphrodisiac."

There was silence after Alisa's confession.

Lara was the first to speak. "I can understand that. You're the one making the decisions."

"I was in complete control."

"That's the one thing Henry hasn't let you have in the business." Brenna's voice was musing. "In the bedroom, it's a different story."

Alisa nodded. "I love Henry and our sex life is great, but that was the first time I'd ever experienced that sense of supremacy."

"What are you going to suggest to Henry?" Lara knotted her thread. "Join a club that caters to willing partners?"

"I want Trent to become a part of our household so that we can have a ménage in the truest sense." Alisa straightened her shoulders.

Ella frowned. "What will you tell people?"

"Nobody else needs to know the private details of our sex life." Alisa took a couple of stitches in her fabric. "Trent can continue to live at the apartment."

"Will Henry let you sleep with Trent when he's away?" Lara started another daisy chain. "I imagine that is where things will go if you insist on pursuing this."

"Right now Henry doesn't want either of us to see Trent again." Alisa laughed. "I'm going to take it one step at a time."

Chapter 11

Alisa sipped her coffee and stared out the French doors overlooking the pool and patio. It had been five days since the evening she'd spent with Henry and Trent. Shivers of pleasure still shot through her when she remembered that night. No matter what she tried, Henry refused to discuss anything about Trent or their time together.

She heard Henry's approach.

She continued to sip her coffee.

He hugged her from behind and nuzzled her neck. "What are you thinking about?"

"Trent."

Henry tensed. "That subject is closed."

Alisa took another sip. "Not for me."

Henry dropped his arms and turned her to face him. "I did what you wanted. That's the end of it. Our life goes back to its regular routine now."

"I want a new normal."

Henry ran his hand through his hair. "That's not possible."

"Why?"

"We can't have another man living with us. You have to think about the business and our image."

"You never let me near the business, so why should that be my concern?"

Henry's nostril's flared. "Don't be obtuse. Fairman's is ours. If it goes down the toilet, so does our future and Bert's inheritance."

"You refuse to let me have a position in the company, and now you're going to use it against me?" Alisa shook her head. "We have enough money without Fairman's Hotels."

"Think about Bert." Henry's tone was harsh. "Our son deserves better."

"He needs love and parents who are happy."

"We were content." Henry went to the window. "At least until you demanded we invite Trent into our bedroom."

"It was your suggestion." Alisa put her coffee down on the table and walked over to her husband. "We were both searching for something, and I think we found it with Trent."

"I threw it out as a joke." Henry's voice was pained. "You were complaining about being bored, and I thought I could show you how absurd you were being."

Anger ripped through her. "You thought my feelings were ridiculous?"

"That's not what I meant." Exasperation filled Henry's voice. "I just wanted you to be happy. You have a beautiful home, a wonderful son, and a husband who loves you to distraction. That should be enough."

"You have all of those things too." Alisa squeezed Henry's arm. "Yet you continue to strive for more with the business. I'm no different."

"Why can't you be happy?" Henry shook his head. "It's a brutal world out there. When I come home, I want you here, not off at a meeting."

"I could take a position that wouldn't require travel."

"You'd be absorbed with working and business." Henry turned to her. "I know you Alisa. When you take something on, you are obsessed."

"And that's wrong?"

Henry exhaled a long breath. "We can't have everything in life."

Alisa's heart constricted at the sadness in his voice. He sounded defeated. She knew that there was something else bothering him, not just the idea of continuing a relationship with Trent.

Alisa put her hands on his chest. "Is there a problem with the company?"

"Everything is great at Fairman's." Henry clasped her hands. "I work hard every day to increase the legacy your father left you. I don't want to disappoint him, or you."

"You could never do that."

"My family lost all of their money through bad management." Henry closed his eyes for a few seconds. "You don't understand how devastating that was. One moment we were at the pinnacle of society and then suddenly, I was parking cars for them."

"My father never treated you like that."

Henry's lips twisted into a smile. "He hated trust fund kids, yet he looked past that with me."

Alisa squeezed his hands. "Maybe because your father gutted your trust fund?"

Henry rolled his eyes. "He still gave me a chance. I want to prove that I'm worthy of his faith in me."

Even after knowing Henry for fifteen years, she'd never guessed how much his self-esteem had been destroyed by his family's carelessness. His need to continue to prove himself had become the overriding goal of his life. He worked too hard. The only thing he was achieving was pushing her away.

"My father never doubted you." Alisa's voice held tears. "The last thing he said to me on the night he died was that the best thing I ever did was marry you. You were the son he never had, and he could die in peace knowing that you were taking care of me."

Henry's eyes widened. "You never told me that."

"You must have known how much my father cared for you." Alisa cleared her throat. "He left you a percentage of the business."

"I thought it was to insure that I would work harder."

"Never." Alisa shook her head. "It was his way of showing that he considered you family."

Henry swallowed. "Thank you for telling me."

"My father would never have wanted you to work yourself to death." Alisa leaned up and kissed him. "I want you to enjoy our life together. There's no point to any of this if you end up killing yourself with the stress."

"I'll try and ease up." Henry gave her hug. "I still don't want both of us tied to the business."

"I understand your reasons. That doesn't mean I agree." Henry started to speak, but Alisa raised her hand for him to wait. "I think that we can find a compromise."

"You mean by including Trent in our marriage?" Henry put his hands on his hips.

"That would be part of it." Alisa straightened her shoulders. "I've trusted you to run the business and never interfered."

Henry nodded. "What does that have to do with our relationship?"

"You've always allowed me to organize the household and our social life." Alisa raised an eyebrow. "Why is this different?"

"If our sexual exploits become public knowledge, we'll be social pariahs." Henry gripped her shoulders. "No one will speak to us."

"I think you're wrong." Alisa didn't let her gaze leave her husband. "Why would you even care about what people say? I would have thought you'd be thumbing your nose at them after the way they treated you when your father lost all of the family fortune."

A muscle in Henry's jaw tightened. "I don't want you or Bert to ever have to go through that."

"My father didn't let others dictate to him what he should do." Alisa lifted her chin. "I am my father's daughter."

"What about Bert?"

"We don't have to tell him anything until he's old enough to understand." Alisa's voice was firm. "Who knows where things will be by that time."

Henry shook his head. "I know you want this. I'm not certain that I can accept you sleeping with another man on a regular basis."

"You didn't have a problem on Saturday."

"That was different."

"Only because you gave yourself permission to enjoy it." Alisa's voice was low. "I was so uncertain about how that night would turn out that I was shaking. Something told me it was right, and I let myself relax."

Henry turned away. "I don't have time to think about this right now."

Alisa's shoulders sagged. "Let me guess. You have another meeting."

"In Seattle." Henry cleared his throat. "I won't be back until Saturday."

"Do you need me to pack?"

Alisa's voice was devoid of emotion. She'd thought that she was getting through to Henry. Now, he was all business again. Fairman's was killing both of them, and why? So they could leave more money to Bert? She understood Henry's feelings of inadequacy, yet what was the purpose of money if they couldn't enjoy life.

"I already threw a bag together." Henry's voice was apologetic. "I would have told you sooner. I just found out."

"That's what the call this morning was about." She should have guessed when she heard Henry's assistant's voice on the phone.

Henry sighed and pulled her into his arms. "I don't want to leave when you're unhappy."

"It's always business first." Alisa didn't bother to hide her disappointment. "At least when Bert was home, I had company."

"That's not fair." Henry looked down at her. "I do my best to be home for you."

"You're away more than you are home." Alisa didn't try to soften her words.

Henry frowned and then looked at his watch. "I'm going to be late for the airport. The car is probably already outside."

"Go." Alisa moved away. "I'll be here when you return. We'll continue our conversation then."

Henry hesitated for a second. "I don't want you upset."

"It's too late for that." Alisa gave him a quick kiss on the cheek. "Phone me when you land."

She followed Henry to the door. His bag and briefcase were waiting for him in the foyer. Henry threw his overcoat over his arm and picked up his luggage. He gave her one last peck on the lips before opening the door. She watched him hand his gear to his driver and then he turned back to her. He raced up the stairs and pulled her into his arms for another kiss. It was full of heat and passion. A spark of excitement twisted through her. He ended the kiss and gazed at her, his eyes filled with love.

"Don't ever forget how much I love you." Henry kissed her forehead before releasing her. "I promise to think about your suggestion concerning Trent when I'm away."

Chapter 12

Another Friday night alone.

Alisa walked from room to room, picking up things, and then putting them down in another place. Everything was picture perfect. She just wished her life was the same. Henry had called earlier to tell her his meetings had gone well, and that he'd be home later Saturday afternoon. That left her with nothing to do until then.

She jumped at the sharp ring of the doorbell.

She wasn't expecting anyone.

She went to the door and checked the security camera. Trent was standing on the porch. He was smiling up at the camera and waving a bottle of wine in the air. Her heart skipped a beat, and she had to force herself to breath as she unlocked the door.

"I thought you had a rehearsal tonight."

"Carlos ended it early." Trent walked into the house. "I have a perfect view of your house from my apartment and the drapes are open. I couldn't help but notice you wandering around the house."

"I'm restless." Alisa motioned Trent to follow her into the kitchen. "Henry's gone until tomorrow, and I'm afraid we didn't part on the best of terms."

"I hope our night together wasn't the problem."

"That night was special." Alisa handed Trent a corkscrew. "It did trigger the discussion, though."

"You both seemed fine with it in the morning."

"More than okay." Alisa took two long stemmed wine glasses down from the cupboard and put them on the granite countertop.

"Then what's the problem?" Trent filled the glasses and handed Alisa one.

She took her glass and grabbed the open bottle. "Let's sit out on the patio. It's a beautiful night and now that I have company, I can enjoy it."

"Are you worried about security?"

Alisa shook her head. "Not me. Henry insists I keep inside with the doors locked when he's away. He's a worrier."

"I like Henry." Trent shut the door to the house and followed Alisa to the cushioned lounge chairs.

Alisa gave Trent a lazy smile over her shoulder. "So do I. That's why we're having a disagreement right now."

"Explain."

"Henry grew up rich and then his father lost the family fortune." Alisa sat down on the lounger and stretched out her legs. "He lives in fear that he'll be destitute again."

"Makes sense." Trent sat beside her. "Sometimes it's better to have nothing. There's less disappointment that way."

"Is that what happened to you?"

"I grew up poor by anybody's standards. My mother died when I was young, and my father was out of the picture before I was born."

"That must have been devastating." Alisa shivered at the thought of a young boy all alone in the world. "What happened to you?"

"I was seven, and I missed my mom like crazy." Trent leaned back in the chair. "I was too old to be adopted, so I was in foster care until I ran away at sixteen."

"Is that when you started modeling?" Alisa tried not to let her shock show. It was a parent's worst nightmare to think that their child was alone and a runaway.

"I was lucky." Trent took a sip of wine. "A kid like me on the streets doesn't usually last very long. I was in New York without a penny to my name when Bob, my agent, found me."

"How?"

"He was picking up a client at the bus depot when I arrived." Trent's voice dropped. "I was being hustled, and he stepped in. He took me home, and his wife insisted I stay with them. Bob got me a modeling contract and the rest is history."

"Your life could have been ruined." Alisa's voice was filled with horror.

"To say the least." Trent looked up at the sky. "I learned from that."

"Not to run away?" Alisa tried to keep her voice light.

"To trust in fate and my instincts."

Alisa digested his words. "You think you were meant to meet Bob?"

"Definitely." Trent looked at her. "I was a typical teenager, and I defied authority every chance I got. Bob was insistent I come with him, and I could have refused. A tiny voice in my head told me to trust."

Alisa nodded. "I'm glad you did. Bob and his wife must be very special people."

"They are. Even though I'm close to them, they have their own family." Trent sighed. "I'm always invited for the holidays, and I'll be forever grateful. It's not the same as having your own family. It feels like being alone in a crowd."

"You haven't been able to fill the emptiness your mother's death left." Alisa's voice was soft.

Trent took a sip of wine. "When I first saw you in that café, I knew I'd found what I was looking for."

Shock rippled through Alisa. There had been an instant connection with Trent for her, and he'd told her that he felt attracted to her. His feelings went deeper than she'd ever suspected. She understood his need for a family. Would he contemplate the unconventional one she had to offer?

"So that's why you agreed to the threesome."

"A part of me thought you were joking." Trent grinned at her. "I mean, you're a beautiful woman. Why would you have to approach a stranger with a proposition like that? I wanted to see where it was going."

Alisa groaned. "It did start out as a joke. Henry's dare, and my friends' encouragement forced me to risk everything. I thought I would die of embarrassment. You made it easy."

"You told me you felt a connection to me. Were you lying?"

"I was serious." Alisa rubbed a finger over the edge of her wine glass. She needed to be completely honest with Trent. "After Saturday night, it's even stronger."

"Is that a problem?"

"I love Henry." Alisa cleared her throat and looked over at Trent. "I think I might be falling in love with you too."

"And that scares you."

"I can't leave Henry."

"I wouldn't want you to." Trent's voice was serious. "Henry is a good man. He doesn't deserve to be hurt."

"Thank you for understanding that." Alisa's voice cracked. "I've talked to him about making what happened Saturday night a permanent arrangement. I want you to be a part of our family. Henry's uncertain."

"He doesn't want to share you." Trent gave a self-deprecating laugh. "In his place, I probably wouldn't want to either."

"Henry wants me to be happy. At the same time, he worries about what others will say."

"It's not something that we have to publicize."

"Henry is always thinking further down the road." Alisa took another sip of wine. "He wants to know how this arrangement will look after a year."

"It could be damn wonderful."

"You might find someone else." Alisa kept her voice neutral. "Henry doesn't want me to be hurt."

"He's a decent man." Trent drank the rest of his wine and put the empty glass on the table. "I could never do something he didn't agree with."

"Neither could I."

"So an affair is out of the question." Trent's voice was definite. "I suppose that leaves us in limbo right now."

"Until Henry can see his way around this."

"Do you want me to move out?"

"Never." Alisa's voice was filled with shock. "Just knowing that you're here has given me such peace this last week. Henry is away frequently and having you so near has eased my mind."

"I'm glad of that." Trent stood. "I can't stay here with you right now."

"There's still more wine." Alisa picked up the bottle. "Have another glass."

"If I have another drink, I'm going to forget all my good intentions."

Alisa's heart skipped a beat at the intense hunger in Trent's eyes. Heat rushed through her body and at that moment she didn't care about what she'd promised Henry. She wanted Trent to gather her close and not let her go. She forced herself to breath.

"I'll walk you out."

"You don't have to." Trent went toward the side walkway.

"I have to set the security system anyway." Alisa picked up the empty glasses and bottle of unfinished Riesling. "It's quicker this way."

Trent shrugged and followed her into the house. She put the glasses and wine on the kitchen island and met Trent at the front door. He already had it open and was waiting for her to punch in the code.

"Thanks for the wine."

"My pleasure." Trent hesitated before continuing. "I'm a phone call away if things change."

Alisa hugged herself tight to keep from grabbing him.

Trent was right. They couldn't do this without Henry's permission. She'd uncovered a part of herself that she'd never known existed before. She was in love with two men, and she didn't want to have to choose between them. It was better if she let Trent go now, while she was still capable of rational thought.

"Your number is on speed dial."

Trent sauntered down the stairs and toward the garage. She watched him until he disappeared through the door to his apartment. Only then, did she shut the door and key in the code. She leaned against the entry wall and slid to the floor. She buried her head in her hands and gave way to the tears that had been threatening all day.

She didn't want to lose Henry, but there was a connection to Trent that she couldn't deny. A rational woman would have sent Trent away. She was her father's daughter. She wanted both men. She dried her tears with the back of her hand. She was certain that Trent was meant to be part of her life. She knew what she needed, and she'd figure out a way to get it.

Chapter 13

Henry's flight was delayed.

Alisa had gone to the airport to meet him. She'd canceled the limo service because she couldn't wait alone in the house any longer. This morning when he'd called, he said he needed to talk, and she'd been on edge all day. She could tell by the tone in his voice that he'd come to a decision.

She paced in front of the arrival doors, her stomach in knots as she waited for a sign of Henry. When he finally appeared, she could see the lines of exhaustion on his face. He passed through the sliding doors and stood looking around. She ran to meet him and flung her arms around him.

"You look tired." She hugged him and took his suitcase. "I canceled the car service and came instead."

Henry kissed her cheek and put his arm around her shoulders. "You didn't have to do that."

"It was lonely at the house." Alisa turned the suitcase on its wheels and rolled it beside them as they walked to the exit doors. "The drive gave me something to do."

Henry squeezed her shoulder. "I prefer seeing your face when I land than a driver's"

Alisa smiled up at him. "I bet you do. The car is parked on the second level."

They walked in silence, arm in arm, until they reached their vehicle. Alisa opened the trunk and left Henry to load the luggage while she started the car. She'd been right to come and meet him. His face had lit up the moment he'd seen her. He worked hard to keep the business going, and he deserved to be appreciated.

She no longer cared what his decision was. She loved her husband, and she would do whatever he wanted. He sacrificed so much for her. He refused to let her share the load right now, but hopefully someday, he might change his mind. Until he did, she would ease his life and worries in whatever way possible.

The drive home was quiet. Henry had fallen asleep the moment she'd merged onto the highway, and Alisa focused on her driving. When she pulled up in front of the house, Henry woke with a start.

"That was quick."

"I'll get the bags." Alisa turned the car off. "You go upstairs and get a shower."

"Not until we talk."

Alisa's chest tightened. "We can do that tomorrow after you've rested."

Henry shook his head. "I'm hungry. We'll talk while we eat."

Henry took his luggage upstairs while she went to the kitchen to prepare a quick meal of soup and salad. By the time Henry came down, the meal was ready, and they sat at the kitchen island to eat.

"I missed you." Alisa took a forkful of lettuce. "The house was too quiet."

"You should have met up with one of your friends for lunch."

"They were too busy." Alisa cleared her throat. "They either have jobs or have gone back to school."

Henry put his spoon down. "I'm sorry I made you feel like you couldn't handle a job. I know you're capable. I never thought of myself as old fashioned. I guess a certain part of me must be."

"Your mother didn't work."

"My mother did charity work, socialized, and spent time at the Country Club." Henry frowned. "She was devastated when Father lost his money."

"She's doing fine now."

"Because I set her up with an annuity." Henry pushed his soup away. "I never told you that."

"We have more than enough. I don't begrudge what you give to your family." Alisa's tone was loving.

"Most women would." Henry reached out and clasped her hand. "You're the most generous person I know."

"The company stays running because of you." Alisa squeezed his hand. "You work hard, and I love you even more because of that."

"I wasn't sure if you still felt that way after I left on Thursday." Henry's voice was doubtful.

"We've argued before, and you've never doubted my love."

"It was never about another man." Henry brushed a finger over her knuckles.

"You're my husband." Alisa held his gaze. "I would never do anything that you didn't want. Trent can live in the apartment. If you don't want anything more to happen between us, then it won't."

Henry cleared his throat. "I may have been wrong."

Alisa's breath caught in her throat.

Henry's decision was worse than she'd thought.

"You don't want Trent living here?" She blew a strand of hair off her face. "It's only for a couple of months. You can trust me."

Henry shook his head. "I trust you."

"Then what's the problem?"

"I had a lot of time to think on the plane." Henry grimaced. "The truth is, I worry about you being here alone."

"You think I'm going to have an affair?" Alisa's voice cracked. "You should know me better than that. I'm as loyal as they come."

"You're the best thing that ever happened to me." Henry looked up at her. "I still remember the day you ran across the university quad and introduced yourself."

Alisa laughed. "I couldn't let you get away."

"You had a feeling, or as you put it, an instinct, that we were meant to meet." Henry shook his head. "You were right."

"My intuition is always right."

"That's how you feel about Trent." Henry's words were a statement not an accusation.

Alisa inhaled a sharp breath. Henry was looking at her with a steady gaze while still holding her hand. She bit her lower lip. She couldn't lie, not even to spare Henry's feelings.

"It was almost identical to the sensation I had when I first saw you."

"That's why you invited him into our home and bedroom." Henry nodded. "I figured it out on the plane. You might have set out to show me that you were capable of taking charge, but I know you would never have let a stranger touch you the way Trent did."

"I considered it." Alisa's voice was low. "I even answered a personal ad."

"Do you know how dangerous that could have been?" Henry's voice was horrified.

"I do now." Alisa gave a small laugh. "Lara was with me when the guy and his buddies showed up."

Henry rubbed a hand over his face. "You could have been killed."

"I wasn't." Alisa shrugged. "Lara found Trent through one of her contacts."

"That makes my decision easier." Henry lifted her chin with his finger. "I don't want you doing anything that silly ever again. If I suggest you're not capable of doing something, you remind me of tonight."

"I will."

"I couldn't bear to lose you." Henry's eyes locked with hers. "I don't want you looking for another man to sleep with ever again. Is that clear."

Alisa nodded. She'd never seen Henry this serious before. Her heart constricted at the love she saw in his eyes. She'd been a fool to even consider ruining her marriage.

"Good." Henry released her chin. "I've decided that Trent can stay."

Alisa blinked. "What?"

"I don't want you searching for love anywhere else." Henry's voice was firm. "You want Trent to be part of our lives. I'm not going to fight it."

"You don't have to agree to this just because I want it." Alisa's voice was firm. "It's a decision that both of us have to be comfortable with or it won't work."

Henry cleared his throat. "I've thought about this a lot. I'm away from home all the time. When Bert was here, there was plenty for you to do. Now I sense that you are bored."

"I could get a job like I suggested in the beginning."

"You can do that too."

Alisa frowned. "Then there's no reason for you to want Trent to stay here."

"It has nothing to do with whether you work or not." Henry's voice was insistent. "I like Trent, and I know you do too."

"I would never choose him over you."

Henry gave her a sheepish grin. "You were right about me being uptight. I was worried about how others would view our lifestyle. I've become too focused on business and doing things proper. I've forgotten about what's important. You're the only thing that matters to me."

Tears pricked Alisa's eyes. "I appreciate that you want to do this for me. There are two of us in this marriage, and I don't want you sacrificing anything."

"I won't be." A tinge of red filled Henry's cheeks. "I have to confess I enjoyed watching Trent with you. It was the most erotic charge I've ever had. You're a beautiful woman and to watch you enjoying yourself, turned me on. I don't think I've ever been so aroused."

Alisa sat back. "Why didn't you tell me?"

"I was embarrassed to admit it." Henry cleared his throat. "I also like knowing who you're going to be sleeping with when I'm not here."

"I'm not going to betray you by having an affair."

"Maybe not now, but sometime in the future you might be bored enough to consider it." Alisa tried to interrupt him. He stopped her by touching a finger to her lips. "I've seen it in other marriages, and I don't want that for us."

"Are you saying that you're going to find a mistress?"

"You're more than enough woman for me." Henry's voice was hoarse. "Everything I do, is to please you. It gave me joy to see you so sexually confident and free."

"So you won't feel cheated by this arrangement?" Alisa couldn't hide her doubt.

Henry shook his head. "All three of us will be in this lifestyle together, though. I know I will be faithful, and I believe you will be too. You need to see if Trent is willing to commit."

"Honesty is vital for this to succeed."

"Let me know what Trent decides." Henry stood and kissed her. "I'm going to take a shower. I'll be waiting for you upstairs."

Alisa stroked her hand down his cheek. "Give me a few minutes to clean up."

"You might ask Trent if he wants to join us."

Alisa's heart raced.

Henry winked and then headed upstairs.

After Henry left, Alisa picked up the phone and hit the number seven. It was her lucky number, and the one she'd set the speed dial on for Trent. Henry had given his permission, and now she needed to know if Trent was willing. She was just about to hang up when Trent answered.

"It's Alisa. Can you come over now?"

Chapter 14

Alisa could hear the shower running in the master ensuite. She undressed and joined her husband. She picked up a bath scrubber and lathered it up before rubbing his back. Henry turned around and pulled her into a kiss. He devoured her mouth with his, setting her blood on fire and shudders of desire throughout her body.

Before the kiss ended, the shower door opened. Henry ended the kiss.

"Glad you could join us." He handed Trent a scrubber. "I don't think Alisa will need much coaching to accommodate us."

"The seduction is the best part." Trent's voice was low and husky.

Henry turned Alisa so that she was facing Trent. His arousal was obvious. Henry's erection was hard against her backside. She eased back against her husband and ran her hand down the long length of Trent's penis. He shivered and then joined them under the shower head. Alisa sighed with satisfaction as she found herself sandwiched between the two men she cared for.

Her dreams had come true.

She had a husband who loved her, and a lover ready to satisfy her.

Henry's hands reached around and stroked her breasts. Trent's tongue licked across her mouth before he pushed inside and sucked and nipped until she was limp. His hand reached between her legs and stroked her until she exploded with her first orgasm of the night. He eased away from her as Henry pushed her into Trent's arms.

This time Trent held her back and Henry was given access to her front. Trent's fingers caressed her breasts and his lips kissed her neck and shoulders. Henry ran his hands down her abdomen and then across her inner core before he knelt and spread her legs. His tongue darted inside her folds and licked. She groaned as he tasted her.

Strong arms held her safe.

Love filled her soul.

Henry circled and sucked until she was at the edge of climax. He held her there until she was screaming for release. Only then, did he increase his pace and let her reach orgasm. She came hard and with such an explosive climax that her body shook with the force of it. Trent and Henry both held her until her body recovered. Then all three lathered each other's bodies and rinsed off before shutting the shower off.

"Still think you can handle two of us?" Henry whispered in her ear as he handed her a towel.

"Watch me."

Alisa pulled both of the men out of the bathroom and pushed Henry down on the bed. She leaned over him and ran her tongue down his fully aroused penis. It looked painful. She wasn't about to let him have any relief. She intended to enjoy his discomfort for a while.

She climbed onto the bed and motioned for Trent to get behind her. Trent didn't need any further encouragement. He positioned her so that he could enter from behind and then eased his throbbing penis into her vagina. Alisa savored every inch of him. She leaned back and took his full length inside her before moving forward to focus on Henry.

Trent thrust deep as she clasped Henry's penis. She stroked down and then took him into her mouth. He tensed as she began to suck and lick him. Trent set the pace. With each thrust, Alisa stroked down on Henry until they hit a rhythm that had all three of them frantic for completion.

Trent reached around and brushed a finger across her clitoris and that was the last conscious thought that Alisa had. Waves of bliss exploded throughout her just as Henry released into her mouth. A few seconds later, Trent clasped her hips close to him as he shuddered his own release. They all collapsed on the bed.

It was several minutes before any of them moved. Trent was the first. He eased Alisa up onto the pillows beside Henry and climbed onto the bed beside them.

"You really should dare Alisa more often Henry." Trent sounded exhausted. "I like the results."

"When you've known her as long as me, you'll know which buttons to push too." Henry chuckled and turned to Alisa. "You can prove me wrong any time you like."

Alisa leaned over and kissed his cheek. "That was fun."

"That was the best homecoming I've ever had." Henry yawned and pulled the bedsheets over them. "I'm exhausted. I hope you don't mind if I sleep."

Trent turned Alisa onto her side and spooned her. "As long as I can still play with your wife."

Henry bunched a pillow under his head and turned the bedside light off. "Be my guest."

Alisa thought Trent had been kidding until she felt his fingers between her legs. He caressed and fingered her until she shook with release. His erection was hard against her back as he continued to fondle her until she'd had another two orgasms. Only then, did he reposition her one leg higher and enter her. He set a slow and lazy pace, thrusting and withdrawing to a rhythm that kept him on the edge of release and had her quivering with multiple orgasms.

When she was limp with exhaustion, he increased his pace, deepening his penetration until he shook with his own release. He was still connected to her when he pulled her close into his arms, and they both fell asleep.

Hours later she was awakened by the caress of lips against her breasts.

She moaned and moved closer to the sensation.

Her other breast was stroked and kneaded, causing jolts of pleasure to shoot to her womb. She moved onto her back and spread her legs wide. Her eyes opened to the still darkened room and the familiar feel of her husband's lovemaking. She arched her hips to meet him. He was hard and throbbing when he pushed into her and his pace was fast. They were both panting with release within minutes and a delicious spiral of ecstasy shattered through her. Henry followed close behind with his own climax.

Alisa awoke to an empty bed.

For a few seconds she thought she'd dreamt the whole night, but the pillows on either side of her were flattened from use. Her ears strained to hear a noise. The house was quiet. The shower wasn't running and there were no radio or television sounds. Then a whiff of coffee reached her nose.

The next second, the door of the bedroom opened and Henry and Trent both came in. Trent was carrying a tray with coffee, cream and sugar, and mugs. Henry had a basket of croissants and jams. Alisa stretched her arms over her head and punched the pillows into shape behind her back. Almost as good as making love to two men was being served breakfast by them.

"It's about time you woke up." Henry held out a plate and the basket. "I thought you were going to waste a beautiful day by staying in bed."

"There's nothing wrong with bed." Alisa took a croissant and put it on the plate. "As long as you're with the right men."

"I like how you think." Trent held up a cup of coffee. "What do you take?"

"Just cream."

"I'll remember that for next time." Trent fixed the coffee and handed it to her. "Did you have a good sleep?"

"Fantastic." Alisa sipped the delicious brew and sighed. "I could get used to a night filled with loving."

Henry cleared his throat as he climbed into the bed beside her. "That's what Trent and I have been discussing."

"Am I going to regret getting you two together?"

"We only want to increase your pleasure." Trent sat on the other side of her. "Henry and I have reached an understanding."

"As long as I have the final say."

"Always." Henry leaned back against the headboard. "Trent has agreed to a committed and exclusive relationship with us."

"I promise not to cheat." Trent turned to her. "I don't see myself getting interested in anyone else. If I do, I'll be honest with both of you."

"Thank you."

Alisa blinked back tears. In her heart she'd known that Trent was the right man for them. It had just taken Henry a little more time to come to the same realization. To hear Trent commit to their arrangement made her heart soar. Relief and possibilities filled her mind.

"What else did you gentlemen decide?"

"You have the final say with the household arrangements." Henry cleared his throat. "I'm so busy with the business and travel that I don't want to have to make decisions when I come home. I trust my wife to do that."

"I have a career that I want to build." Trent exhaled a deep breath. "I'm hoping that I can make a serious living with acting in the future. I need a home base to work from and a woman I can love."

A spark of elation took hold within her. What they were asking was doable. They were giving Alisa everything she wanted. Complete control, freedom, and most important, their trust. There was only one other thing she needed to know.

"Can I work if I want?"

"As long as we come first." Henry's voice was apologetic. "I don't want to stop you from doing what you desire. Neither Trent, nor I will be available all the time or even at the same time. Can you work around that? Most women find it difficult to juggle a job with one man. You'll have two of us to consider."

"What if I promise to stop working if it interferes?"

"I can live with that." Trent raised an eyebrow at Henry.

"So can I."

"Let's all shake on it." Alisa held out a hand to Henry and then to Trent. "Honesty always. That's the only way this will work."

"Agreed." Both men shook hands with each other.

Alisa leaned back on the pillows and finished her coffee. She held her cup out to Trent for more. He jumped up and brought her a refill. This arrangement was going to work better than she'd ever imagined. She bit into her croissant and considered the day ahead. They'd said she had complete control. What a better time to test their resolve.

"It looks like a warm day outside."

Henry brushed crumbs off his fingers. "Sunny and hot all day."

"I have this sudden urge to swim and make love in the pool."

"That sounds like a perfect plan." Trent jumped up from the bed and held his hand out to her.

"Did I mention how much I love you?" Henry leaned over and kissed her.

Alisa kissed him back. "You can show me all day long."

Chapter 15

The quilting circle was meeting at Alisa's house this week. She'd set them up in her living room and moved in a portable sewing table for any cutting. Henry was away at another business meeting, and Trent was at rehearsals. She had the house to herself for the first time in days.

Keeping two men sexually satisfied was fun and exhausting. She was looking forward to time with Trent, one on one. It would be the first time, and Henry had agreed to it. She smoothed out her completed star block and put it aside to match colors for a second block.

"You're glowing Alisa." Lara snipped a section of red embroidery floss off. "You better share with us. What happened?"

"Henry agreed to a permanent ménage." Alisa's voice was filled with joy.

"So there are three of you living at your house?" Ella's eyes widened. "Don't you have a problem with jealousy?"

Alisa shook her head. "Henry just wants me to be happy."

"So he gave you Trent instead of letting you go to work." Brenna voice was dry. "Was that worth the trade off?"

Alisa picked up a blue, tie-dyed fabric. "I didn't have to give anything up. All I had to promise was to put both of the men first."

"How can you do that and work?" Lara took the first stitch in a padded leaf chain. "A career always interferes."

"I'm still debating on what type of business would keep me free for the men in my life." Alisa shrugged. "It will come to me and if it doesn't, I'm enjoying life too much to worry about it."

"I'm happy for you." Ella's voice was sincere. "Not many men would be as generous as Henry about this situation."

"There are benefits for him." Alisa grinned. "He's never had so many sexual adventures or fantasies fulfilled. He comes home to a romantic interlude every night and more sex than he ever dreamed of."

"That will keep a man satisfied." Lara laughed. "You seemed to have figured out the best of both worlds."

"They've given me complete control, and I love it." Alisa picked up a cream fabric to match with the blue. "As long as we're honest and committed, it will work."

"What happens when someone wants out?" Brenna's frowned.

Alisa shrugged. "I'll worry about that when it happens. Trent has promised to talk to us if he finds another partner, and Henry knows that he will always be first in my life."

"It sounds good." Ella handed Alisa a micro-floral print from her stash. "This might make a better match."

Brenna cleared her throat. "You all did what we set out to do, and it seems to have worked out for the best."

"Are you having doubts about following through on Peter's fantasy?" Alisa put Ella's fabric next to hers.

"No," Brenna added. "It's a big step."

"We understand how frightening it can be." Alisa's voice was full of sympathy. "The thought of finding another man terrified me. From the moment Trent walked into my life everything changed. I'm never at a loss for what to do, and I don't feel lonely kicking around this big house."

"Finding the courage to follow through with having an affair has brought real love into my life." Ella's voice was firm. "I'm independent and strong now. If I hadn't moved out of my comfort zone I would be alone and destitute, exactly like Gerry planned for me."

Lara reached over and squeezed Ella's hand. "Taking control of my life was the best thing I ever did. Who knows how many more years I would have wasted with David and his lies?"

"I have to take charge." Brenna tightened her grip on her quilt block. "That's why I signed up for dominatrix school."

Brenna

Chapter 1

Brenna was happily married.

She and Peter had fallen in love in their teens, and after he finished law school they wed. Twenty-four years and three sons later, they were still blissfully in love and living their own fairy tale of happily ever after. At least, that was what Brenna had believed until she'd checked Peter's pockets before sending his suits to the drycleaners.

That's when she'd found the business card that had shattered her life.

Mistress Elise was printed in bold script on one side.

Peter had written an address on the back, and at first, she'd assumed the woman was a client. She'd checked with her husband's assistant. There was no record of her. If Mistress Elise wasn't a business associate, why did he have her contact information? The card had burned a hole in her hand, and memory, until she'd researched Elise online. That's when her world had come crashing down.

Mistress Elise was a dominatrix.

The address on the back of the card was to her dungeon.

Now, her goal was simple. If Peter wanted a dominatrix, then she would become one.

"The only way I'm going to understand what Peter needs is to train with someone who knows how to do it." Brenna's hand shook as she pinned her miniature Dresden plate onto its backing. "The school is for three days, and it starts next week."

"Does Peter know?" Lara looked up from her crazy-quilt block.

"He'll be out of town. I'll tell him I'm visiting a friend." Brenna watched Lara and Alisa exchange glances. "Do you think I'm wrong to keep it a secret?"

"When I arranged for a threesome with Trent, I didn't tell Henry until I had set everything in motion." Alisa grimaced. "It took him by surprise, and he almost didn't go through with it."

"It was a shock when David set up our first swinger's party without telling me." Lara's voice was low with pain. "I had no control over the situation, and that made it more difficult for me."

"Isn't that the point of Peter going to a dominatrix?" Ella's voice was matter of fact. "He wants someone else to take control."

Brenna nodded. "His fantasy is to be submissive."

"Then don't tell him." Ella jabbed her needle into her quilt block. "The surprise could be part of the pleasure for him."

"You're tough." Alisa laughed. "I remember when we started this journey together. You were afraid to confront Gerry about his mistress."

"Having Jesse in my life has taught me a lot." Ella's expression turned dreamy. Jesse was the younger man that Ella had met after her marriage had dissolved. There was no doubt that Ella was deeply in love with her younger man.

Brenna smiled as she remembered how she'd felt when she'd first fallen in love with Peter. That feeling had only deepened over the years. That's why she was determined to give her husband what he fantasized about. If he wanted a dominatrix, then she'd do that for him.

Ella picked up a floral print. "Being in love with a wonderful man is perfect for boosting a woman's confidence."

"Try being in love with two men," Alisa said. "The best part is, I don't have to choose."

"Do you love Trent as well?" Brenna didn't keep the shock from her voice. "Is it even possible to know so soon?"

"I knew almost from the beginning." Alisa said. "I don't think he's in love with me, but I'm okay with that. I have Henry's love to support me no matter what happens."

"I always thought I could count on Peter's love." Brenna sighed. "I'm not so sure now."

"Seeing a dominatrix doesn't stop him from loving you." Lara's voice was muffled as she bent over her block. "He might be too embarrassed to be honest with you about his needs and fantasies."

"That's why I'm not telling him what I'm doing." Brenna knotted her thread and buried the needle in her background fabric. "He won't be able to deny it, or stop me."

"I hope you know what you're doing." Lara looked up from her work. "Some of the things I've heard about these dungeons are pretty shocking."

"Do they actually call them dungeons?" Ella frowned. "That's not very encouraging."

Brenna straightened her shoulders. "I'll have to get used to it."

"What if you can't?" Alisa's voice was serious. "We may have started this journey to please our husbands, but we've found our own happiness along the way. You can't force yourself to do something that you're not comfortable with."

Brenna frowned. "You've all done what you said you would. If I don't want Peter going to a dominatrix, then I have to take this step."

"Going to a school?" Alisa shivered. "Anything could happen there."

"Will you be safe?" Lara's voice was filled with concern.

Brenna shrugged. "I never thought about danger. It's a school with references."

"That doesn't mean you'll like what you see." Lara's voice was hesitant. "This is a lifestyle that you're not familiar with."

"You don't think I can handle it?"

"Lara didn't say that." Alisa said. "I think one of us should go with you."

"No." Brenna inhaled a deep breath. "If I can't face this alone, then how will I be able to give Peter what he wants?"

"Taking one of us with you isn't a sign of weakness." Ella put her sewing down on her lap. "We've all reached out for help to accomplish our missions."

"That was for a date, or advice." Brenna shook her head.

"I'll go," Ella said. "Lara has a business to run, and Alisa has her hands full with two men. I'm the logical choice."

"What about Jesse?" Lara's tone was doubtful. "You're just starting a new relationship. Won't he object?"

"He's out of town next week." Ella shrugged. "I'll tell him what I'm doing. I don't think he'll mind."

"He might think differently when you come back ready to dominate him." Alisa chuckled. "You've become a tiger since dumping Gerry."

Ella grinned. "It's wonderful. I used to be frightened of my own shadow."

Lara pulled a thread through her work. "I'd feel better if Brenna had someone with her. I'm up to my eyeballs with work right now or I'd go."

"I don't think burying yourself with work is a good thing. You suffered enough after what David did to you." Alisa shook her head. "Maybe you should take a break."

"Work calms me." Lara shrugged. "Besides, David is history."

"Good." Brenna had never thought that David had treated Lara properly. She was glad David was soon to be divorced from Lara. His behavior with the swinging and sex clubs had proved her right. The man was abusive. "You deserve a good man."

"I think I may have found one." Lara's voice held a note of hope.

Alisa gasped. "Already?"

"Who?" Ella leaned forward in her chair. "You have to give us the details."

"Did I mention I had dinner with one of my clients?" Her soft voice echoed in the quiet of Alisa's living room. When the others shook their head, Lara continued. "I've seen Vince several times now, and he treats me wonderfully. He's a true gentleman."

"What does that mean?" Alisa's voice was suspicious. "Being nice could be a cover for not being interested in you."

"He's hard to read." Lara shook her head. "There's an attraction. I think he wants to take it slow."

Ella frowned. "Because you just left David?"

"That's part of it." Lara snipped her thread. "His wife died a couple of years ago, and this is the first time he's dated."

"So you're both on a rebound." Alisa pursed her lips. "That could be a problem."

"He also has two adorable children." Lara smiled. "He's being careful about any new relationships because he can't risk them getting hurt."

"You love children." Ella's voice was defensive. "You'd never hurt them."

Lara nodded. "Slow is good right now. His children are sweet. I don't know how I feel about men after the experiences I went through with David."

"Don't tell me you're swearing off them?" Alisa's eyes widened with surprise.

"I just want to be certain this time." Lara leaned back in her chair. "You and Brenna have happy marriages. That's what I want."

"Then take it slow." Ella leaned over and squeezed Lara's arm. "You'll know when it's right."

Alisa tilted her head. "I can't argue with that. I knew immediately that Trent would fit in with Henry and me."

"So that just leaves me." Brenna pushed away her fears. "I need to finish what we started."

"You could ignore Mistress Elise's business card. Throw it away and pretend you never found it." Alisa's voice was quiet. "You have a perfect marriage with Peter. None of us would blame you if you decided not to go through with this."

"I would never forgive myself." Brenna straightened her shoulders. "No relationship can have secrets, especially not a marriage."

"Are you certain?" There was a hint of doubt in Ella's voice. "Peter has been very discreet about it. He's never even hinted that he has these fantasies."

"Loving someone doesn't mean you have to change yourself." Lara's voice shook with emotion. "I tried to change for David, and I nearly destroyed myself."

"I would never have agreed to let Trent into my home if I hadn't felt it was the right thing to do. You have to trust your instincts," Alisa added.

Brenna exhaled in exasperation. "I agreed to do this. I won't back out now."

Ella shrugged. "Then I'll go to the school with you."

"That's not necessary." Brenna's voice was firm. "I have to do this on my own. After all, none of you will be with me when I confront Peter."

"Then it's decided." Lara picked up her embroidery. "You are going to be the dominatrix that Peter needs."

A chill of misgiving raced across Brenna's skin. She ignored it. There should be no secrets between a couple, and Peter had hidden this from her for a reason. She couldn't ignore that. She would do what was needed to keep her marriage together and her husband happy. The only way to do that was by going to dominatrix school.

Chapter 2

Brenna was debating what clothes to bring.

She had nothing in her closet that fit her vision of a dominatrix.

"Are you certain you don't want a ride to the airport? I could go early and wait for my flight."

"You'd be stuck there for five hours." Brenna looked up from the suitcase she was packing. "I've ordered a shuttle."

Her husband, Peter, leaned over her shoulder. "I thought you were only going for a couple of days. You've got enough clothes there for a month."

Brenna stood back and frowned down at her case. Peter was right. She'd over packed. The problem was she didn't know what to wear in a dungeon. The literature from the school had said that a special outfit wasn't needed. Did that mean jeans and a T-shirt were okay, or was something sexy and clingy more appropriate.

With a huff of exasperation, she pulled clothes out of the case and tossed them onto the bed. A pair of stretch jeans and comfortable cotton slacks with a couple of nice tops was all that she kept. She rearranged her stuff and then shut the case. She'd already wasted too much energy on clothes. Focusing on that had helped her forget her real problem.

She was going to a dominatrix school.

Mistress Patricia's dungeon to be exact.

Training started tomorrow morning at nine sharp.

A shiver went through her. Her life would never be the same after this and she still wasn't certain it was what she wanted. Her marriage was important, and she'd always thought she'd do anything to keep it together. This was the first time she'd been tested, though.

She looked over at Peter who was arranging a couple of suits and dress shirts in his garment bag. Travel was routine for him. He was in demand as a lawyer and out-of-town court appearances were part of the territory. He was an excellent defense attorney. A surge of love went through her. He worked so hard for his clients and his family. He was worth the effort of pushing her comfort zone.

She reached for him and hugged him close. "I love you."

Peter straightened up and looked down at her, his brown eyes warming with a spark of desire. "Is that an invitation?"

Brenna stood on her tip-toes and kissed his chin. "I could be persuaded."

"You don't have to ask me twice."

Peter pulled her into his arms and kissed her. It was familiar and welcomed. Sex with Peter was never disappointing and right now she needed the comfort of his arms to reassure her that she was doing the right thing.

"Let's clear the bed." Brenna's voice was low and seductive.

"I love having the house to ourselves." Peter released her, picked up his bag and put it on the floor, before reaching for her case and doing the same. "I never thought I'd get used to the boys being gone. At times like this, it's wonderful."

Brenna pulled her top over her head. "It's nice having the freedom to do what we like."

Peter yanked the bed sheets back and undid his pants. "Spontaneity adds to the excitement." Peter stepped out of his pants and sat on the bed.

Brenna finished undressing and climbed up beside Peter. Her fingers feathered across his broad shoulders and down his chest. He was still in great shape with firm, defined muscles. There were a few more inches around his middle —and grey was spattered amongst his brown chest hairs, but he was essentially the same man she'd married over twenty-four years ago. She leaned closer and kissed along his shoulder and up his neck.

He groaned and pulled her down with him onto the bed. He let her roam across his chin with her lips. When she'd reached his mouth, he took over. He flipped her onto her back and started the familiar seduction of her body. His hands caressed her breasts, thighs, and backside. His tongue dueled with hers and when the fire within her burned, he heightened it by pushing his hand between her legs and rubbing a finger against her clitoris.

Within seconds she exploded.

Peter thrust into her while she was still riding the crest of her climax. He moved with a steady rhythm that had her rushing towards her second orgasm just as Peter found his own. Together they floated down from the heights of bliss. It was comforting to be held in his arms and know everything was as usual. Years of marriage had taught them exactly what the other liked. Peter was intimately familiar with her body and knew how to excite and fulfill her.

"Are you happy?" Brenna looked up at Peter.

He kissed the top of her head. "Very. We have a good life."

"Is that all that matters?" Brenna knew it was foolish to push. She needed to know what it was that had driven Peter to a dominatrix.

Peter frowned. "We've worked hard for everything. Don't tell me you're unhappy?"

Brenna shook her head. "I'm the luckiest person in the world. I'm married to a man I love more and more each day, I have three wonderful sons, a beautiful house, and my dogs."

Peter hugged her closer. "You're a wonderful wife and mother. I have no complaints."

"Do you ever wonder if we're in a rut?"

"Sometimes." Peter shrugged. "Usually, things are too hectic to consider it. There's nothing wrong with life running smoothly."

"I suppose." Brenna sighed. "I know you're busy at work and travelling. I want you to know you can talk to me about anything."

"What's this about?" Peter's voice held a serious tone. "You're not upset because I'm away from home so often? It's never bothered you in the past."

Brenna shook her head. "It's nothing like that. I want you to remember that you can come to me with any problem."

Peter chuckled. "There's nothing wrong. We've been blessed with abundance. Life is good."

"You're not bored?"

"Boring is good." Peter pushed upright and put his feet on the floor. "We've been married a long time. Things are bound to feel like a routine."

Brenna leaned up on her arm and watched Peter pick up his pants before he turned to look at her. "What about experimenting with different lifestyles?"

Peter frowned. "What kind?"

Brenna picked at a loose thread on the blue toile bed covering. "Like swapping and threesomes. Maybe even BDSM."

Peter's eyes widened. "Are you serious? We don't have fireworks, but life isn't meant to be lived on a constant high. We're not teenagers anymore."

Peter walked into the ensuite and a few seconds later, she heard the shower start. She flopped back onto her pillow. He'd lied. He didn't trust her enough to be honest. Instead, he wanted to keep that part of his life hidden from her.

What he had admitted was more damning. He was satisfied with their life, even if there was no excitement. Were contentment and familiarity enough of a reason to stay together? What about intimacy and desire? She'd given Peter a chance to open up about his secret life and fantasies, and he'd avoided it.

She didn't want routine. That's what her parents and grandparents had. She wasn't ready to settle for a life dictated by ignorance and playing it safe. She refused to see her marriage drift into boredom and stagnation. Passion and excitement were worth fighting for. She pushed out of bed and finished packing her suitcase.

Her mission was clear.

She was going to be the dominant woman that Peter needed.

Chapter 3

The clinical chill of the meeting room was a disappointment.

It was furnished in a contemporary style with white leather couches, glass tabletops, and stainless steel chairs. It was a stark contrast to her expectations of dark shadows and chains on the walls. Brenna pulled out a chair and sat down at a table with two other women. The metal was cold against her body.

A petite brunette held out her hand. "I'm Amy."

The woman beside her nodded. "Connie." She was blonde with an inch of dark roots showing.

"Brenna." Her voice was low. She cleared her throat. "Have you been waiting long?"

Amy shook her head. "Mistress Patricia said she'd be back in five minutes. There's one more person in the class."

Only four women were brave enough to take the training?

Brenna clenched her hands around her notebook. She took a couple of deep breaths and forced the tension to ease from her shoulders. She had been hoping for a larger class so that she could hide in the background. Four students meant she'd be forced to participate.

The door opened and two women entered.

One was tall and wearing a designer suit. The other had her hair pulled back in a ponytail and was wearing shorts with a T shirt. Brenna wasn't surprised when the woman wearing shorts walked to the table. She pulled a chair out and plopped down beside her.

"Now that everyone is here, we can begin." The well-polished woman in the suit picked up a remote control from one of the side tables and pointed it at the wall. A screen slid down from the ceiling.

"I am Pat Bently, better known as Mistress Patricia to my clients." She used the remote as a pointer and aimed it at their table. "Introduce yourself and tell us why you want to be a mistress?"

The controller was aimed at the woman with the ponytail. She leaned back in her chair. "I'm Debra, and I want to make money as a professional dominatrix."

"You'll need more than this class for that. This is a short introduction to BDSM. It's not meant to teach you everything, just the basics." Mistress Patricia gaze was intent. "There's so much more you need to know before becoming a professional dominatrix. My advice would be to work in a dungeon as an assistant and let them mentor you with further training."

Debra waved away the suggestion. "I've already lined that up with a friend in the business."

Pat nodded and then moved on to Amy. "My boyfriend thinks I'm too timid in bed."

"So what do you expect to happen by taking this course?" Pat crossed her arms over her chest.

Amy shrugged. "He thinks it will make me open to new sexual experiences. He bought me the classes for my birthday."

"Classes will not make you a dominant." Pat's voice was firm. "We can help you with your desire to be more daring and experimental in the bedroom only if that's what you want."

Pat turned to Brenna.

Her mouth went dry.

She cleared her throat. "My name is Brenna Stuart, and I'm here because I want to fulfill my husband's fantasies."

"Has he told you he wants to be dominated?"

Brenna shook her head. "No. He's seeing a dominatrix, and I would prefer that he come to me with his needs."

"Understood." Pat moved onto Connie.

"I've always desired to control men." Connie jutted out her chin. "I thought it was wrong until I started looking online for information."

Pat nodded and then turned back to the screen. A picture of a dark curtained room appeared on the viewer. The camera panned over the walls which had bars secured to them and chains hanging from the ceiling. It went on to show a couch with leather straps attached, a chair, and a rounded stool with a cushion on top and leather straps at the side. The next wall had an assortment of paddles, whips, belts, handcuffs, and ropes hanging from hooks. There were canes, and prods, along with pads attached to electrical devices.

A shiver went through Brenna at the sheer number of instruments of torture in the room. How could Peter step into a place like that? Everything was designed for pain and humiliation. She continued to watch as the camera panned into another area where there was an iron cage big enough to hold a large dog. Then they were showing a padded chair that looked like something from a dentist's office. When the video finished, there was silence in the room.

"That is what a typical dungeon looks like." Pat clicked the video off. "Only a professional needs this much equipment for their playroom."

"Do we have to use all of it?" Amy's voice cracked in the middle of her question.

"You don't have to use any of it." Pat put her remote down and pulled out a chair to sit on. "You should feel comfortable with what you are doing at all times."

"You will show us how to use them, right?" Debra's voice was insistent.

"Tomorrow. Today we're going to discuss the role and rules." Pat waited for a few seconds and then spoke. "Why do you think men would pay to see a dominatrix?"

"They need an escape from their stressful lives." Debra threw out.

"They want to be punished?" Connie shrugged.

"They want someone else to take control." Amy's voice was doubtful.

Pat nodded and then looked at Brenna. "You said your husband was seeing a dominatrix. Why do you think he's going?"

Brenna thought about all the years she'd known Peter and what motivated him. He never did anything he didn't want to, and that included visiting her family at the holidays. She could only come up with one answer. "It must give him pleasure."

"Bingo." Pat tapped the table with a finger. "You're all right with your reasons. For a successful relationship, there has to be pleasure. Your submissive, must be satisfied."

"I thought they did what you asked them to. Why does it matter if that doesn't give them pleasure?" Connie put her elbows on the table.

"You're in control, so it's your responsibility to ensure that the session goes as your client or significant other wants it to." Pat looked at each of them for a few seconds before continuing. "You are not doing this to abuse your partner. It's their fantasy, and you're role playing it for them."

Pat stood. "Let's get started with the general rules."

Brenna opened her notebook before looking at the other women. Connie and Debra had leaned back in their chairs and boredom flickered across their features. Amy was wide-eyed and biting her lower lip. Her expression was a mixture of uncertainty and fear. Brenna gripped her pen and took a deep breath. She had to remember that she was here because she loved her husband.

Peter desired this.

To refuse to help was inexcusable.

She would never deny Peter anything that he needed. If there was an obstacle to him getting assistance, she wouldn't stop until he was better. This wasn't an illness, yet he required it to be happy and fulfilled, and she was going to get it for him. She would have to dig deep within herself to find the strength. She would succeed.

"The first thing is to be patient." Mistress Patricia's voice cut through her thoughts. "Your client or partner won't find being a submissive easy. Give them the time they need to accept and enjoy the role."

"That seems a contradiction." Brenna frowned. "Why do something you don't want?"

"They may have fantasized about this for years. That doesn't mean they're ready for all of the elements of being submissive." Pat leaned against the table. "That's why communication is so important. You need to find out what their fantasies are and give that to them."

"So it's about their needs, not ours?" Debra shook her head. "What do we get out of it?"

"Your role is to help them achieve their fantasies in a controlled and safe environment." Pat's voice took on a hard edge. "If your desire is to inflict pain, then this isn't the right place for you. By being humble and open to listening to your submissive, you will learn."

"So communication is vital." Brenna nodded. "What if they won't tell you what they need?"

"You have to be sensitive and build trust in order for them to be open with you." Pat looked at each of them for a few seconds before moving to the next point. "Some men have hidden their fantasies for so long that even though they've come to you for help, they still can't get past their discomfort and open up."

Sympathy filled Brenna.

To have to hide what you want because you're afraid of being judged must be a living hell. She didn't want to think of that happening to Peter. Guilt gnawed at her at the thought that he might have lived like that for years, and she was totally oblivious to it. No wonder he wouldn't open up to her.

"That must be horrible for them."

Pat nodded. "That's why your ability to help them express their desires is so important. Both of you benefit if you're able to get them to be honest about what they need. That's the only way you will have a successful relationship with your submissive."

"What if you can't give them what they want?" Debra's voice was doubtful. "I've heard of some strange requests."

"They may seem strange to you. Always remember these are your client's or significant other's fantasies. Try not to make judgements about them."

There was a moment of silence and then Mistress Patricia continued. "You have to be honest with what you're comfortable doing." Her voice was serious. "You need to know your limits. You might not be the right dominatrix for your client. Recognize that, and hopefully you can direct them to someone who will do the role playing they need."

"So it's okay to say no."

"Definitely," Pat said. "Just as your submissive has a safe word, you can have hard limits that you do not go beyond."

"What about sex?" Amy's voice had a catch in it.

"That is not allowed." Pat's voice was forceful. "We are not selling sex to our clients."

"Never?" Amy moved forward in her chair. "I don't think my boyfriend is going to like that."

"A consensual relationship is different from one with a client. You may still have a sexual component, but not in the dungeon. Once you've finished with aftercare, the client leaves. If you are having a relationship with your submissive then you could add a sexual component. It depends on what you've agreed to before the scene."

Brenna's head started to spin. "What's aftercare?"

"That's the emotional support you give to your partner or client after a session." Pat's voice gentled. "It might be hugging, cuddling, or praising them. It will strengthen the bond between you and should never be overlooked after a session."

"So it's more than just inflicting pain?"

"Your clients will have endorphins released after being in subspace. They need care and help to return from this."

"Do you do this with every client?" Debra's voice had a hard edge of scorn. "That must take forever."

"It's part of a session, or as I like to call it, a *scene*." Pat's tone became stern. "You have to have boundaries in place before you begin. This is about fulfilling their needs and along the way, if you have fun, then great. The client comes first."

"This sounds harder than I thought." Debra sounded perplexed.

"It's exhausting work." Pat crossed her arms over her chest. "This isn't about making a fast buck. Have you sat in on any sessions at the dungeon where you're going to be trained?"

Debra shook her head. "My friend said to take your course first, and then she would let me help in the dungeon."

"Has she explained that you'll probably have to be a bottom for a few months before they'll let you start dominating?" Pat tilted her head. "An effective dominatrix needs to have sympathy and empathy."

"Are you saying that I'll have to let them hurt me?" Debra's voice was a high-pitched screech.

"That's normal in most houses." Pat's tone was neutral. "I'm assuming that you're training at a house and not a private studio."

Debra nodded. "I didn't sign on for someone else to give me pain."

"How could you possibly appreciate your clients' needs if you haven't been through it yourself?"

Debra pushed back her chair. "This isn't for me. All I want is to make some money."

Debra stood and walked out.

The door shut behind her with a slam.

Brenna released the breath she'd been holding. She didn't understand everything that Mistress Patricia had been talking about. It made sense that you couldn't let someone strike a person if they didn't have a clue about the pain they might be inflicting. That would be torture.

A shiver went through Brenna.

Would they have to let someone hit them?

She cleared her throat. "Are we going to have to be submissive here?"

Pat shook her head. "This course is too short and general for anything like that. If you're serious about the lifestyle, I would recommend you experiment with both roles."

A collective sigh went up from the group.

"Is anyone else having doubts?" Pat raised an eyebrow.

"What if we can't be dominant? The thought of hitting my husband makes me nauseous." Brenna expressed the concern that had been playing over and over in her mind. She wanted to help Peter. What if she wasn't able to? She'd never raised her hand to any of her sons when they were growing up. She didn't believe in physical punishment.

Pat smiled. "You're here. That's more than most wives would do for their husbands. This lifestyle doesn't have to involve physical pain if the two of you are uncomfortable with it. The best advice I can give, is to take it slow, especially in the beginning. There are other ways to dominate."

"I hope so." Amy shuddered. "My boyfriend is so much stronger that I'd be afraid he'd come after me if I hit him."

"That's why we have restraints." Mistress Pat clicked on the screen. "If your boyfriend sent you here, trust me, he wants to be dominated. Now let's look at what is necessary for a scene."

Brenna forced herself to focus on the screen.

There was so much information coming at her that she didn't know if she'd be able to keep any of it straight. The rest of the day passed in a blur of rules, limits, types of domination and humiliation, and equipment. It was almost five in the afternoon by the time the class was dismissed.

Brenna stood and was stretching her arms behind her back when she was stopped by Mistress Patricia's voice. "Wear comfortable clothes tomorrow. We're going to start practicing in the dungeon."

Chapter 4

The dungeon was dimly lit with shadows in the corners.

Brenna rubbed the chill from her arms.

How had she come to be here? This was so far from her comfort zone that she had to be in an alternative universe. Ropes and chains hung from hooks on the wall, along with paddles, canes, and whips next to them. It was exactly like the photo from the day before. Steel cross-bars were bolted to the opposite wall, and beside them was a ladder-like contraption. There was a cushioned stool in the center of the room that had restraints attached to the legs.

Today, Mistress Patricia was in full dominatrix costume. She had a black leather bustier that snugged in her waist and made her hips flare in a flattering manner. Black thigh-high leather boots, thong panties, garters, and fishnet stockings finished the look. There was no denying she was a beautiful woman and the outfit gave her presence. Brenna was thankful that she wouldn't be at the receiving end of her domination.

"You won't have to do anything you're not comfortable with today." Mistress Patricia's voice directed. "I know this might be a lot to take in for the first time. Try and remember that this is what the people who come here want."

"Should we be wearing a costume also?" Brenna's voice was hesitant. The only thing she had that was close to what Patricia was wearing was a pair of shorts and a T-shirt.

"I have some outfits in the change room. You can borrow one for today." Mistress Patricia looked at all three of them before pointing to Brenna. "This is going to be the room you play in today. Once you have changed, I will show the rest of you to your rooms."

Brenna found a pair of thigh-high shorts and a tight-fitting, stretch top to wear before coming back to explore the dungeon room that would be hers. She walked to the wall with the paddles and whips, and moved her fingers across the leather flat-lashes of one of the floggers. It looked deadly. The one beside it looked worse.

It had braided lashes.

That would inflict serious pain.

"Why would anyone want this?" Brenna's whisper echoed in the room. "It has to hurt."

"This isn't about pain for most people." Mistress Patricia's voice interrupted Brenna. "It's about playing out fantasies and trust."

"So they're trusting you not to inflict too much pain?" Brenna shook her head. "I'm still having difficulties understanding all of this."

"Pain can be pleasurable." Mistress Patricia took the flogger that Brenna had been touching off the hook. "Hold out your hand."

Brenna hesitated for a second and then presented her palm. Mistress Patricia swung the flogger and the lashes brushed against her fingers. There was no force in the swing, and a slight tingle was all Brenna felt. It was more of a tickle, than a hit.

"You trusted, and I honored that." She hung the flogger back on its hook. "I have a slave that is willing to let you practice on him. Are you ready for your first lesson?"

Brenna took a deep breath and nodded.

She was here to learn.

"We're going to start with the basics of spanking today."

The door opened and a naked man walked in. He was looking at his feet, shoulders slouched forward, and hands in front of his private parts. His posture screamed submission. He stood at the entry and waited.

"Over here slave," Mistress Patricia barked.

She pointed to a metal bench attached to the wall. It was at waist height, and the man leaned over it and spread his legs. His naked buttocks were fully exposed. Mistress Patricia secured his ankles to the base of the contraption, and his wrists to the top with leather cuffs.

"This is a safe position that allows for longer playtime," Mistress Patricia explained. "He is exposed and yet comfortable."

Mistress Patricia motioned for her to come close.

Brenna had to force her feet to move. Seeing another man's bare bottom wasn't her idea of fun. She had to remind herself that this was what Peter wanted, so she had to learn.

"You have to warm him up first before you start getting serious." The dominatrix smoothed her hand over the man's bottom. "Try a few slaps before you use any of the equipment."

Brenna moved her hand over the man's cold bum until it felt warm, and then she gave a quick flick of her wrist and slapped. It was more play than pain.

"Good." Mistress Patricia's voice held approval. "A few warm ups and then move on to the paddle or strap. Make sure you aim for the fleshy area."

Brenna followed the instructions, alternating between light and heavy swats until the slave's bottom was a nice rosy color. That's when Mistress Patricia handed her a paddle. It was heavy in her hand and even a light tap on bare skin made an ominous noise.

"You can start putting a bit more weight behind your swings."

Brenna grimaced. "I don't want to hurt him."

"You won't. Watch your aim and stay clear of his back." Mistress Patricia took the paddle from her and gave a couple of firm whacks to the man's bottom. "Vary the pressure in the beginning until he's able to handle the pain, and then you can increase it."

Brenna watched as the dominatrix worked the paddle and then moved to a strap. The man seemed to be enjoying it. When his buttock cheeks were a nice red, Mistress Patricia handed her the flogger to continue. Brenna took a few swings and winced at sound of the leather hitting flesh.

"Get comfortable and keep a steady rhythm."

Brenna put more weight behind her next swing.

The man groaned.

She jumped back.

"It's fine." Mistress Patricia nodded. "He's starting to enjoy it."

Brenna continued to spank until her arms ached from swinging the flogger.

Sweat beaded on her forehead.

Her stomach felt hollow.

Part way through the lesson, she'd realized that it wasn't as difficult to do as she'd imagined. She had been careful and kept her pressure light. She found a rhythm that she was comfortable with. Mistress Patricia had watched and encouraged the whole time. Half-way through the session, Brenna realized that she was doing exactly what the client wanted. That's when her tension eased. She never got to the point of enjoying it, and yet she didn't feel guilty about inflicting pain on someone else.

When the time was up, Mistress Patricia released her slave and let him kiss her feet. She rubbed his backside and made certain there were no cuts, before helping him leave the room. Brenna followed and watched as the dominatrix held her slave and praised him. For a few seconds, the man looked as if he were in another world until his eyes started to focus, and his breathing evened out.

When he was able to stand on his own, Mistress Patricia led Brenna back into the dungeon.

"We need to clean the equipment." She picked up the paddle, strap, and flogger. "There are some cleaning cloths in the cupboard. Wipe down the equipment including the metal rack."

Brenna was relieved that the session was over.

It had been an intense scene.

She turned to get the cleaning cloths when Mistress Patricia's voice stopped her. "You're a quick learner Brenna. Your husband is a lucky man."

Chapter 5

"You have to tell us what happened." Alisa lowered her voice to a whisper. "The suspense is killing me."

They were outside Erotic Dreams. It was the only sex shop within miles of Dearston. They often drove into the city to buy fabric, and Alisa had suggested this trip should include a visit to the specialty shop. This is where the quilting group had decided to meet this week.

Sex toys instead of fabric would be their goal.

Brenna hadn't spoken to any of the women since she'd returned from Mistress Patricia's studio, and she knew they wouldn't let it rest until she'd given them a full report. A part of her was hesitant to reveal everything she had learned at the school. She wanted to forget the uncomfortable scenes, but that wouldn't be fair to the others.

Ella opened the door to the store. "Did you have to whip someone?"

Brenna started giggling. "Sort of."

"Are you serious?" Ella's eyes widened. "I was joking."

"It was a school to learn to be a dominatrix." Lara's voice was matter of fact. "What did you expect?"

"Pictures." Ella waited for all of them to enter the store before shutting the door. "Maybe some classroom stuff."

"We had one day in the class." Brenna waited for her eyes to adjust from the bright sunshine of the outdoors, to the interior lighting of the store.

"Did you learn techniques in class?" Lara frowned. "I would have thought that was more of a hands on thing."

"The classroom was for the rules of play."

"They consider that play?" Ella shuddered. "I can think of other terms for pain."

Brenna smiled at the look of disgust on Ella's face. "I used to think the same thing. Now I'm not so sure."

"You liked it?" Alisa questioned. "I knew you were a closet dominatrix."

Brenna shook her head. "I have a better understanding of what it's about. I might even be able to give Peter what he needs."

"Then school was a good thing." Lara's voice held a note of approval. "What did you learn?"

"That you have to be honest with yourself and your partner."

"You mean you tell them ahead of time how much pain you're going to give them?" Ella whispered.

Brenna looked around the shop and walked toward the BDSM equipment at the rear of the store. "You have to sit down with your partner and discuss what you plan to do and what is off limits before you start playing."

Alisa stopped in front of a display of restraints. "Is that when you find out what their safe word is?"

"It's more than just safe words. You also have to understand what your partner wants and their hard limits." Brenna fingered a pair of metal handcuffs and then moved to a roll of bondage tape.

"Hard limits?" Alisa leaned close. "That doesn't have anything to do with the size of their erection does it?"

Ella gasped and looked behind her. "We shouldn't be talking like that here."

"This is the perfect spot for a frank discussion about sex." Lara motioned her hand around the store. "How else would you know what to buy?"

"You're right." Ella shrugged. "The clerks have probably heard and seen everything."

"So what is a hard limit?" Alisa asked.

"It's what you won't do." Brenna moved to a display of clothing. "I don't want to physically humiliate anyone, not even if they beg."

"Did someone beg you in the dungeon?" Lara's voice was full of concern.

"No." Brenna shivered as she remembered the scene that Mistress Patricia had let them watch. One of the client's fantasies had involved humiliation and water play. It had been an eye-opening experience— not one she wanted to repeat.

"Did you have clients?" Ella pulled out a see-through, black, baby-doll set.

"Two volunteers and one of Mistress Patricia's slaves."

"She had a slave?" Ella clasped the hanger close to her body. "Is that legal?"

"They want to be slaves." Lara shook her head. "This is really a different world from what we're used to."

"The terms are strange for us. The people into these fetishes are serious about it," Brenna said.

Brenna looked at the rack of dominatrix costumes of leather and rubber and moved over to a section of corsets. She wasn't ready for the leather look yet. She flipped through a number of black and red corsets until she found a red one with a black flirty skirt attached. She held it in front of her.

"What do you think?"

"You don't want leather?" Alisa had pulled out a black, leather, body-hugging dress.

"I have to ease into this." Brenna bit her lower lip. "It might be what Peter wants, but I'm not comfortable in the full gear yet. I figure a less dominant look with high heels is the best way to give me confidence in the role. Otherwise, I'll feel ridiculous."

Lara stood back and examined the outfit. "If you find a pair of red heels, I think you'll look in control. It'll be a softer edge."

"You could almost go to a party in that." Ella approved. "I'd even wear it."

"What about a whip?" Alisa pointed to a riding crop that was hanging from a hook.

Brenna shook her head. "I tried that in the dungeon and it takes a lot of practice."

"So what will you use?"

"A paddle to start with." Brenna put the dress over her arm and walked to the display that held a number of spanking implements. "I want a small leather paddle, and at least one flogger."

"Wow, you really know your stuff." Ella's voice held awe. "You've had practice with both of those?"

Brenna nodded. "We all participated in several scenes where spanking was involved."

Lara handed her a leather flogger. "Do you think Peter will like this one?"

Brenna held it by its corded handle and swung it in an arc. It had a nice weight, and its leather and suede tresses were smooth. "This will do nicely."

Alisa picked up a small paddle and wacked it against her palm. "Ouch. That hurts."

"I think that's the point." Lara's voice was dry. "When do you plan on using this with Peter?"

"He's away until this weekend." Brenna took the paddle from Alisa. "When he gets home, I'm planning a special evening. After that we need to have a direct conversation about how far I'm willing to go with this role."

"Is that what Mistress Patricia suggested?" Ella ran a finger over the bristles of a wooden hairbrush before handing it to Brenna.

"She said that I might not be able to do this for Peter. Trying was the first step, though. There should be some common ground between the two of us."

"What does that mean?" Lara frowned. "You won't be a dominatrix?"

Brenna shook her head. "She suggested that I start with a gentler approach until I was comfortable with the role. It should be play, and that it's meant to bring pleasure to both of us."

"So don't force yourself."

"Exactly." Brenna was grateful that Lara understood.

"Try the costume on." Alisa urged Brenna to the change room. "I'm dying to see what you look like all dommed up."

Brenna handed the equipment she'd picked out to Alisa, and took the dress into the small cubicle. Once it was on, she tightened the front laces and tucked them into the top. She took a deep breath, making the costume shift. It was too loose. She flipped the skirt as she turned to look at the back in the mirror. It was obvious that she still had her panties on. She would have to remove them when she was with Peter.

All three of her friends were waiting. Their eyes widened when she stepped out of the room. "I need someone to tighten the back laces."

"Turn around." Lara grabbed the laces and pulled. Within seconds, the front of the garment came together and cinched in her waist.

Brenna looked into the store mirror. She didn't' recognize the person who stood there. She looked like a softer version of Mistress Patricia. There would be no mistaking her role. She was a dominant. A flicker of excitement twisted in her lower abdomen. For the first time since she'd started this fantasy, she wondered if it might not be enjoyable. She exhaled and smiled.

This role was starting to feel like fun.

Maybe she was a closet Dominatrix.

"There's some thigh-high, silk stockings here. They have elastic at the top." Ella handed her the package.

"You could go with a garter." Lara looked at the dress with a critical eye. "It definitely needs red stilettos. That will set it off perfectly."

"I'll take the silk nylons and a garter belt." There was mischief in Brenna's voice. "Peter won't know what hit him."

"Leather or vinyl for the garter?" Ella was at the accessory shelf.

"Leather," Brenna and Lara answered at the same time.

"It's going to cost a fortune. I don't care." Brenna gave the outfit one last twirl and then went back to the change room. "I'm going to try the leather dress on too."

"Why not. You'll need a couple of pairs of stockings then." Lara held the change room curtain open.

The black leather dress hugged her body and stopped at her upper thigh. There was a zipper down the front and Brenna zipped it up to just above her breasts. There were possibilities here for a lot of teasing. She zipped it lower and nodded. She was getting this outfit. She wanted to see the look on Peter's face when she opened the zipper to her navel.

She smoothed her hands down the front of the dress before she stepped outside.

"It's perfect." Alisa nodded. "You look like a professional dominatrix. Peter's not going to know what hit him."

"I'll say," Ella exclaimed. "I thought I was being risqué by buying baby doll lingerie."

"That outfit needs boots." Lara's voice was definite.

"Next trip." Brenna sighed. "Good leather boots cost a fortune."

"The outfits are perfect." Lara took the stuff that Alisa had been holding. "What else do you need?"

"A restraint kit for the bedroom." Brenna pointed to the wall where the other restraints were. "I saw a kit over there."

By the time she'd changed and rejoined the others, they'd found three different kits to choose from. She picked one that worked with the mattress of her bed and had soft covered wrist and ankle restraints. She had everything she needed to create an evening of domination and pleasure for Peter.

"That school taught you a lot." Lara's voice held approval. "Maybe we should all go."

"It wouldn't hurt." Brenna walked to the checkout. "Do you want to continue looking around for some toys for yourselves?"

Ella giggled. "Lingerie is enough for me this trip."

"My two men keep me pretty happy." Alisa gave the store a once over. "Give me a few months, and I'm sure I'll be wanting a few toys to liven things up."

"I'm without a man right now." Lara's tone was wry. "I'll wait."

"Is everyone up for some shoe shopping?" Brenna put her wallet away and gathered her purchases.

"Red stilettos, lunch, and then fabric." Lara was the first one out of the store. "Is there anything else you need Brenna?"

"Just for Peter to come home."

Chapter 6

Everything was perfect.

Brenna gave a last look at the dining room table. She'd set it earlier in the day. The lasagna had almost finished baking, and the salad was on the table. She could relax. Peter had called from the airport when he landed. He would be home in ten minutes.

The stage was set.

She had a wonderful evening planned for him.

Brenna readjusted the front lacing on the black corset dress she was wearing. She swung her hips so that the cool silk of the flirty red skirt brushed against the bare skin of her upper thighs. She wasn't wearing any panties under the dress, only a garter and silk nylons. A delicious thrill of anticipation twisted in her womb.

A car door slammed shut.

Peter was home.

She smoothed her hands down the front of the outfit and inhaled a deep breath. It was show time. She slipped into her red stilettos and straightened her shoulders. Peter needed to see a woman in control the minute he walked into the house, or the scene would be destroyed. She'd put too much effort into preparing this evening to have it ruined.

Tonight she was in control.

After that, she'd do what Peter wanted. If he wanted her to spank, humiliate, or use bondage, she would. She didn't know his fantasies, yet if he trusted her, he would open up about his desires. They needed to establish the bond between a dominatrix and her submissive before they could move forward.

The front door opened. "Something smells good."

Brenna walked into the foyer. "It's a special meal."

Her stomach knotted with desire. Even after all these years, he still had the ability to excite her. His hair was white now, but his brown eyes were just as vibrant and alive as when he'd been a teenager. She loved him with her whole body, that's why tonight was going to be so difficult. Their roles would be reversed.

He was the man always in control.

A powerful presence.

Peter's eyes widened, and he dropped his garment bag on the floor. "What are you wearing?"

"Do you like it?"

Brenna swirled around so that her husband could get the full effect of the dress. When she stopped, he was watching her with his mouth open. For a second, doubt threatened to overwhelm her. Then she saw the flicker of interest in Peter's eyes. He was definitely intrigued.

"Get into something more comfortable."

Peter shook his head. "I don't think I have anything that will rival what you're wearing."

Brenna pointed to his garment bag. "Take that into the bedroom. I've put your outfit on the bed."

Peter lifted an eyebrow.

"Now." Brenna used her most authoritative voice.

Peter grinned. "What happened to my sweet wife?"

"Do you have a problem?" Brenna put her hands on her hips.

"Not at all." Peter picked up his suitcase raced to the bedroom.

Brenna followed him. She leaned against the door jam and watched as he picked up the red silk robe that she'd left for him. She'd chosen it especially for this evening. It matched the color of her dress and shoes, and there were no fasteners. It would hang open, giving her easy access.

"You can't be serious?" Peter gave a short laugh. "This thing will barely cover me."

"That's the idea." Brenna entered the room and took the robe from her husband's hands. "You need a shower. When you've cleaned up, put this on and come to the dining room."

"What about briefs."

"If I wanted you to wear briefs, they would be out," Brenna reprimanded. "Do as I ask."

Brenna kept her face straight as she watched Peter struggle with her commands. He gave her a long look and then shrugged. He took the robe and went into the bathroom. Brenna went back to the kitchen and sagged against the counter.

Dominating was harder than it looked.

She had to maintain the role if her scene was going to succeed tonight.

Everything depended on Peter accepting her as a dominant. She needed to engage his interest before she could gain his trust. Only then, would he open up to her about what his real desires were.

If she could convince him that she could dominate him, maybe he would agree to give up Mistress Elise.

The oven timer went off. She pulled the lasagna out and placed it on the table. The water in the shower was turned off, and she knew that she had only seconds before Peter would reappear. She grabbed the bottle of wine and put it on the table. She stood back and waited.

Peter came into the room pulling the sides of the robe together.

It did very little to hide his body from her view and that was exactly what she wanted. There would be no way for Peter to hide his reaction to her commands and voice. If he was excited, it would show. She picked up the bottle and handed it to him.

"You may pour." She sat at her place.

Peter grinned and reached for the corkscrew. "What game are you playing?"

"Dinner isn't a game."

The cork released from the bottle. "Your outfit is over the top."

Brenna leaned back in her chair and let her eyes wander over Peter. "I like what I see. If you continue to please me, I might be generous later on."

"Is that how it is?" Peter chuckled as he poured out a glass of wine. "Okay, I'll play along."

"You may sit."

"As you wish."

Brenna filled her plate with salad before handing the bowl to Peter. She took a small portion of lasagna and moved the dish toward her husband. Her stomach was tight with tension, and she doubted that she'd be able to eat anything. That didn't stop the game. She had to continue to play her part.

When Peter was finished eating, she sat back and moved her plate away.

"You may clear the table." She took a sip of wine.

"Did you want the dishes washed also?" Peter pushed up from the table. His robe hung open and the evidence of his excitement was displayed.

"Yes." Brenna cleared her throat. "When you're finished, I'll inspect your work."

She listened to the sound of water running, and dishes being stacked into the dishwasher as she sipped her wine. Peter was humming. She couldn't believe her ears. She'd ordered him to clean up, and he had. Better yet, he was enjoying it. Maybe there was something to this domination stuff. She wasn't about to try the whole BDSM tonight, though.

Tonight was a soft introduction.

It was meant to be fun.

The sound of the dishwasher starting alerted Brenna to her husband's approach. She straightened in her chair and took a deep breath. She needed to be strong, for the next part of the evening to succeed. Firm and dominant was the role she was to play, and she couldn't let Peter know how nervous she was.

She stood and went into the kitchen. Peter had just wiped the counter dry and had balled up the towel. He aimed it like a basketball and shot it into the sink. "Not bad for an old guy." Peter turned around with a grin. "Tonight is for the young at heart."

Brenna shrugged. "That depends on how well you listen."

Peter put his hands on his hips, which pushed the robe open farther. "How would you rate my performance so far?"

"I haven't seen anything yet." Brenna took a step closer to her husband and ran a finger down his chest. She stopped just short of his obvious erection. "There's more to keeping a wife happy than doing dishes."

Peter inhaled a sharp breath. Brenna raised an eyebrow and leaned in for a kiss. Her tongue caressed his open lips. Flickers of excitement shot through her body.

Intense.

Delightful.

Sinful.

She relished the shiver of reaction that raced through Peter. His body didn't lie. He was aroused and fully involved in the scene. A surge of pure pleasure coursed through her.

She was in control.

Peter was at her mercy.

She began to relax and enjoy the sensation.

She darted her tongue into his mouth, letting it slide and stroke over his, until he grabbed her close and poured his whole being into the kiss. He held her head and deepened the embrace. Her body flamed with desire, and for a second, she considered letting him take her right now in the kitchen.

It was too soon.

She pushed away.

When Peter tried to pull her back, she held him at bay with one hand. She was the one in control this evening, and she had to remember one of Mistress Patricia's rules. Never let the submissive dominate from the bottom. It was time for her to regain her position in this scene.

"That was your reward for a job well done."

"If that's the case, what else do you want me to do?" Peter's voice was husky.

"First you have to agree that I am in control this evening."

"Anything you want." Peter's body shook with need.

"On your knees and kiss my shoe."

Peter dropped immediately.

He grinned up at her, and then bent to kiss her stilettos.

A twist of delight flowed through Brenna. Knowing that she could bring her husband to such a state of arousal was a first for her. Peter had always been in control of their lovemaking. He was a generous and thoughtful lover, and she had no reason to complain, but maybe, Peter had needed something different. Now was her chance to show him that she could give him what he wanted.

"Stand."

Peter obeyed.

"Drop your robe and go to the bedroom."

Peter shrugged his shoulders and was nude within a second. He reached a hand out for her, and she moved back a step.

"Aren't you coming?" Peter coaxed.

"You can wait for me." Brenna kept her voice neutral. "I expect to find you standing beside the bed."

Peter chuckled. "As you wish."

"Do you think this is a game?" Brenna used the voice she had practiced in Mistress Patricia's dungeon.

Peter shook his head. "No."

"Good." Brenna moved closer to Peter. "You are following my orders tonight. Is that clear."

A shiver of reaction went through Peter. His body flared and a spark of excitement glittered in his eyes. Brenna had Peter's complete attention. She was in control, and he had no problem with it. His body did not lie.

"Go and wait."

Peter nodded and left the kitchen.

Brenna released the breath she'd been holding and leaned against the kitchen counter. She'd made it through the first part of the evening. Peter had obeyed her commands. Rather than resent what she was doing, he seemed to be enjoying it.

Brenna loved it.

She'd never felt so alive before. Her husband had done her bidding, and never once had he complained. It was fantastic. Now all she had to do was translate that into the bedroom, and she would have everything a woman could ask for.

She picked up Peter's discarded robe and smiled.

Tonight was going to be spectacular.

Chapter 7

Peter was stroking his erection when she entered the bedroom.

"Did I say you could do that?"

Peter's hand dropped away. "I was keeping myself ready."

Brenna hid her smile.

It was a brilliant idea, and one she would remember for next time.

"As long as you don't come." Brenna tapped her husband's chest. "You can only climax if and when I command it."

Peter grinned.

"Do you understand?" Brenna used her dominatrix voice, which echoed through the room.

A visible shock of arousal shook Peter's body. "Yes."

Brenna turned and pulled the sheets back from the bed. "Lie down."

Peter was on his side patting the mattress for her to join him before she could blink. He had a surprise coming if he thought that was all she had in store for this evening. She shook her head and knelt by the bed. She pulled out the cuffs that were attached to the bed restraint kit she'd bought at Erotic Dreams. She'd secured the straps under the mattress earlier in the day so that everything would be ready for Peter.

"Get on your back." Brenna opened her bedside table and pulled out the leather blindfold she'd picked up from Mistress Patricia. She leaned over Peter. "Close your eyes."

"What are you going to do?" Doubt was evident in Peter's voice.

"Do you trust me?"

Now was the moment of truth. If Peter couldn't relax and trust her, then there would be no pleasure for either of them. She held her breath and waited for the wariness to leave his eyes. He relaxed. He was ready to continue.

"Always." His words sounded like a vow.

"Then don't question me."

Brenna gave him a light kiss on the lips and then secured the blindfold. Her husband was hers for the evening. Tonight was all about pleasure. Giving and receiving. If he wanted pain, then they would discuss that later.

After the mask was secure, she moved her hand down his right arm and picked up the soft cuff restraint that was secured by straps under the bed. It had a hook and loop fastener that would adjust to Peter's wrist perfectly. Peter jerked his arm away when she put the cuff on his wrist.

"Trust me." Brenna eased his arm back onto the bed and secured the restraint.

"What have you done with my wife?" Peter's voice was uncertain. "I was only away for a week."

"A lot can happen in that time." Brenna's voice was soft as she fastened Peter's other wrist and then moved to his ankles. "Now we're ready."

Peter gave a nervous laugh. "I feel totally exposed."

"You're surrendering your enjoyment to me." Brenna picked up a feather that she'd put on her dresser.

She brushed the soft tip across Peter's abdomen. His muscles tensed as she moved the feather to his chest.

"Relax." She whispered into his ear. "Enjoy the sensations."

"It tickles."

Brenna moved the feather over his face and down his neck. The tension released from his body. She continued stroking and touching him until every inch of his skin had been feathered. When she was finished, Peter was groaning with delight. His body was receptive to her touch.

She replaced the feather with her lips.

She placed soft kisses across his body. Peter was quivering. Her tongue darted out and replaced her lips. She licked every inch of him. She left the best to last. Peter tried to jump off the bed and pulled on his restraints when she flicked the tip of his penis with her tongue.

Her hand eased him back down.

"Remember the rule."

"What rule?" Peter groaned.

"I control your climax." Brenna's tongue twirled over the tip of him. "You come only when I allow you to."

"I can't hold back."

Brenna pressed her thumb below the head of his penis. "You can and you will." Her voice was firm. "Understood."

She continued to apply pressure until Peter nodded. She eased her thumb away. "Inhale...take a deep breath."

Peter inhaled and tightened his abdominal muscles. "Ready?"

When Peter nodded, she moved back to kissing him. This time she focused on his neck and shoulders as she let her fingers roam over the rest of his body. Peter was aroused to almost breaking point when she stopped.

"I'm going to get a glass of wine." Brenna eased off the bed. "I'll be back later."

"You're going to leave me like this."

Brenna brushed a finger down his cheek. "Think about how much you'll want to please me when I return."

She shut the door behind her and sagged against it.

She was in full arousal herself.

She walked to the kitchen and poured another glass of wine. Fifteen minutes should give Peter enough time to calm down. Everything she had read in preparation for this evening had said that delaying a man's orgasm increased his pleasure. At the rate she was going, it would be a night to remember.

When she returned to the room, Peter was still in the center of the bed, and he was fully aroused. The time alone hadn't dulled his excitement. Brenna closed the door behind her and walked to the bed. She leaned over her husband and gave his shaft a gentle squeeze.

"I see you employed your time productively."

"That was your intention." Peter's voice was hoarse. "Are you going to put both of us out of our misery?"

"Perhaps."

Brenna had waited long enough.

She climbed onto the bed and straddled him. The tip of his erection was at the entrance to her moist vagina. She eased herself down onto him. Extreme sensations of bliss overtook her body. She'd been in a state of constant arousal since she'd planned this scene. Her body wanted release.

"This is for me only."

"As you wish." Peter took a deep breath.

She moved her hips up and down again. Her body quivered at the edge of climax. Spirals of delicious ecstasy raced through her, each more intense than the last. Her body moved on its own volition, taking what it needed, selfishly demanding her own release.

She rode him hard.

Her breathing became rapid, her body flushed as her heart pounded. The world splintered into shards of rapture as she reached climax and collapsed onto of Peter as the aftershocks of pleasure hummed through her body. It had been a glimpse of heaven.

Peter moved beneath her.

She remembered her role.

She pushed upward, and lifted herself off her husband. He was still erect. He'd kept his promise and held back his need to come. She smiled.

"You please me." She stroked a hand down his penis. "You may wait here until I require further attention. Make sure you're ready for me."

Peter moaned. "Again?"

She kissed his chest and then licked his nipple.

Her tongue twirled around the hardened peak, and then she nipped him.

"Was that a complaint I heard?"

"Never." Peter's breathing was ragged. "I don't know how much longer I can hold off."

"Until I say." Brenna moved onto his other nipple and licked it. "I'm doing this because I love you."

He jumped when she teased him with her teeth.

She stood and left the room.

This time she waited only ten minutes before returning. Peter was still erect and waiting. He turned his head the moment she came into the room. He was still blindfolded.

"Are you comfortable?" Brenna's voice was soft.

"Hell no." Peter's voice was filled with frustration. "You've got me on edge, and I don't like it."

"Think how great your reward will be." Brenna walked to the bed and stroked her husband's throbbing penis. "Are you ready to play again?"

Peter nodded. His breathing hitched up a notch, and Brenna could see the rise and fall of his chest as his heart pounded faster. Her husband was more than primed.

She began with an exploration of his inner thighs.

Stroking.

Teasing.

Arousing.

He tried to move away. There was no escape. She increased the pressure of her hands, massaging as she moved higher. A groan let her know that Peter was enjoying her efforts. She skipped his obvious erection and moved to his abdomen. She continued her fondling and caressing until her husband was writhing in ecstasy. It was hard to control her own need as Peter's excitement grew. She desired release as much as he.

She straddled him again.

Positioned him close to her entrance.

"Are you going to follow the rule?"

No hesitation this time. "Yes." His voice was firm.

"Then let's play." Brenna pushed down onto him and moved her hips in a rocking motion.

"You can come only when I tell you."

"As you wish." Peter's voice was strained.

His body was tense as he let her ride him until she had climaxed twice. Each time she exploded with shivers of ecstasy until she could handle it no more. Both times, she paused and let him gather his strength. She waited until his breathing had eased, and she had recomposed herself, before she started her rhythmic motion again.

Her next climax built fast. Beads of sweat had formed on Peter's forehead. When she knew that she was close to the edge, she leaned back and released his legs from the restraining cuffs before removing his blindfold. She wanted to see his eyes when he reached his peak. She kissed his lips before whispering her command.

"You may come now."

That was all it took. Peter lifted his hips from the bed and met her downward stroke with all of his might. It was only seconds before Brenna fell over the edge into a mind shattering climax. Peter was right behind her as she felt his body shudder his own release. Before she collapsed onto him, she released his hands from the restraints.

Peter hugged her close and then rolled her onto her back.

He was still inside of her.

His hips thrust deep. Brenna looked up at him, mesmerized by the determination she saw on his face. He clasped her hands above her head and drove into her again. His strokes were deep and powerful. Never had he been ready to go so soon after a climax. This was a side of Peter she was seeing for the first time.

She relaxed and let her husband control their heated spiral into renewed ecstasy. He pulled at the front laces of her bodice and freed her breasts, taking one into his mouth and licking and sucking until her body shook with need. His free hand massaged and kneaded the other breast until she writhed with bliss.

They reached the peak together.

Peter collapsed onto her.

"That should teach you not to tease a man unmercifully." Peter's words came out between gasps for air.

It was several seconds before his breathing returned to normal. He rolled them onto their sides and gave her a lazy smile of satisfaction before falling asleep. Brenna got up, changed into a nightgown, and turned off the lights before joining her husband in bed. There would be plenty of time for discussion in the morning.

When she awoke, Peter was staring down at her with a puzzled look. She rubbed the sleep from her eyes and stretched her arms over her head. She felt great.

Relaxed.

Totally satiated.

"Morning."

"What the hell was last night about?" Peter wasn't angry. He was using his best assertive tone. The one he usually reserved for the boys, or the courtroom.

"I thought you enjoyed it." Brenna wanted to avoid the confrontation about him seeing a dominatrix for as long as possible.

"It was spectacular." Peter's voice held a note of awe. "That doesn't explain where you got the idea from."

"I went to dominatrix school."

Silence and a blank look were all she got from Peter.

Finally, he spoke. "Why?"

"You don't have to lie anymore. I've shown you that I can be trusted so you need to tell me the truth."

"What am I lying about?" His voice was full of confusion.

"I know you've been seeing a dominatrix. I found Mistress Elise's business card in your pocket."

Peter shook his head. "She asked me to help her out one time. I have never visited her as a client."

Chapter 8

Brenna's stomach dropped. "I thought you were going to a dominatrix behind my back."

Peter laid his head back on his pillow and started laughing. "That's the last thing I'd do. I have absolutely no desire to be someone's whipping boy, much less their slave."

Brenna's mind spun.

She tried to focus.

How could she have been so wrong? She'd never considered the possibility that Peter wasn't seeing a dominatrix. All of the effort and training she'd put into fulfilling her husband's fantasies had been for nothing. Peter didn't want to be dominated.

"I was so certain." Brenna's voice was a breathy whisper.

"After all these years of marriage, do you think I'd keep something like that a secret from you?" Peter sounded hurt.

"At first I couldn't believe it." Brenna's voice cracked. "When I found out that she wasn't listed as one of your clients, the only other explanation was that you used her professional services."

"She was never on the books because it was a personal favor."

"So it wasn't just business." Brenna grabbed onto Peter's confession as if it were a lifeline.

"Joe Franks asked me to help her." Peter shrugged. "I was too embarrassed to ask the specifics of their relationship. I gave her the legal advice she needed and that was the end of it."

"You must have visited her dungeon because her address was on the back of the card."

"Once." Peter's voice was defensive. "I met her in the office. I never saw any other rooms."

How could she have misjudged the situation and what did that say about her marriage. What did it say about her? If Peter didn't want to play the game anymore, where did that leave them?

She'd enjoyed dominating her husband.

He'd had fun. There was no way for him to disguise his sheer enjoyment of last evening. A memory of the explosive sex they'd experienced flooded her brain. It had been the most erotically stimulating thing she'd ever experienced. There had to be a way to take the lessons she learned from Mistress Patricia and use them in her life. Maybe all wasn't lost.

"You enjoyed last night." Brenna sat up in bed. "You've never been able to do it twice in a row, not even in your teens."

"Last night was hot." Peter didn't hide his enthusiasm.

"That's because you trusted me." Brenna leaned back against the pillows. "I planned the whole evening so that you'd enjoy it."

Peter looked over at her. "You succeeded. I don't remember the last time I was so aroused. God, you were magnificent. Where the hell did you buy that outfit?"

"That's my secret." The tension in Brenna's stomach eased. Her effort hadn't been a complete waste.

"Probably at dominatrix school." Peter snorted. "Why didn't you talk to me first before you took a course that we'd have no use for?"

"Do you think it was wasted?" Brenna lowered her voice and leaned toward Peter. "I thought you quite liked obeying my commands."

Peter jerked. "That's not fair. I hadn't seen you in over a week."

"Since when was pleasure about fairness?" Brenna kept her voice sultry. "I bet I can make you just as eager this morning as you were last night."

There was a visible tent forming under the bedcovers. "How?"

"You can start by getting me a coffee." Brenna leaned over and stroked her husband's burgeoning erection. "After that, a shower for two."

Peter's eyes widened. "We're too old for that."

"Age has nothing to do with pleasure." Brenna tilted her head. "Trust me."

She rubbed her foot up the side of Peter's leg. A visible shudder went through him. She ran her fingers down his chest and under the covers. A couple of strokes and he was in full arousal. She leaned back against her pillows and stretched.

"Coffee."

Peter shook his head and threw his covers off. "I'm not sure I like this new you."

"You don't have to like it." Brenna stopped him from putting on his robe. "You just have to please me. I like to see my man nude."

"You're kidding."

Brenna shook her head. "I always reward obedience."

Peter stared at her for a few seconds and then threw the robe down. "I'm not answering the door if the bell rings."

He left in a huff.

Brenna waited until she was alone before she sagged back against the pillows. It had worked. Peter might not like to think of himself as being submissive, but he'd gone to get her coffee in the nude. He had obeyed. Never in her wildest dreams had she thought he would do something like that. This wasn't what had been taught in dominatrix school. The basic premise was the same.

She had to be firm and dominant.

Peter had to submit.

The thought made her wet. She was as aroused as Peter by their play. It didn't matter that she hadn't planned this type of scene. She was going to continue it.

Peter came in with the coffee. He was half aroused and there was a sheepish grin on his face. It was obvious he couldn't believe that he obeyed her. It was also obvious that he liked it. She motioned for him to stand beside her. He handed her the coffee, and she put it on the bedside table.

"You please me very much." She reached over and stroked his penis. "Did you bring yourself one?"

He shook his head. "I didn't know if I was allowed."

She ran her fingers up his erection.

"Perfect answer. Come closer."

Peter hesitated a second and then moved to within inches of her. She clasped his penis with one hand and stroked him up and down until he was close to climax. She stopped and leaned back against the pillows.

"You remembered the rule."

Peter's voice cracked. "You control my climax."

Brenna nodded. "Get yourself a coffee and come sit beside me."

When he left the room, Brenna exhaled the breath that she'd been holding. She couldn't remember when she'd been so aroused. If Peter was half as excited as she was, they were going to have one heck of a wonderful weekend.

Peter was back in record time.

He climbed into the bed. "So how long do you intend to keep playing this game?"

"Who said I was playing." Brenna sipped her coffee. "I love having my coffee delivered to me in bed."

Peter shook his head. "What else did you learn in dominatrix school?"

Brenna shrugged. "I learned how to spank a man and then take care of him afterwards."

"We are not going down that road." Peter crossed his arms over his chest. "I'm not even sure I like this coffee stuff."

Brenna smiled. "I like it. That's all that matters."

Peter turned to look at her. "You can't expect me to accept this."

Brenna shrugged. "We're having fun."

Peter huffed and pushed back into his pillows. "Real men don't become slaves."

"Some men like it." Brenna's voice was hesitant. "It helps them relieve their stress."

"A good round of golf will do the same thing."

"For you maybe. Some men need to go to a place where they don't have to make decisions; all they have to do is feel. They relinquish control to a person they trust."

"It sounds as if you learned the lingo." Peter finished drinking his coffee and put it on the table. He reached over and took Brenna's half-finished cup and put it down beside his. "Now it's time for the man of the house to take over."

Before Brenna could protest, Peter had pulled her into his arms and started kissing her. Within seconds, she was lost in the power of his passion. Thoughts of dominance were forgotten as she surrendered to her husband's expertise. He had her body singing with pleasure as he stroked and teased her to several climaxes before he entered her. He took his time, pushing her to the edge of bliss time and again, until he let them both shatter in ecstasy.

It was several minutes before either of them was able to move.

"Now tell me who is in control?" Peter's voice was smug.

Peter's lovemaking had been a reassertion of his dominance in bed.

Brenna was too replete with satisfaction to care.

"The sex was just as fantastic last night as it was this morning. I'm not ready for any crazy lifestyle changes." Peter got out of bed and headed for the shower. "I have a golf game at noon. I'll be back for supper."

Brenna sighed. If she'd been thinking properly when she found Mistress Elise's business card she would have realized that Peter wasn't the type of man to want to be dominated. Even if Peter had enjoyed the game last night, there wasn't going to be any way to convince him to continue playing. Now that she'd had a taste of being in control, she liked it.

Where did that leave her?

She'd have to come up with another plan.

Chapter 9

"It was a complete disaster." Brenna lifted the box of dishes from the floor to the countertop.

Lara pulled out a handful of paper-wrapped plates from the box. "Peter didn't like the surprise?"

"Surprise is the operative word." Brenna crossed her arms and leaned back against the counter. "He didn't have a clue about what I was doing."

Lara paused in her unpacking. "I don't understand."

"It turns out that Peter was never seeing a dominatrix."

Lara's mouth dropped open. "No!"

Brenna nodded. She had promised Lara that she would help her unpack her new apartment, so after Peter had left for his golf game, she had come over to Lara's place. The movers had dropped everything off the day before, and the place was littered with boxes. Lara's new furniture would be arriving later in the day so they had to clear the mess away.

"He'd given Mistress Elise legal advice as a favor for one of his friends."

Lara shook her head and started to laugh. "That's perfect. If you hadn't believed that Peter was seeing a dominatrix you would never have mentioned it to the group. None of us would have tackled our marriage woes if not for you."

Brenna pushed away a twinge of guilt. "I started all of this and it turns out my husband is satisfied with our life."

Lara put the china plates in the sink. "I always thought it strange that Peter wouldn't have opened up to you about his needs."

"Why?"

"You seemed to have a wonderful marriage." Lara shrugged. "Peter has always been considerate of you and he's a wonderful father. He's your typical alpha male and driven to succeed, yet there's never been any doubt that he loved you."

Brenna moved to the sink and started to fill it with water. "That's almost exactly what Peter said. He told me there was no way he would have gone to a dominatrix without talking to me first."

"That's because you two have true intimacy in your marriage." Lara reached into the box for more china. "I envy that."

"Just because David was a jerk doesn't mean you won't find a man to love."

"That's what I keep telling myself. I have to learn to trust my instincts again." Lara handed a stack of teacups to Brenna. "When I first met David, I was reluctant to let him into my life. He was so persistent he eventually wore me down and I mistook his motive as love."

"He was a fool." Brenna added dish soap to the water. "I'm glad you're free of him."

"So am I."

"I can't believe David won't let you have any of the wedding presents or kitchen things."

"It's not in the prenup." Lara's voice was a few octaves lower in an imitation of David.

"It's a good thing that you kept some of your stuff from before the marriage."

Lara picked up one of the cleaned plates and placed it in the cupboard. "I couldn't get rid of my grandmother's china. It was too old-fashioned for David, and he refused to store it at the house. I was forced to rent a storage locker. There was room in the unit so I kept some of my other things too."

"At least you're not starting from scratch."

"True." Lara laughed. "I'll use that as a gauge in the future. No man is going to take over my life so completely that there isn't room for my past."

For several hours they continued to unpack and wash the china. Once everything was put away in the cupboards they moved on to the box of pots and pans. The boxes were broken down and put aside to recycle. They still had an hour before the new furniture arrived, so Lara put the kettle on, and they settled down for tea in the freshly washed china.

They sat on the floor, leaning against the living room wall with a plate of cookies and tarts. Brenna savored the sweet heat of the tea as she sipped it between nibbles on a shortbread cookie.

"Tell me what's bothering you."

Lara's voice broke into Brenna's thoughts.

"How did you guess?"

"You're too quiet." Lara's cup clattered in its saucer as she put it down on the floor. "I would have thought you'd be ecstatic about Peter."

Brenna shrugged. "At first I was too shocked to give it much consideration. Now I'm not so sure."

"You want Peter to see a dominatrix?" Lara's voice held confusion.

Brenna tapped a finger against her teacup. "It's not that. I'm happy that he trusts me enough to be honest. I suppose I feel disappointed by the whole experience."

"You had a scene planned for Peter's return home." Lara frowned. "Wasn't your roleplaying as a dominatrix a success?"

"That's the problem." Brenna looked at Lara. "It was fantastic. Peter loved it and so did I."

Lara smiled. "I thought you didn't like the dominatrix school."

"I wasn't comfortable having to spank and humiliate men. Until I had Peter alone, I didn't realize how much I loved having control."

"It aroused you."

"I loved it." Brenna's stomach flipped as she admitted the truth for the first time. "I don't think I've ever been so aroused before."

"Was it the power that excited you, or the scene you had set up?"

Brenna let her mind wander back to the previous night. The setting had been romantic, the food perfect, and Peter had been home. The clothes she's worn had added an extra element of excitement. The real thrill had been the scene she'd planned. She'd had complete control over what they would be doing that night.

"Both. I loved the scene, and the fact that I had orchestrated it."

"What did you do?"

"I wore the corset dress with the flirty red skirt, my stilettos, and the garter with silk nylons." Brenna inhaled as the memory wove its magic. "Peter was surprised, but he played along. I had set up the bondage set under the mattress, and I insisted that Peter obey me."

"So you used everything you learned at Mistress Patricia's." Lara took a sip of tea. "It sounds like a safe and gentle introduction into the BDSM lifestyle."

"I wanted to gain Peter's trust." Brenna hesitated a second before continuing. "I wasn't confident that I'd be able to carry out a totally dominant scene, so I did what Mistress Patricia had recommended."

Lara rubbed her fingertip over the top of her teacup. "I never told any of the others, but when I was in college I dated a man that was a Dom."

"You were a submissive?" Brenna didn't hide her shock. "Why didn't you say so earlier?"

"I was only with him a short time." Lara shrugged. "I wasn't a very good submissive, and I couldn't envision myself as a slave. My biggest problem was that even though it was sexually exciting, I couldn't let myself trust completely."

"Maybe he wasn't a man you should have trusted." Brenna's voice was quiet. "Remember what you just said about trusting your instincts."

Lara nodded. "My question is whether you pushed yourself too hard to be what you thought Peter wanted? Maybe you'd be more comfortable if he was the dominant one?"

Brenna let the idea sink in.

Did she want to relinquish control to Peter?

The scene from the previous night played through her memory. She'd enjoyed teasing and then denying Peter until he was frantic with need. She'd had a sense of pride over the fact that she'd driven him wild enough that he came twice. She alone was responsible for making that possible. Even thinking about it now was giving her an erotic charge.

"I liked the power of being able to drive my husband wild with need." Brenna blurted the truth out and then looked at Lara with wide eyes. "I know I was hesitant to try this in the beginning, but it was fun. Is that terrible of me?"

"There's nothing to be ashamed of." Lara smiled. "Now that you know what you like, you can devise a plan."

"Peter refuses to play."

"There's more than one way to approach a man about this." Lara picked up a cookie and took a bite.

"You don't understand Peter. You can only push him so far before he digs his feet in. There's no budging him after that."

"He's a man." Lara's voice was matter of fact. "There's always a way."

Just then the buzzer rang.

For the next hour, they were busy with delivery men and arranging furniture. When they were finally alone, the apartment had the basic elements necessary for a comfortable home. There was a sectional, dining table and chairs, and a bedroom set. The walls were still bare. Brenna was certain that Lara would have that fixed soon enough.

When they'd finished arranging the furniture, they both plopped on the sectional.

"What did you mean by saying Peter was a man?" Brenna glanced at Lara.

"You can work around the fact that Peter doesn't like bondage. There are other ways that he can be submissive."

"You mean spanking?"

"You can dominate your husband without physical restraints." Lara kicked off her shoes and tucked her feet under her legs. "Have you ever heard of female led relationships?"

Brenna shook her head.

"There are many levels, and you don't have to use pain."

A flicker of excitement stirred within Brenna. Maybe there was a way that she could take what she'd learned from Mistress Patricia and apply it to her life with Peter.

"Does that mean you can do it some of the time?"

"You decide how you want to incorporate it into your life."

Brenna frowned. "That might be a good compromise. The problem is that Peter wants things the way they usually are."

"Then deny him."

Brenna tilted her head. "Are you suggesting what I think you are?"

Lara nodded. "He's a man and just like any other man, he has wants and needs."

Brenna giggled. "So if I control his climaxes, then I'll control him."

"And eventually he'll come to see that your way of doing things benefits him."

"That seems so unfair." A twinge of doubt raced through her. "I love him. If I deny him, am I denying myself too?"

Lara gave her a wicked grin. "No one said that pleasure has to be equal."

It took Brenna a second to realize what Lara meant. "He won't go for that."

"You're doing him a favor." Lara's voice was sincere. "For men, the longer between their orgasms and the larger the buildup, the better it is."

Brenna frowned. "Are you certain?"

"You've never denied Peter before." Lara twisted around to face Brenna. "You said that last night the sex was fantastic. Did Peter get to come when he wanted?"

Brenna shook her head.

"You had control, and you made certain that he had a wonderful experience."

"I never thought of it like that."

"You gave him the night of his life." Lara's voice was quietly persuasive. "Now you have to convince him that's what he wants all the time."

"Do you think he'll go for it?"

"All you can do is ask." Lara pushed off the sectional. "If he's hesitant and it's something you really want to do, then start slow. Don't do anything drastic, just a bit of play now and then."

Brenna stood. "I had him get me coffee this morning."

"That's a great way to begin." Lara went to the new television console. "Make sure you reward him."

"I did." Brenna's voice was low with laughter. "I think he enjoyed it, even though he complained."

"There's a lot of places online where you can research this stuff." Lara connected a cable to the television. "Have all the information ready before you approach him."

"I'll try it."

"If that fails, you could always open up a dungeon to compete with Mistress Elise."

Brenna laughed. "Wouldn't' that make Peter's day. I might threaten him with it."

"An education is a horrible thing to waste." Lara winked. "Now where should I put these speakers?"

The rest of the afternoon was spent organizing Lara's space. By the time Brenna left, the apartment was looking livable. She drove home and replayed the conversation she'd had with Lara. It sounded like fun. All she had to do was convince Peter that a bit of roleplaying would improve their sex life.

Chapter 10

Brenna had done her research.

Tonight she was going to speak to Peter about role playing in their marriage. Nothing too serious, just a bit of chore play, along with teasing and denial. It had been a week since she'd sprung the dominatrix scenario on him, and by her estimation, he was more than ready to be in the mood to listen to her suggestion.

She'd taken care with her attire this evening, putting on a pair of brown slacks, a peach silk blouse, and a pair of dressy loafers. It was casual, yet elegant. There wasn't a hint of the dominatrix in the outfit because she was hoping to ease Peter into accepting her suggestion.

She was in the kitchen when he came home.

If all went as planned, in the future she'd be spending less time cooking.

"Smells good." Peter dropped his briefcase on the table. "What's for dinner?"

"Chateaubriand."

Peter's eyes widened. "Did I forget we're having company?"

Brenna switched the burner on for the vegetables and turned to Peter. He pulled her in for a hug, and she relaxed in his embrace. He'd always made her feel safe with his self-assurance and strength. Would he be able to switch roles and let her have control?

Peter patted her bum and released her. "You don't have another wild night planned?"

Brenna shook her head. "Not unless you want one."

"That night has haunted my thoughts all week. It was stupendous." Peter's gruff admission sent a shiver of anticipation through her. "I had a hard time concentrating at work because my mind kept wondering back to it."

Brenna twirled a finger around Peter's silk tie. "I might be able to improvise something."

"Your imagination could be the death of me." Peter's voice cracked. "I don't think I could handle that on a regular basis."

"What if we tried something a little less dominating?"

Brenna held her breath and waited for his reaction. When he didn't say anything she glanced up at his face. He was looking at her with sparkles in his eyes. She hadn't seen that look of intense interest in years. Maybe there was hope for her plan.

"You sly devil." He gave her a quick kiss. "You do have something planned."

Brenna shrugged. "I thought we could discuss options over dinner and a bottle of wine."

"Where are you coming up with all of these ideas?"

"I have sources." Brenna said in a flippant tone. "Why don't you change?"

"You don't have to ask me twice." Peter grabbed his briefcase and left.

Brenna let out a shaky breath.

He was almost hooked.

Now for the hard part. She had to tell him what her plan was. First, she'd make sure he was well-fed and a bit tipsy. From her research she knew that he might be hesitant at first. All it would take was the proper presentation and persuasion, then he'd be eager for the role playing. They'd both benefit from switching up their relationship and letting her take the lead.

After dinner, they retired to the living room with their second bottle of wine. Peter lit the fireplace and the ambiance in the room was perfect for their discussion. Brenna kicked her shoes off and tucked her feet up beside her on the couch. Peter sat down beside her and offered a refill on the wine.

She took a sip and waited for him to get comfortable. He kept giving her sideways looks and the tingle of arousal that had been with her all day grew intense. There was only one way for her to approach the subject and that was head on.

"Have you ever heard of chore play?"

Peter frowned. "It sounds like work."

"Work with benefits." Brenna ran her finger over the edge of her crystal wine glass. The high-pitched ring pierced the silence.

"Go on," Peter coaxed.

"You'd have to do certain things and if your performance is good, then you get a reward." Brenna stole a glance at Peter. He was frowning as if he were trying to understand what she was saying.

"It sounds like you'd be bribing me."

"Not quite." Brenna's voice was hesitant.

"You'll have to be more explicit." Peter reached over and clasped her hand. "If there's something you want from me, then ask. After all these years, you must know that I'd do anything for you."

Brenna swallowed back her hesitation. She knew this would be difficult to discuss with Peter because he had always taken the lead in their relationship. She'd never been disappointed with his direction in the past.

Now, she desired more.

"I want to have control in our relationship."

"Don't you like how I handle things?" Peter's voice held a note of hurt.

"I love what you've done for us and the boys." Brenna put her glass of wine down. "This has nothing to do with that. I just want you to allow me more control with the direction our relationship is taking."

Peter nodded. "This is about the dominatrix thing."

Brenna ran her finger down her husband's cheek. "It's also about what is best for both of us. I think I've found a compromise if you're willing to consider it."

"They really did a number on you at that school." Peter exhaled a heavy breath. "I'm not saying I didn't enjoy the other night. That's not what our relationship is about. We are equals."

"Are we?"

Peter frowned. "What do you mean?"

"You always take the lead when we make love."

Peter shook his head. "That's not true. If you're not in the mood, we don't have sex."

"So I take the lead by being negative?" Brenna asked. "Does that seem fair?"

"It's the truth." Peter huffed with exasperation.

"I want that to change." Brenna spoke in a firmer voice. "If you love me, then you'll consider what I'm going to suggest."

"Do I have a choice?" Peter's voice was tinged with anger.

"Always."

Brenna picked up her wine glass and leaned back into the soft cushions of the couch. She sipped her wine and waited for Peter to calm down. It took several moments before he rubbed a hand over his face and gave her a crooked grin.

"I'm being unreasonable. Tell me what you want."

"I want to experiment with chore play."

The tension in Brenna's shoulders eased. Peter hadn't failed her. He always took a while with something new. In the end, he usually came around. It was one of the reasons their marriage had lasted so long.

"Why do I think that means work for me?" Peter leaned close and lowered his voice. "And pleasure for you?"

"I always said you were a smart man." Brenna giggled. Things were already heating up, and they hadn't started yet.

"Give me the broad strokes, no pun intended." Peter picked up his wine and took a gulp.

"Like I said before, you do the things I ask, and then you get rewarded." Brenna shrugged. "What could be simpler?"

"What kind of things?"

"You already told me you weren't into any of the bondage stuff, so I thought we'd start with housework and see how that goes."

"I help with the dishes when I'm home." Peter frowned. "What more do you want?"

"Dinner, grocery shopping, vacuuming, washing the floors." Brenna was counting the chores off on her fingers. "I'd like you to bring me coffee in the morning."

"Is that all."

Brenna shook her head.

She'd left the best to last.

"You have to give me an orgasm whenever I ask."

Peter's hand jerked and his wine splashed about in his glass. "You're kidding."

Brenna forced her face to remain expressionless. She was using all of her dominatrix training to stay in control of this situation.

"There is one more condition which is for your benefit."

"Finally something for me." Peter shook his head. "What is it?"

"I control your orgasms."

Peter stared at her with his mouth open. "No."

Brenna hid her disappointment. She knew this wasn't going to be easy. She still had one trick up her sleeve. She'd use Peter's logical mind against him.

"That's the only way this will work." Brenna waited a second before continuing, "Your pleasure will be dependent on how well you perform."

"That's blackmail." Peter's voice was curt.

"It's no different than what I did last weekend." Brenna dropped her voice to a sultry whisper and ran a finger down Peter's chest. "I controlled everything."

Peter watched as she moved to his crotch. She rubbed against him and hid her smile as his arousal grew. He was definitely interested.

Peter cleared his throat. "What if I don't like it?"

"Then we stop." She squeezed him, relishing his burgeoning erection.

"I could cheat." Peter's voice was full of bravado. "There's no way to monitor me."

Brenna sat back. "I'd know. There's no way you could hide it."

Peter considered her words for a few seconds and then shook his head. "Are you planning on putting camera's in the shower and following me when I travel?"

"No." Brenna took another sip of wine. "You're going to have to sign a contract."

Peter threw his head back and laughed. "Do you think I won't break a contract like that?"

"I trust you." Brenna said in her most innocent voice. "Once you see the benefits of this, I'm certain you won't want to stray."

"So I sign this contract and you trust me to follow it." Peter shook his head. "You really think the benefits of delaying my orgasm are worth all of this effort."

"It's supposed to be fun." Brenna said. "There's no reason to start this if you going to be negative from the start."

"I didn't say I wouldn't do it." Peter's voice was a growl. "Let me get used to this first."

"Answer me one thing." Brenna's voice was a sharp command. "Did you enjoy last weekend?"

Peter's face softened. "You know I did."

"Then trust me."

Peter took another gulp of wine. "Do you have the contract drawn up?"

Brenna pulled a sheet of paper off the coffee table. "You can read it."

Peter gave a quick perusal of the short contract she'd written.

"Basically you want me to do the housework on the weekends I'm home. If we're having company, then you'll take over."

"Correct." Brenna waited for him to finish the list she'd prepared.

"Coffee and orgasms seem to be at the top of your demands. Are you trying to tell me something?" Peter looked at her with a raised brow. "I thought you enjoyed our sex life?"

"You're a wonderful lover, and I've never had a complaint." Brenna pointed to the paper. "This is for fun and to give us a bit more excitement in our lives. The boys are away most of the time, so we can let loose and enjoy ourselves."

"I'll be walking into walls if you don't let me have regular orgasms." Peter's tone was half serious.

"You'll be thinking about me," Brenna countered. "And all the fun you'll have when you get home."

"I wish I'd never left that card in my pocket." Peter chuckled. "I created a monster."

"Maybe that's what you subconsciously wanted all along." Brenna handed Peter a pen. "When you're ready."

Peter gave the contract another quick glance and then signed it.

"I hope you read the fine print."

"I know everything that I need to." Peter stood and reached his hand out to her. "Let's get to work and give you one of those orgasms you're so concerned about."

"The dishes need to be cleaned. You will have to do that afterwards."

Brenna shook with the delicious sense of power and excitement that filled her. She would be in control. The most exciting part was knowing that Peter was going to be so happy and eager once he embraced the lifestyle. When she reached the bedroom, she lit a couple of candles and pulled the sheets back.

"Are you going to have mercy on a first timer and let me enjoy myself too?"

Brenna shook her head. "You'll have to earn that."

Peter groaned. "I still don't know how you plan on ensuring that I don't masturbate?"

"It was in the fine print." Brenna unbuttoned her blouse. "I did ask if you'd read it."

Peter gave her a sheepish grin. "I missed it."

"You won't be able to hide it because you'll have no interest in our game." Brenna kicked off her shoes. "If you don't honor the contract, I'll lock you up in a chastity device."

Chapter 11

"They have such a thing?"

Brenna nodded. "It looks painful too."

"I'll bet." Peter pulled her close. "You're enjoying this a bit too much."

Brenna shrugged. "It's fun."

"From my perspective, you're the only one having a good time."

"I thought you enjoyed giving me pleasure." Brenna kissed his chin.

"Honey, there's nothing I like more." Peter's voice dropped to a seductive whisper. "How about you get nice and comfortable on the pillows, and let me take care of your needs."

Brenna leaned back in his arms. "You're the expert."

"Don't you forget it."

Peter backed her up against the side of the bed. He helped with getting her blouse off her shoulders and then unfastened her bra. His fingers massaged and kneaded the tension from her shoulders before he moved lower. He caressed and stroked, sending jolts of sweet pleasure through her body. Moist heat filled her as he moved lower and undid her pants. Within seconds, she stood before him naked.

Peter rubbed a finger between her legs.

She shook with need.

He knelt in front of her and spread her legs. She fell back against the bed, giving her husband complete access. He kissed and licked her sensitive inner thighs before his tongue touched her clitoris. Bliss sizzled through her. She writhed with excitement as he teased, tasted, and sucked her until she shuddered with an explosive climax.

Peter eased away from her. "Is that what you had in mind?"

Brenna chuckled. "You know it is."

"Are you ready for another one?"

"Always." Her voice was soft with satisfaction.

Peter shrugged out of his shirt and undid his pants. She inhaled as he dropped his trousers and kicked them off. He was superb in full arousal. She trembled with the need to feel the full length of him inside of her. She pushed it away. Tonight was about denying Peter, and she knew that if she let him near her, she'd forget her good intentions and give him whatever he desired.

Peter ran his hand down his penis. "Are you sure you don't want some of this?"

Brenna shook her head.

She sat back against the pillows. "You have to earn that privilege."

"As you wish."

Peter positioned himself between her legs and let his tongue work its magic. Two orgasms later she was boneless with satiation. All she wanted was to curl up and sleep. There was still Peter's needs to think about. He was holding her close in his arms, his fingers trailing fire over her body. His heavy arousal pressed against her legs.

"Did I earn my reward?"

Brenna kissed his chest.

Dare she relent so soon?

Her body screamed for the fulfillment that being joined with Peter gave her. She craved the communion of feeling one with her husband and moving together in their own unique dance of lovemaking. It was intimacy at its purest. The reward for years of hard work spent on their relationship.

She pushed away.

"The table needs to be cleared."

Peter groaned and flopped back on the pillows. "You're killing me."

Brenna stroked her hand up his erection. "You'll live."

Peter exhaled. "I hope so."

He pushed out of bed and pulled the covers over her before stalking out the room nude. Brenna smiled. Peter hadn't given a second thought to how he was dressed. He was upset about not getting his own way.

He was motivated.

She was making progress.

Was this what she really wanted? That was the last thing she thought before falling asleep.

The next day Brenna was relaxing on the couch. She stretched her legs out in front of her. She was reading and waiting for Peter to finish scrubbing the kitchen. He'd spent the previous night tossing and turning, and he had been grumpy when he'd presented her with her coffee this morning. She was enjoying the role reversal too much to relent. Peter had signed the contract and she intended for him to honor it.

At least for the weekend.

After that, she wasn't so sure.

It was fun teasing her husband. At some point, she wanted the sense of familiar comradery they'd always had between them. Keeping the balance of sexual power uneven might be exciting, but it was exhausting. She shut her book when she heard Peter approaching.

"Time for your lunch."

She looked up and gasped.

Her six foot four inch husband was holding a plate out to her with nothing on but a frilly floral apron. The apron reached mid-thigh and did nothing to conceal the tent of his arousal. He bent closer when she didn't move to take the plate from him. He tugged the book from her limp hands and replaced it with the plate.

"Is there anything else?" His voice was sweet as honey. His eyes sparkled with mischief.

Brenna shook her head. She wasn't hungry, but she had no intention of turning the sandwich away after Peter had put so much effort into the presentation.

"The flowers are a nice touch." Brenna took a bite of the ham and cheese on rye bread. "Where did you find that apron?"

"It was buried at the back of one of the kitchen drawers I was cleaning out."

Brenna choked on her food. It took a second for her to swallow and then she glared at Peter. "I just finished straightening those drawers last month."

Peter shrugged. "They needed organizing."

A sliver of panic shot through her. "You didn't throw anything away?"

"I set it aside for the charity donation box." Peter put his hands on his hips. "You told me to clean the kitchen."

Brenna took a deep sigh before settling back against the couch cushions. She'd told him that an hour ago because he was hovering. She would give him a task, and he'd be back within minutes demanding more to do. Usually Peter was too busy doing his own work on the weekends to bother her. Not today. Since they'd started playing this game, all he could think about was getting tasks done so he could get a chance for release.

Sex was a powerful motivator.

Brenna wasn't certain she'd survive the experience.

"Don't you like the sandwich?" Peter's voice was filled with exasperation. "I spent a lot of time making it the way you like. I cut the crusts cut off and added just the right amount of mayo."

"It's wonderful." Brenna took another bite. "Is there one for you?"

"I'll eat when you're finished."

"Did you bring some work home this weekend?" Brenna kept her voice neutral.

"Yes." Peter's eyes narrowed as he watched her take another bite.

"You could take a break from working around the house."

"Do you want another orgasm?" Peter's voice was eager. "That will make three today. Surely that's enough for me to have earned a release."

"Not quite." Brenna's voice was dry.

She needed to find him another task. Preferably one that would keep him busy for several hours. He'd done the vacuuming, the dusting, and cleaning the kitchen. That left only one area of the house untouched.

"The bathrooms need to be scrubbed."

"You're kidding?" Peter tilted his head. "You'd rather I clean than give you an orgasm?"

Brenna picked up her book. "Yes."

Peter left in a huff.

She sighed.

Being dominant was hard work. She had almost given in and let him talk her into doing what he wanted, which was another trip to the bedroom. She needed a break, even if Peter didn't. He'd been plying her with food and drinks all day. Constantly demanding her attention and then upset when she asked for space. Here she was eating a sandwich she didn't want, just because Peter had made a point of insisting.

She was a failure as a dominatrix.

Who was in charge?

It was fun in the beginning to have control over Peter. Getting him to do small tasks for her was great. Controlling his orgasms by tying it to her pleasure was insane. All he thought about was sex. He was in a constant state of arousal.

He'd taken the task of serving her to the extreme.

He wasn't unhappy, though.

She had to be doing something right. Brenna left her lunch half-eaten and went back to reading her book. She'd barely finished a chapter when Peter was back for new orders. So much for a relaxing day. She was almost to the point where she was going to let him have an orgasm just to get him out of her hair. Instead she closed her book and stood.

"Let's go."

Peter grinned. "To the bedroom?"

"Where else?"

"We've never done it in the kitchen and now that it's clean...." Peter's voice trailed off.

Brenna shook her head. "You're enjoying this way too much."

"Wasn't that the point?' Peter took her hand. "Just think, you'll be able to make me clean it again afterwards."

"I'm beginning to see why you're such a good lawyer." Brenna let Peter lead her out of the living room. "You're goal-oriented, and you never give up."

"After all our years together, you're only now figuring that out?"

"I've never blocked you before." Brenna gave a short laugh. "I feel like a twig trying to withstand a tornado."

"Honey, you're the only real goal I've ever had." Peter's voice was a husky assertion.

A gust of desire overtook her senses.

Peter's gaze was heated and sincere.

"Where should we do it?" Brenna's voice shook with need. "I've always wondered if it would be difficult on the countertop."

"It's perfect." Peter wiggled his eyebrows. "The better to eat you my dear."

The kitchen sparkled.

The countertop and table were cleared of clutter and the floor was clean. Peter grabbed her close to him and nuzzled her neck. A tremor of excitement raced through her. He was eager and attentive. It was everything she had hoped for when she started this game. She leaned back into his arms and let him lift her to the counter.

He pulled her pants off and bent to taste her.

She was wet and ready for him.

His tongue licked and teased her until she exploded with ecstasy.

She had barely caught her breath when he gathered her into his arms. "Let's try the table."

He carried her across the kitchen and positioned her close to the table's edge. He spread her legs and moved his lips over her inner thighs. By the time he had reached her sensitive core, Brenna was shaking with need.

She lay back on the tabletop and let her husband shatter her with another orgasm. She had never seen Peter so adept in the kitchen before, and when he pulled a chair over and sat in front of her, she surrendered to the delightfully erotic afternoon of explosive pleasure that Peter's hunger provided.

Chapter 12

Brenna stepped out of the shower and into the arms of her husband.

Peter was holding a large bath towel out for her. Drops of water clung to his hair, shoulders, and body. Still, he stood there and tended to her needs. She let him hold her close and rub her dry, luxuriating in every tingling sensation that he was creating within her. His touch was tender and seductive, sending quivers of anticipation through her. All day he had pleasured her, catered to her needs, and made her his total focus.

He was naked and aroused.

Tonight would be his reward.

When she was dry, she took the towel from him and started to rub his back and abdomen dry. He was still in great shape. The years had added a few extra pounds and muscles, and changed his hair from brown to gray. Underneath it all, he was the boy she'd fallen in love with in high school. When he was toweled dry, she reached up and kissed him.

"Feel better?"

"Nothing like cleaning up after a long day of work." Peter clasped her chin between her fingers and held her gaze. "What say we take this somewhere more comfortable? The kitchen hurt my back."

"You can cross that off your bucket list." Brenna laughed. "Antics like that are for the young."

"Hey we're not in our dotage yet."

"Prove it." Brenna's tone was a challenge.

Without missing a beat, Peter picked her up in his arms and carried her out of the bathroom and into their bedroom. He stopped at the bed and plopped her down on the mattress. She was laughing too hard to notice she'd bounced a couple of times. When she stopped and looked up at her husband, her heart skipped a beat.

Peter was leaning over her, his brown eyes unblinking.

He wasn't hiding his hunger.

She swallowed back her surprise. In all of their years together, he'd never looked at her with such passion or intensity. All day he'd done her bidding, and her reward was his complete and devoted attention. It was a revelation. Teasing and denying him had intensified his desire. It had also increased her pleasure.

She brushed her hand against his cheek. "You worked hard today."

"I'm glad you noticed." Peter lay down beside her. "I ache for you desperately. Are we going to continue playing the game?"

"You've earned a reprieve."

"Good." Peter gathered her close. "I've been dying all day to kiss you properly."

"No more words," Brenna whispered.

Peter's tongue flicked over her lips before seizing her mouth in a heated kiss. Their lips clung as if they were both starving. It was all consuming. She let herself get lost in his urgency. Brenna surrendered to Peter's expert touch as his hands roamed over her back and down her thighs. He brushed his fingers against her sensitive skin, sending shivers of delight through her.

He moved so that she had access to his body.

She ran her hand up his heavy arousal. He shook when she clasped him tight. He was close to the breaking point, and she knew that it wouldn't take much to push him over the edge. When she released him, he growled and pushed her onto her back. His lips left her mouth and started an erotic descent down her neck.

Her heart raced as his fingers caressed and teased her, moving up her thigh as his lips continued down her neck to her breasts. He touched her inner core and her body throbbed with need. He rubbed her clitoris until she was panting for release.

His tongue licked and tasted the sensitive skin of her breasts before circling her areola. A flick across her nipple had her on the screaming edge of climax. Peter positioned her so that he could enter her.

One thrust.

She shook with an explosive release.

Peter moved within her, setting a heated pace that rekindled the flames of arousal. Within seconds, Brenna was pulsing with renewed arousal. She marveled at his control and energy. He continued to hold back his own pleasure as he waited for her to join him. Together, they weaved a taut coil of rapture until it broke, sending both of them spiraling into ecstasy.

Peter collapsed on top of her and she held him close.

She was one with him.

Complete union.

"I love you."

Peter chuckled and rolled off her. "That's easy to say after a day of total devotion."

"Not every husband would have agreed to my demands."

"How could I refuse you?" Peter leaned over and kissed her. "You weren't wrong about making it better. That was one of the most stupendous orgasms I've ever had."

"So you're ready to do this again tomorrow?"

Peter leaned up on one elbow. "Is this lifestyle what you want?"

Brenna brushed a lock of hair from Peter's forehead. It had been ages since they'd had this much fun. Still, she missed the joy of being joined with him when they made love. She had numerous orgasms today, yet nothing had been as wonderful as when they'd been together, moving as one. She just wanted to enjoy making love with her husband.

"I want to make you happy." Brenna gave him the truth. "That's all I've ever wanted."

"It's been fun." Peter shook his head. "Shocking, erotic, mind-blowing, and sensual. I don't think I've ever spent a day where I was more aroused. You could have asked me for anything, and I would have given it to you."

"That sounds like bribery."

"Most women wouldn't care how they got it." Peter gave her a gentle kiss. "Today made me realize how much I love you. There's only ever been one woman for me, and if you want to pursue this game, then I'll do it."

"But you didn't really like it." Brenna could hear the reservation in her husband's voice.

"Who likes cleaning?" Peter said. "I wouldn't be able to concentrate on anything but you if we did this full-time. When would I get any work done?"

"What about me." Brenna's voice rose in indignation. "You were hovering around me all day. I barely had a minute alone."

"I thought that was the point." Peter's voice was strident. "I was there to do your bidding."

"It didn't work out like I envisioned." Brenna stopped short of pouting. "I thought I'd have more time for myself if you did all the work."

"So neither of us got what we expected." Peter's voice was tinged with laughter. "Can we call it quits?"

"I'll rip the contract up in the morning."

Peter jumped out of bed. "I'm not taking any chances. Where is that damn thing? I want it destroyed now while you're in the mood."

He left and was back within seconds. He handed her the contract and waited until she'd ripped it in two before taking the paper and throwing it in the garbage. Then he jumped back in bed and gathered her close.

"Now I can keep my golf game tomorrow."

Brenna swatted him on the chest. "Is that the only reason you don't want to play."

Peter gave her a heated look. "I like the freedom of making love to my wife. I adore you, and if you feel that I'm neglecting you, all you have to do is tell me."

"Complete honesty."

"If you find strange cards in my suits, ask me." Peter nibbled at her ear. "We've had miscommunication in the past, but this one was a doozy."

"So if I want a bit of excitement in our marriage, you'll provide it?"

"Always." Peter gave her a searing kiss. "I was thinking that we should plan a second honeymoon for our twenty-fifth anniversary this fall."

"Just the two of us."

"How about a Mediterranean cruise?" Peter's fingers fluttered against her back, sending a tremor of awareness through her body.

"It sounds wonderful."

"No cooking or cleaning, just the two of us making love all day long." Peter nipped at her bottom lip. "I could give you as many orgasms as you wanted, and I might even allow you to tease me for a few days."

Brenna was finding it hard to concentrate on Peter's words. "It sounds delightful."

"Good." Peter ran his hand up her thigh. "I'll book it tomorrow."

"I still think we could make the chore play work." Brenna didn't want to lose all the ground she'd won today.

"How about we set aside one weekend a month for some fun." Peter's voice was serious. "I've let work interfere too much lately. As long as I know ahead of time, I can make certain you have my complete and devoted attention. I don't need a contract for that."

"You'll do whatever I ask?"

"As long as there are no whips or chains." Peter's voice held a hint of laughter. "You planned one hell of a sensual evening last week and today was over the top. It would be a shame to let your training go to waste."

"You have no objection to role-playing scenes?"

"I'm here to fulfill your heart's desire." Peter inhaled a sharp breath. "I can't remember being that turned-on since we were teens."

"When we had to sneak away to make love?" Brenna smiled at the memories of their sexual explorations in the back seat of Peter's car.

"There was such an intensity to our love-making that my whole body shook."

"I seem to remember a few tremors today."

"There were more than a few." Peter's voice was wry. "You sure have a talent for renewing the passion in our marriage."

"I thought you'd never notice." Brenna smoothed a hand over Peter's chest.

"I adore you." Peter clasped her hand. "It's my turn to play."

His fingers caressed her until the passion flared between them again. All thought of domination was banished as she melted under her husband's sensual onslaught. She might regret tearing up the contract tomorrow. Tonight, all she could focus on was the exquisite rapture she felt in Peter's arms.

Chapter 13

"The suspense is killing me." Alisa plopped her bag of quilting supplies down on the floor before sitting in a burgundy leather chair. "What happened with Peter?"

"Did he like the outfit?" Ella slid into the wingchair near the fireplace. "I bet you wowed him."

"Give Brenna a chance to speak." Lara shook her head and sat on the couch. "She'll tell us in her own time."

"I told Jesse your plans." Ella pulled out her floral Dresden Plate block. "I think he was jealous. I might have to borrow some of your equipment."

"I'd love to see that scenario." Alisa laughed. "I can remember four months ago when we started our plan, you couldn't even tell Gerry that you wanted a divorce."

Ella shrugged. "I've come a long way since then."

"We all have," Lara said.

Lara's quiet voice gave Brenna the opportunity she needed. "Peter wasn't seeing a dominatrix."

The confession caused a few seconds silence before Alisa spoke. "You're kidding?"

Brenna shook her head. "A client of his had asked him to speak to Mistress Elise as a favor. There was never any sneaking behind my back—or wishing to be submissive."

"What happened when you sprung your scenario on him?" Ella's voice was full of horror. "Was he angry?"

"He was surprised and a bit reluctant." Brenna pulled out her miniature spool quilt. "Thank goodness I'd only planned a tame scene."

"Start from the beginning." Alisa pulled out her half-finished star block.

Ella leaned forward. "Please."

Lara separated her red embroidery floss into strands.

"I made a special dinner and when Peter came home I was dressed in the red and black corset dress with heels. I told him to change. After dinner, I tied him up and made passionate love to him."

"He let you?" Ella's voice was full of awe.

"He thought it was funny," Brenna said. "I thought it was what he wanted."

"So what happened afterwards?" Alisa waved Brenna on.

"Peter had a good laugh, and insisted he wasn't interested." Brenna looked over at Lara. "The problem was I enjoyed it."

"I knew it." Alisa grinned. "You've been a closet dominatrix all along."

"That's when Brenna came to see me." Lara threaded her needle. "I gave her some advice. I'm not certain what happened afterwards."

"What advice?" Ella's eyes widened. "I can't imagine that you could coerce a man like Peter into being submissive if he didn't want to."

"Not coerce, convince." Lara knotted her thread. "There are certain lifestyles that would allow you to dominate a man without playing with BDSM."

"Like what?" Ella frowned.

"Female-led relationships and chore play." Brenna smoothed her quilt on her lap. "I talked Peter into signing a contract where he allowed me to control his orgasms, and then I teased and denied him in exchange for things like cleaning the house."

"You did that?" Ella's eyes were round with wonder.

"The house sparkles." Lara gave her a meaningful look. "I take it the contract was signed."

"We played at it for one weekend, and then we both decided it wasn't for us." Brenna laughed. "We hired a housekeeper."

"That doesn't sound like a bad exchange."

"Peter realized just what it took to maintain the house." Brenna's voice softened as she remembered his exact words. "He said that he wasn't here often enough to help, and he didn't want me too exhausted to make love in the evenings."

"It sounds as if this whole misunderstanding improved your marriage." Lara buried her knot in the seam of her patchwork.

"It has," Brenna agreed. "Peter booked us a cruise for our anniversary, and our sex life is better than when we were first married. We've agreed to set aside one weekend a month for us to explore role-playing."

"Then everything worked out for all of us." Lara nodded. "Soon we'll be wondering what to talk about on Wednesday."

"I have a confession." Ella's voice was quiet.

"Don't tell me you've let Gerry back into your life." Alisa's voice was full of exasperation. "That's the worst thing you could do."

"No matter what the future holds for me, Gerry is the last person I'd let near me."

"That sounds ominous." Brenna felt a twinge of concern when she noticed Ella's hesitation. "We're your friends. There's nothing you could say that would upset us."

Ella took a deep breath. "I'm pregnant."

"It's Jesse's baby?" Lara put her block on her lap.

"Of course." Ella clasped her hands in her lap. "We were careful about birth control most of the time."

"But mistakes happen." Alisa's voice was matter of fact. "What are you going to do?"

"Jesse wants to get married as soon as the divorce comes through."

"What do you want?" Lara asked.

"I want to wait." Ella exhaled. "Things are different than when Gerry and I were young. There's no need to be married to your baby's father. I don't want to make the same mistake again."

"I'm glad you're taking the time you need. Have you told your children yet?" Lara's question was asked in a delicate tone.

Ella shook her head. "I'm going to wait a few more weeks. We want to be certain that we past the first trimester before we announce it."

"That's wise." Alisa nodded. "That should solve the problem you're having with them wanting you to get back together with their father."

"At least there's no chance of that happening." Brenna pulled her needle out of the binding of her quilt. "Are you happy about the baby?"

Ella rubbed her lower abdomen. "Extremely. I feel like I've been given a second chance."

"Gerry is going to go ballistic when he finds out." Alisa snorted. "He'll probably insist that his mistress have a baby just to show you up."

"There's no chance of that happening." Ella smiled. "Marta left Gerry once he lost control of the money and the company."

Brenna shook her head. "That's such a cliché. There's no one more deserving than Gerry."

"Agreed." Lara cleared her throat. "I have a confession to make also. You know I've been seeing more of Vince."

"The man with the children?" Alisa looked up from her star quilt block. "I thought you were going to take it slow."

"We are."

"I sense that's a problem." Alisa's tone was wry. "A woman has needs."

Lara nodded. "I ran into Sam last week."

"The man from the sex club." Ella's eyes widened in surprise. "What happened?"

"He asked me to dinner."

"Is that all he wanted?" Alisa pursed her lips.

Lara shook her head. "He thought we should hook up again."

"What did you do?" Brenna kept her tone neutral.

"I said no." Lara sighed. "I was so tempted, but that isn't what I desire. I want to settle down and have children."

"What did Sam do?" Brenna leaned back.

"He asked me out again." Lara shook her head. "What is it about men? You tell them no and they think that means the chase is on."

"Is that so bad?" Alisa's voice was gleeful. "I can tell you there's nothing better for a woman's confidence than to know that two men lust after her."

"I suppose." Lara smiled. "I told Sam I wanted children and stability. He didn't seem to care."

"Does Vince know about Sam?" Brenna asked.

Lara nodded. "I told him I had dinner with someone else. He was upset at first. Now he seems to think of it as a competition. I'm tired of feeling like a prize."

"Find a man who makes your heart beat fast and loves you more than life." Ella's voice was adamant.

"It's too soon to tell." Brenna's voice was matter of fact. "You're young Lara. Take your time and find the right man. Ella's right, you want a man that gives you passion, devotion, and a lifetime of companionship."

"I'm worth it." Lara's voice was decisive. "I need a man who doesn't look at me as a trophy."

"I have some news too." Alisa pulled out another diamond piece from her stash. "Trent is going for an audition in Hollywood."

"Does that mean he's leaving you?" Brenna's voice was full of concern.

"He's not in a hurry to leave." Alisa looked up at them. Her green eyes were aglow with excitement. "He's confessed that he loves me."

"How does Henry feel?" Ella's voice was hesitant. "I know he supports you. To have another man in love with your wife must be difficult."

Alisa shrugged. "We've grown comfortable together. I know it isn't a typical household."

"So you are in love with two men and both of them love you." Brenna was sincerely glad for Alisa. She'd taken what had seemed like an impossible situation and succeeded. "Everything has worked out. I'm glad."

"I still have the desire to work in the business, but I've solved that." Alisa put her elbows on her knees and leaned forward. "I'm opening an online-dating service."

"Won't the competition be brutal?" Lara frowned. "There must be thousands of similar businesses."

"Not ones connecting people looking for alternative lifestyles." Alisa's voice was full of glee. "It came to me when Trent announced that he had to stay in Hollywood for a couple of months."

"So you're replacing the men in your life with work?" Ella's voice was doubtful. "That doesn't sound like much fun."

"I'm setting up the first office in Hollywood." Alisa's voice held a note of glee. "It's a big city, and there's lots of diversity there."

"You're moving?" Brenna's voice rose in shock.

"Only for a month. I'll be back after that." Alisa waved away any concerns. "I'll run the business from home, but I need an office where applicants can go if they want to. An administrator and a couple of assistants should be able to handle the walk-in clients."

"So you get to live with two men and have a business." Brenna nodded. "Ella found true love and has a baby on the way. Lara is dating again and waiting for the right man."

"And your marriage is rejuvenated," Alisa added.

"Everything sounds perfect to me." Brenna picked up her quilt. "If I hadn't announced that Peter was seeing a dominatrix, none of this would have happened."

"Finding the courage to leave Gerry was difficult at times. Looking back, it is the best thing I ever did." Ella glanced up from her quilt block. "Thank you for helping me see the plan through."

"I would never have left David if I hadn't tried swapping." Lara's voice was soft with gratitude. "Swapping is what finally let me see the truth about him."

"I would have ignored Henry's request for a threesome." Alisa reached over and squeezed Brenna's hand. "I have a much fuller life and love surrounds me. There are no mistakes. You found that card in Peter's pocket for a reason."

They were right.

All of them had found fulfillment.

She pulled out the small spool quilt she'd been working on for months. There were only a few stitches left on the binding, and then it would be finished. She'd begun this quilt the day the group had first discussed what to do about their marriages. It was only fitting that it be finished after all of their journeys were complete.

A sense of peace filled Brenna as she pulled the thread through the quilt backing. Life was in order. She felt the love surrounded by her best friends. Together they had challenged their preconceived ideas of what it meant to be a wife. They had fought their doubts and found the courage to demand more of their lives and relationships. In the process not all of their marriages had survived.

All of them had found their own definition of happiness.

They had all succeeded.

THE END

Author's Note

Quilting was always one of my favorite pastimes. It's something I taught myself, and over the years, taught many others to do. Shopping for the perfect material is relaxing and when you're with others, lots of fun. I still treasure the memories of the forays I made into quilting stores with my sisters and mother. Even on a family trip to Hawaii, my sisters and I visited fabric shops.

When I began quilting, everything was done by tracing a template and then cutting out the blocks, one by one. Strip piecing and rotary cutters hadn't been invented yet. That's why the first quilt I taught myself to make was very easy. It was six by six inch squares of white and patterned cotton. I placed the blocks so that a design was created in the center and the four corners. It was simple, quick, and even though I hand quilted it, done in record time.

I progressed from large squares to the small ones for double and triple Irish Chain quilts. From there I moved to triangles, curves, and diamonds. I lost count of the number of lone star baby quilts I made and hand quilted. Many years, and a couple of shoulder and neck injuries later, I find it difficult to hold a needle in my hand for any length of time. I've moved to machine quilting and for the joy of hand work, I do crazy patchwork and embroidery.

When you piece a quilt together you try to keep a scant quarter-inch seam allowance so that all your corners and points meet at exactly the right place. The beauty of a crazy quilt is that you don't have to be exact. Everything is bits and scraps of fabric sewn together in a haphazard fashion. The end result is a completed quilt.

Crazy quilts were popular in the Victorian era when women of the upper class would use their scraps of expensive fabrics, such as silk and velvet, to create a quilt. They embellished the seams and fabric with embroidery. It was the perfect venue for displaying their expert needlework, and quilts from this era are masterpieces of creativity.

When you are learning to design quilts, it is easiest to matching two colors in the beginning. There are many examples of antique quilts that only consist of two color schemes, such as the red and white quilts popular in the 1800's and into the twentieth century. Two color quilts are distinctive and memorable.

As one becomes more adventurous with their designs, other colors are added. Care has to be taken when adding additional colors. You can choose colors on the opposite sides of the color wheel, or those beside each other. You have to look for similar hues and tones of color also. The last thing you want, is one fabric that doesn't fit with the others.

Creating quilts is joyous. Combining fabrics and colors into a harmonious design is deeply gratifying. Quilting with friends makes the experience even more special. There is always a new technique or pattern waiting to be learned. A quilter may choose to use the same patterns over and over, but with a little imagination and effort, a whole new world of options opens up to them.

I believe the evolution of a quilt is much like that of a marriage. We tackle the broad strokes first and once we have those mastered, we move onto the finer details. Along the way, compromise is necessary. Just like a two-colored quilt, the two people in the relationship shine bright together when they complement each other and form a harmonious union. It is a thing of beauty; positive and prosperous.

Adding another person to a relationship or household requires the same consideration as combining fabrics. Everyone needs to work together and live in accord with each other. Honesty, and the desire to build a strong and committed family is necessary for success.

Like a crazy quilt, a marriage is seldom a precise fit. Two people come together with their gifts and flaws, and they hope to create something new and viable. Sometimes a masterpiece is created and it is truly beautiful. We've all known couples who are as much in love after fifty years together as when they began their journey on their wedding day.

Other marriages are not pretty. Nothing between the pair seems to work in harmony or balance. Stitches may be added to try and strengthen the bonds, but it doesn't keep the fabric of their lives together. Some couples stay together and may eventually achieve success in their relationship, but most rip apart at the seams.

Variety and experimentation can bring joy and pleasure. Communication is key for each spouse to understand the needs and desires of the other. A solid relationship will stand the test of time and change. Adventure can bring an element of laughter and fun, especially when love and respect are present between the partners.

Every marriage is unique and no one solution works for everyone. I believe that as women find their own empowerment and strength, that a good marriage becomes stronger. It is only with trust that we will have the love and sense of belonging that is necessary for true intimacy to flourish.

About the Author

Cynthia Clement is an award winning and bestselling author who began writing stories in her teens, but it wasn't until her forties that she became serious about writing. She believes in second chances, exploring new ideas, and bringing the impossible to life. Her novels, whether contemporary, historical, or science fiction, all focus on love, honor, and intrigue.

She lives in Canada with her husband of thirty-two years, her teenaged son, and Norman, their dachshund. She has an eclectic range of interests including paranormal phenomena, ghost hunting, quilting, reading, gardening, and great conversation.

Her first book, The Seduction of Sarah, was a finalist in the HOLT Medallion Best First Book Category. Her Science Fiction Romance book, aHunter4Rescue, has placed first in the 2014 International Digital Awards in the Paranormal Category and received third place in the 2014 ACRA Heart of Excellence Reader's Choice Award, Paranormal Romance Category

Books Available

Science Fiction

aHunter4Hire series

aHunter4Rescue
aHunter4Saken
aHunter4Life
aHunter4Ever
aHunter4Trust
aHunter4Gotten

Historical

Caldern Family

The Seduction of Sarah
The Seduction of Madalyn

Novellas
Pleasuring Emily
Christmas Kisses

Contemporary

Wednesday Wives Club

www.ingramcontent.com/pod-product-compliance
Lightning Source LLC
Chambersburg PA
CBHW031059260626
47172CB00001B/137